W9-BEC-949

WARRIORS

A LIGHT IN THE MIST

THE BROKEN CODE

THE BROKEN CODE

WARRIORS

A LIGHT IN THE MIST

ERIN HUNTER

An Imprint of HarperCollinsPublishers

Library of Congress Cataloging-in-Publication Data
Names: Hunter, Erin, author.
Title: A light in the mist / Erin Hunter.
Description: First edition. | New York : Harper, [2021] | Series: Warriors: the broken code ; book
    six | Audience: Ages 8–12. | Audience: Grades 4–6. | Summary: "StarClan, the Dark Forest,
    and all five warrior Clans band together for a final battle that seeks to destroy Bramblestar's
    impostor before he destroys everything they hold dear"— Provided by publisher.
Identifiers: LCCN 2021024286 | ISBN 978-0-06-282388-5 (hardcover) | ISBN 978-0-06-
    282389-2 (library binding)
Subjects: CYAC: Cats—Fiction. | Fantasy.
Classification: LCC PZ7.H916625 Li 2021 | DDC [Fic]—dc23
LC record available at https://lccn.loc.gov/2021024286

Typography by Jessie Gang
21 22 23 24 25   PC/LSCH   10 9 8 7 6 5 4 3 2 1
❖
First Edition

Special thanks to Kate Cary

ALLEGIANCES

THUNDERCLAN

LEADER
BRAMBLESTAR—dark brown tabby tom with amber eyes

DEPUTY
SQUIRRELFLIGHT—dark ginger she-cat with green eyes and one white paw

MEDICINE CATS
JAYFEATHER—gray tabby tom with blind blue eyes

ALDERHEART—dark ginger tom with amber eyes

WARRIORS
(toms and she-cats without kits)

THORNCLAW—golden-brown tabby tom

WHITEWING—white she-cat with green eyes

BIRCHFALL—light brown tabby tom

MOUSEWHISKER—gray-and-white tom
APPRENTICE, BAYPAW (golden tabby tom)

POPPYFROST—pale tortoiseshell-and-white she-cat

BRISTLEFROST—pale gray she-cat

LILYHEART—small, dark tabby she-cat with white patches and blue eyes
APPRENTICE, FLAMEPAW (black tom)

BUMBLESTRIPE—very pale gray tom with black stripes

CHERRYFALL—ginger she-cat

MOLEWHISKER—brown-and-cream tom

CINDERHEART—gray tabby she-cat
APPRENTICE, FINCHPAW (tortoiseshell she-cat)

BLOSSOMFALL—tortoiseshell-and-white she-cat with petal-shaped white patches

IVYPOOL—silver-and-white tabby she-cat with dark blue eyes

EAGLEWING—ginger she-cat

APPRENTICE, MYRTLEPAW (pale brown she-cat)

DEWNOSE—gray-and-white tom

THRIFTEAR—dark gray she-cat

STORMCLOUD—gray tabby tom

HOLLYTUFT—black she-cat

FERNSONG—yellow tabby tom

HONEYFUR—white she-cat with yellow splotches

SPARKPELT—orange tabby she-cat

SORRELSTRIPE—dark brown she-cat

TWIGBRANCH—gray she-cat with green eyes

FINLEAP—brown tom

SHELLFUR—tortoiseshell tom

PLUMSTONE—black-and-ginger she-cat

LEAFSHADE—tortoiseshell she-cat

LIONBLAZE—golden tabby tom with amber eyes

QUEENS (she-cats expecting or nursing kits)

DAISY—cream long-furred cat from the horseplace

SPOTFUR—spotted tabby she-cat

ELDERS   (former warriors and queens, now retired)

GRAYSTRIPE—long-haired gray tom

CLOUDTAIL—long-haired white tom with blue eyes

BRIGHTHEART—white she-cat with ginger patches

BRACKENFUR—golden-brown tabby tom

SHADOWCLAN

LEADER   TIGERSTAR—dark brown tabby tom

DEPUTY   CLOVERFOOT—gray tabby she-cat

MEDICINE CATS   PUDDLESHINE—brown tom with white splotches

SHADOWSIGHT—gray tabby tom

MOTHWING—dappled golden she-cat

WARRIORS   TAWNYPELT—tortoiseshell she-cat with green eyes

DOVEWING—pale gray she-cat with green eyes

HARELIGHT—white tom

ICEWING—white she-cat with blue eyes

STONEWING—white tom

SCORCHFUR—dark gray tom with slashed ears

FLAXFOOT—brown tabby tom

SPARROWTAIL—large brown tabby tom

SNOWBIRD—pure white she-cat with green eyes

YARROWLEAF—ginger she-cat with yellow eyes

BERRYHEART—black-and-white she-cat

GRASSHEART—pale brown tabby she-cat

WHORLPELT—gray-and-white tom

HOPWHISKER—calico she-cat

BLAZEFIRE—white-and-ginger tom

CINNAMONTAIL—brown tabby she-cat with white paws

FLOWERSTEM—silver she-cat

SNAKETOOTH—honey-colored tabby she-cat

SLATEFUR—sleek gray tom

POUNCESTEP—gray tabby she-cat

LIGHTLEAP—brown tabby she-cat

GULLSWOOP—white she-cat

SPIRECLAW—black-and-white tom

HOLLOWSPRING—black tom

SUNBEAM—brown-and-white tabby she-cat

ELDERS   **OAKFUR**—small brown tom

SKYCLAN

LEADER   **LEAFSTAR**—brown-and-cream tabby she-cat with amber eyes

DEPUTY   **HAWKWING**—dark gray tom with yellow eyes

MEDICINE CATS   **FRECKLEWISH**—mottled light brown tabby she-cat with spotted legs

FIDGETFLAKE—black-and-white tom

MEDIATOR   **TREE**—yellow tom with amber eyes

WARRIORS

SPARROWPELT—dark brown tabby tom

MACGYVER—black-and-white tom

DEWSPRING—sturdy gray tom

ROOTSPRING—yellow tom

NEEDLECLAW—black-and-white she-cat

PLUMWILLOW—dark gray she-cat

SAGENOSE—pale gray tom

KITESCRATCH—reddish-brown tom

HARRYBROOK—gray tom

CHERRYTAIL—fluffy tortoiseshell and white she-cat

CLOUDMIST—white she-cat with yellow eyes

BLOSSOMHEART—ginger and white she-cat

TURTLECRAWL—tortoiseshell she-cat

RABBITLEAP—brown tom
APPRENTICE, WRENPAW (golden tabby she-cat)

REEDCLAW—small pale tabby she-cat

MINTFUR—gray tabby she-cat with blue eyes

NETTLESPLASH—pale brown tom

TINYCLOUD—small white she-cat

PALESKY—black-and-white she-cat

VIOLETSHINE—black-and-white she-cat with yellow eyes

BELLALEAF—pale orange she-cat with green eyes

QUAILFEATHER—white tom with crow-black ears

PIGEONFOOT—gray-and-white she-cat

FRINGEWHISKER—white she-cat with brown splotches

GRAVELNOSE—tan tom

SUNNYPELT—ginger she-cat

QUEENS   **NECTARSONG**—brown she-cat (mother to Beekit, a white-and-tabby she-kit, and Beetlekit, a tabby tom)

ELDERS   **FALLOWFERN**—pale brown she-cat who has lost her hearing

WINDCLAN

LEADER   **HARESTAR**—brown-and-white tom

DEPUTY   **CROWFEATHER**—dark gray tom

MEDICINE CAT   **KESTRELFLIGHT**—mottled gray tom with white splotches like kestrel feathers

WARRIORS   **NIGHTCLOUD**—black she-cat

BRINDLEWING—mottled brown she-cat

APPLESHINE—yellow tabby she-cat

LEAFTAIL—dark tabby tom with amber eyes

WOODSONG—brown she-cat

EMBERFOOT—gray tom with two dark paws

BREEZEPELT—black tom with amber eyes

HEATHERTAIL—light brown tabby she-cat with blue eyes

FEATHERPELT—gray tabby she-cat

CROUCHFOOT—ginger tom

APPRENTICE, SONGPAW (tortoiseshell she-cat)

LARKWING—pale brown tabby she-cat

SEDGEWHISKER—light brown tabby she-cat
APPRENTICE, FLUTTERPAW (brown-and-white tom)

SLIGHTFOOT—black tom with white flash on his chest

OATCLAW—pale brown tabby tom

HOOTWHISKER—dark gray tom
APPRENTICE, WHISTLEPAW (gray tabby she-cat)

FERNSTRIPE—gray tabby she-cat

ELDERS   **WHISKERNOSE**—light brown tom

GORSETAIL—very pale gray-and-white she-cat with blue eyes

RIVERCLAN

LEADER   **MISTYSTAR**—gray she-cat with blue eyes

DEPUTY   **REEDWHISKER**—black tom

WARRIORS   **DUSKFUR**—brown tabby she-cat

MINNOWTAIL—dark gray-and-white she-cat
APPRENTICE, SPLASHPAW (brown tabby tom)

MALLOWNOSE—light brown tabby tom

HAVENPELT—black-and-white she-cat

PODLIGHT—gray-and-white tom

SHIMMERPELT—silver she-cat

LIZARDTAIL—light brown tom
APPRENTICE, FOGPAW (gray-and-white she-cat)

SNEEZECLOUD—gray-and-white tom

BRACKENPELT—tortoiseshell she-cat

JAYCLAW—gray tom

OWLNOSE—brown tabby tom

GORSECLAW—white tom with gray ears

NIGHTSKY—dark gray she-cat with blue eyes

BREEZEHEART—brown-and-white she-cat

QUEENS   **CURLFEATHER**—pale brown she-cat (mother to Frostkit, a she-kit; Mistkit, a she-kit; and Graykit, a tom)

ELDERS   **MOSSPELT**—tortoiseshell-and-white she-cat

THE BROKEN CODE

WARRIORS

A LIGHT IN THE MIST

TWOLEG NEST
GREENLEAF
TWOLEGPLACE
CLEARIN
TWOLEG PATH
TWOLEG PATH
SHADOWCLAN
CAMP
SMALL
THUNDERPATH
HALFBRIDGE
GREENLEAF
TWOLEGPLACE
HALFBRIDGE
CAT VIEW
ISLAND
STREAM
RIVERCLAN
CAMP
HORSEPLACE

HAREVIEW
CAMPSITE

SANCTUARY
COTTAGE

SADLER WOODS

LITTLEPINE
SAILING
CENTER

LITTLEPINE ROAD

TWOLEG V

LITTLEPIN
ISLAND

RIVER ALBA

WHITECHURCH ROAD

KNIGH
COPSE

PROLOGUE

❧

At the edge of the clearing, beneath the starless sky, the Dark Forest cats watched. Around them, mist billowed in the darkness like warm breath in the ice-cold air. They stared at a warrior. His pelt was bloody and ragged from fighting. It rippled now as he pressed his belly harder against the ground. A white tom circled him slowly.

The white cat's flanks showed the scars of countless battles. His eyes shimmered with menace. And yet he did not attack.

The watching cats shifted impatiently but did not speak.

Ashfur lashed his tail. Weren't they enjoying the fight? Was it because Snowtuft was hesitating? The fool was tiptoeing around Rootspring like a nervous kit! "Get on with it, you mangy white coward!"

Snowtuft glanced at him. Was that doubt in his gaze? Rage surged like fire in Ashfur's chest. Did he have to make *every* move for these mouse-hearts?

Rootspring must die! Without speaking, he flicked the simple, vicious instruction at the spirit cats. It energized them, his thought becoming theirs. Their pelts spiked, their ears flattened, their tails bushed as they began to yowl.

"Kill him!"

"Slit his throat!"

"Rip him to shreds!"

As their screeches filled the darkness, Snowtuft slid into an attack crouch, as fluid as a snake. Eyes wide with panic, Rootspring backed away.

Ashfur's rage cooled and hardened until it sat like granite in his belly. He had known this fury for as long as he could remember; it was like an old friend. With it came the certainty that the warriors who thought they'd defeated him would one day pay for their treachery. They'd ignored his suffering, but he would relish theirs. He would end a grudge born long before his death. One that death itself had not ended.

How could StarClan have been so stupid? They'd actually believed he'd repented, that he'd forgiven his enemies—even Hollyleaf, his murderer. *What fools!* They'd had no idea what he'd been planning as he'd pretended to care about their warrior life—hunting, dozing in the sunshine, sharing tongues with friends and kin. It had been enough to make them believe he was one of them, while in secret he'd been exploring every tail-length of StarClan's hunting grounds, learning all he could about them. Had they really thought he was going to let Bramblestar and Squirrelflight live in peace?

It hadn't taken long to work out that StarClan's power came from its connection to the living Clans. If he could disrupt that link, he could expose StarClan for the pathetic bunch of elders they were. Even though their youth and strength had been restored, their minds were feeble with age. Without the connection to their descendants, the StarClan warriors would be nothing but memories, and the living Clans, separated from their ancestors, would become as vulnerable as prey.

It had been easier than he'd expected to close off the existing path to the Dark Forest and the living Clans at the edge of StarClan's territory. But he'd known he couldn't seal himself in with the StarClan cats. He'd clawed a tunnel near the heart of StarClan's lands that led deep into the Place of No Stars. No cat knew of it but him. Slowly, deliberately, he had begun to concentrate power into his own paws. But he still hadn't known how to reach into the living Clans.

Moons had passed, and, all the time, Ashfur's rage had grown. Yet he'd swallowed it, like bitter prey, and waited. And then Mistystar had lost her first life and Ashfur had at last seen a way to return to the lake.

He'd watched the dying RiverClan leader appear in StarClan, shimmering like a ghost among the star-specked warriors. Leopardstar had greeted her. Her Clanmates had clustered around her, eager for a glimpse of their leader before she returned to the living Clans to begin her next life. That was when Ashfur realized that while her soul was in StarClan, her body was defenseless: no more than flesh beneath a pelt, waiting only for a spirit to inhabit it.

Finally, he knew how he could return to the living Clans. Still pretending to be one of them, Ashfur persuaded the other StarClan cats to let him leave their hunting grounds and return to observe the Clans by the lake, promising he would make sure they were staying true to their precious warrior code. Free from StarClan at last, he blocked his secret tunnel with weeds and branches. Soon the living Clans were despairing over their lost connection with their ancestors, and losing their faith in StarClan. The barrier grew stronger and thicker until StarClan's connection with the living was broken.

Without StarClan's guidance, the lake Clans had been lost. How he'd enjoyed filling the ShadowClan medicine-cat apprentice's mind with fear. When Bramblestar had become sick, Ashfur had tricked the young mouse-brain into making the ThunderClan leader sicker, and then Bramblestar had died in the snow. At last, Ashfur had found a way back! Undetected, like slow poison entering a wound, he'd slipped into Bramblestar's empty body.

He'd shuddered as he did, repulsed by the sudden, unfamiliar restrictions of Bramblestar's ill-fitting pelt. But he'd ignored the discomfort. Finally, he was going to have everything that should have always been his.

And yet it had all gone wrong. The Clans had changed. And Squirrelflight wasn't his mate; she was Bramblestar's. Her gentle purrs, her loving glances, hadn't been for Ashfur— *never* for Ashfur. Her love had always been for Bramblestar.

Rage rose now like bile in Ashfur's throat, almost choking him. He jerked his attention back to the clearing and glared at the yellow SkyClan warrior. Rootspring would pay for trying to stand in his way. Ashfur let his fury surge into the spirit cats, his thoughts exploding from their mouths in yowls of hate.

"Claw his pelt off!"

"Rip his ears!"

Snowtuft lunged at Rootspring and, holding him down, drew bloody claw marks along the warrior's spine.

Pleasure bubbled in Ashfur's chest. *I'm not cruel,* he told himself. This was all Squirrelflight's fault. *She drove me to this. I only wanted the Clans to see what hypocrites they are.* It had been satisfying to turn them against each other. He'd watched as spite blossomed among the lake Clans as they tried to prove what good and loyal warriors they were. If nothing else, he'd looked forward to watching them realize they were no better than he was. But then Squirrelflight had faked her own death to escape him, and the living Clans had turned against him. They'd *betrayed* him. He could do nothing but flee to the Dark Forest. He had allies here—cats too mean or cruel to make it to StarClan. Since he'd blocked off StarClan, the spirits of dead cats who belonged there but could no longer find their way had also collected in the Dark Forest. He'd made sure they would fight for him as well—whether they wanted to or not.

He'd thought he still had a chance. If he brought Squirrelflight here, he could make her see her Clan in a new light—that they were nothing but a gang of murderous fox-hearts pretending to be special. She'd see they were no different from him. Surely then she could love him?

Yet, even here, she'd defied him. She'd escaped and taken Bramblestar with her.

Ashfur flexed his claws. He wasn't going to hope any

longer. This time he wouldn't hold back. He was going to punish Rootspring, and then he would destroy whatever he could—the Dark Forest, StarClan, the living Clans. If he couldn't have what he wanted, then why should any cat in the Clans? He'd take everything from them. By the time he was finished, they'd be nothing but loners and rogues.

A deep thrill shivered beneath his pelt. Curling his lip, he watched Snowtuft throw Rootspring to the ground. The scarred white tom's claws tightened on the warrior's throat, digging deeper into already-bloody fur. Snowtuft lifted his gaze to meet Ashfur's questioningly.

Spittle dripped from Ashfur's mouth and splashed onto the dark earth. "Kill him," he snarled.

CHAPTER 1

"Kill him."

Ashfur's snarl set fresh panic sparking through Root-spring's pelt. Bloodlust sharpened the malice in the dark warrior's eyes. *He's enjoying this.* The Dark Forest cats at the edge of the clearing screeched in excitement. They were spurring Snowtuft on, as pitiless as a pack of dogs. Snowtuft's claws curled like burning thorns into Rootspring's throat.

The pain brought focus. He wasn't ready to die. He pulled up his hind paws, tucked them beneath the scarred tom's belly, and, with every whisker of energy left in his body, heaved him away.

Agony seared through Rootspring as Snowtuft's claws ripped clumps of fur from his neck. He scrambled up, but Snowtuft had already found his paws and was facing him in a crouch, his muscles bunched so tightly that, when he leaped to attack, Rootspring knew he would strike faster than a hawk. And yet he could see helpless desperation in Snowtuft's eyes. *He doesn't want to hurt me. But he has no choice.*

Rootspring narrowed his eyes. Snowtuft's gaze once more was on his neck. *I have to stop him.* As Snowtuft leaped,

7

Rootspring ducked beneath him, slamming his head into the white tom's chest and thrusting upward with a grunt. As Snowtuft struggled to keep his balance, Rootspring twisted quickly and hooked his claws into the white tom's pelt, hauling him to the ground with a thud.

Around him, the Dark Forest and spirit cats' eyes flashed with anger as they saw Snowtuft fall.

Ashfur flattened his ears. "Get up, you mouse-brain!"

The watching cats hissed.

One cat's yowl rose above the others. "Rip his pelt off!"

Rootspring stiffened. Was that Sandynose? Grief jabbed his belly. His former Clanmate was cheering Snowtuft on, as though he'd never patrolled beside Rootspring, or shared prey with him after a long day's hunting. Rootspring glanced up.

The stocky brown tom's face was twisted with hate. Beside him, Stemleaf was yowling too. It would break Bristlefrost's heart to see her friend and Clanmate like this.

"Finish him!"

Despair hollowed Rootspring's belly. Dappletuft, Softpelt, and Conefoot were beside them; Strikestone and Frondwhisker too.

As he hesitated, Snowtuft tore free of his grip and sprang to his paws. The white tom's eyes glistened with an apology as he lunged again at Rootspring.

Rootspring reared to meet the attack, lashing out with swipe after swipe, letting his training guide his paws as his thoughts whirled. Stemleaf had been a loyal Thunder-Clan warrior; he'd been Bristlefrost's friend and part of the

rebellion against Ashfur when he had used Bramblestar's body
to control ThunderClan. Dappletuft, Softpelt, and Conefoot
had been rebels too. They'd died fighting Ashfur beside the
lake. They'd *never* act this way if they had even the slightest
choice. Did Ashfur have so much power that he could make
loyal warriors turn against their allies?

Claws raked Rootspring's jaw. The pain shocked him.
Snowtuft was still fighting back. Rootspring blocked out the
cries of his former friends. He couldn't let Ashfur win. He
was fighting not just for his own life, but for the spirits of the
cats Ashfur had already killed. He dropped onto his belly as
Snowtuft aimed another blow at his muzzle, then rolled over
and hooked his claws into Snowtuft's shoulders. Holding the
white tom tight, he curled around him and churned sharp
claws at his spine.

Snowtuft twisted free with a shriek, leaving tufts of fur
between Rootspring's claws. He turned and hurled himself
at Rootspring. The power of the white tom's attack caught
Rootspring off balance. As he thumped to the ground, he
glimpsed Mapleshade glowering among the encircling cats.
Not all the cats here were being controlled by Ashfur. Some
had been in the Dark Forest for moons and wanted to hurt
the living as much as their leader did.

Rootspring grunted as Snowtuft landed on top of him. As
the weight of the white tom knocked the breath from his body,
he saw a familiar tabby tom watching the fight, his whiskers
twitching with cruel excitement. Rootspring was startled.
What was *Darkstripe* doing here? Hadn't Rootspring pushed

the fox-hearted warrior into the dark water that was flooding the Dark Forest? Rage sparked in his chest. Darkstripe was the reason Rootspring was stranded in this place.

You should be dead.

Grunting, Rootspring rolled and curled his claws into the earth, dragging himself along the ground as Snowtuft's claws drew arcs of fire in his flank. He'd been trying to make his way back to the living world behind Bristlefrost and Shadowsight when Darkstripe had attacked him. His rage hardened and, suddenly, pure, murderous hatred for the tabby tom flashed like fire in his thoughts.

The intensity of it shocked Rootspring. He froze for a moment. He'd never felt such loathing for any cat. He shook himself free from Snowtuft's grip and, as quick as cornered prey, turned on the white tom and raked his claws across his muzzle. The Dark Forest must be getting to him. He couldn't let it. He would not allow the evil that had festered and grown in this place to infect him. He pushed hard into the earth with his hind paws and flung himself at Snowtuft. As he sent the white tom staggering backward, Rootspring ducked low and knocked his paws from beneath him. Rootspring leaped on top of Snowtuft as he fell, and pinned his shoulders to the ground, trembling with the effort as Snowtuft squirmed beneath his grip.

He stared into the white tom's frightened eyes, pushing anger away. *What do I do now?* He couldn't kill this cat. Snowtuft had tried to help him. A cat who died in the Dark Forest would be gone forever, never to see kin or Clanmates again; he would be nothing but a memory. The thought sent a tremor down Rootspring's spine. What could be worse than that? Besides, hadn't he secretly been hoping to get Snowtuft out of this place? If he could defeat Ashfur, he might be able to persuade StarClan to take him in. Whatever terrible sins the Dark Forest cat had committed in life, he'd committed them long ago, and he had since helped Rootspring to fight Ashfur. Didn't he deserve some reward?

Snowtuft's gaze reached for his, shimmering with desperation.

Can I kill another cat to save myself? Rootspring wondered. As he hesitated, Snowtuft's gaze flashed toward Ashfur.

"Can't you do anything right?" The dark warrior's yowl seemed to make even the darkness shiver. His eyes flitted toward the watching mob. "One of you, kill him!"

The cats rushed forward, jostling and almost tripping over one another as they competed to obey Ashfur's command. Panic shrilled through Rootspring's blood. He let Snowtuft wriggle free and faced the encircling horde as they closed in on him, pelts bristling and gazes glittering with violence.

Through his panic, Rootspring remembered Dewspring's words. *Look for the weakest part and break through.* His mentor had taught him what to do if he was surrounded. Rootspring scanned the advancing cats. Conefoot had drawn back his lips. Beside him, Stemleaf flattened his ears. Dappletuft snarled, his eyes dark with menace, but Rootspring could see that the RiverClan warrior was limping. The deep claw marks that had ended his life still showed on his chest. Rootspring's heart leaped. That was his way out.

He charged at Dappletuft and, shoving the unsteady RiverClan tom into Stemleaf, barged through the line. As Dappletuft fell and Stemleaf stumbled, Rootspring slid past them like a rabbit slipping through brambles. Hope surged in his chest as he saw shadows of the Dark Forest open before him. They would swallow and hide him if he reached them. He raced across the clearing, his flanks heaving as he fled.

Then teeth sank into his hind leg. His breath caught in his throat as they hauled him backward. Pain seared his fur as claws sank into every part of his pelt and dragged him screeching into the mob. As he flailed in desperation, trying to fight his way free, he saw Ashfur's eyes glinting among the blur of teeth and pelts.

I'm going to die here. Rootspring felt hope drain away. Terror dragged him into a darkness he felt sure must be death. His thoughts flashed to memories of Bristlefrost: how she'd pulled him from the lake when he was still a 'paw, and how she'd looked at him as they sat in the moonlight in the shadow of a willow, far away from the lake and their duty to their Clans. The way her gentle face had shone like starlight.

His breath slowed as grief swallowed his heart. It swept away the fear as he realized he would never see her again. It numbed the pain of the claws and teeth and drowned out the growls and hisses of the Dark Forest cats. He could no longer feel their hot breath or smell their rancid fur. Going limp, he gave himself up to death. What else could he do?

Out of the corner of his eye, he saw a pale gray pelt moving in the darkness beyond the cats. Rootspring twitched as he recognized it. *Bristlefrost.* It seemed like mist, soft against the shadows of the forest. *I'm seeing things.* His heart ached for her. He gazed at the mirage, thankful that this would be his last memory. But the mirage didn't fade. It moved closer. *Bristlefrost?* She was charging toward him, her blue-green eyes wide with outrage. *Are you really here?*

Rootspring yelped as pain cut once more into his consciousness. The Dark Forest cats were tearing at his pelt. Then, suddenly, they let go and turned on a new enemy. *Bristlefrost!* She was actually here!

Swiping one way, then the other, she cleared a path through the mob. Rootspring scrambled to his paws, ignoring the sting of his wounds. *Bristlefrost!* He could still hardly believe it. He watched her knock Conefoot aside, her gaze fixing on him. *She's come to rescue me!*

"Run!" Her screech sent fresh energy surging beneath his pelt.

But he wasn't going to let any of these mangy fox-hearts hurt her. With a snarl, he pushed his way between two warriors and shoved another off its paws. He had to reach Bristlefrost. She wasn't going to die here. And neither was he.

CHAPTER 2

Shadowsight blinked open his eyes. I'm in the Dark Forest again! He looked around, scanning for danger. Twilight lit the twisted trees with an eerie glow. Only a few moments ago, he'd been following Bristlefrost through darkness, the Sisters' singing echoing in his mind as they guided them here. Now he flattened his ears against the sounds of battle. Yowls tore the dank air and the scent of blood touched his nose.

He looked around for Bristlefrost, and alarm crackled through his pelt as he saw her streak away from him, leap a tree root, and dodge around a trunk, running at full speed toward the sounds of battle.

"Wait!" He raced after her, pulling up where the forest opened and dim light showed a clearing. A mob of cats seethed there like swarming eels. Pelts rippled; tails lashed; eyes flashed with aggression. Shadowsight's breath caught in his throat as Bristlefrost hurled herself at the throng. *Does she have bees in her brain?* She hauled a tabby away from the group and flung him aside, then plunged deeper into the crowd.

Shadowsight watched her, hardly able to believe his eyes. *What in StarClan are you doing?* Then he recognized a yellow tom at the center of the battle. *Rootspring.* He looked beaten, but as Bristlefrost fought her way closer, the SkyClan warrior lifted his head. Fresh light sparked in his blue gaze as he saw her.

I have to help them. But how? Shadowsight had never been a good fighter; his training had been in herbs, not in battle moves. And this mob was clearly under the control of Ashfur. What else could be driving them to this frenzy but the dark warrior's hunger for revenge?

Shadowsight's paws seemed rooted to the earth. He could still feel the lingering stiffness in his leg from his fight with Ashfur. If he leaped in now, he might be more trouble to his friends than help. His heart pounded in his ears. *What can I do?*

Scanning the fighting cats, he spotted Ashfur. The dark warrior hung back from the battle and watched through slitted eyes. His ears and tail were rigid, as though he was concentrating hard. Shadowsight backed further into the shadows.

Another pelt caught his eye. He recognized at once the ragged black cat pressed between two spirit cats as they lashed out at Bristlefrost. *Spiresight.* The skinny tom had saved his life twice now. His eyes were dull, as though he hardly saw. And yet he yowled and lunged like a warrior, his body moving though his gaze betrayed no consciousness. Did he even realize what he was doing?

Bristlefrost reached Rootspring. Wordlessly, as though they'd trained side by side for moons, they pressed together, tail to tail; rearing, they lashed out with their forepaws, swiping viciously at every muzzle they could reach as the fought their way through the mob. With a speed and strength that amazed Shadowsight, they opened a path to the edge, then dropped down on all fours and swapped glances.

"We can do this," Bristlefrost growled.

Rootspring nodded, and they turned back to face their attackers.

A white-and-ginger tom shot from the advancing mob and dived at Bristlefrost. *Stemleaf?* Shadowsight's ears twitched with surprise. Hadn't he trained alongside Bristlefrost in Thunder-Clan? The tom swiped at her muzzle. She ducked and knocked him away with a powerful blow to his cheek. He reeled, taking a moment to regain his balance, then turned his gaze on her. His eyes were cold and vicious. A chill ran along Shadowsight's spine as Bristlefrost hesitated. It must go against all her instincts to fight a Clanmate she'd sworn to defend.

Then Stemleaf's eyes widened, as though awareness had returned for a moment. He paused, looking as hesitant as Bristlefrost, and Shadowsight's heart quickened. Was the ThunderClan warrior coming to his senses? How strong, he wondered, was Ashfur's hold on these cats? Especially if they'd been loyal warriors in life—surely that loyalty must still be buried somewhere in their hearts. Shadowsight's thoughts quickened. He had been able to break Ashfur's control over Bramblestar by interrupting the evil cat's concentration.

He looked again at the dark warrior and saw that his gaze had not wavered. It was fixed on the fighting cats, his tail as stiff as dead prey as he seemed to focus every whisker of energy on them. Controlling so many cats had to be taking a huge amount of effort.

Stemleaf's gaze emptied once more, as though the part of him that recognized Bristlefrost had died, and he leaped at her, sinking his teeth into her scruff and dragging her to the ground. Rootspring's pelt bushed. He leaped toward her, but Softpelt darted in front of him and batted him away. As Rootspring fought to keep his balance, the RiverClan she-cat knocked his paws from beneath him, rolled him onto his spine, and began clawing his belly with vicious hind paws.

Shadowsight looked at Ashfur again. The evil tom's flanks were trembling as he focused on the fight. *It is hard for him.* Shadowsight shifted his paws, his thoughts whirling in his mind. *Can I distract him?* What would be the best way to draw his attention?

Shadowsight spread his claws and hooked them into the chilly soil. He felt dampness beneath them and sank into it, allowing his thoughts to unfurl toward Ashfur. He'd tended to the dark warrior when he'd been a prisoner in ShadowClan; he'd dressed his wounds and sat with him and spoken with him more than any other Clan cat had. During that moon, he'd forged a connection with Ashfur that made Shadowsight shudder as he remembered it—how naive he'd been. . . .

But now he had to reach for that connection again.

He opened his heart to it and let it roll over him, until it seemed to seep into every hair on his pelt. A deep, brooding anger, darkened by jealousy, bloomed inside him. Shadowsight felt queasy. Suddenly he could see anger in the tiny quiver in Ashfur's whiskers. He could read jealousy in the blackness of the dark warrior's eyes. It was vengeance that was driving him. Vengeance, because Squirrelflight had dared to love some other cat!

How could that be an excuse for the kind of malice Ashfur had inflicted on the Clans? A true warrior accepted defeat and moved on. Protecting their Clan was more important. But Ashfur had let his bitterness grow until it tainted his whole life. He must have nursed it in StarClan so that it poisoned his mind even after death. And now he was determined to make all the Clans suffer, and all because Squirrelflight had chosen Bramblestar instead of him.

Shadowsight shook out his pelt, eager to break the connection that had let Ashfur's emotions invade his thoughts for a moment. At least now he knew what to do.

In the clearing, Bristlefrost screeched, pain sharpening her yowl. Stemleaf had sunk his teeth into her shoulder. He was dragging her across the forest floor, toward the other spirit cats, whose eyes glittered with excitement. Ashfur flicked his gaze toward a mottled tom near the front. The tom darted across the clearing and clawed Bristlefrost's ear. Another followed and bit into her flailing hind leg.

"Let her go!" Rootspring struggled free of Softpelt's grip and raced for Bristlefrost.

As he reached her, Ashfur swept his gaze over the mob, and a moment later, they all surged forward. Their hisses filled the air. Shadowsight smelled fear-scent as Bristlefrost and Rootspring disappeared beneath the teeming pelts. Panic flared like lightning through his fur. He had to stop this.

"Squirrelflight loves Bramblestar!" He glared at Ashfur as

his yowl rang out over the clearing. "She'll never love you."
He knew that the dark warrior's fury was not a strength, but
a weakness; his jealousy was a wound that could be hollowed
out until the pain was so intense that he couldn't think of anything else. Shadowsight yowled again. "She chose Bramblestar
and she always will. They are happy together and you can't
change that." He held his breath as he watched for the dark
warrior's response. Ashfur's vicious glare stayed on the spirit
cats, but his tail was quivering.

Hope pricked in Shadowsight's chest. "If you truly loved
Squirrelflight, you'd want her to be happy," he went on. "You
wouldn't be trying to destroy everything she loves." Was the
fur along Ashfur's spine twitching? "You have no idea what
love really is." Fear churned in Shadowsight's belly. He was
deliberately provoking a warrior capable of the worst cruelty.
But he had to break Ashfur's concentration, no matter the
cost. Rootspring's and Bristlefrost's lives depended on it. He
forced himself to go on. "How could a warrior like Squirrelflight ever love a warrior like you? No wonder she chose
Bramblestar. He's everything you're not. He's brave and loyal.
He's a true warrior in a way you could never be."

The spirit cats were slowing, their pelts smoothing, their
tails growing limp. A few of them straightened and looked
around, confusion in their eyes, as though they'd woken from a
dream. *It's working!* Shadowsight edged forward so they could see
him. "Ashfur is controlling you!" he yowled at them. "You have
to fight it." Recognition was sparking in their eyes, as though
they were seeing each other for the first time and suddenly

understood what they were doing here. Shadowsight's throat
tightened as Ashfur's gaze turned slowly toward him. He
forced himself not to tremble. "Quick!" he called to the spirit
cats. "He's lost concentration! Run away while you can."

Some of the cats turned and fled toward the trees. Others seemed frozen to the earth. They glanced fearfully toward
Ashfur, as though too frightened to escape him. Only the cats
at the farthest edge of the battle seemed unafraid. They glared
at the milling spirit cats with undisguised fury. *They must be
true Dark Forest warriors,* Shadowsight thought. These weren't
cats who had died recently and found their path to StarClan
blocked. They belonged here. They were fighting for Ashfur
because they *wanted* to.

Bristlefrost and Rootspring were staggering to their paws.
Rootspring shook out his bloody pelt and began anxiously
sniffing Bristlefrost, as though checking her wounds. Stemleaf stood like stone and watched them, his eyes wide with
shock. He seemed to flinch as Bristlefrost turned toward him.
He blinked at her helplessly. "I'm sorry."

"Shadowsight's right," she told him. Her mew was gentle.
Pity welled in her eyes. "Ashfur was controlling you. You have
to fight it. . . ."

Stemleaf took a step back, shaking out his pelt. He wouldn't
meet her eyes. *Doesn't he believe me?*

Bristlefrost added softly, "Spotfur needs you to watch over
her from StarClan. She's missed you so much."

Now Stemleaf's eyes met hers, glistening. "I'd have stayed
with her if I'd had the choice."

"I know," Bristlefrost told him.

"Tell her I love her."

Bristlefrost nodded. "Come with us." She flicked her tail. "We need to get away while we can." As she turned toward the trees, the remaining spirit cats finally began to scatter, racing for the cover of the forest.

Ashfur bristled with fury. "Don't let them get away!" he growled.

Shadowsight's belly tightened as the Dark Forest warriors charged after the spirit cats. Dappletuft tried to duck beneath a bramble, but a Dark Forest she-cat with a scar running along her spine grabbed his tail between her teeth and hauled him back. Softpelt darted into the shadows. A burly tom charged after her, and Shadowsight heard a screech. A moment later he saw the tom dragging Softpelt back into the clearing by her scruff.

Shadowsight's heart sank. Slowly, the Dark Forest warriors were herding the spirit cats back into the clearing. Their escape thwarted, the defeated cats cowered in front of the bared teeth and unsheathed claws of their captors. He looked back toward Bristlefrost, relief pricking in his paws as he saw her already haring toward the trees, Rootspring and Stemleaf at her tail. *Run!* he urged silently. Ashfur wouldn't miss a second chance to kill them.

Bristlefrost's gray pelt was quickly swallowed by the forest's shadow. Rootspring disappeared after her. Stemleaf was trailing, his frightened eyes fixed on Rootspring's tail as it snaked away into darkness.

No! Shadowsight froze as he saw Mapleshade pelt after them. She swooped across the dark earth as fast as a hawk, her pelt flat against her powerful frame. *Hurry!* Shadowsight urged Stemleaf on, panic bursting like fire in his chest as the ThunderClan warrior stumbled, his paw buckling on a root. Mapleshade's eyes lit with satisfaction as he faltered. She leaped and flung her paws toward him, grabbing his hindquarters and rolling with him as he tumbled to the ground. Stemleaf tried to struggle free, but Mapleshade was too strong. Holding him down with one paw, she slashed his chest with her other. The ThunderClan warrior's eyes widened with shock and he fell limp.

Please don't die here! Shadowsight could hardly believe his eyes. Stemleaf mustn't disappear forever. Spotfur needed him, even if only in StarClan. How could Mapleshade be so cruel? Shadowsight had heard tales of her nastiness as a Dark Forest mentor during the Great Battle. But if she'd been so tough, why was she following Ashfur's orders now? She clearly wasn't being controlled by him like the other spirit cats. What could she possibly have to gain by helping Ashfur wreak his revenge on the living Clans?

Shadowsight peered at Stemleaf's body. Was he dead or just injured? Shadowsight couldn't make out any blood. He began to skirt the clearing to get a better look as Mapleshade tried to nudge the limp tom roughly to his paws.

As he neared, Shadowsight saw the she-cat glance at him. His blood ran cold as her gaze flicked past him, satisfaction flashing in her eyes. What had she seen? Shadowsight glanced over his shoulder. Blood roared in his ears as he saw Ashfur padding after him, ears flat, eyes slitted with menace. Shadowsight froze for a moment, terror pulsing through his paws. *I have to escape.* He darted between the trees, hoping the shadows would hide him.

The steady thumping of Ashfur's paws behind grew louder as the dark warrior drew closer. Terror threatened to overwhelm Shadowsight. His pads slithered on the damp earth. He felt hot breath on his tail. *Help me!* If only StarClan could come to his aid. He felt powerless. The only thing he could do now was fight. Panic-stricken, he turned to face his attacker.

Ashfur's lip twisted in a snarl, his face a whisker from Shadowsight's. Breathless with horror, Shadowsight backed away until he felt rough bark against his spine. A tree trunk. If only it could swallow him and protect him from Ashfur's rage. The dark warrior loomed over him, his face twitching as though he could barely control the anger welling inside him. Shadowsight closed his eyes. Time seemed to slow as he braced himself for the claws that would rip open his muzzle.

He just hoped he'd given Bristlefrost and Rootspring enough time to get away.

CHAPTER 3

Bristlefrost glanced back. "Where's Stemleaf?" She slithered to a halt. There was no sign of the white-and-ginger tom. "We can't leave him behind."

Rootspring pulled up beside her. "I'll find him." As he began to race toward the clearing, movement deeper in the forest caught Bristlefrost's eye.

Alarm sparked through her fur. "Wait!"

Through the trees, she saw Ashfur grab Shadowsight by the scruff and fling him against a tree. The medicine cat hit the trunk with a thud and slid, dazed, among its roots. Bristlefrost's heart seemed to stop as the dark warrior padded toward Shadowsight. "We have to help him!" She darted toward Shadowsight as he struggled to find his paws, but Rootspring hooked her tail and tugged her back. "I'll take care of Ashfur," he mewed. "You find Stemleaf!"

Before she could argue, Rootspring pelted away, zigzagging between the trees. Bristlefrost held her breath as she watched him barrel into Ashfur and knock the dark warrior off his paws. She wanted to help him, but she *had* to find Stemleaf.

She raced for the clearing and reached it, breathless. *Where is he?* The Dark Forest warriors were pressing the spirit cats toward the middle of the clearing. Softpelt and Dappletuft huddled together. Strikestone and Conefoot shrank back in terror, the rest eyeing each other helplessly as the snarling warriors stalked around them.

Then she saw him. In the shadows at the side of the clearing, Mapleshade was shaking Stemleaf by his scruff. When the tortoiseshell-and-white she-cat let go, he dropped to the ground with a groan. "Get up, you mouse-heart!" she snarled.

Stemleaf lifted his head. Blood from a torn ear ran into his eyes, coloring them crimson. He blinked at Mapleshade and began to haul himself to his paws.

"Get over there with the others." Mapleshade nudged him roughly with her muzzle. "Did you really think you could escape?"

Anger surged through Bristlefrost. She drew her lips back into a snarl and charged toward the Dark Forest she-cat. Her paws moved so lightly over the ground that Mapleshade didn't seem to hear her. Bristlefrost leaped and felt a surge of satisfaction as she slammed into the other she-cat, claws outstretched, ears flat. Mapleshade fell, rolling onto her side like a helpless kit. Bristlefrost rolled with her, surprised that it had been so easy to knock the Dark Forest cat from her paws. Surely a seasoned warrior wouldn't be defeated so quickly? Her heart lurched at the feel of claws hooking her pelt. The sting made her wince, and she realized that Mapleshade hadn't fallen at all—the old she-cat had dropped into a defensive roll and was pulling Bristlefrost with her. A moment later, Bristlefrost's shoulders were pinned to the earth. She yelped in pain as hind claws raked her belly. Mapleshade's breath bathed her muzzle, and triumph sparked in the evil cat's gaze.

Bristlefrost gritted her teeth. Mapleshade wasn't the only warrior who knew battle moves. She let herself fall limp—only for a moment, but long enough for Mapleshade's grip to loosen with surprise. As it did, Bristlefrost darted from beneath the Dark Forest warrior, her lithe body quicker and nimbler than the more powerful she-cat. She spun and swung a blow at the she-cat's muzzle before Mapleshade could move. She felt fur and blood clump beneath her claws. Mapleshade recoiled and Bristlefrost raked her cheek with her other paw, delivering blow after blow before Mapleshade could regain her balance. "Run!" she hissed at Stemleaf.

The white-and-ginger tom had found his paws and was watching, his eyes wide. As he hesitated, Bristlefrost threw her whole strength into a fresh blow that sent Mapleshade reeling.

"Run!" she yowled again. But Stemleaf was staring into the forest, where Rootspring was guiding Shadowsight between the trees. The medicine cat's paws were unsteady and he was leaning heavily on the SkyClan tom.

Bristlefrost followed Stemleaf's gaze. Ashfur was standing motionless as the two toms limped away. Bristlefrost frowned, puzzled. *Why isn't he stopping them?* He stared toward the clearing, his gaze dark with intent, his body stiff, as he focused his attention on the spirit cats.

Bristlefrost's pelt grew cold as fear left the spirit cats' eyes. Their pelts smoothed; their ears pricked. Noiselessly, they turned and began to head into the forest.

She glanced back to Stemleaf. The warrior's eyes had begun to cloud. He turned his face toward her. "Get away from here," he croaked. "I can't promise I won't hurt you."

Bristlefrost swallowed back panic. Ashfur was taking control of his mind again. "Fight it!" she mewed.

"I'm trying." Stemleaf was trembling.

Bristlefrost watched, her paws frozen to the earth as she saw the familiar spark she'd recognized in his eyes disappear, and once more Stemleaf became a stranger.

He glowered at her. "You shouldn't have come here."

Bristlefrost's heart sank. She couldn't save him while he was like this. As he bared his teeth, she scrambled away, racing toward Rootspring. They had to get out of here. But the forest was already rippling with pelts as Ashfur's spirit cats moved through it. The Dark Forest cats who moments ago had blocked their escape walked among them; they were allies once more.

Bristlefrost skidded to a halt beside Rootspring. He was propping Shadowsight up, one shoulder tucked beneath the medicine cat's. Shadowsight's eyes were glazed. "Is he okay?" Bristlefrost mewed.

"He's pretty out of it," Rootspring told her.

Bristlefrost glanced at the advancing cats. "We have to escape this place."

"How?" Rootspring glanced around, fear glittering in his eyes. The forest was alive with cats. They were surrounded.

Ashfur's head was low, like a snake about to strike. His eyes were as black as night as he guided the spirit cats into a tighter circle around Bristlefrost, Rootspring, and Shadowsight.

Bristlefrost forced her pelt to stay flat. She could feel every one of her wounds burning, and her limbs felt heavy after the battle they'd already fought. "I'm not sure I can fight them again," she whispered to Rootspring.

"We don't have a choice." Rootspring lodged his shoulder more firmly beneath Shadowsight's.

The dazed medicine cat seemed unaware of the danger. How could they protect him and themselves at the same time? Bristlefrost moved closer to Rootspring. She dared not look at him, her heart breaking at the thought that he might die. *Perhaps I can give him enough time to escape*, she hoped desperately.

Suddenly, a white pelt flashed through the shadows, moving like lightning from among the spirit cats. It streaked toward Ashfur.

Bristlefrost stared at the scarred tom, her eyes widening with surprise. "Snowtuft!"

The white warrior lunged at Ashfur, crashing into him like a Twoleg monster smashing into carrion on the Thunderpath. Staggering backward, Ashfur slammed against a tree. His eyes flashed with surprise. Then rage returned to light the blackness once more.

As it did, the spirit cats stopped in their tracks. They stared, surprised to be free again. Softpelt and Dappletuft blinked at each other. Sandynose and Strikestone jerked their muzzles around, puzzled. Conefoot scanned the forest as though he'd forgotten where he was.

Snowtuft reared, lashing out at Ashfur with a yowl. "Run while you can!" he called to the spirit cats.

Ashfur batted him back. "Stop them!"

On his command, the Dark Forest warriors turned on the spirit cats once more as they began to flee. Softpelt dodged past a tabby tom. Conefoot leaped over a gray she-cat, twisting neatly out of reach of her claws as she leaped to stop him.

Bristlefrost stared at the jumble of pelts. Would they manage to escape this time? "Should we help them to get away?" She glanced at Rootspring.

"We can't risk it," he told her. "We have to get Shadowsight out of here." He began guiding the medicine cat away from the chaos.

She hurried after him and pressed in beside Shadowsight. The medicine cat limped between them, staring blankly ahead. At least he could put one paw in front of the other. Her ears flinched against the battle sounds behind her. *Please let them escape.* Were the spirit cats any match for the powerful Dark Forest warriors? And what about Snowtuft? The white tom had been reckless to take on Ashfur directly. But his attack had let them escape, and gratitude fought grief as Bristlefrost wondered what would happen to him.

An agonized shriek rose above the other yowls. The dark trees seemed to tremble as it split the air. Bristlefrost felt sick. Was that Snowtuft's dying wail? As she tried to block the thought out, paw steps thrummed behind them. She snapped her muzzle around, glancing fearfully over her shoulder. Had Ashfur sent a patrol after them already? She tried to quicken their pace. "I think they're chasing us," she whispered.

Rootspring was already looking back, his ears pricked nervously. She saw fur lift along his spine and unsheathed her claws, preparing to fight. Arching her back, she snarled as she saw Stemleaf darting toward her. Rootspring lined up beside her, flattening his ears threateningly. Bristlefrost didn't want to hurt her former Clanmate or the skinny black tom who was racing at his side. She knew they wouldn't be attacking if they had a choice.

The black tom pulled up a few tail-lengths away. Stemleaf slithered to a halt beside him. "It's okay," he mewed. "He's not controlling us."

Bristlefrost eyed the two cats. Was Stemleaf telling the truth? Rootspring was scanning the forest around them warily, as though wondering the same thing.

The skinny black tom stared anxiously at Shadowsight, who was shaking his head as though trying to get water out of his ears. "Is he hurt?"

"He's just dazed." Bristlefrost shifted her paws uneasily. Was this a trap?

"Do I know you?" Rootspring frowned at the skinny tom as though he vaguely recognized him.

Shadowsight lifted his muzzle and blinked at the black tom. His eyes cleared. "Spiresight!"

Spiresight padded closer. "Are you okay?"

Shadowsight shook out his pelt. "There's some ringing in my ears now, and I feel a little dizzy, but that's all." He looked at Spiresight and broke into a purr. "It's good to see you." He nuzzled the skinny tom affectionately. "Did Ashfur hurt you?"

"No," Spiresight assured him, purring in return.

Bristlefrost's chest tightened. She knew that Shadowsight had been named for Spiresight, the city cat who'd saved his life when Tigerheart and his family returned to ShadowClan's lake territory. And Spiresight's spirit had nurtured Shadowsight when he was recovering from the impostor's attempt to kill him. The warmth of the two toms' reunion touched her. Even in this dark place, friendship and loyalty could endure. She glanced at Stemleaf. His eyes were bright. Her shoulders loosened. These cats weren't being controlled by Ashfur.

Rootspring swished his tail. "We should keep moving."

Bristlefrost nodded. "It won't be long before Ashfur sends a search patrol." She led the way, following a trail of flattened earth between the trees. She glanced back, anxiety rippling through her fur as she noticed Shadowsight swaying. Spiresight stepped in to steady him with his shoulder, but it was clear from the medicine cat's faltering steps that the blow to his head was still affecting him.

Rootspring fell in beside her. "Where are we heading?"

Bristlefrost kept her voice low. "We have to get you back to the living world. Shadowsight isn't fit to be in such a dangerous place." She glanced at Rootspring's bloodstained pelt. There was a scratch beneath his eye, and one of his ears was torn. *Neither are you.* "There are too many enemies here," she mewed. "We need to get help."

Shadowsight nodded. "But it won't be easy. You were dragged here in your body, which means you can't just wake up in the living world, like we could. Squirrelflight and Bramblestar were able to escape back through the Moonpool—maybe you could do the same."

"Great. Do you know how to get to the Moonpool? I mean, how do we find it from the Dark Forest?" Rootspring blinked at her hopefully.

Bristlefrost's pelt rippled along her spine. She had no idea.

"I think I know how we might get Stemleaf and Spiresight out of here." Shadowsight's mew took her by surprise.

She pricked her ears. "How?"

"There's a path from the Dark Forest to StarClan," Shadowsight explained. "Stemleaf and Spiresight might be able to use it to get back to where they belong."

"Where is it?" Bristlefrost asked eagerly.

"It's near the edge of the Dark Forest," Shadowsight explained. "I found it the first time I was here. It was blocked by branches, but if we can unblock it, Stemleaf and Spiresight might be able to get through, and then perhaps the other spirit cats can escape that way, and then Ashfur wouldn't have so much power. . . ." His mew trailed away. Was he sure about this, Bristlefrost wondered, or was he just hoping?

Rootspring was looking doubtfully at the medicine cat, too. "I thought your first visit here was in your dreams?"

Shadowsight looked puzzled, as though he didn't understand why Rootspring was asking. "So?"

"So, how can you be sure that this blocked entrance is real?" Rootspring pressed.

"Just because it was a dream doesn't mean I wasn't here." Shadowsight looked from Rootspring to Bristlefrost. "*You're* here, right?"

"I'm *here* here I was dragged through the Moonpool by Willowshine, remember. My *body* is here. But even for you, this isn't a dream," Rootspring reminded him.

"You're right," Shadowsight answered tartly. "This is just a forest full of dead cats."

Rootspring's pelt ruffled.

Bristlefrost flicked her tail. "I think we can all agree that nothing about the Dark Forest is simple." She wanted to find the mound of tangled branches. "It doesn't matter *how* we got here—we're here now, and I think we should find this blocked entrance." Surely it would be better than stumbling around looking for a way to the Moonpool.

She hung back and let Shadowsight take the lead, then followed with Rootspring.

His pelt was still ruffled. "I just hope he knows where he's going," he whispered in Bristlefrost's ear.

"We have to trust him," she whispered back.

Shadowsight followed the trail of trodden earth until it forked, and paused. He hesitated, then took the path that led uphill. With only tree trunks and shadows to mark the way, it was hard to tell how far they'd come. Shadowsight seemed tentative as he led them along a twisting route, and Bristlefrost began to worry that they were traveling in circles. The only thing she could be sure of was that more and more streams of crow-black water were crisscrossing the forest floor.

"Does he really know where this entrance is?" Stemleaf whispered from behind.

Bristlefrost glanced back at the white-and-ginger tom. "Give him space," she whispered. "I'm sure he'll find the way." She hoped she was right. Peering ahead, past Shadowsight and Spiresight, she saw dense fog pressing between the trees. Shadowsight halted as he reached it. Cautiously, he poked a paw into the murky cloud; then he snatched it out quickly. "It's freezing."

"It marks the edge of the Dark Forest," Spiresight told him.

Bristlefrost stopped beside them. "Can't we go through it?"

"There's nothing beyond," Spiresight explained. "Just fog." He narrowed his eyes. "But I've never seen it reach this deep into the forest before."

Shadowsight edged backward as the fog brushed his muzzle. "It's closing in."

Spiresight glanced around nervously. "Is the Dark Forest shrinking?"

Bristlefrost lifted her tail. "Let's try another route."

Stemleaf shifted his paws and glanced at the medicine cat. "You *do* know which way to go, don't you?"

Shadowsight tasted the air. "It's hard to tell," he mewed. "But if we keep going, I'm sure I'll recognize something soon."

Bristlefrost whisked her tail. "The path to StarClan must

be *somewhere*," she mewed, trying to sound hopeful. But she wasn't sure what would happen if they *did* find the entrance. Shadowsight had said it was blocked. If Stemleaf and Spiresight could get through, there wouldn't be so many spirit cats trapped in the Dark Forest. But they couldn't just wait here for Ashfur and his followers to track them down. "Come on." She turned away from the fog and nodded Shadowsight into the lead once more. "Let's try this way."

She fell in beside Rootspring, following the others as they retraced their steps. "Do you think the Dark Forest is really shrinking?" she whispered.

"I'm afraid it is," Rootspring answered. "Snowtuft told me as much, when he was helping me."

Bristlefrost pressed back a shiver. If the Dark Forest *was* disappearing, would they disappear along with it? Spiresight's words from a moment ago came back to her now. *There's nothing beyond.* She tried not to think about what that could possibly be like. Instead she told herself that Shadowsight *would* find the way to StarClan. When he did, they would work out what to do next.

Ahead, a stream of dark water showed among the trees. It was wider than the others and crossed their path. Shadowsight hopped over it and the rest of them followed. Bristlefrost glanced down as she jumped it. Her belly tightened. The water was so black that it didn't even show her reflection.

"This water's strange," she whispered to Rootspring as she landed.

"Keep your paws clear of it," Rootspring warned her.

Bristlefrost stiffened. "Why?"

"I fell in last time I was here," he told her. "It felt like it was draining my strength. I think I was lucky to survive."

Bristlefrost stopped, alarmed, and stared at him, her eyes pricking with grief. How many times had Rootspring come close to dying in this dreadful place?

He paused beside her. "In the fight back there"—he glanced the way they'd come—"I thought I was going to die. And all I could think of was you." His eyes shone with love. "I was so glad to see you—not just because you saved me, but because the thought of never seeing you again seemed worse than death."

It felt as if her heart swelled in her chest until she could barely speak. "I'm glad I got to you in time," she breathed.

He touched his muzzle to hers, then seemed to force himself to break away and begin walking again. She understood; they had work to do. He was limping a little, and as she noticed again his torn and bloody pelt, anxiety flashed through her. She couldn't ever lose him. He meant too much to her. The thought made her breathless with fear. At least the bloodstains had dried and no fresh blood was oozing from his cuts.

She hurried after him. "Do your scratches still hurt?"

He shrugged. "A little."

She guessed he was being brave.

"I'll be okay," he told her.

She moved closer, letting her pelt brush his. Here, where they faced so much danger, it didn't matter that they were from different Clans. Along with Shadowsight, they were the only living cats in the Dark Forest, and all they had right now was each other. They walked in silence for a while as Shadowsight led them along first one trail and then another. Fog seemed to hem them in more and more, and the dark streams seemed to be a little wider each time they crossed one.

The silence felt eerie. A forest without birds made her paws prick uneasily. But at least the silence was better than the shriek of battle. Bristlefrost remembered the screech she'd heard as they'd fled Ashfur and the Dark Forest cats. She shuddered.

Rootspring glanced at her. "What's wrong?"

She kept her gaze ahead. "Do you think Snowtuft is dead?"

Rootspring hesitated. "I don't think Ashfur would spare any cat who challenged his authority." His ears twitched nervously.

"So you think Ashfur killed him?"

Rootspring avoided her gaze. "I wanted to get him out of this place," he mewed quietly. "He saved me more than once. He didn't deserve to be here anymore. I kind of hoped he'd be given a place in StarClan."

Bristlefrost moved closer, pressing her flank against his. "If he is dead, he died a true warrior's death," she murmured.

Ahead, Shadowsight and Spiresight were heading over a rise. Stemleaf turned and waited for Bristlefrost and Rootspring to catch up. As he watched them, Bristlefrost was suddenly aware how close she was walking to Rootspring, and quickly pulled away.

Stemleaf's whiskers twitched with amusement. "Don't act

cool for me," he mewed. "I think it's cute how close you two have become." When Stemleaf had died, she and Rootspring had hardly even been friends. He sidled up beside them as they followed Shadowsight and Spiresight over the rise and glanced mischievously at Bristlefrost. "I guess you're over your crush on me."

Bristlefrost's ears grew hot. "That was moons ago," she mumbled.

"I know." Stemleaf nudged her with his shoulder. "I'm just teasing." He turned to Rootspring. "But it seems like you're mates now."

"We're not mates," Bristlefrost mewed quickly.

Rootspring moved closer, letting their pelts brush once more. "We love each other," he told Stemleaf simply. "But we love our Clans too."

"Really?" Stemleaf looked surprised. "Spotfur was the brightest part of my life." He gazed ahead thoughtfully. "Since I died, I've been surer of that than ever. I know it was easy for us to be together, but I think that if she'd belonged to another Clan, I would have chosen *her.*"

Bristlefrost blinked at him, surprised. "You'd have given up ThunderClan?"

He shrugged. "Clans have many warriors, but you only love one cat."

Bristlefrost looked away, her chest tightening. For a long time, she'd been determined to choose her Clan over Rootspring. Could Stemleaf tell she was having doubts? She felt

Rootspring's pelt, warm against her, and wondered if he was thinking the same thing.

Ahead, the trees were beginning to thin. A wide, dark stream lay at the bottom of a slope. It didn't tumble or chatter like a stream in the living forest but spread silently across the forest floor like a pool of blood. Bristlefrost pressed back a shudder and hurried after Shadowsight and Spiresight as they stopped at the edge.

Shadowsight gazed across the dark water. On the other side, blackened tree stumps stuck up from the earth like claws. "I think we're heading in the right direction," the medicine cat mewed. "I saw this hollow in my dream." He glanced at the stream. "But this wasn't here then."

"Why is the Dark Forest changing?" Spiresight wondered.

"It must be something to do with Ashfur." Shadowsight leaned down and sniffed the water.

Stemleaf shivered. "I just hope we can get out before there's so much fog and water that there's no path left."

"Let's cross this stream and find the entrance to StarClan." Bristlefrost lifted her chin. They didn't have time to worry about what might happen. Perhaps they *would* be able to get Spiresight and Stemleaf back where they belonged. She leaped the stream, trying not to look down, and stumbled as she landed.

"Look out!" Rootspring darted forward, teetering at the far edge, his eyes wide with panic.

She snapped her head around and saw her tail skimming

the water. With a gasp, she flicked it up. She was sure she'd leaped far enough to clear it. How fast was the dark water rising? "Quick!" She beckoned the others over with a jerk of her muzzle.

As Stemleaf and Spiresight leaped the stream, Rootspring hung back. Shadowsight hesitated at the edge. Was he still dazed?

"You can do it," Bristlefrost called across the water.

"Just be careful not to touch it," Rootspring warned.

Shadowsight tensed, bunching his muscles as he prepared to jump. Narrowing his eyes, he leaped and cleared the stream with his forepaws. But as one hind paw reached dry land, he seemed to lose his balance, wobbling as he landed so that his trailing paw splashed into the water.

Bristlefrost gasped. As quick as a flash, she snatched Shadowsight's scruff between her teeth and hauled him clear. She let go and sniffed his hind leg, relieved to find that it was only wet.

Rootspring jumped after him and landed beside them, his pelt spiked. "Are you okay?"

"I'm fine." Shadowsight shook the water from his hind paw. His pelt rippled self-consciously as he padded up the slope. Spiresight followed, catching up and staying close. Stemleaf glanced uneasily at Bristlefrost, then hurried after them.

Bristlefrost looked back at the stream. She was sure it had spread even further across the forest floor. Foreboding pricked beneath her pelt. The dark water was definitely rising.

"I hope we find the entrance soon," she mewed.

Rootspring folded his tail across her spine. "We will," he promised, and Bristlefrost hoped he was right.

Shadowsight, Spiresight, and Stemleaf had stopped at the top of the rise. Bristlefrost slowed as she saw Stemleaf's pelt lift along his spine. Shadowsight's ears were twitching. What had they seen? Bristlefrost hurried to catch up, wary as a familiar scent touched her nose. *RiverClan?* She stopped at the top, her paws pricking in surprise. A familiar cat was standing between the blackened tree stumps.

It was Willowshine.

Bristlefrost's hackles lifted. Was the dead RiverClan medicine cat still under Ashfur's control? She scanned the shadows behind her, half expecting to see eyes gleaming in the darkness as a patrol of Dark Forest warriors prepared an ambush, but nothing was there. She tasted the air. Willowshine was alone.

"It's okay." Willowshine seemed to sense her fear. "Ashfur's not controlling me."

Rootspring narrowed his eyes at the RiverClan medicine cat. "You've lied about that before," he growled.

"That wasn't me." She stared at the yellow tom with clear, bright eyes.

Bristlefrost studied her cautiously. There was no sign of the malice Bristlefrost had seen in the cats Ashfur had been controlling in battle. "I think she's telling the truth," she whispered to Rootspring.

"I am." Willowshine whisked her tail. "I promise."

Rootspring padded closer and sniffed; then, apparently satisfied, he dipped his head. "How did you get free?"

"I ran away when Snowtuft attacked Ashfur," she told him. "His control seems to be stronger over medicine cats, but usually, Ashfur can't force cats to do his bidding when he's not close to them."

Bristlefrost's tail twitched nervously. "Did you see what happened to Snowtuft?" she asked, dread weighing like a stone in her chest.

Willowshine's gaze darkened. "Ashfur broke his neck," she mewed bleakly. "I'm sorry to say that he's dead."

Bristlefrost felt sick.

Rootspring stiffened. "He deserved to make it to StarClan." Bitterness edged his mew. "Now he won't exist at all, not even here."

"He'll exist for us," Bristlefrost mewed softly. "We'll remember him, even if he isn't in StarClan."

Rootspring looked suddenly weary, his bloodstained pelt dull and ragged.

Pity stabbed Bristlefrost's heart. "Can you check Rootspring's wounds?" she asked Willowshine. She sat down, aware of the sting of her own injuries, of her aching muscles. She wasn't sure it was wise to stop here, but she knew she wasn't the only cat who needed to catch their breath.

Willowshine sniffed Rootspring's pelt, pausing at every claw scratch and bite mark to examine it. Then she looked at Spiresight. "I know there are no herbs here to treat wounds, but have you seen any moss? I can at least clean some of the blood away."

Spiresight got to his paws. "I'll look for some." As he hurried away to search cracks and crevices in the tree trunks, Stemleaf began to tend to his own cuts and scratches, washing them thoroughly. Shadowsight rested on his belly and, tucking his paws under him, closed his eyes for a moment.

Willowshine glanced at him anxiously. "You shouldn't sleep here," she advised, sniffing behind his ear. Even Bristlefrost could see swelling there. "You might not be able to wake up." Willowshine looked into Shadowsight's eyes as he opened them. "Are you feeling dizzy?"

"A little," Shadowsight told her.

Willowshine's gaze flicked to the tip of Bristlefrost's ear, where Bristlefrost could feel stinging. "You look like you could do with treatment too. That was a vicious battle. You three ought to get back to the living forest so you can get some proper care."

I wish it were that easy. Bristlefrost's tail twitched irritably as the RiverClan medicine cat went on.

"I don't know why you thought you could fight the Dark Forest cats alone."

"It's not like we had a choice," Bristlefrost snapped.

Spiresight padded from the shadows and dropped a wad of damp moss at Willowshine's paws. "That's all I can find, but at least it looks clean," he mewed.

"Thank you." Willowshine dipped her head, picked up the moss between her jaws, and began to press it into the deepest wound on Rootspring's flank. Rootspring grimaced but made no sound.

Bristlefrost was still smarting from Willowshine's words. "We've been trying to find the entrance to StarClan so we can get Stemleaf and Spiresight back there."

"It's blocked," Willowshine mewed. She didn't look up from her work.

Bristlefrost blinked. "Do you know where it is?" she asked, surprised.

Willowshine jerked her muzzle toward the shadows beyond the tree stumps. "That way."

The medicine cat sounded so sure. Bristlefrost felt suddenly hopeful again. "How do you know?"

"I just feel it." Willowshine shrugged. "It's like StarClan is pulling me toward them." She blinked at Stemleaf and Spiresight. "Can't *you* feel it?"

Stemleaf frowned as though concentrating. Then his eyes widened. "Yes!" He sounded surprised. "I hadn't noticed it before, but I do now. . . . It's like a tug in my chest."

Spiresight padded a few steps between the stumps and stared toward the shadows where Willowshine had pointed. "I feel something," he mewed. "Like a longing . . ." His mew trailed away.

"That's it." Willowshine sat back on her haunches and brushed away a few crumbs of moss caught in Rootspring's pelt. "We just need to follow that feeling."

Bristlefrost felt hope rising in her chest once more. "Then

let's go." She got to her paws and started to head toward the shadows.

Willowshine slid past her. "I'll show you the way," she mewed.

Bristlefrost was happy to let the medicine cat take the lead. She felt tired despite the brief rest, and her wounds were throbbing. Shadowsight hurried after the RiverClan medicine cat, and as Spiresight and Stemleaf followed, Bristlefrost caught up to Rootspring.

"Did the moss help?" she asked.

"Kind of." Rootspring shrugged, and Bristlefrost guessed he must still be in pain. She wanted to get him home as soon as possible so that Frecklewish could give him herbs that would make him feel better.

Willowshine led them up a rocky hillside and onto a narrow ledge, which they followed around a cliff where overhanging trees reached for them with dangling branches. Bristlefrost shuddered as twigs scraped her spine and was relieved when the ledge opened onto another rocky slope. She scrambled down it after the others, one eye on Rootspring, who winced as he fought to keep his footing on the slippery gravel. The slope flattened onto marshy ground where rivulets of dark water twined between muddy hummocks. Bristlefrost fought back fear as the group picked its way from mound to mound, careful not to let a paw or tail slip into the streams. Her pelt smoothed with relief as more level ground came into view in the forest beyond.

They followed a narrow path through a wall of twisted brambles, the prickles scratching Bristlefrost's pelt as she padded after the others. On the far side a large, gnarled tree sprouted among slender beeches. Shadowsight lifted his tail excitedly. "I remember this place. The entrance to StarClan is this way!" He broke into a run. Bristlefrost's belly sparked with alarm as he disappeared into the shadows.

"Wait!" She quickened her step, signaling to the others with a flick of her tail to keep up. But Stemleaf was already racing after the ShadowClan medicine cat. As Bristlefrost caught up to them, she saw among the shadows a wall of branches piled between the trees. They were woven tightly together with vines, twisted together like a swarm of snakes.

Stemleaf stared at it, his eyes wide. Spiresight began to sniff anxiously at the vines.

Bristlefrost padded closer. "Does this lead to StarClan?"

"Yes," Willowshine mewed heavily. "At least, I guess it *used to.*"

Rootspring stopped beside Bristlefrost. His ears were pricked. He frowned. "Can you hear a voice?"

Bristlefrost looked at him. His ears swiveled toward the entrance. She strained to hear, listening for a sound from among the twisted branches, but heard nothing except the eerie silence of the Dark Forest.

Willowshine poked a vine with a paw. "How in StarClan did Ashfur manage to weave this shut?"

"I'm not sure." Shadowsight stood back and looked thoughtful. "But it looks way more tangled than it was in my dreams. It's like the vines and branches have knotted together even more tightly."

Stemleaf's pelt pricked nervously. "How can we get through?"

"It looks like we're stuck here." Spiresight's tail drooped.

"When Ashfur finds us, he'll control us again." Stemleaf shuddered. "It feels like drowning and there's nothing we can do to stop it." He looked at Bristlefrost with round eyes. "There's no way to fight it," he mewed.

Bristlefrost whisked her tail. This couldn't be the end. The living Clans were depending on them, the spirit cats too. "There has to be a way," she told him. "We need to defeat Ashfur for good." She wasn't going to let Stemleaf despair. "Think of your kits."

"My kits?" Stemleaf blinked at her.

Doesn't he know? Bristlefrost had assumed a StarClan cat would know everything. But then she remembered, StarClan hadn't communicated with the living cats in a long time—and Stemleaf wasn't a StarClan cat. At least, not yet.

"Spotfur is carrying your kits," she explained. "She'll need you to watch over them."

"I'm going to have kits?" Stemleaf's whiskers were twitching excitedly. "Really?"

"Yes." Bristlefrost felt a glimmer of hope. His excitement was infectious.

Rootspring shifted beside her. "You can't let them grow up in a forest destroyed by Ashfur," he mewed.

Stemleaf lifted his chin. "You're right. I can't let that

happen. I'll do anything to protect them. I'll stop Ashfur, whatever it takes."

As he spoke, a vine in the tangles blocking the entrance seemed to loosen from the branch it was smothering. Slipping suddenly, it snapped, and the branch bulged from the barrier, straining at the rest of its bonds.

Bristlefrost's breath caught in her throat. "Is that a good omen?"

Shadowsight hurried closer to the barrier and sniffed it. "I think it may be more than a good omen." He faced the group. "This place is full of fear, rage and spite. It thrives on dark energy." He looked at Bristlefrost. "The only way I could get here was to feel angry and frightened. I had to feel hopeless."

Bristlefrost narrowed her eyes thoughtfully. Was that how the Sisters had helped them find their way here? By attuning their emotions to match the energy of the Dark Forest?

Shadowsight went on. "I had to work hard to make sure I never lost sight of myself, so that those dark emotions couldn't take me over entirely."

Of course! When they'd brought her here, the Sisters had shown her how to center herself so that there was always a place inside her heart that the Dark Forest could not reach, a part of herself that would remain safe from its influence.

Rootspring curled his claws into the earth. "I hadn't thought about it before, but you're right," he told Shadowsight. "It's the same when I connect with dead spirits. I have to anchor myself to the earth to stop me slipping entirely into their world."

Shadowsight began to pace eagerly in front of the barrier. "Ashfur never centered himself or tried to protect any part of himself from his darkest thoughts. He let them grow. He encouraged them until they possessed him entirely. And now he's so in tune with the Dark Forest that he can shape it to his will."

Bristlefrost's pelt was tingling with excitement. "But if *he* can shape it, so can we!" She nodded toward the snapped vine. It was withering. "Look what happened when Stemleaf decided Ashfur could be stopped. He began to hope, and that vine snapped."

Rootspring swished his tail. "Here, hope is our greatest strength."

"It might be our only strength," Spiresight mewed darkly.

"If it is, we have to make the most of it." Bristlefrost darted forward and hooked her forepaws around a vine. Tugging it, she yowled out loud. "StarClan is still with us," she mewed. "And we're going to reach them."

Willowshine grabbed another vine and pulled. "I know I'll get to StarClan," she yowled. "I'll see my ancestors again."

"I'll watch my kits grow up!" Stemleaf sank his teeth into a thick tendril and jerked it away from the branch it was holding. Rootspring grunted as he freed a bunch of knotted sticks.

Bristlefrost felt the vine between her paws give a little. "It's working!" Hope was surging beneath her pelt now. But time was running out. Untangling the barrier was going to take ages—far longer than they had. If Ashfur and his allies didn't find them first, the fog and dark water that were swallowing the Dark Forest would overwhelm them. She let go of the vine and sat back on her haunches. "It would be quicker if we had help."

Shadowsight paused. "We need more cats," he agreed.

Bristlefrost frowned thoughtfully. "Perhaps we could free some of the spirit cats from Ashfur's control. If we explain to them that StarClan never abandoned us—that they *belong* in StarClan's hunting grounds—their hope could open the way to StarClan."

"How will you free them?" Willowshine glanced around the group. "None of you look like you're up to confronting Ashfur right now."

"We couldn't do it alone," Stemleaf conceded.

Bristlefrost felt a prickle of frustration, but she knew that they were right. "We could get help from more living cats," she suggested.

Rootspring looked at her. "You mean, bring more Clan cats here?"

Bristlefrost's heart was pounding. "Well, yes. After all, if *we* can get here, so can others. We just have to find a way to let them—"

"Bristlefrost? Is that you?"

Bristlefrost jerked around. Someone was calling her name. Had Ashfur or his warriors caught up to them? Hackles rising, she scanned the shadowy forest.

The voice called again. "Bristlefrost? Are you there?" The voice sounded excited.

Bristlefrost turned further around, completing a circle, and saw Shadowsight staring at the barrier. His eyes were wide with amazement.

Willowshine pricked her ears. "Leafpool? Is that you?"

Bristlefrost hurried closer. She'd been an apprentice when Leafpool had died. She remembered the pale tabby she-cat crossing the camp clearing, or nosing her way from the medicine den. She knew from Squirrelflight that Leafpool had made it into StarClan before they lost communication with the living cats. Was ThunderClan's former medicine cat really behind the tangle of branches and vines? "Leafpool?" she mewed tentatively.

"Yes!" Leafpool sounded delighted. "It's me!"

Bristlefrost strained harder to see through the crisscrossed branches. She glimpsed a light brown tabby pelt, and the scent of ThunderClan flooded between the vines. It really was her! This was the first contact any cat had made with StarClan in moons, and the thought that StarClan was so close, even if they couldn't reach it, made her fur tingle with excitement. She pressed harder against the barrier, listening for Leafpool's voice, and felt another vine loosen.

Stemleaf and Rootspring hurried nearer, their whiskers quivering.

"What's happening out there?" Leafpool called. "We've heard nothing for so long. Is everything okay?"

Bristlefrost swapped looks with Rootspring. What should she tell the StarClan cat?

"Ashfur took over Bramblestar's body," Rootspring called.

"We knew that cat was up to no good." Leafpool sounded frustrated. "But how?"

"He stole it when Bramblestar lost a life," Bristlefrost explained.

"We were able to drive Ashfur out," Shadowsight told her. "Bramblestar has his body back now, but Ashfur has taken over the Dark Forest. He's trying to hurt the Clans."

Leafpool didn't speak, and Bristlefrost guessed the StarClan cat was struggling to take this all in.

Willowshine stretched her muzzle closer. "We haven't been able to reach you for moons," she mewed. "We thought you'd abandoned us."

The barrier trembled. "StarClan would never abandon you!" Leafpool exclaimed. Bristlefrost felt weak with relief as Leafpool went on. "The pool where we watch our loved ones is clogged with vines, just like this tunnel. We've been trying to reach you, but with no success. Somehow, by blocking our connection to the Dark Forest, Ashfur has cut us off from you. . . . We should have realized he was planning something when he asked to go to the living world to find out why we were losing touch with you. We had no idea that he would cut us off, or that he wanted to take over Bramblestar's body!"

"So Ashfur destroyed our connection with you?" Shadowsight mewed. "By building this barrier between StarClan's hunting grounds and the Dark Forest? The tangle of vines looks like it's getting stronger."

"Exactly. He's the one who dug this entrance in the first

place," Leafpool called through the branches. "He blocked the old one that led through the woods to the Dark Forest. He wanted a connection that only he knew about, one that only he could use." Leafpool sounded exasperated. "Now we realize that's because he intended to block it. And because all three worlds are interconnected—the Dark Forest, our hunting grounds, and the living world—it also prevented us from communicating with you. But Ashfur didn't want StarClan to see what he was doing. We're trapped in here and there's no way through. We've tried to break the barrier down, but it's too strong for us."

"We have to find a way soon," Bristlefrost urged. "The Dark Forest is disappearing!"

"That doesn't surprise me. Things are changing in StarClan, too," Leafpool answered. "Some of our warriors are starting to feel weak. Their memories of the living world are fading, and they're fading along with them."

Bristlefrost pressed back a surge of alarm. "Things are bad here, too. There's dark water, and fog, and it's closing in." She felt her breath hot against the barrier as she leaned closer, waiting to hear Leafpool's response. But Leafpool was silent. Bristlefrost's heart was pounding so hard, she wondered if the other cats could hear it. "Are you still there?"

"I'm here," Leafpool answered. "I'm afraid Ashfur has upset the balance between the worlds. Light and shadow cannot exist without each other, and now Ashfur has broken the connection . . ." She sighed. "I fear things will only get worse in the living world, too."

"We can fix it, though, can't we?" Bristlefrost's throat felt tight.

"We have to." Leafpool's mew was firm. "It's time we started to set things right."

Bristlefrost rested her cheek against the barrier as renewed relief overwhelmed her. Their ancestors hadn't abandoned them; StarClan was going to help the living Clans. She hadn't realized how much moon after moon of being told by Ashfur that the Clans were being punished for breaking the warrior code had put a chill in her heart. Now she knew it wasn't true—it had never been true. StarClan was still on their side.

She looked at the other cats and saw hope glistening in their eyes. They were as relieved as she was. Beside them, the vines creaked as they loosened a little more. But the branches were still firmly in place. They would need more help than this to break the barrier between StarClan and the Dark Forest.

She flicked her tail eagerly. "We have to get back and tell the Clans," she mewed to Rootspring. "If *they* know that StarClan never abandoned them, their hope might be enough to break down this wall."

He nodded. "We have to get—"

Before he could finish, Willowshine jerked around, her pelt spiking as she stared into the shadows between the trees. "Ashfur is near," she breathed. Fear sparked in her eyes. "I can feel him. He's trying to take control of my mind."

Spiresight was backing away, his tail bushed. "I can feel it too."

Stemleaf frowned. "Are you sure? I can't sense anything."

"Willowshine told us that she thinks medicine cats might be more sensitive to his control," Shadowsight mewed.

Leafpool called through the barrier. "Quick! You must get away."

Willowshine's tail trembled. "Let's go before he gets any closer."

Spiresight blinked at Shadowsight. "Come on."

Shadowsight dipped his head. "You'll be faster without me," he mewed. "I'm still a little dizzy. Besides, Ashfur can't control the minds of living cats."

"He can still hurt you," Spiresight warned.

Stemleaf's pelt ruffled along his spine. "I can sense Ashfur. He must be getting closer." He backed away. "We shouldn't be near any living cat. If Ashfur takes over our minds again, we'll try to attack you."

Bristlefrost felt an ache of pity for the white-and-orange tom. She couldn't imagine what it would be like to be forced to attack her Clanmates. "Okay. You'd better go." She turned to Shadowsight. "You should leave, too. Go another way."

He blinked at her. "On my own?"

She nodded. It would be safer for all of them.

Shadowsight's eyes glittered with fear. "What about you and Rootspring?"

"We'll divert Ashfur to give you time to escape." She met Rootspring's gaze. "Okay?"

"Okay." Rootspring nodded.

"It's up to you now, Shadowsight—can you try to wake up?" she asked hopefully.

Shadowsight shook his head. "I'm not sure." He closed his eyes tight, and Bristlefrost watched as his forehead wrinkled in concentration. She held her breath, waiting for the small gray tom to fade as he awoke by the Moonpool. But nothing happened.

After a few moments, he opened his eyes. "I can't do it," he mewed sadly. "Something is different . . . maybe because the Sisters helped us in."

Bristlefrost tried to hide her disappointment. *This will be harder, then.* "You have to go out like Bramblestar and Squirrelflight, then. Can find your way back to the Moonpool?" she asked.

The medicine cat glanced nervously between the trees. "I . . ."

Rootspring stepped forward. "When I fell through, there was a gnarled tree," he explained. "And the light was odd, reflected through the water above."

Shadowsight nodded. "That sounds like enough for me to look for. I'm sure I can find it. I'll have to."

"Good." Bristlefrost spoke quickly. "Thank you, Shadowsight. Get back to the living Clans and tell them what Leafpool said. Tell them that we need help dismantling this barrier." She called through the branches to Leafpool. "We'll let the Clans know that you're still on their side," she promised.

"Stay safe," Leafpool mewed back.

"Be as quick as you can," Bristlefrost told Shadowsight.

"If the Dark Forest is shrinking, then there isn't much time. Before long we might not be able to reach this place again."

Shadowsight nodded and, without another word, slipped away into the shadowy forest.

Stemleaf paced anxiously. "I can hear paw steps," he mewed.

"Quick, go!" Bristlefrost told him. She could hear them too.

Willowshine hesitated. "Will you be all right?" she asked.

"We have to be," Bristlefrost told her. "The Clans are depending on us." As the three spirit cats disappeared between the trees, she glanced at Rootspring. "We should split up too," she told him.

His eyes widened. "Wouldn't it be safer if we stayed together?"

"The more trails we leave, the harder it will be for Ashfur to find us." Bristlefrost scanned the shadows, her heart pounding. "One of us has to survive. We'll have more of a chance if we separate."

Rootspring's pelt spiked. "I can't leave you."

Bristlefrost could hear the rustling of the twisted brambles getting closer. "There's no time to discuss it. You head that way." She nodded toward the shadows beside the barrier. "I'll go this way." Before he could argue, she touched her muzzle quickly to his. "We'll meet back here once we lose Ashfur." Her chest pricked with fear as she hurried away, breaking into a run as angry growls sounded behind her. *Please let Rootspring be okay.* What if he didn't make it back to the barrier? Her belly tightened. *What if I don't make it back?* What if the dark water rose so much there was no way to *get* back? She could see thin streams cutting between the trees. If the Dark Forest flooded completely, they would never be able to free StarClan.

She pushed the thought away. She could not let herself despair. Hope was her only weapon here, and she had to cling to it no matter what.

CHAPTER 4

Rootspring pulled up sharply, sending leaves fluttering as he slid to a halt. Pricking his ears, he peered back the way he'd run, straining to see any sign of Ashfur's patrol. Relief washed his pelt. He thought he'd lost them, but he tasted the air anyway just to be sure. His shoulders loosened. The only scents here were the musty odor of decay and the sour tang of the blood dried into his fur.

He crouched low, his flanks heaving, his paws hot. He was breathless from the chase. Twice he'd thought Ashfur's warriors would catch him as he led them away from the StarClan barrier. The first time, he'd hit a stretch of rough ground dotted with pools of dark water. He'd dodged around the water, careful not to get his paws wet. The patrol chasing him had split up and tried to cut him off, but he'd given them the slip, leaping the last two pools and diving into a patch of nettles before switching course. It had thrown them off only for a few moments; they were on his tail again by the time he reached a rocky gully that cut the forest in two. He'd led them along it, his muscles burning with the effort. Panic had clutched his chest until he felt he could hardly breathe. But he'd known that, with every paw step, he was leading them farther from the barrier and from Bristlefrost.

Bristlefrost. He hoped he had drawn off all their pursuers and she was clear of danger by now. Perhaps she'd even made it back to the barrier and was waiting for him there already. *Please let her be safe.* His belly tightened. What if she didn't make it? What if he never saw her again? *No!* He pushed the thought away. *I can't think like that.* It hurt too much.

The second time they'd nearly caught him, he'd been scrabbling out of the gully. As he'd hauled himself up a wall of crumbling earth and rock, he'd felt claws hook his tail. He'd ripped free, but a tail-length from the top, the ledge he'd scrambled onto had collapsed. As it dropped away beneath him, he'd grabbed the cliff top and dangled for a moment by a single claw. Terror had flared through every hair of his pelt, but he'd made it, pulling himself up and collapsing at the top while he watched Ashfur's patrol pace angrily beneath, unable to follow.

He hadn't stopped running since then, crossing damp earth where he could so the rank smell would hide his scent, doubling back every so often to confuse the trail. And now he was sure he must have lost the Dark Forest warriors.

He caught his breath and let it slow, forcing his pelt to smooth. As his panic eased, he became aware of his wounds once more. Fresh blood was welling on his shoulder where a scratch had reopened. He turned to lick it, wincing at the sting.

Rootspring.

He froze as he heard someone call his name. Slowly, careful not to shift the leaves, he stretched up and craned his neck to peer around. The trees were slender here, their narrow trunks hard to hide behind, and there was no undergrowth but creeping weeds, which wound around their roots. He couldn't see any cat. But he'd definitely heard his name. Had Ashfur's patrol tracked him down? He tasted the air again and smelled nothing new.

Nervously, Rootspring began to pick his way between the trees, hardly breathing in case he gave himself away.

The voice sounded again.

Rootspring.

This time, he answered. "Who *are* you?" He scanned the forest again, uneasy as he saw no sign of life. He swallowed back fear. "*What* are you?" Whatever it was, it was tracking him, and being stalked by something in the Dark Forest couldn't be good.

Rootspring.

The voice was inside his head. Hadn't Bramblestar's spirit spoken to him like this beside the lake—calling to him inside his mind? He'd thought he had bees in his brain until he'd realized who it was, and even then he hadn't trusted the ghost as it had trailed him through the forest.

Rootspring.

But it couldn't be Bramblestar. The ThunderClan leader was alive and in the living forest with Squirrelflight. His thoughts whirled. Was it Leafpool? But how could it be? She was trapped behind the barrier, far from here.

A thought flashed in his mind. Was this what it had felt like for Shadowsight, when Ashfur had spoken to him from StarClan? *Is this* Ashfur *who's trying to reach me the same way?* Rootspring felt queasy. The dark warrior might be seeking to influence him. Or, even worse, possess him.

Rootspring quickened his step, ignoring the dread pressing in his chest. *Just act like you can't hear it,* he told himself. Ashfur couldn't take over living cats, as far as they knew. And Rootspring would never allow him to.

He remembered Dewspring's advice. *If you don't want to be hunted, become the hunter.* His mentor's words rang in his mind. *If you can't escape your enemy, face them.* It would be foolish to *face* Ashfur right now; Rootspring was outnumbered and in unfamiliar territory, and he'd seen how powerful the dark warrior was. But that didn't mean he couldn't find out what Ashfur was up to. It would be better than waiting here, imagining voices and jumping out of his fur every time he heard a noise. Besides, he wanted to know if it was safe to return to the barrier. In case Bristlefrost really was waiting for him there.

Rootspring shook out his pelt. He'd retrace his steps and see if he could sneak up on Ashfur and his warriors. If he could find out what Ashfur was planning, he might be able to get one step ahead. He ignored the fear churning in his belly. He would be careful. He wouldn't get caught.

Rootspring headed for the gully, pausing at the top when he reached it and peering down into the bushes and trees clustered at the bottom. There was no sign of Dark Forest warriors, and he found an easy way down and made his way along it, ears pricked for signs of danger.

Rootspring!

He stopped as he heard the voice again. He was sure now that it was in his head. There was something soft and almost familiar about it, and it was growing more urgent.

What are you doing? it asked.

Why was it trying to distract him? Irritation pricked his pelt. *It's none of your business,* he thought crossly. Focusing hard on the path and keeping alert for signs of Dark Forest warriors, Rootspring retraced his steps. He kept low as he crossed the open ground, picking his way around the pools of dark water. Did the paths between them seem narrower?

As he reached woodland once more, cat-scents touched his nose. He tasted the air, relieved that the wind was blowing toward him, and recognized Ashfur's scent and the musky smell of Darkstripe. There were other cat-scents too. He didn't recognize them all, but they were steeped in the stench of the Dark Forest. He could smell Softpelt and Strikestone among them. Disappointment tugged at his belly. At least he couldn't detect Stemleaf, Willowshine, or Spiresight. They must still be free.

He ducked down as he reached the trees and picked his way toward the scents. His ears twitched as he heard sounds coming from beyond a thick swath of bracken. The Dark Forest cats were talking there, their mews grumpy. Stealthily, Rootspring nosed his way among the rotting stems and crept nearer. Belly pressed to the ground, he wriggled as close as he dared and peered between the stalks.

In the damp glade ahead, a bedraggled group of spirit cats stared blankly at Ashfur, their eyes showing nothing but blind obedience as he paced in front of them. Rootspring's heart sank as he saw his Clanmate Sandynose. The clever brown tom's gaze was unquestioning. He would have hated what he'd become.

As Ashfur talked, Darkstripe's tail flicked restlessly back and forth. Beside him, the other Dark Forest warriors listened, attentive. Mapleshade sat back on her haunches and licked her belly absently. But her ears were pricked and turned toward the dark warrior. A gray-and-white tabby Rootspring didn't recognize was flexing his claws as though he couldn't wait to carry out Ashfur's orders.

Ashfur nodded toward a different ragged tom, this one a pale gray tabby. "Silverhawk, take Clawface and guard the Moonpool tree."

That's where Shadowsight was headed. Rootspring tensed. Had the ShadowClan medicine cat managed to find his way back to the living Clans yet?

The Dark Forest warrior blinked at Ashfur. "Isn't it a bit late to—"

"Just do it!" Ashfur snapped. "I don't want any more intruders in my forest."

Silverhawk dipped his head and beckoned to a battle-scarred brown tom with a flick of his tail. Together, the two cats headed away between the trees.

Rootspring watched them disappear into the shadows, his heart pounding. Shadowsight had to get news to the Clans. Should he follow the two warriors and make sure the medicine cat made it out safely, if he hadn't already? He hesitated. Wouldn't it be better to stay here and find out what Ashfur was planning?

"Houndleap." Ashfur was staring at a scrawny black tom.

Houndleap returned his gaze eagerly.

"Take Mapleshade and Rushtooth and search for Rootspring and the others."

Houndleap nodded.

"And keep an eye out for Stemleaf and his *friends.*" Ashfur's lip twitched angrily. "They can't hide from me forever."

Especially if the Dark Forest is shrinking. Rootspring shivered. Ashfur's gaze flashed toward the bracken. Rootspring pressed himself harder against the earth as the dark warrior narrowed his eyes. Rootspring held his breath. *Can he see me?*

"Hey." Mapleshade rolled onto her paws. She stared indignantly at Ashfur.

He glanced at the tortoiseshell-and-white she-cat, his ears flattening as he saw her expression. "What?" he snapped.

"Why are you putting *him* in charge of the patrol?" Mapleshade jerked her muzzle toward Houndleap.

Ashfur's eyes sparked with fury. "Because you let Stemleaf escape!"

Mapleshade flexed her claws but said nothing.

Houndleap slid a superior look at the she-cat. "Don't worry, Ashfur," he mewed smoothly. "*I* won't let Rootspring get away."

The dark warrior glanced at him. "You'd better not," he snarled.

Houndleap led the patrol into the woods, Mapleshade glowering as she padded heavily behind. Ashfur headed in the other direction, where the trees thinned and dying bushes lined the path. Darkstripe followed, while the Dark Forest warriors nudged the spirit cats into action. The gray-and-white tabby hissed as Conefoot stumbled, then gave his captive a sharp nip behind the ear. Conefoot yelped and turned on the Dark Forest cat. Hope sparked in Rootspring's chest as he saw anger flicker for a moment in Conefoot's eyes, but they glazed over again and he hurried quickly after Sandynose and the others. Rootspring shifted his paws thoughtfully. *Conefoot seemed to throw off Ashfur's control there for a moment, when he was angry. Does that mean a strong emotion can break his hold?* Rootspring wondered. He remembered the vines snapping in the barrier that blocked off StarClan when the surrounding cats felt hope. *Could hope be the key to fighting off Ashfur?*

It was a fascinating idea, but Rootspring had to focus on getting back to Bristlefrost. He could discuss it with her when they reunited. As soon as they were out of sight, he slid from the cover of the bracken and crept after them. The undergrowth here was thick, its rotting leaves hiding the Dark Forest cats from view, but Rootspring followed their paw steps, his ears pricked. He skirted bushes and trees, keeping low as he tracked the party downslope.

"Do you smell something?" Darkstripe mewed suddenly.

Rootspring froze. Had the wind changed? Was it carrying his scent toward the Dark Forest cats? He tasted the breeze; no, he was safe.

Ashfur growled. "Everything stinks in this place."

Rootspring heard the undergrowth rustle. His pelt rippled nervously. Was Darkstripe pushing his way through the bushes? He glanced back, dismayed that the slope behind him was bare. The undergrowth was the only cover in reach, but where would Darkstripe push through? As it shivered in front of him, Rootspring chose a random spot and ducked under the twisted branches, hoping fervently that he wouldn't be seen. As Rootspring's heart pounded, Darkstripe padded into the open a few tail-lengths away and looked around. The tom's yellow eyes were narrow with suspicion, but he didn't seem to spot Rootspring.

"You're imagining things." Ashfur's mew sounded from the path. "There's no cat here. After the shredding we gave them, they wouldn't dare come within striking distance."

Darkstripe's eyes glittered. He glanced around once more, then pushed his way back through the bush.

Rootspring drew in a shuddering breath and waited until he heard the patrol move off. Then he crept out from beneath the bush and began to track them again, this time keeping further back. Fear grew in his belly. He tried to push it away, but it hardened and rooted itself in his chest until he could hardly breathe. Around him the bushes grew more scraggly, and as the slope flattened, twisted trunks replaced them, so black they looked burnt.

With a sickening sense of dread, Rootspring realized where he was. Between the trunks, he could see a dark lake stretching beneath the starless sky. This was the island where Ashfur had held him and Squirrelflight hostage. He shuddered as he remembered the soul-aching despair he'd felt when he'd fallen into the lake.

But there wasn't an island anymore. There was only water. All that remained of the island was trees, their branches sticking up from the lake's surface like misshapen limbs, their roots lost in the swallowed earth.

Rootspring felt his gut twist as his heart pounded faster in his chest. The water was rising even more quickly than he'd feared! It hadn't been long since he'd been imprisoned there, and yet the entire island had disappeared. How long did they have before the path back to the Moonpool was cut off by flooding? Or the whole of the Dark Forest disappeared beneath the dark waters? He had to get himself, Bristlefrost, and the spirit cats out while they still had a chance.

Ashfur had stopped on the shore. His tail twitched uneasily. "What's happened here?" He stared at the water. "Thistleclaw, where's the island?"

"Don't ask me." The gray-and-white tabby's gaze narrowed as it flitted like a nervous bird over the half-drowned trees. "You're the one who started this."

Ashfur padded warily to the water. Thistleclaw, Darkstripe, and the other Dark Forest warriors were staring in undisguised alarm at the lake. But the spirit cats clustered behind Ashfur like chicks following their mother. As Ashfur neared the edge, they huddled closer. Berrynose almost stepped on the dark warrior's paws. Ashfur waved them away with an irritable flick of his tail, but a stone shifted beneath his paw and he stumbled. His forepaw splashed into the water. Tail bushing, he jerked back and barged clumsily into the spirit cats under his control. They scattered in panic, then stopped a few tail-lengths away, staring at him, confused.

Ashfur's pelt lifted self-consciously along his spine. "Can't you stop them crowding around me?" he snapped at Darkstripe.

Darkstripe eyed him coldly. "I don't control them. You do."

Ashfur flattened his ears. "Watch your tone."

Darkstripe held his gaze for a moment, then looked away. "Sure," he mumbled.

Ashfur snorted and stumbled in his haste to retreat from the water. Seeming to panic, he jumped to his paws and jerked away, then took in a breath. "This place is no use to us now that the island is gone," he remarked, his voice smooth again. He padded back toward the forest.

Darkstripe followed with the other Dark Forest warriors, the spirit cats padding obediently between them.

Rootspring ducked lower and waited for them to disappear among the trees, then crept out from his hiding place. Should he keep following them? As he gazed at the forest, he felt the tug of the water. He padded to the edge, his pelt tingling. Curiosity was pulling him closer to the lake. He had to know what darkness lay there. As he neared it, he felt cold, suddenly light-headed, his strength ebbing as though he'd traveled for days without rest or food. Dread rose in his belly, seeming to twine like ivy around his throat until he could hardly breathe.

He pulled away, his paws tingling with fear. How could *water* make him feel like this?

He had to get away. Turning, he raced across the shore, hardly aware of the damp earth beneath his paws.

Stop! The voice in his head rang like the cry of a fox in the night. It shrilled through his pelt, setting it on end, and he pulled up, his breath catching as he looked down and saw dark water a muzzle-length from his paws. A wide stream had spilled from the lake and reached across the shore.

Shock sparked along his tail. He'd nearly run straight into it! The strange voice had saved him.

He backed away, his heart pounding. *I need to find the others.* The water was spreading fast. He had to warn them, and he wanted to tell someone about the voice that had saved him. Perhaps together they could work out who would be speaking to him here in the Dark Forest.

His thoughts spinning, Rootspring veered away from the water and into the bushes. If he followed the route he'd come by, it would lead him through the woods and back to the StarClan barrier. He pushed his way eagerly between the decaying branches, forcing back a shudder as the wilting leaves slid along his spine.

He pitied the warriors who came here after death. Did any of them regret the actions that had brought them to the Dark

Forest? His thoughts flitted to Snowtuft and he felt a sudden jab of grief. If only the scarred tom had had a chance to see StarClan; he'd deserved a chance at happiness after sacrificing himself to save the spirit cats. Instead, he'd disappeared forever.

Rootspring shook out his pelt, remembering what Shadowsight had said about the Dark Forest. This place fed on misery. He had to keep hoping. Lifting his muzzle, he focused on finding the others. *I'm going to get to them before Ashfur's cats can.* He wasn't going to let Bristlefrost, or any of them, fall into the paws of the Dark Forest warriors. They were going to get out of this place and find a way to defeat Ashfur.

Breaking from the bushes, he raced between the trees. Surely Shadowsight must have found his way back to the Moonpool by now. Keeping low, Rootspring began to push his way between the brambles. Beyond them, a swath of ferns filled a dip in the forest floor and Rootspring plunged in, half closing his eyes against the fronds as he pushed his way through. He burst out, relieved to be clear of them, and shook the leaf dust from his ears.

I'm coming, Bristlefrost. With a rush of hope, he pictured finding her at the barrier, with Stemleaf, Spiresight, and Willowshine. Between them, they would find a way to save StarClan. Once they had the help of the living Clans, they could free the rest of the spirit cats and break down the barrier that had cut them off from StarClan.

As he began to head upslope, he saw something move. He froze. A cat was slinking out from behind a tree. Rootspring's chest tightened as he recognized the wide face. He'd met this warrior before.

Her round amber eyes shimmered with satisfaction as she unsheathed her claws. "Hi, Rootspring," she snarled, blocking his path.

Rootspring stepped back, forcing his pelt not to spike as he stared at the vicious she-cat. *Mapleshade.*

CHAPTER 5

Shadowsight peered along the path snaking ahead of him. This part of the forest looked exactly like the last. How was he meant to find his way to the Moonpool when every tree was as twisted as the last and the moss, which seemed to cover every trunk and root, turned everything to the same miserable color?

He stiffened as something caught his eye. *What's that?* Was the shape ahead a shadow or a Dark Forest warrior? He held his breath, not daring to move, and strained his eyes until he could see that its rough pelt was not matted fur, but bark. *It's a branch.* Relieved, he padded on once more, wincing a little. As his dizziness had faded and the throbbing behind his ear had begun to ease, he'd become more and more aware of the wound in his leg. Mothwing had treated it after his last visit to the Dark Forest, but it had reopened when Ashfur had attacked him and was burning now.

Ignore it. Rootspring and Bristlefrost had been far more badly injured, and they were racing through the forest right at this very moment, leading Ashfur and his warriors on a wild rabbit hunt so that he'd have time to reach the Moonpool. He just hoped Ashfur hadn't managed to catch up with them. *I can be as brave as they are.*

Shadowsight lifted his muzzle and pushed on. He had to get back to the living Clans. They would have to send help if they wanted to destroy the barrier that had cut them off from StarClan. There was no time to waste. The rivulets of dark water were cutting ever more deeply into the forest floor. And Shadowsight could see fog always pressing at the edge of his vision, as though at any moment it would rush in and swallow up the trees.

I just wish this were a real forest. At least then he'd be able to use scent to find his way. Back home, he'd always known where he was, even with his eyes closed. The smell of fresh chervil or a patch of coltsfoot or the brush of soft borage leaves against his paws would orient him even faster than his sight could. Here everything smelled of rot.

Shadowsight hopped over another dark stream and scanned the trees, hoping to find a clue that he was going in the right direction. Was this really the way to the Moonpool? He stopped where a boulder forced the path to curve and sniffed the stone, hoping to smell his own scent, or perhaps Rootspring's. If this was the path to the Moonpool, he would have passed this way too, surely?

He flicked his tail in frustration as he breathed in only the dank smell of decay and lifted his wounded leg, hopping on three paws to ease the jabbing pain that shot up his tail with every step.

Anxiety prickled in his gut. The path was stretching into

deeper shadow. What if he was nowhere near the Moonpool? What if he'd been traveling in entirely the wrong direction and only getting farther away? His heart sank at the thought but he pushed on, feeling suddenly weary as the hope he'd been clinging to seemed to drain into the damp earth.

The path led to a hollow where dark water pooled at the bottom. Shadowsight picked his way around the water and leaped over the stream that fed it. He slid between rocks as the forest sloped up, hardly bothering to look for the path when he reached the top, sure now that he'd come the wrong way.

He almost tripped over the thick root that twisted across his path. Its bark smelled fresh, and he glanced at it, wondering why no moss grew over it. Curious, he sniffed his way along it until he reached the point where it twined into the trunk of a great tree that stood like a guardian in the darkness. His heart quickened. This was it! The way to the Moonpool!

He looked up, trying to make out the top. Instead of sky, the tree reached into water. Even from here, he could see the pool rippling at the tips of the highest branches, floating above the air. The Moonpool! He'd finally found the shimmering entrance to the living world.

It was a long way to the top, and his wounded leg throbbed at the thought of the climb as he traced a possible route through the branches. *Can I make it?* He shook out his pelt defiantly. He *had* to, no matter what. StarClan, Rootspring, Bristlefrost, and the trapped spirit cats were all depending on him.

Hooking his claws into the bark, Shadowsight hauled himself up, grimacing as he pressed his hind paws into the trunk.

Tentatively, he worked himself into the crook where the tree began to branch. The open wound on his leg stung as though Mothwing had dressed it with nettles instead of cobwebs, but he could bear it. He'd have to.

Trying not to think about the pain, he followed the thickest branch to where it skimmed a higher one and climbed onto the next. This branch twisted upward to reach past another. He padded carefully to where the branches crossed. It was only a small hop from one to the other; then he could climb up for quite a way before he'd have to jump again. *I can do this.*

He crouched, bunching his muscles, then leaped across the gap. Pain sliced through his wounded leg. Panic sparked in his chest as he lost his footing. He felt himself falling and grabbed the bark with his foreclaws, fighting to hang on. But his hind legs were dangling, the weight of them dragging him down as the bark crumbled beneath his paws. Fear burst behind his eyes as he felt the branch slide from his grip. He slithered down onto the lower branch, blinded by the pain in his leg. His flailing paws caught the branch, then lost it, and he felt air rush around him as he dropped from the tree and landed with a thump on the ground.

He didn't move for a moment, the breath knocked from him. Aware only of the pain in his throbbing leg, he lay still. When Ashfur had first attacked him, the pain had sent him back to the living world, but it wasn't forcing him into unconsciousness and escape now. Would he be stuck here in the Dark Forest, so badly hurt that he could never climb out? He felt his flanks rise and fall, his breath the only noise in the silence. Then relief began to loosen the fear in his belly. The pain in his leg was easing. Gingerly he pushed himself to his paws, keeping off this injured hind leg at first, then testing it by pressing it gently against the earth.

He winced as pain shot through it again. He stretched it, then forced himself to pad around the tree. His leg hurt, but it could take his weight. But was it strong enough to push him to the top of the tree?

He grunted. Why had he let himself fall? *I'm dumber than a pigeon!* He looked up again toward the shimmering Moonpool, his heart aching to see how close it was. And yet he might not be able to reach it. If he couldn't climb the tree, should he return to the barrier and wait for the others?

He pictured their disappointment when they saw him. *They're depending on me.* They had risked their lives to give him time to escape. He couldn't let them down.

Gritting his teeth, Shadowsight climbed once more onto the lowest branch. He let his wounded leg hang limp, using only his three good legs to haul himself up to the next. He hopped along it like injured prey, then pulled himself onto the next branch and carefully made the jump he'd missed last time.

He was panting by the time he'd made it halfway across the branch, and, when he glanced down at the forest floor, he was surprised by how far he'd climbed. His pelt burned with the effort, and he paused to catch his breath. His hind leg throbbed, but he pushed on, struggling from one branch to the next and gritting his teeth against the pain every time his injured leg banged against the bark or caught on a knot.

Only when he heard the rippling of water did he look up, his heart pulsing with excitement as he saw that the Moonpool was now only a few tail-lengths above him. He limped along the curving branch at the top of the tree where the pool met the air and, after taking a deep breath, pushed his forepaws up into the water and drew himself into the Moonpool.

The chill of it took him by surprise. It was so dark he could hardly see, and the water pressed around him so powerfully that he felt the air being forced from his lungs. Would he have enough breath to reach the surface? Dizzy with fear, he gazed up at the distant glimmer of sunshine. *Keep going!* He had no choice.

Fighting the weight of the water, he kicked out with his good leg and flailed with his forepaws. The light seemed too far out of reach. Lungs aching, he pushed on, fighting the urge to breathe. Bubbles escaped his mouth, rippling through his whiskers and past his ears as they shot upward. He chased them, pulling harder until the darkness began to clear and a few muffled sounds reached him. Suddenly light flooded the water around him, and a moment later he broke the surface. Happiness burst in his chest as, gasping, he splashed across the pool. He was home!

Sunshine filled the hollow, blinding after the gloom of the Dark Forest. He crouched in the shallows at the edge of the Moonpool, weak with relief, and then rushed toward his body, still sleeping beside Bristlefrost's at the pool's edge. Warmth filled him as he felt his spirit reconnect to his physical form. He drew in gulp after gulp of cold, clean air. It was heavy with the scent of moorland and forest, and he relished the taste. *I made it! I'm whole again!* When he'd caught his breath, he pushed himself to his paws. He glanced around eagerly, surprised to find cats from every Clan gathered in the hollow.

Why were they glaring at each other? They were standing a few tail-lengths from the pool, their ears and tails twitching with annoyance. Graystripe, Bramblestar, Squirrelflight, and Jayfeather stood together. Tigerstar glowered at them, his forehead furrowed in a frown.

I'm back! Shadowsight wanted to call to his father, but then he noticed the leaders of the other Clans, each with their medicine cat, staring so coldly at the ThunderClan cats that he didn't dare interrupt.

Ivypool and Dovewing were here too, and Tree. A few tail-lengths away, the Sisters kept their distance, watching the Clan cats, their eyes narrow with interest.

No cat noticed Shadowsight. Perhaps he should clear his throat to let them know he'd made it back. Or he could just limp between them and let them see him for themselves.

Bramblestar's tail swished impatiently. "It's clear what we need to do—"

But Leafstar cut him off before he could explain. "Wait a moment, Bramblestar. You've only just returned from the Dark Forest. Perhaps you should let the other leaders handle this."

Squirrelflight whirled on the SkyClan leader. "You should be glad to have him back!"

But Leafstar eyed her calmly. "I am. But let's not forget, he was away from us for a long time."

"What does that mean?" Squirrelflight demanded with a glare.

"Isn't it possible he might have been tainted by his time there?" Leafstar mewed.

"Tainted?" Squirrelflight bristled.

Shadowsight blinked in surprise. How could the SkyClan leader believe that Bramblestar could be anything but brave and honorable?

Mistystar moved closer to Leafstar. "The Dark Forest breeds evil," she mewed. "We've witnessed it time after time."

Tigerstar stiffened. "Oh, have we?" he shot back. "Because I trained there during the Great Battle, and somehow I emerged a sensible cat."

Mistystar snorted.

As he watched their interaction, Harestar's whiskers quivered. "That may be up for debate," he added, "but I, too, trained there. I'm not sure you understand what you're implying, Leafstar."

The SkyClan leader's neck fur ruffled. "I understand perfectly well, thank you. There's never before been a living cat who spent so much time in the Dark Forest, has there? Even in the Great Battle, the warriors returned home after their training—at least, that's what I understand?" Leafstar glanced around at the other leaders.

"That's correct," Dovewing mewed softly.

"And don't forget Ashfur lived in Bramblestar's body for

over a moon," Leafstar mewed. "I'm only saying—we can't be *sure* his influence is gone."

Bramblestar's eyes widened. "But I am myself now, not Ashfur!" he exclaimed. "I've never been anything like him!"

Squirrelflight pressed against her mate and stared indignantly at the other leaders. "Bramblestar is a true warrior!"

Mistystar's ears twitched. "He was in the past, maybe."

"And now!" Squirrelflight insisted.

Leafstar looked doubtful. "Why would we take *your* word for it?"

"You were in the Dark Forest with him," Tigerstar reminded Squirrelflight.

Ivypool glared at the ShadowClan leader. "*I've* been in the Dark Forest too, and I'm growing tired of this argument." She'd been one of the ThunderClan apprentices who had sneaked into the Dark Forest many moons ago when it threatened war on the living Clans. "I have a kit in the Dark Forest right now, and I certainly hope you're not going to reject her when she returns. Because being in the Place of No Stars didn't make me evil. If anything, seeing the cruelty there made me a *better* warrior. Bramblestar would never let it change who he was."

Squirrelflight dipped her head gratefully to Ivypool.

Bramblestar lifted his chin. "I'm the same cat I've always been. The Dark Forest didn't change me, or Squirrelflight."

But Leafstar still looked uncertain. "How can we be sure?"

Shadowsight stared at the leaders. What a ridiculous

conversation. Why were they being so difficult? There wasn't time! "I was with them," he called out as he limped from the edge of the Moonpool. "I know what happened there. Bramblestar and Squirrelflight were true warriors! They couldn't change even if they wanted to. They would die for their Clan and for each other and you know it."

"Shadowsight!" Dovewing pushed past them, her tail quivering with excitement. "You're awake! You're back!" She hurried to his side and pressed her muzzle against his ear, purring so loudly that he could hardly hear the mews of the other cats. Tigerstar wound around them, his purr drowning out Dovewing's, and Shadowsight's throat tightened with emotion. He was home, and he was safe again. He rested against his mother for a moment before pulling away. He was here on a mission.

Tigerstar stared at him eagerly. "What happened?"

"Was there a battle?" Harestar asked.

Mothwing whisked her tail. "Did you defeat Ashfur?"

Mistystar pricked her ears. "Is he dead?"

Excited mews rippled around the other cats.

Tree shouldered his way to the front. "Where's Rootspring?" He glanced anxiously toward the Moonpool as though he expected his kit to appear any moment.

"Where's Bristlefrost?" Ivypool left her kit's sleeping body to stand beside him. "Why hasn't she come back with you?"

Shadowsight hesitated. How could he tell them that their kits were still in danger? "They're still in the Dark Forest," he mewed, adding quickly, "But they're okay." *At least they were when I last saw them.*

Ivypool and Tree exchanged glances, fear showing in their eyes.

Dovewing sniffed Shadowsight's pelt, recoiling as she spotted the fresh blood where his leg wound had reopened. "You're hurt!"

"I'm fine," Shadowsight promised. He shifted his paws, feeling suddenly overwhelmed as more cats crowded around him.

Graystripe padded to his side and gently waved them away with his tail. "We can deal with his injuries later." He blinked reassuringly at Dovewing. "For now, give him space, and let's hear what he has to say."

Shadowsight dipped his head gratefully at the elder. He could see why he'd been ThunderClan's leader while Bramblestar and Squirrelflight had been lost in the Dark Forest.

Mistystar stared solemnly at Shadowsight. "What happened?"

Taking a deep breath, Shadowsight began. "Bramblestar must have already told you what Ashfur's been doing in the Dark Forest," he mewed. "How he's been controlling the spirits of cats who've died and not been able to reach StarClan."

Bramblestar looked grave. "He's also persuaded a lot of the Dark Forest warriors to join him."

Shadowsight nodded. "There were too many cats for us to fight," he mewed.

Tigerstar glanced at Shadowsight's bleeding leg. "It looks like you tried to fight them anyway," he mewed anxiously.

"We had no choice," Shadowsight told him. "We had to stop them from killing Rootspring." Tree's eyes widened in alarm. "When we reached the Dark Forest," he went on, "Ashfur had already set his cats on Rootspring. Bristlefrost fought them off and I distracted Ashfur and broke his concentration for long enough that his control over the spirits slipped and they could get away. But we weren't fast enough, and Ashfur and his warriors attacked again."

Dovewing tried to hurry back to his side, but Graystripe waved her back with his tail.

"Let him finish," the ThunderClan elder mewed.

"I'm okay." Shadowsight blinked at his mother reassuringly. His leg was throbbing, but telling the Clans what he knew was more important. "We thought we were going to die for sure. But then Snowtuft attacked Ashfur and gave us chance to escape—"

Ivypool interrupted. "Snowtuft?" She looked puzzled. "But he was a Dark Forest warrior. He wasn't on Ashfur's side?"

"He was pretending to support Ashfur," Squirrelflight explained. "But he was fighting on our side when Bramblestar and I were there. He helped us escape."

Shadowsight nodded. "And he saved me. He saved all of us."

Bramblestar's ears pricked eagerly. "So Ashfur doesn't have *every* Dark Forest warrior on his side. . . ."

"He has enough," Shadowsight told him grimly.

Bramblestar's gaze darkened. Leafstar, Mistystar, and

Harestar stared at Shadowsight in dismay.

"There *is* good news, though." Their plan rested on Shadowsight's convincing the living cats to join the fight. And he was about to share the most important discovery of all.

Mistystar leaned forward. Harestar's tail twitched.

Shadowsight dipped his head. "We spoke to StarClan," he mewed.

Shadowsight's heart seemed to grow at the sight of their faces brightening.

"*StarClan!*" Jayfeather spoke for the first time, his blind blue eyes shining.

Puddleshine padded forward. "Are they okay?"

Alderheart's pelt prickled excitedly. "Who did you speak to?"

"Leafpool." Shadowsight paused as he remembered how happy he'd been to hear the StarClan she-cat's voice echoing through the barrier.

Squirrelflight's eyes glistened with apprehension. "Is she okay?"

"She's fine," Shadowsight told her. "StarClan's fine. They never abandoned us."

The gathered cats looked at each other, ears pricking and pelts twitching with hope. Shadowsight felt a surge of pride as he saw his father's eyes light up. Harestar lifted his tail, a purr rumbling in his throat. Their relief seemed brighter than the sunshine that flooded the hollow.

Shadowsight explained. "StarClan couldn't reach us. They tried, but Ashfur has blocked the path between StarClan and the Dark Forest, and somehow that's blocked StarClan's connection with us as well. Leafpool told us that the pool they watch us through is clogged with vines so they can't see us. I'm still not sure how it all works, but he's trapped them inside their hunting grounds and they can't communicate with the living Clans. That's why they've been silent."

Harestar frowned. "Can't they unblock the path?"

Shadowsight shook his head. "They've been trying, but Ashfur's built a barrier so strong that they can't break through it alone, and it's been growing stronger all the time."

"Why?" Mistystar stared at him.

"It seems that the more the Clans lose hope in StarClan, the stronger the barrier becomes," Shadowsight told her.

"But we've *never* lost hope in StarClan!" Mistystar objected.

Harestar shot her a stunned look. "We thought they'd *abandoned* us," he mewed. "That they were punishing us for breaking the warrior code. That's losing hope, isn't it?"

"But we kept trying to get them back," the RiverClan leader insisted.

Tigerstar grunted. "We did some terrible things to get them back," he mewed darkly.

Shadowsight flicked his tail. He knew that his father was right. When Ashfur had been in control of Bramblestar's body, he had forced the other leaders to punish the "codebreakers" in their Clans. Ashfur had identified Dovewing, Shadowsight's mother, as one of the cats meriting punishment, but Tigerstar had refused to follow the false Bramblestar's orders. Still, other cats were exiled, or given absurd punishments. . . .

But we don't have time to dwell on the past. Shadowsight needed cats to help them fight *now*, before the dark waters cut off the Dark Forest, and any chance of reconnecting with StarClan, forever. "We think we've found a way to break the barrier down."

"'We'?" Bramblestar blinked at him.

"Me and Bristlefrost and Rootspring," Shadowsight explained. "We were at the barrier. We saw the vines knotting it together. They looked impossible to break, but then Bristlefrost told Stemleaf that Spotfur was expecting kits. . . ." Shadowsight hesitated. Would this make any sense to these cats? He knew it must sound terribly bizarre, even to his fellow medicine cats. But he had no choice. He just hoped they'd understand. "Stemleaf was so happy that one of the vines snapped."

Leafstar looked dubious. "Isn't that just a coincidence?"

"No," Shadowsight pressed. "We think it's related to hope. When we tried thinking positive thoughts, we found we could break through even more vines."

Mistystar frowned. "Not enough to break the barrier completely, though."

"That's because there weren't enough of us," Shadowsight told her. "If we could take more living cats to the Dark Forest, we might be able to weaken it enough to pull it apart. Then the spirits trapped there can find their way to StarClan, and everything can go back to normal." Shadowsight gazed hopefully around at the gathered cats. *We have to try.* He blinked at his father. Surely Tigerstar would support him?

His father eyed him cautiously. "How *many* cats would

have to go to the Dark Forest?"

"Well, a lot," Shadowsight admitted. "We need enough cats to feel hope to break down the barrier . . . and then we'd still have to defeat Ashfur and his army."

"It's a big risk to take." Leafstar's pelt pricked along her spine. "Even if you're able to free StarClan and convince them to help you . . . it sounds like Ashfur has a lot of Dark Forest warriors on his side."

Mistystar shifted her paws uneasily. "If a warrior dies in that place, they're gone forever, aren't they? How many Clan-mates would we be willing to lose to a death like that?"

"Haven't we lost enough already?" Harestar mewed.

Shadowsight puffed out his chest. "The cats you've already lost are trapped in the Dark Forest. They don't deserve to be there. They died fighting for their Clan. They should be in StarClan." The leaders exchanged glances. "And we need to rescue Bristlefrost and Rootspring," he went on. How could they hesitate after their warriors had been willing to risk their lives? "They put themselves in great danger so I could come back. They led Ashfur and his warriors away to give me time. We can't let them die there."

Ivypool's eyes rounded with fear.

Tree padded forward. "We have to send help."

Tigerstar's shoulders were stiff. Shadowsight knew that his father wasn't going to be easily persuaded. "I think we should take some time to think about this," the ShadowClan leader mewed.

"We don't *have* time!" Shadowsight wailed. "There's water

everywhere in the Dark Forest, *and* fog, and it's swallowing everything up. We have to unblock the barrier so the spirit cats can get to StarClan before the Dark Forest disappears!"

But Tigerstar didn't look moved by Shadowsight's plea. In fact, his eyes brightened. "Wouldn't that solve all our problems? If the Dark Forest disappears, then Ashfur will disappear with it, along with whatever's blocking the way to StarClan."

Squirrelflight eyed Tigerstar sharply. "Of course you don't want to do anything," she growled. "*Your* kit is back with the living."

"Is that so wrong?" Tigerstar mewed.

Squirrelflight stiffened, her hackles rising. "Of course it's wrong!"

Ivypool stepped closer to Tree and lashed her tail. "Meanwhile, *our* kits are still stuck there!"

Tree gazed steadily at the ShadowClan leader. "If the Dark Forest disappears, Bristlefrost and Rootspring will disappear with it."

"So many spirit cats are trapped too." Shadowsight stared pleadingly at his father. "Strikestone's there, and Conefoot."

Tigerstar stared at him for a moment, then shook his head. "I don't mean to sound callous," he said, "but those cats are already gone. Let's think about this for a moment. It would be a dreadful sacrifice, of course"—here he nodded at Tree and Ivypool, who glared back at him—"but imagine being free of the Dark Forest and all the evil cats it holds . . . *forever!*"

Tree shook out his pelt as if he were trying to recover from a chill. "I know you're not serious," he mewed. "What separates Clan cats from the rogues? We care about each other—we protect each other! But why not *my* kit?"

"Rootspring knew he was taking a risk," Mistystar pointed out. "But this isn't about any one cat! It would be irresponsible of us not to consider what Tigerstar is saying. . . ."

Shadowsight shook his head, unable to believe what he was hearing. Would Tigerstar let even his own warriors disappear for good? Shadowsight took a breath. *If they know how much is at stake, they'll have to do something.* "When we spoke to Leafpool through the barrier, she said the living world, the Dark Forest, and StarClan are all balanced. By blocking off one, Ashfur has caused disturbances in the others. And if one disappears . . ." At last, he saw Tigerstar's ears twitch. *Have I gotten through to him?*

The ShadowClan leader dipped his head. "Okay," he conceded. "If even the living world is threatened, let's say we have to do something." He glanced around at the other leaders. "But is this a fight we can even win? How can we send in enough cats to outnumber Ashfur and his warriors?"

Puddleshine suddenly padded forward, his pale blue eyes glittering, and at the sight of his mentor Shadowsight felt a relief so strong that he let out a heavy breath. "Perhaps we don't need to. Weren't you listening to Shadowsight?" the ShadowClan medicine cat mewed. "First we destroy the barrier. And to do that, we don't have to fight; we just need to *hope.*" He pointed his muzzle toward Shadowsight. "What if our cats don't have to do all the *hoping?* You said the spirit cats could help if we could free enough of them."

"Yes," Shadowsight mewed eagerly, feeling weak with gratitude for Puddleshine's problem-solving. Even if his mentor didn't support sending in a horde of strong warriors, his alternate plan might work. "If we can free the spirit cats, their hope might be enough to break the vines."

Jayfeather looked thoughtful. "The spirit cats aren't the only cats in the Dark Forest who might help."

Tigerstar blinked at the ThunderClan medicine cat. "Are you saying that we could persuade Dark Forest cats to join us?"

"Why not?" Jayfeather mewed. "Snowtuft did. Why shouldn't others? They don't even have to fight. We only need them to hope. And surely Dark Forest warriors must hope for *something?*"

Shadowsight's paws pricked excitedly. "Because the worlds are all connected, the barrier Ashfur has built is destroying their home too," he mewed. "If we can make them see that, surely they'll want to break it down."

Mistystar grunted. "Why would any cat want to save the Dark Forest?"

Bramblestar looked at her. "Living in the Dark Forest is still better than disappearing altogether." The ThunderClan leader's expression was grim, his eyes as dark as prey holes, as though he was still haunted by his time there.

Squirrelflight's tail was flicking eagerly. "Okay. So we send in a small team of cats. If they can persuade enough spirit and Dark Forest cats to help destroy the barrier," she mewed, "we can free StarClan. With them beside us, we could defeat Ashfur once and for all."

Shadowsight sensed the gathered cats shifting, their movement hardly noticeable, and yet something seemed to change. Had Squirrelflight's words inspired them? Harestar's whiskers quivered. Leafstar glanced eagerly at the Moonpool. Only Mistystar's gaze remained dark.

"That sounds like a lot of *ifs* and *maybes*," she growled. "We've already lost so much."

Shadowsight saw grief in her wide blue eyes and guessed that she was thinking of Willowshine. She must feel guilty that she'd allowed her medicine cat to take a risk so dangerous that it had killed her. He met the RiverClan leader's gaze. "We've lost cats very precious to us," he acknowledged. "But if we stop now, we're going to lose them forever."

Mistystar's ears twitched with alarm.

"We might be able to keep them close if we *try*," he pressed. "We have to save something more important than any of our lives. Something that means no cat can ever truly die."

Harestar frowned. "You mean . . . "

"StarClan," Shadowsight finished, looking around, relieved to see hope lighting up the other cats' eyes. Even Tigerstar lifted his tail, and Shadowsight felt his heart miss a beat.

Had he done it? Had he convinced the Clans to send help?

CHAPTER 6

Bristlefrost slowed and glanced over her shoulder. Was it safe to stop? She couldn't hear any cats in the woods behind her; the sound of her paw steps echoed alone through the forest. She pulled up, relieved to catch her breath at last. Her belly tightened. *Was Rootspring still running? Had he managed to keep ahead of the Dark Forest warriors? He's a fast runner,* she told herself. *And smart. He'll have found somewhere safe.* She had to believe it. Believing anything else was too painful. *He'll be waiting for me right there at the barrier.*

The idea comforted her, and she padded onward, wondering how far she'd come and how to get back. As her heart slowed and her pelt began to cool, she glanced over her shoulder again. She frowned. Had the woods changed behind her? The trees looked denser than before, and the smooth forest floor seemed to have contracted somehow and pushed up into haphazard hills. How would she be able to retrace her steps now?

She turned to keep going, her heart lurching as she saw a ditch torn open at her paws, in ground that had been level a moment ago. Surprised, she nearly stumbled into it, managing to hop the gap just in time and climb the short, steep slope beyond. As she paused at the top, her sense of foreboding deepened. Running between the sharp dips and rises, she could see veins of dark water.

Feeling utterly lost, she was more grateful than ever that she'd managed to outrun Ashfur's warriors. They must be accustomed to the unsettling landscape; they probably knew how to navigate its shifting nature. She scanned the trees again warily. Perhaps she hadn't lost them after all. Perhaps they'd known where she was heading and had run to cut her off. Were they watching her now?

Keeping low, she picked her way past a bramble, careful not to let its thorns catch in her pelt. There was something menacing about its gnarly stems, as though a prick from them could poison her. The thought made her shudder. *Keep hoping,* she told herself. She knew from what she'd witnessed at the barrier that hope was very powerful in this dark place. Perhaps it was even her best defense.

The ground here was littered with leaves. She stepped lightly, trying not to disturb them. She didn't want to leave a trail or make a sound that might give her position away.

Her ears twitched. Muffled mews sounded nearby. Heart pounding, she stopped and strained to hear. Cats were whispering somewhere close. Bristlefrost dropped into a crouch and crept across the leaves, lifting her tail, careful not to make them rustle. She stopped as the forest floor opened in front of her and peeped over the edge. A narrow gully ran below, and she could make out three Dark Forest warriors at the bottom. They huddled together, their pelts flattened against their bony frames.

A mottled brown-and-ginger tom glanced nervously over his shoulder before turning his gaze back to a gray tabby who seemed to fade in and out, becoming temporarily insubstantial, like a shadow. "But you've seen it for yourself, Maggottail," the tom mewed. "The Dark Forest is shrinking."

"So?" Maggottail shrugged. "Soon we won't have to worry about the Dark Forest. What Ashfur's promised is *huge*. That's why every cat is following him, even Mapleshade."

"But it's shrinking *fast*," the mottled tom growled. "We'll be standing on top of each other soon."

"Just wait," Maggottail urged. "As soon as Ashfur delivers on his promise, we won't need this place anymore."

Bristlefrost's breath quickened. What did they mean? She stretched her head farther over the edge, trying not to miss a word.

The mottled brown she-cat's pelt was twitching nervously. "How much longer do we have to wait?" she asked.

Maggottail rolled his eyes. "Stop worrying so much, Sparrowfeather."

"I might be right to worry," Sparrowfeather argued. "Redwillow's right. The Dark Forest *is* shrinking. We can't wait much longer."

Redwillow twitched his tail. "Ashfur's been promising things for a long time. So far, he's only taken care of himself.

Now these new cats have shown up to fight us. Did Ashfur know they'd come?"

"He didn't seem very prepared for them," Sparrowfeather chimed. "I don't think things are going exactly how he planned."

"Then what if he doesn't keep his promise?" Redwillow stared at Maggottail. "What if he *can't*? Even the best hunter can't wish a pigeon out of the sky."

Maggottail looked thoughtful. "What choice do we have? If the Dark Forest is disappearing, Ashfur is our only way out. It's not like StarClan is going to help us. We have to help ourselves." He lowered his voice even more. "And if Ashfur *does* come through—"

Bristlefrost edged a little farther forward, desperate to hear.

"—we'll be able to—"

Her paw slipped, sending a flurry of leaves fluttering into the gully.

Three muzzles jerked toward her. Three pairs of eyes locked onto hers.

Tail bushing, Bristlefrost scrabbled out of sight. But it was too late.

"Spy!"

The dark warriors' paw steps were already thrumming over the earth below. In a few moments, they'd reach the end of the gully and be tearing up the slope toward her. Bristlefrost fled, her paws skidding over the leaves. Digging in her claws, she hared downslope. As she gained momentum, she pushed harder, trying to pick a straight line between the tightly packed trees. The dips and rises made it hard to find her rhythm. She slithered down one slope and scrambled up the next, slow, then fast, then slow again as she met a new ridge. The path that had seemed clear a moment ago was now dotted with trees, and she had to zigzag between them, never quite able to pick up speed.

She could hear the paw steps of the Dark Forest warriors behind her. They must know this terrain like their own markings. Their steps sounded surer, pounding over the ground with an even beat. She heard distance opening between them and she guessed what they were doing. How many times had she used this tactic when hunting rabbit with a patrol? *When prey bolts, spread out.* It was a hunting move every warrior learned. To one side she glimpsed mottled ginger fur where Redwillow was cutting off one escape route, and she glanced the other way, her heart sinking, to find Sparrowfeather rounding a bramble to block her path.

Ahead, the land sloped down again, and she raced across it, wind streaming in her fur. A narrow passage between the trees gave her a chance to pick up speed. She pressed harder against the earth, and followed the passage as it became a channel, the ground rising on either side as she fled deeper into it. Panic flared beneath her pelt. The warriors had skillfully driven her this way just as a patrol would drive a rabbit into a hollow. She could hear paw steps behind her and fought desperation as she saw a steep rock wall blocking the end of the deep ditch they'd chased her into. She slowed to a halt in front of it and turned, ears flat, teeth bared. She'd have to fight.

Claws unsheathed, she glared at her pursuers as they came to a stop. Blood roared in her ears as she saw them exchange glances. Saw them silently discuss how they would attack. She braced herself, trying not to tremble. Redwillow stared at her for a moment, then raced toward her. She ducked low, expecting claws, but instead the warrior crashed clumsily into her. His head butted hers with a thump, sending her reeling. She winced, stars flashing before her. That was no battle move she'd ever learned. What in StarClan was he doing?

Confused, she shook away the pain, her pelt bushing as she saw Sparrowfeather charge, then leap. Bristlefrost crouched as the she-cat landed clumsily on her back. She braced for the sting of claws. But none came. Instead, Sparrowfeather wobbled like a squirrel trying to balance on a branch, then slithered off and landed on the ground beside her.

Bristlefrost backed away. Had these cats ever been warriors? She blinked at them, wondering what they would do next. Hope bubbled in her chest. If this was their idea of fighting, she might escape after all.

Sparrowfeather got to her paws, looking bemused. Redwillow shrugged.

Maggottail snorted at them scornfully. "Let *me* try."

Bristlefrost could hardly believe her eyes. The gray tabby was padding calmly toward her. She wondered whether to take a swipe at the mouse-brain, but he seemed so uninterested in fighting that she held back. Instead she watched as he stopped beside her and pressed his head into her flank. He began pushing, and pushed until her paws skidded over the earth and he was pressing her against the stone cliff. She didn't resist. She was too confused. There was no point starting a fight if these cats were too featherbrained to use even the simplest battle moves.

"Is it working?" Maggottail called to the others as he squashed her against the stone.

"No." Sparrowfeather sat down.

Redwillow was frowning. "Perhaps she has to be asleep."

Bristlefrost wriggled free and looked around at the Dark Forest cats. "What in StarClan are you trying to do?"

Maggottail's ears twitched. "We're trying to take over your body, mouse-brain."

Bristlefrost blinked at him. "You're *what*?"

"Like Ashfur did with Bramblestar," Sparrowfeather explained.

Bristlefrost swallowed back a purr, surprised that anything could be funny in this place. These cats seemed to have heads stuffed with thistledown. Did they really think this was how Ashfur had stolen Bramblestar's body? She didn't even know how to begin to explain that her body wasn't really *here*, anyway—it was fast asleep in the living world. "You can't just step into my body like you're stepping into a den."

Redwillow tipped his head to one side. "Why not? We've done the ritual."

"Ritual?" Bristlefrost stared at him.

"Ashfur told us we'd be able to once we'd followed the ritual," Redwillow explained.

"What ritual?" Bristlefrost wanted to know exactly what Ashfur had told these cats.

"We had to pull out three of our whiskers," Maggottail explained. "Then close our eyes and wait while he took them to the barrier blocking off StarClan and buried them."

Redwillow narrowed his eyes. "He said the ritual was how he'd gained enough power to take over a living cat."

Bristlefrost searched his gaze. "And you believed him?"

Sparrowfeather nodded. "We tried it as soon as we heard there were living cats in the Dark Forest," she told Bristlefrost. "So we should be able to take over your body now." She looked puzzled again. "But it's not working."

Redwillow was frowning. "Perhaps Ashfur has to be here for it to work," he mused.

Bristlefrost stifled a snort. *My body would have to be here for it to work, too,* she thought with amusement. Still, she felt sorry for these cats. They'd fallen for Ashfur's ridiculous lies. But hadn't her own Clan fallen for them too? At least she understood now why the Dark Forest warriors were so willing to follow Ashfur—he'd promised them a new life among the living Clans in return for their support. Her amusement faded as she realized how desperate they must be to escape the Dark Forest. Sympathy swelled in her chest. "I'm so sorry."

Sparrowfeather and Redwillow looked at her, surprised.

Maggottail narrowed his eyes. "What for?"

"Ashfur lied to you," Bristlefrost mewed. "He can't give you the power to take over the bodies of living cats."

"But *he* did it," Redwillow reminded her. "He took over Bramblestar's body."

"That's because Bramblestar had nine lives," Bristlefrost explained. "Ashfur worked out that there was a moment between losing one life and returning with the next when his spirit could slip into Bramblestar's body and take his place. But I'm not a leader. You couldn't use my body, even if I died."

"We could take over a leader, like he did," Maggottail pointed out.

"I suppose." Bristlefrost frowned, wondering if all the leaders were vulnerable now. "But there are only five leaders. Even if they all died, how would you decide which Dark Forest warriors would get their bodies?"

The Dark Forest warriors glanced at each other, uneasy.

Maggottail bristled. "You're lying!"

Bristlefrost met his gaze steadily. "Don't you think that if pulling out your whiskers and burying them was enough to give a dead cat the power to take over a living cat, a Dark Forest warrior would have figured it out already?"

Sparrowfeather sniffed. "Perhaps Ashfur's the only one clever enough."

"Then why is he back here in the Dark Forest and not living beside the lake in some other warrior's body?" Bristlefrost watched the tabby she-cat.

Sparrowfeather's eyes clouded for a moment. Then her shoulders slumped. "So we *can't* just take over any cat when we want to?"

Redwillow growled. "Are you saying Ashfur made it up? The ritual and everything?"

"What do you think?" Bristlefrost shrugged, trying to look calmer than she felt. "You know Ashfur as well as I do."

Sparrowfeather lashed her tail. "We should have guessed a ritual that made us pull out our whiskers and sit around forever with our eyes closed was a lie," she snarled. "That worm-weasel just wanted to see how dumb we were."

"We should stick to his plan anyway," Maggottail mewed.

"Why?" Sparrowfeather looked at him. "What's in it for us if we can't take over living cats?"

"Even if Ashfur can't get us into the living Clans," Maggottail mewed, "he still might be able to make life here better for us."

"How?" Bristlefrost argued. "You've seen what's happening to the Dark Forest. It's shrinking and it might disappear altogether. What do you think is going to happen to you when it does?"

Maggottail didn't answer. Sparrowfeather and Redwillow glanced uneasily at each other.

Bristlefrost pressed on. "If you help us instead of helping Ashfur, we might be able to put things back the way they were."

Maggottail's tail was flicking back and forth. Sparrowfeather's pelt lifted along her spine.

Bristlefrost hesitated. Was there any point trying to convince Dark Forest warriors to do something good? After all, they weren't here because of their kind hearts or noble sacrifice. Perhaps she was wasting her breath. Worse, she might be making them angry, and she was outnumbered three to one. But what else could she do? They wouldn't just let her walk away. Her best chance was to win them over.

Excitement fluttered in her chest. She *had* to persuade them. Puffing out her fur, she tried to imagine what Bramblestar would say.

"Ashfur can't be trusted," she began. "Look what he's done to the Dark Forest." She glanced around. "You must have noticed the water rising. It's so creepy, you can't even see your reflection in it. And there's fog too. It's going to swallow everything soon. Was any of that here before Ashfur arrived?"

Maggottail watched her through slitted eyes. Sparrowfeather and Redwillow didn't answer. She pressed on.

"And you've seen how quickly he turns on his allies," she mewed. "Look what he did to Snowtuft."

"Snowtuft attacked him," Maggottail grunted.

"But Ashfur *killed* him," Bristlefrost mewed. "Snowtuft doesn't exist anymore. Not even as a spirit. Is that fair?" This time, she didn't give them chance to answer. "I know how much you want to return to the living Clans. I'd hate to end up here, but you made your choices while you were alive and did things you can't take back. And being here must be better than not existing at all. Don't you think Snowtuft would settle for being here right now instead of nowhere?" Did

Sparrowfeather wince? Was she actually getting through to one of these cats?

"Before Ashfur came along," Bristlefrost went on, "you had a—" She was about to say *life*, but stopped herself. "You had somewhere to rest and just *be*. Ashfur will take that away from you, and for what? Some absurd revenge that has nothing to do with you. Do you really care whether Squirrelflight and Bramblestar are happy? It makes no difference to you what happens to the living Clans. What matters to you is what happens here in the Dark Forest; and if you follow Ashfur, he will destroy it along with everything else you've ever known."

Redwillow was leaning closer now. Sparrowfeather had pricked her ears.

"You have a chance to do something you never did in the living forest," Bristlefrost pressed. "You have a chance to fight on the side of goodness and courage and loyalty. You have a last chance to be true warriors."

Did they even want that? She tried to read their gazes but saw nothing except wary curiosity.

"Join us." She was going to persuade them. She had to. "Join the Clan cats and help us defeat Ashfur. Protect your home. Protect the cats who've become your Clan—protect the Dark Forest." She finished, finally out of words, and stared at the three warriors.

Redwillow's eyes were bright. Sparrowfeather's tail was swishing eagerly. Had she done it? Had she convinced them?

Maggottail looked dubious. "What if we end up like Snowtuft?"

"If we can get enough allies," Bristlefrost told him, "the only cat who'll end up like Snowtuft is Ashfur."

"But Ashfur has every cat on his side," Sparrowfeather mewed anxiously. "Fighting him is hopeless."

"Don't say that. There *is* hope, even in the Dark Forest." Bristlefrost blinked at the cats encouragingly. "And, if you help me get to the barrier between the Dark Forest and StarClan, I'll show you what it looks like."

CHAPTER 7

❧

Rootspring's belly churned with frustration. He examined the sheer rock walls that marked the edges of his prison. Surely there was a crack or ridge where he could find a clawhold and heave himself to the top of the towering boulders? He growled to himself when he saw only smooth stone. *I don't have time for this!* The Dark Forest was shrinking, and Bristlefrost was out there alone.

Through the only gap in the stone walls, he could see Mapleshade and Houndleap. They'd brought him here and were guarding him. *I should have fought them.* But when they'd trapped him near the lake of dark water, escape had seemed hopeless. He was already wounded, and they outnumbered him. It had seemed smarter to play for time and wait for a chance to escape without injury. But perhaps he should have tried. It was going to be impossible to escape from here. His heart felt so heavy he could feel it like a stone in his chest.

Above him the black, starless sky gave no clue to how much time had passed. Was Bristlefrost waiting for him beside the StarClan barrier? Had Shadowsight made it to the Moonpool? Perhaps a patrol of living Clan cats was already on its

way to the Dark Forest. He flexed his claws. If it was, he could
do nothing but wait for them.

He jerked around as he heard hushed mews outside.

"He's on his way." Rushtooth sounded breathless, as though
he'd been running.

Rootspring padded softly toward the entrance and peered
out. Where had the slippery brown tom come from?

Mapleshade was watching the forest. "Was he pleased when
you told him we'd caught one of them?"

"*Really* pleased," the tom panted.

"*Of course* he was pleased." Houndleap padded toward the
trees. "That's what he asked us to do." He pricked his ears
eagerly as Ashfur padded from the shadows. "Hi, Ashfur."

"Tail-licker," Mapleshade muttered as Houndleap greeted
Ashfur with a dip of his head and followed him toward the
boulders. She glowered at Houndleap as Ashfur stopped at
the prison entrance. "Why don't you offer to groom him for
fleas while you're at it?"

Houndleap glowered back. "Shut up!"

"Both of you shut up," Ashfur hissed as he padded inside.

Rootspring froze as the dark warrior locked eyes with him.
There was menace in his gaze. Rootspring forced his pelt to
stay smooth. He wasn't going to let this fox-heart see his fear.
"Why are you doing this?" he demanded.

Ashfur blinked at him. "Doing what?"

"Trying to hurt StarClan!" Rootspring glared back. "Trying to hurt *us*! We've never done anything to harm you."

Ashfur padded closer and Rootspring unsheathed his

claws. Had the dark warrior come here to kill him? If he had, Rootspring vowed not to let it be an easy fight. Perhaps he'd be able to finish Ashfur off once and for all. He tore his gaze away from the evil tom's dark blue eyes and tried to gauge the strength in his well-muscled shoulders, wondering how long he'd have to launch an attack before Mapleshade and the others rushed in to help.

Ashfur's muzzle twitched in a smirk. "Do you really think you can hurt me?"

"I'd like to try!" Rootspring showed his teeth. "You've tried to destroy the Clans I love."

"They shouldn't have gotten in my way," Ashfur mewed icily.

"What do you think you'll win by destroying us?" Rootspring stared at him. He was acting like he didn't know he was already dead. "You can never live again."

"Is that so?" Ashfur padded lazily around Rootspring. "I thought I already had. Through Bramblestar."

Rootspring snorted. "And how did that work out for you?"

Ashfur thrust his muzzle toward him. "Why are you all so full of yourselves?" he hissed. "ThunderClan was just the same when I was alive. So smug. Just like you are now. You all think you're so loyal, but when Squirrelflight dumped me for Bramblestar, none of my Clanmates stood by me. Not one." He straightened, as though recovering his composure. "But I showed them. I ruled them all." He whisked his tail. "They did whatever I told them to do. They exiled their Clanmates and fought each other, just to please me." His gaze darkened.

"And yet Squirrelflight *still* didn't appreciate how powerful I was. She acted like I was an ordinary warrior." Anger edged his mew. "She dismissed me like I was an apprentice. But I didn't give up. I brought her here. I thought we could be mates at last. I thought we could rule the Dark Forest together."

Rootspring stared at him. "Why would a *living* warrior want to live in the Dark Forest?"

"To be with me, of course." Ashfur's eyes darkened with rage. "But she only wanted Bramblestar."

"Of course she wanted Bramblestar!" Rootspring couldn't stop himself. This cat was getting more ridiculous by the moment. "Bramblestar's her mate, and you're just a dead warrior who's done nothing but hurt every cat. She doesn't *owe* you anything—and the more you try to destroy the Clans, the more she'll hate you."

Ashfur narrowed his eyes. "I'm going to destroy more than the Clans." He padded closer, dropping his mew and breathing into Rootspring's ear. "I'm going to destroy the Dark Forest and StarClan along with it."

Rootspring drew back sharply, eyeing the entrance to his prison. Houndleap was standing there, his ears pricked with interest. But there was no way he could have heard Ashfur's whisper.

Ashfur spoke again, so quietly that his voice wouldn't reach the pale brown tom. "StarClan can't survive without the Dark Forest. This place is no more than a miserable reflection of StarClan, and as it vanishes, so will StarClan. I bet it's already started. The fog will be swallowing up their precious hunting grounds. They have so much territory, they probably haven't even noticed yet—but, when they do, they won't be able to stop it. Once this place is gone, StarClan won't be far behind. It won't be long until they've all disappeared."

Rootspring could hardly believe his ears. Ashfur was destroying the Dark Forest *on purpose*, and he knew that he would destroy StarClan with it. What kind of cat would do something so cruel, and so devastating? Horror swept over Rootspring like freezing water. How had Ashfur ever managed to become a StarClan warrior?

He glanced past the cruel tom to where Houndleap was still straining to hear. He clearly couldn't. If he had, he wouldn't still be listening with such wide, hopeful eyes. Behind him, Rushtooth hovered, his ears twitching with interest. Rootspring felt a twinge of pity. *They don't know the truth.* These cats were helping Ashfur without realizing what it would mean. They must have thought he was going to reward them somehow, but he was plotting to destroy their very existence. He blinked at Houndleap. *If they knew the truth, would they turn against him?*

Ashfur was still talking, cooing softly like a dove, seeming hardly aware that Rootspring was staring at him with disgust. "Once the Dark Forest is gone, I'll be free to return to the lake."

How? Rootspring wondered. Wouldn't he just disappear with the other Dark Forest warriors and StarClan?

But Ashfur clearly believed he could do anything. "I'll make Squirrelflight suffer," he hissed. "She'll pay for betraying me, along with every cat she's ever cared about. Eventually she'll beg me to stop and become my mate. I wonder how many cats will have to suffer before she—"

Rootspring stiffened as another voice drowned out Ashfur's. It was the voice he'd heard earlier in his head, as clear now as the sound of a stone dropping into a still pool.

I'm going to get you out of this.

Rootspring's pelt lifted along his spine.

But you'll have to trust me.

He blinked slowly. *I will,* he promised in return.

The voice sounded again. *Good. Now look Ashfur right in his eyes, and say these words—exactly as you hear them.*

Rootspring listened, his heart thumping so loudly he had to concentrate to hear what the voice told him. He repeated the words, interrupting Ashfur's raving. "You betrayed StarClan's trust in you. They shouldn't have let you go."

Ashfur stopped, his mouth hanging open as he stared at Rootspring, his eyes wide with shock, as though he was watching prey talk. He backed away, his tail quivering, and ducked out of the prison.

"Ashfur?" Houndleap hopped aside as the dark warrior pushed past him. "Are you okay?"

Ashfur hardly looked at the Dark Forest warrior. "Keep an eye on him," he growled. "I need to check the barrier."

"Why?" Houndleap looked puzzled. "It looked fine last time we were there."

But Ashfur was already sprinting into the forest. "I need to check that it's not broken," he yowled over his shoulder.

The barrier! Alarm sparked in Rootspring's fur as he watched the dark warrior disappear among the trees. That was where he was supposed to meet Bristlefrost. Hardly breathing, he hurried to the opening.

Mapleshade blocked his way. "You're not going anywhere." She glared at him menacingly and butted him roughly back into his prison.

As she turned to leave, Rootspring curled his claws into the earth. He had to get out of here. What if Bristlefrost was at the barrier when Ashfur arrived? She'd have to face him alone.

He had to do something. He had to keep her safe. He turned and padded back into the shadow of the rocks. "So?" he whispered softly to the voice inside his head. "What now?"

CHAPTER 8

❧

The blue sky that had welcomed Shadowsight back from the Dark Forest was disappearing fast. As clouds drifted across the sun, darkness slid over the Moonpool hollow. Shadowsight looked hopefully at the leaders. "So you'll send help?"

Harestar shifted his paws. Mistystar glanced uneasily at the Moonpool. Tigerstar eyed Bramblestar and Leafstar warily, as though fearing their reply.

Why was no cat answering? Shadowsight felt as though his heart would burst from his chest. "You have to!" Alarm sparked through his pelt. Surely he'd convinced them to rescue Bristlefrost and Rootspring, and tear down the barrier that had broken the connection between the living and the dead, before the Dark Forest disappeared altogether. What about the spirit cats? They couldn't risk losing them. He'd told them what Leafpool had said—that the Dark Forest and StarClan were balanced, and if one disappeared, so would the other. She had told them that the living world would be affected, too, that all three worlds were connected. He blinked at Tigerstar. "I promised Rootspring and Bristlefrost that I'd get help," he pleaded. "You can't let them down."

Tigerstar stared back, his gaze as blank as that of a mind-controlled spirit cat.

Leafstar looked thoughtful. "We have to do something."

Shadowsight jerked his muzzle toward her. "You have to *save* them!"

Leafstar went on as though he hadn't spoken. "If what Shadowsight told us is true—"

"Of course it's true!" There wasn't time for doubt.

"*If* it's true," she repeated slowly, "we have no choice but to send in more warriors."

Shadowsight felt a flash of relief. He glanced around at the others, trying to read their gazes. Graystripe stared at the earth beneath his paws, looking thoughtful but calm. Next to him, Mothwing frowned, agitated.

"Is it worth the risk?" she asked. "What if it's too late to save Bristlefrost and Rootspring? The Dark Forest is dangerous. We could lose *more* cats if we go in after them."

Shadowsight could hardly believe his ears. Was his fellow *medicine* cat really telling them to give up on Rootspring and Bristlefrost? His mouth suddenly seemed as dry as shriveled leaves. Why wasn't any cat objecting?

Mothwing went on. "Ashfur's gone. Bramblestar's back. The Clans are safe now. How many cats are we willing to lose in the hope that we might reconnect with StarClan? We've done fine without them these past moons."

Jayfeather's ears were twitching. "That's not true!"

"We survived without StarClan's help," Mothwing pointed out. "And we got rid of Ashfur."

"Only after we let him steal a leader's life and turn us against each other," Jayfeather snapped.

"There were losses," Mothwing conceded calmly. "But we proved that we can manage without StarClan."

"You *managed*, yes," Bramblestar mewed darkly. "But at what cost?"

Mistystar padded to her Clanmate's side and met Bramblestar's gaze. "Do you want us to sacrifice more? Isn't it enough that I've lost a medicine cat?"

"I'm not willing to sacrifice Bristlefrost and Rootspring," Bramblestar snapped. "Don't forget, I've just come from the Dark Forest. You have no idea how cruel it is there, and it's getting worse because of Ashfur. Do you really think we should abandon our Clanmates to that place? They deserve better. We need to get them out."

"And the spirit cats too," Shadowsight pressed. "They should be in StarClan."

"They're already gone, but my remaining warriors are very much alive," Mistystar growled.

Bramblestar flattened his ears. "Are you saying we should let Rootspring and Bristlefrost die?"

"We can't be sure they haven't yet," the RiverClan leader pointed out.

"We have to try to save them!" Squirrelflight's tail was quivering. "If we abandon our Clanmates, we're no better than rogues."

"This might be our last chance to reconnect with StarClan," Shadowsight reminded them. Even if they were willing to sacrifice warriors, had they forgotten there was even more at stake?

Harestar's pelt ruffled along his spine. "How many cats need to die for StarClan's sake?"

"Would StarClan even *want* cats to die so that they can survive?" Mothwing mewed. "They've already lived long lives. Perhaps it's time we let go of the dead and focus on the living."

Puddleshine stared at the RiverClan medicine cat. "Surely you can't be serious!" he mewed. "I know you've never put your faith in StarClan, but I hoped at least that you'd come to understand how important our ancestors are to the rest of us. I can't let StarClan go that easily, and I won't give up what I believe in. It doesn't matter if saving them means risking lives. There's more to lose than you're admitting. If we let go of StarClan, we let go of what it means to be a warrior. We would be threatening the whole future of the Clans. You may not value them, but I'm willing to fight for them. I *won't* let StarClan go. I will risk my own life, if I have to."

Mothwing eyed him calmly. "You're letting emotion get the better of you."

"We can take care of ourselves," Harestar put in.

"StarClan doesn't hunt our prey," Mistystar chimed. "*We* do!"

Leafstar's tail flicked angrily. "Hold on. Are you saying that being a warrior means nothing more than catching prey?"

Squirrelflight puffed out her chest. "StarClan guides our paws!"

Shadowsight glanced at his father. Tigerstar hadn't spoken,

but he was watching Harestar and Mistystar thoughtfully. Did he agree that it wasn't worth risking more cats to save their dead ancestors? Shadowsight felt queasy. This discussion had to stop. The Clans had to see sense. They had to send help.

He pictured Leafpool calling desperately through the barrier. He'd promised her he'd bring help.

"Listen!" Shadowsight looked at the cats. "If no one goes back in, Ashfur will have won." They blinked at him. Paws trembling, he went on. "He wanted to destroy the Clans and cut us off from our ancestors, and unless we do something, that's exactly what he'll have achieved."

"That's true," Puddleshine raised his tail defiantly. "This is exactly what Ashfur wanted."

"We can't let him destroy StarClan." Alderheart stepped forward, his whiskers quivering. "They have protected us so many times. It's our turn to protect them."

"Without StarClan, we medicine cats are just herb gatherers and poultice mixers." Jayfeather raised his blind blue gaze to Mothwing.

Mothwing retorted, "That's all we need to be."

"What about loyalty?" Shadowsight demanded. "Rootspring and Bristlefrost think we're coming to help. It's probably the only thing giving them hope right now."

"You're not the one who will have to order more warriors to their deaths!" Mistystar snapped.

At the edge of the group, Tree cleared his throat, drawing every cat's eyes to him. "You all know that I have never entirely embraced Clan life." The yellow tom padded to the middle. He spoke softly, but his clear amber gaze was hard. "I've found your ways strange, and I haven't always respected your belief in StarClan. It seemed strange to me at times—these dead cats that you allow to control the lives of the living. I have felt that your beliefs sometimes get in the way of what seems logical and practical. But when I *have* questioned you, you've steadfastly defended your belief in StarClan. You believe that it's what separates the Clans from rogues or kittypets. And I must admit . . . the longer I live among you, the more of StarClan I see, the more I understand." He paused, his eyes traveling over the group. "What I'm asking you now is, if you don't have StarClan, what *are* you?" He studied the face of each leader, as though waiting for them to answer. But no cat spoke. He went on. "They have been the center of everything the Clans have ever believed. Now, more than ever, you need to stand by your ways and beliefs, no matter how difficult it might seem. You must fight for your way of life. If you don't, then can you truly call yourself warriors?"

"How dare you?" Harestar's hackles lifted.

A growl rumbled in Mistystar's throat.

Tree blinked at them calmly. "You've saved Tigerstar's kit. Won't you accept the same risks to save mine? Rootspring never intended to go into the Dark Forest, but he's there, and he helped rescue Bramblestar, and now he's trying to save all the Clans. Are you really going to abandon him while he fights to keep your way of life alive?"

Harestar looked away.

Dovewing padded to Tree's side.

Ivypool followed. "Bristlefrost is there too." The silver-and-white tabby's eyes brimmed with emotion. "She chose to go. She chose to help her friend rather than let him die." Her mew trembled as she went on, and Dovewing pressed her flank against her littermate's supportively. "I've been to the Dark Forest, so I know what she's facing. I couldn't abandon any cat to that place, especially not my own kit. I will go there gladly, whatever the cost, to save her."

Shadowsight eyed his father hopefully. Tree and Ivypool had made a stronger case even than Bramblestar for saving the cats who were trapped in the Dark Forest. Even Mothwing wasn't arguing now. But Tigerstar only glanced at his paws.

Dovewing blinked at her mate. "Listen to me," she told him. "We're just lucky Shadowsight came home safely." The ShadowClan leader's ears twitched uneasily as she went on. "Are you really going to stand by while these cats condemn another cat's kits to death?"

Shadowsight held his breath. Dovewing had a power over Tigerstar even StarClan could not match, and she was willing to stand up for Rootspring and Bristlefrost. They weren't her kits, but his mother would fight for them. But his father still didn't speak.

Shadowsight puffed out his fur. His wounded leg was throbbing, but he ignored it. "There's one thing I've learned from seeing Ashfur control the Dark Forest cats," he mewed. "His control can be broken, and the more good cats who challenge him, the more we can disrupt it. I'm sure that if we send in a large enough patrol, we can defeat Ashfur for good."

"If we betray StarClan, we give up what it means to be true warriors." Bramblestar swished his tail. "I won't let Ashfur change ThunderClan. We must save our Clanmates, both living and dead."

Harestar eyed the ThunderClan leader; then, as though coming to a decision, he dipped his head. "WindClan will do what is right."

Mistystar hesitated as Harestar looked at her expectantly. She met his gaze, her blue eyes clouded with doubt, then gave a grunt. "RiverClan will fight for StarClan," she muttered.

Mothwing's tail twitched. She looked at Tigerstar. "Are you going to agree to this recklessness too?"

Tigerstar glanced at Dovewing. "Yes," he told the River-Clan medicine cat. "ShadowClan will stand by its ancestors." Shadowsight saw determination in his father's face. At last, Tigerstar was willing to do the right thing.

Leafstar looked from one leader to another and then, with a sigh, dipped her head. "SkyClan will stand with the other Clans, and with StarClan."

Mothwing stared boldly at Bramblestar. "How are we supposed to get so many living cats to the Dark Forest?"

"We can help." A mew sounded from the edge of the hollow.

Shadowsight turned, surprised to see Flurry padding toward the group. He'd forgotten the Sisters were here. They'd been silent while the Clan cats discussed what to do next.

The ginger-and-white she-cat stopped at the edge of the group. Snow and Sunrise followed her, their long fur rippling. "We sang Bristlefrost and Shadowsight into the Dark Forest," Flurry reminded them. "We can do the same for others."

"Thank you." Bramblestar dipped his head gratefully. He caught Leafstar's eye. "But we mustn't send a large patrol. Shadowsight is right about the Dark Forest. It's shrinking fast. We have to act quickly, but wisely. A small patrol has a better chance of getting in undetected and moving quickly once they get there."

Leafstar nodded. "The fewer cats we risk, the better."

"Who should we send?" Squirrelflight asked.

Tigerstar frowned. "This mission is so dangerous, how can a leader *send* any cat?"

Bramblestar whisked his tail. "I agree. Any cat who goes must volunteer."

Ivypool's eyes widened eagerly. "I'll go—"

"No." Bramblestar cut her off. "Your kit is already there. We cannot risk you too."

"Then let me."

Shadowsight blinked in surprise as Squirrelflight stepped forward. Hadn't she seen enough of the Dark Forest?

"I want to be the one to finish this thing with Ashfur." Squirrelflight's mew was unwavering. "Once and for all."

Shock showed in Bramblestar's ruffled pelt. "There's no way you're going near Ashfur again, not after everything he's put you through." His eyes glistened. "You know none of this is your fault, don't you? You don't have anything to prove."

"I know," Squirrelflight answered. "Everything Ashfur's done—taking over your body, punishing codebreakers, kidnapping me—they were all his choices. He blames me for rejecting him, but that's no excuse for his cruelty. That's why *I* have to go. He has to see that there can be no reward for his actions, and I have to show him that he has no power over me, over any of us. I've had enough of being scared of him and trying to appease him. He's tried to ruin my life, both when he was alive and after he died—and that gives me the right to be the cat who puts an end to his miserable existence."

Shadowsight felt a rush of admiration for the ThunderClan deputy. After everything she'd been through, she was still ready to fight.

The sound of shifting paws pulled Shadowsight's gaze back to Graystripe. The long-haired ThunderClan elder was finally looking up, his face set in a determined expression as he padded past Bramblestar and looked Squirrelflight in the eye. "That's fair." His mew seemed to rumble around the hollow. "But it would be playing right into Ashfur's paws." Squirrelflight blinked back at him as he went on. "Don't you think he'd be pleased to know that he'd become such a burr in your pelt that you'd risk your life to face him?"

Squirrelflight's gaze clouded. "But I have to do this—"

"No, you don't," Graystripe told her. "It's not just you that Ashfur wants; it's revenge. He wants to make all the Clans—but especially ThunderClan—suffer for what happened to him when he was alive. To beat him, to truly win, we must do more than survive. We must thrive. We must grow stronger,

and prove that we are better warriors than he could ever be."
His gaze burned into Squirrelflight's. "And to do that, we need
you to survive. We can't risk losing you in a battle with Ashfur, on his territory. Think how much satisfaction that would
give him." Squirrelflight glanced away, clearly unable to argue.
"You must stay here," Graystripe mewed, "with Bramblestar.
You must stay and show Ashfur that you and ThunderClan
will survive whatever he tries to do. You are too valuable for
us to lose."

Squirrelflight gazed for a moment at Graystripe. Then she
stretched her muzzle toward him and nuzzled her nose gently
into his thick mane. She pulled away. "Okay," she agreed. "I'll
stay behind. But, if I don't go, who will?"

Graystripe's eyes grew round, amusement glittering in
them. "Isn't it obvious?"

Squirrelflight looked puzzled.

"Me, of course," Graystripe told her.

Bramblestar started forward. "You're too old—"

Graystripe waved him back with a flick of his tail. "The
Tribe told me that I still had an important role to play in the
Clan's fate. This must be it. I can feel it. My heart tells me this
is the time."

Shadowsight's paws tingled. This great warrior was vol-
unteering to risk his life for his Clan. He felt a new rush of
affection for the old tom. ThunderClan was lucky to have
him.

Squirrelflight glanced at Bramblestar. The ThunderClan
leader seemed to swallow, then dipped his head. "All right,"

he told Graystripe. "If it's something you feel you must do, I won't stop you."

Squirrelflight straightened. "If you must go, I want you to give a message to Ashfur."

As she leaned closer and whispered into his ear, Shadowsight strained to make out what she said, but her mew was so soft no cat but Graystripe could hear her.

At last, she pulled away. "Promise you'll tell him those exact words."

Graystripe dipped his head. "I promise. I will."

Bramblestar's tail was twitching. "You must also promise to get out of there if it looks like things aren't going our way."

Graystripe met his leader's gaze. "I can't promise that," he mewed. "Ashfur has had *his* way for far too long. I'm not returning until he's been defeated."

Dread tugged at Shadowsight's heart. The battle ahead seemed suddenly more real than ever. He looked at Tigerstar. "We're not going to let Graystripe go in there alone, are we?"

"Of course we're not." Tigerstar fluffed out his fur. "ThunderClan can't be the only ones to send a warrior. One cat from each Clan must go with him." He looked at the other leaders.

Leafstar frowned. "This is a big decision," she mewed. "We must share it with our Clans. Let's head home and discuss it, then return tomorrow with our volunteers."

Shadowsight's breath quickened. *Tomorrow?* That could be too late. He flexed his claws with frustration. It had been harder than he'd thought to persuade the leaders to send help.

He didn't dare press them more.

Flurry padded forward, her gaze sharpening. "No."

Hope flickered in Shadowsight's chest. Did the Sisters want them to go sooner too?

"You mustn't return with your volunteers," she went on.

Shadowsight's heart sank. Was she going to put *more* obstacles in the way?

Tigerstar glowered at Flurry. "The Sisters don't tell the Clans what to do."

Flurry blinked back at him. "You want our help, don't you?"

"Yes, but—"

She cut him off. "Singing five cats into another realm will require all our concentration," she mewed. "We can't have any distractions." She looked sternly around at the Clan cats. "Your volunteers must come *alone*."

Bramblestar glanced at Tigerstar. "We have to trust them."

Tigerstar shifted his paws. "Okay," he grunted.

Flurry looked satisfied. "The ritual is usually performed at sunset, but we need to get the patrol there as quickly as possible. Make sure your volunteers are here before the sun rises. We'll need to make a start the moment they arrive to be sure we get them in before full daylight."

Shadowsight sat down outside the medicine den and fluffed out his fur against the evening chill. As the stars began to show themselves above the trees, the fresh smell of dew and the musky odor of his Clanmates' dens filled his nose. The familiar scents of the ShadowClan camp comforted him, but he couldn't help wondering what was happening to Bristle-frost and Rootspring in the Dark Forest. Were they still okay? They'd been waiting so long already for help. Were they beginning to think it might not come?

His Clanmates were gathered in the clearing, watching Tigerstar as he stood beneath the drooping pines, his tail high. Dovewing hung back in the shadows, her eyes shimmering in the darkness. Tigerstar had explained what had happened beside the Moonpool, and the ShadowClan warriors had listened gravely as he told them what the Clan leaders had decided.

Shadowsight was relieved that his Clanmates had accepted the news so easily. He'd feared they might question the information he'd brought back from the Dark Forest. But they clearly had faith in their leader, and no cat seemed to doubt that they must face Ashfur and try to break the barrier between StarClan and the Dark Forest.

"Any cat going into the Dark Forest will risk death, with no hope that they'll have a place in StarClan afterward," Tigerstar told them. "I can't order any warrior into that kind of danger, so I need a volunteer."

Nervous mews rippled around the clearing.

"I know how much I'm asking," Tigerstar went on. "And if no cat comes forward, I will go myself."

"No!" Dovewing hurried forward, but Tigerstar motioned her back with a jerk of his muzzle.

Stonewing called from among his Clanmates. "You're our leader," he mewed. "We can't lose you."

"You mustn't risk your lives," Snaketooth mewed.

"ShadowClan needs you here," Scorchfur agreed.

"I'll go." Cloverfoot padded to the front.

"No, let me go." Snowbird hurried forward.

Cinnamontail followed her. "Let me do it. Antfur is trapped there, and if I can help free him from the Dark Forest, I must."

Shadowsight felt a rush of pride. He knew his Clanmates were brave, but he'd never expected so many volunteers. He wished he could be the one to go. He knew the paths and shadows of the Dark Forest better than any cat here. But his injured leg was still sore, even though the herbs Puddleshine had smeared it with had eased the pain and strengthened it a little. He didn't want to be a burden to Bristlefrost and Rootspring, as he had been before. They would need the strongest warriors possible to prevail against Ashfur.

Still, a part of Shadowsight hated to think of Bristlefrost and Rootspring facing danger without him. And, after everything that had happened with Ashfur—how he'd formed a connection with the dark warrior and even helped him escape—he wished he could prove his loyalty again to his Clan and make them, and his father, proud of him.

Tigerstar gazed gratefully at Cloverfoot, Snowbird, and Cinnamontail. "Thank you."

"I'll do it!"

Shadowsight's heart seemed to miss a beat as he saw Lightleap pushing her way to the front. *No!* The mission, which had seemed dangerous before, seemed suddenly deadly. He limped forward as his littermate stopped in front of their father.

"Let me go," she mewed. "I can do it. I know I can."

Tigerstar's ears twitched uncomfortably.

Shadowsight pushed past his Clanmates as Lightleap went on.

"Cloverfoot can't go," she mewed earnestly. "She's our deputy. We can't manage without her. Snowbird is a great warrior, but she's nearly an elder. It's too dangerous for her. And Cinnamontail has learned a lot since she joined ShadowClan, but she hasn't been practicing battle moves with her parents since she was a tiny kit like I have. I'm a good warrior." She glanced back at Stonewing, blinking eagerly at her former mentor. "Aren't I?"

The white tom nodded. His dark blue eyes glittered as though he was torn between pride and fear. "You were one of my best apprentices," he mewed.

"See?" Lightleap looked eagerly at her father.

Grief cut through Tigerstar's gaze.

"You can't say no just because I'm your kit," Lightleap pressed. "I'm strong and I'm clever and I know almost as many battle moves as you now."

"She's right, Tigerstar." Pouncestep padded forward and glanced affectionately at her sister. "I don't envy any Dark Forest warrior who gets in her way. She's got strong claws. She could tear down that barrier in no time."

Lightleap puffed out her chest. "Let me do this. Please."

In the shadows, Dovewing's eyes were wide with fear.

As Tigerstar hesitated, Shadowsight slipped around the edge of the clearing and stopped beside his mother. "He can't say no," he whispered. "It would look like he's protecting his kin above his Clanmates."

"I know," Dovewing mewed huskily. "But why did she have to volunteer?"

"She knows she can do it." Shadowsight realized that he'd been so wrapped up in becoming a medicine cat that he'd hardly noticed what a brave, strong warrior his littermate had become.

Murmurs rippled through the Clan.

"She's the fastest hunter I've seen," Whorlpelt mewed.

Flowerstem nodded. "She defeated me in battle practice last moon."

"Lightleap!" Berryheart called out his denmate's name.

Gullswoop and Slatefur joined in. "Lightleap! Lightleap!"

In a moment, the camp was echoing with her name as her Clanmates shouted their support.

Tigerstar's pelt ruffled uneasily. Shadowsight felt Dovewing tremble beside him.

"He'll have to let her go," she whispered, her mew breaking. She buried her muzzle in Shadowsight's fur. "I was so thankful to have my son back . . . but now I might lose a daughter."

Shadowsight's throat tightened. He'd seen the horrors of the Dark Forest. He knew what Ashfur was prepared to do to have his revenge on the Clans. The dark warrior would not spare Shadowsight's brave littermate just because she was young. He wished he could tell Lightleap not to go. But how could he stop her?

"Lightleap! Lightleap!" Her Clanmates were still calling her name, their eyes shining with pride. There was nothing Shadowsight could do. The Clan had spoken.

CHAPTER 9

Bristlefrost followed the Dark Forest warriors between the trees. She
hung back, keeping them at the edge of her vision even as she
paused to scan the forest. She didn't trust them. This could be
a trap. What if they were leading her straight to Ashfur?

Maggottail glanced over his shoulder. "Keep up," he
growled.

She narrowed her eyes but padded after him. Right now,
this was her best option. These cats knew how to reach the
barrier and she didn't. She wished she had a spirit cat's sensi-
tivity to the pull of StarClan so that she could at least tell if
they were leading her in the right direction.

Maggottail nudged Redwillow sharply out of the way and
hopped over a slippery tree root. Redwillow glowered at him
but said nothing, pushing in front of Sparrowfeather instead.
Sparrowfeather's hackles lifted and she nipped Redwillow's
tail as he passed. Were all Dark Forest patrols this mean to
each other? Bristlefrost pressed back a shudder. *I guess they're
not here because they're kind.* They must have done something bad
when they were alive to end up in the Dark Forest—something
really bad, if StarClan had rejected them yet taken in a cat like

Ashfur. She comforted herself with the thought that, unlike the first Tigerstar, they hadn't been evil enough to inspire nursery tales.

She padded after them, the fog pressing in the distance as she picked her way around twisted roots and black puddles. Her belly churned with unease. There didn't seem to be a stretch of forest left where dark water hadn't seeped into the ditches and hollows.

"I'm not sure we should be doing this."

Maggottail's mew drifted on the stale air.

Doing what? Bristlefrost quickened her step to close the gap between her and the Dark Forest warriors.

"If Ashfur catches us, we can just say we've taken her prisoner," Redwillow mewed.

They didn't seem to care if she could hear them. Her tail ruffled. There was no reason why they should. She was outnumbered and on enemy territory. What could she do?

"Do you think she's really telling the truth?" Sparrowfeather glanced back at Bristlefrost.

"There are plenty of reasons why she'd lie," Maggottail mewed. "After all, she doesn't want us to steal her body."

"But we *tried* already," Sparrowfeather reminded him. "It didn't work."

"Maybe we were doing it wrong," Maggottail mewed. "Perhaps it only works in the living forest."

Bristlefrost's whiskers twitched in amusement. Perhaps these mouse-brains were starting to understand.

"We might need to get rid of her spirit first," Redwillow suggested.

"I suppose no cat can have two spirits in one body." Maggottail agreed. "Perhaps . . ." The Dark Forest warrior lowered his voice now. What was so bad that he finally feared being over-heard? Bristlefrost hurried to catch up, straining to hear as he went on in a hushed mew. "Perhaps we need to kill her first."

A chill ran down her spine.

"If we kill her, we'll lose our chance to help the Clans," Sparrowfeather mewed.

Maggottail scowled at her. "Why do you want to help them, anyway? They only hurt you when you were alive."

"But she says we'll save the Dark Forest, too, if we help them," Sparrowfeather reminded him.

"We only have her word that the Dark Forest *needs* saving," Maggottail argued.

Sparrowfeather glanced at a puddle of dark water as she hopped over it. "Explain why this is here, then. It wasn't here before."

Bristlefrost saw Maggottail's ears twitch. Though he didn't want to show it, he was clearly unnerved by the changes to the Dark Forest.

Sparrowfeather went on. "I think Ashfur *has* been fooling us. I think his promise about new lives beside the lake is a lie."

"But if it's true," Redwillow mewed hopefully, "we'll be able to—"

"You just *want* it to be true," Sparrowfeather mewed sharply.

"And you don't?" Redwillow blinked at her.

"Of course I do, but it seems too easy." Sparrowfeather fluffed out her fur. "I can't help agreeing with Bristlefrost. If it's so simple to take over the bodies of living cats, why is Ashfur here and not living beside the lake inside some Clan cat?"

Maggottail grunted.

Bristlefrost felt a flutter of gratitude toward Sparrowfeather. The Dark Forest she-cat was persistent and pressed on with her argument. "I think Ashfur is stuck here just like we are, and he's just spinning lies because he needs us to fight for him."

"I'm happy to fight for him even if there's only the slightest chance I can live again," Maggottail growled.

Sparrowfeather sniffed. "You just want to have another shot at becoming leader of ShadowClan. You failed when you were alive, and now you're obsessed with getting another chance."

"I'm *not* obsessed," Maggottail snapped, his hackles lifting. Bristlefrost guessed that Sparrowfeather had hit a nerve.

Redwillow's tail twitched. "Before we choose which side we fight on, we should find out if Ashfur really *can* give us new lives. I've been tricked before into fighting for a leader who didn't care whether his warriors lived or died. I'm not falling for it again, not unless I know there's a real reward at the end."

Bristlefrost felt a twinge of disgust. These warriors didn't care what happened to the Dark Forest, or the other cats here; they were only interested in themselves. But perhaps she could use their selfishness to her advantage.

She caught up and fell in beside them. "There's a huge patrol of Clan cats at the Moonpool right now," she mewed casually. There was no harm in exaggerating. Cats like this would want to fight on the most powerful side. "They're preparing to invade the Dark Forest to defeat Ashfur."

Maggottail glanced at her out of the corner of his eye.

She went on. "And they know Ashfur possessed another cat's body, so they are looking out for suspicious behavior. Even if you could sneak out and possess the bodies of living cats, you'd be found out. There's no way the Clans would let you live."

Redwillow's tail twitched nervously, but he didn't speak. Sparrowfeather kept her gaze fixed on the path ahead. But Bristlefrost guessed from their silence that they were thinking about their chances. Had she planted enough doubt about whether Ashfur's plan could succeed, even if it were true?

She wished that there *were*, at this very moment, a patrol of warriors at the Moonpool, preparing to invade the Dark Forest. But she couldn't even be sure that Shadowsight had made it home.

As worry wormed beneath her pelt, she began to recognize the dark stumps that dotted the land around the barrier. Her heart quickened. They were nearly there. Tasting the air, she searched for Rootspring's scent. Had he made it back? Was he here, waiting for her? Disappointment tugged her belly as her gaze landed on the tangled mass of vines and brambles blocking the entrance to StarClan. There was no sign of Rootspring. Her paws pricked with fear. Was he safe?

Redwillow stopped in front of the barrier. Maggottail padded around it, sniffing curiously.

Sparrowfeather lifted a paw and touched one of the vines. "It looks different from the last time we were here," she mewed. "We checked it with Ashfur a while ago and the vines seemed . . ." She hesitated, choosing her words. "Stiffer."

Bristlefrost narrowed her eyes. Sparrowfeather was right. The branches blocking the path to StarClan seemed to be sagging, as though the vines that held them were looser than when she'd been here with Rootspring and Shadowsight. And was that a gap? She padded closer and sniffed at a space that had opened in a clump of knotted brambles. Hope sparked in her fur. She fought to keep it smooth before the Dark Forest warriors noticed her excitement. Light was seeping through the gap. But why? Was it possible that the tangled branches had loosened *more* since they'd left?

Maggottail blinked at Bristlefrost. "You were going to show us what hope looked like," he mewed sourly.

Bristlefrost hooked a vine with her paw, feeling it give a little as she pulled. "It looks like this."

"Yeah, right." Maggottail snorted, but Sparrowfeather was sniffing curiously at the barrier.

Redwillow sat back on his haunches and stared at it. "Is StarClan really on the other side of this?" he mewed.

"Yes," Bristlefrost told him. "We spoke to a StarClan medicine cat last time I was here."

"Why should we help them?" Sparrowfeather backed away from the barrier. "They never helped us."

"I'm not asking you to help *them*," Bristlefrost told her. "I want you to help yourselves."

"How?" Maggottail narrowed his eyes.

"If we can get rid of this barrier, the Dark Forest will stop shrinking," Bristlefrost told him.

Sparrowfeather and Redwillow exchanged glances. Was that hope in their eyes?

Hope! Bristlefrost's paws tingled with excitement. Could the hope of Dark Forest cats really affect the barrier?

Maggottail padded closer, his nose twitching. "How do you know this barrier is the reason the Dark Forest is shrinking?"

"It's broken the connection between your home and StarClan's," Bristlefrost mewed.

"What does StarClan have to do with *us*?" the gray tabby grunted.

"StarClan and the Dark Forest balance each other." Bristlefrost told him what Leafpool had said. She paused, reasoning it out. "I guess it's like hills and valleys. They need each other to exist because what's missing from one creates the other."

"It sounds like a bunch of mouse-dirt to me."

"Think about it," Bristlefrost pressed. "When did the Dark Forest start shrinking?"

As Maggottail frowned, Redwillow blinked at her.

"I first noticed the water just before Ashfur arrived," the mottled tom told her.

"And the fog appeared about the same time," Sparrow-feather mewed.

Bristlefrost's tail twitched. "That was after he'd blocked

the passage between StarClan and the Dark Forest." She looked at Maggottail. He would be the hardest cat to convince. "The Dark Forest is disappearing, and StarClan will disappear too. Both you and the StarClan cats will disappear with your territories."

Maggottail gazed into the forest. In the deep shadows, still some way away, pale fog drifted between the trees, and more dark water pooled around their roots. The gray tabby shivered.

Redwillow peered through the vines. "Perhaps we should do something about it," he murmured.

Sparrowfeather hooked her claws into a vine and tried to shake it.

Bristlefrost's heart quickened. Had she convinced them to help? As she watched the Dark Forest warriors hopefully, a voice beyond the barrier made her stiffen.

"I'm trying, but it's too tight."

She pressed her ear to the knotted brambles. It wasn't Leafpool's mew, but *some* cat was there.

Sparrowfeather jumped away from the barrier as the vines trembled.

Another voice sounded. "It's no good, Needletail. They won't shift."

A small gray nose appeared in a gap between the brambles. A muzzle was trying to push its way through. It pulled back inside.

"Ouch!" A mew sounded again. "They're prickly!"

Bristlefrost darted to the gap and peered through. On the

other side, she could see a sleek gray cat with stars in her fur. *Needletail?* Where had she heard that name before? She tried to remember. The older warriors had mentioned her, hadn't they? She had been a ShadowClan warrior when the Clan had been taken over by a rogue. . . . The gray she-cat looked about the same age as Bristlefrost. It seemed strange to think she'd lived before Bristlefrost had been born.

A low growl sounded behind Bristlefrost. She jerked her muzzle around. Maggottail was staring at the gap, teeth bared, his pelt bushed. Redwillow had dropped into a defensive crouch. Sparrowfeather's eyes were wide with alarm.

"It's okay," she told them. "They're StarClan cats."

Maggottail narrowed his eyes.

"They won't hurt you," she reassured him. But would he try to hurt them? "They might be able to save the Dark Forest."

"Who's there?" Needletail called from behind the barrier.

"I'm Bristlefrost." She pressed her muzzle closer. "I've come from the living Clans. I'm here to try and break down the barrier."

Needletail blinked from between the knotted brambles. "StarClan's collapsing." There was panic in her mew.

Bristlefrost felt a jolt of dismay. She knew parts of it had been fading. But *collapsing?* The situation must be getting worse. "More cats are coming," she mewed quickly. "To help break down the barrier." She hoped it was true. "We just have to wait for them to arrive."

"I don't know if there's time," Needletail called. "The trees here are crumbling and the meadows are fading. Whatever

Ashfur is doing there, we need to stop him. We're helpless here." She poked a paw through the gap and began to tug at the brambles.

Bristlefrost reached up and pulled from the other side. Somehow, she had to help Needletail make this gap big enough to climb through. If a StarClan cat could make it to the Dark Forest, it might weaken the barrier further. She glanced at the Dark Forest cats. They were not the allies she would have chosen. It hadn't been long since they'd discussed killing her so they could take over her body. But there was no one else here to ask. "Can you help me?"

Maggottail stared at her. Sparrowfeather eyed the gap nervously.

"Please!" Bristlefrost tugged harder, ignoring the sharp thorns jabbing at her paws. If they could hope too, she might be able to widen this gap. She strained at the brambles. "With a StarClan warrior on our side, Ashfur won't be able to hurt you," she told them. "And you heard what Needletail said. StarClan's disappearing too now. If we don't get her through, both StarClan *and* the Dark Forest might be gone before we have chance to defeat him."

She caught Maggottail's eye and was surprised to see longing there. *Of course!* she thought. It seemed strange, but it only made sense that these Dark Forest cats, as evil as they might be, wanted *something*. Could she win them to her side if she promised them something they wanted? Certainly she could—wasn't that what Ashfur had done?

But what do they want?

She was hit by a sudden inspiration. "If we can get rid of Ashfur, maybe you could take his place." The brambles didn't give. She pulled harder. "Imagine ruling the Dark Forest. You could be the Clan leader you always wanted to be."

She turned her gaze back to the barrier, groaning as she heaved at the brambles.

Needletail's claws tore at the knots, but the gap wasn't getting any bigger. *Hope is our best weapon.* Bristlefrost gritted her teeth and focused on positive thoughts. *Rootspring will be here soon. Shadowsight will send in a patrol. It may already be on its way.*

Could she feel the brambles shifting?

Suddenly, fur brushed her flank. She jerked her muzzle around, surprised to see Maggottail pulling at the tangled branches. Redwillow hurried to join him, wrapping his paws around a vine. Happiness surged beneath Bristlefrost's pelt as Sparrowfeather reached up beside them and began tugging at the barrier.

They're helping! They're really helping!

Her heart pounding, Bristlefrost pulled harder. The gap where Needletail had poked her muzzle began to widen.

The Dark Forest cats were strong, and the brambles around the gap continued to weaken; the vines loosened and unthreaded until the gap was wide enough for Needletail to poke her entire head through.

Bristlefrost swallowed back a purr. The StarClan cat couldn't pass all the way through yet. She tugged the brambles to one side to stretch open the gap further. Maggottail hauled at the other side. Sparrowfeather and Redwillow worked together, dragging the vines below it closer to the ground until, with a grunt, Needletail pushed her shoulders through and slithered onto the ground.

The StarClan warrior found her paws, the stars shimmering in her pelt as she shook out her fur. She glanced at the Dark Forest cats and looked puzzled. "These aren't Clan cats."

"I persuaded some Dark Forest cats to help," Bristlefrost told her.

Maggottail snorted. "We *decided* to help."

Redwillow nodded. "We want to save our territory as much as you want to save yours."

"Really?" Needletail looked doubtfully at the forest.

Bristlefrost blinked anxiously at her, hoping the StarClan warrior wouldn't offend the Dark Forest cats. A StarClan cat might not respect cats who'd been so bad in their lifetime that they'd been sent here after their death.

But Needletail dipped her head low. "Thank you," she mewed. Bristlefrost felt a rush of relief as the gray she-cat went on. "It takes bravery to stand up to a cat like Ashfur."

Maggottail lifted his muzzle. "We can be brave," he huffed.

Needletail blinked at Bristlefrost. "Where's Rootspring?" she asked. "Leafpool said he was here with you."

Bristlefrost's heart quickened with fear. "I don't know," she admitted. "We split up to confuse Ashfur's patrol. We were going to meet back here, but he hasn't arrived yet." She glanced toward the trees, praying he was on his way. "I hope he's okay."

Needletail swished her tail reassuringly. "I'm an old friend of his mother's. Any kit of Violetshine's must be as tough as old bark. I'm sure he can take care of himself."

Please let her be right. Anxiety churned in Bristlefrost's belly. He should be here by now. Had something happened to him? Suddenly she felt dizzy. The blood rushed to her paws. *Am I going to pass out?* As her vision blurred, she saw Rootspring's face staring at her. He was speaking, his eyes wide with alarm.

Bristlefrost! His voice filled her ears. *Ashfur's coming!*

Panic shrilled through her, dispelling the dizziness. She blinked at the others. "Ashfur's coming!"

Redwillow's pelt bushed. Maggottail scanned the forest, ears flattening.

"We have to get away from here!" Needletail began to nose Sparrowfeather across the clearing.

But the brown tabby seemed to be frozen by fear. "Where is he?" Her gaze flashed with terror.

"I'll head back through the barrier and fetch help," Needletail told them.

"No—don't bring any more StarClan cats yet," Bristlefrost warned. "It's too risky. We need to wait for the patrol from the Clans. If StarClan warriors die here, they'll—*you'll*—disappear forever."

"I know." Needletail fixed her with a determined look. "But some things are worth fighting for, no matter the risk." She glanced at the Dark Forest warriors. "Thank you for bringing these cats here, and for giving them hope. Whatever they've done in life, their courage proves that the spirit of a warrior can never entirely be lost."

Maggottail lifted his chin. Redwillow puffed out his chest.

Sparrowfeather's tail bushed. "I can hear him!"

"Quick!" Bristlefrost nudged Needletail back to the barrier. In the distance, paw steps were thrumming the earth. The dark warrior wasn't alone. From the sound of it, a whole patrol was heading for them.

Needletail thrust her head into the gap and began to push her way through. Her hind paws scrabbled against the earth. The gap was too small. With a grunt she shoved harder. Bristlefrost tucked her shoulder under Needletail and helped her push. "Make the gap wider," she told the Dark Forest warriors.

Redwillow grabbed a bramble and pulled at it. Maggottail tugged a vine with his teeth. Sparrowfeather slid her paws in beside Needletail and tore at the gap.

The sound of paw steps thundered closer, then slowed. Terror pressing in her throat, Bristlefrost turned to face the trees.

Ashfur padded out. He was flanked by Sandynose, Softpelt, and Strikestone. Dappletuft and Conefoot crowded behind with Berrynose and Rosepetal. Even though she'd known her former mentor was among the spirit cats in Ashfur's thrall, Bristlefrost's heart sank at the sight of Rosepetal. She had been a good mentor, and an understanding ear when Bristlefrost had thought her heart would break over Stemleaf. And was that Stemleaf and Willowshine at the rear? Now her heart seemed to drop like a stone in her chest. She'd hoped they'd escaped, but Ashfur had clearly recaptured them.

She unsheathed her claws. Sparrowfeather, Maggottail, and Redwillow let go their hold on the vines. Bristlefrost could smell their fear-scent as they turned to face Ashfur.

Ashfur's eyes narrowed to slits as he saw them. He flattened his ears. "Traitors," he snarled.

At that, Needletail gave up struggling and slid back out of the barrier. She glared defiantly at Ashfur.

As Ashfur met the StarClan warrior's gaze, his hackles lifted. "Ignore the traitors," he hissed to his patrol. Bristlefrost saw now that there was a Dark Forest cat among them—a scrawny black tom she didn't recognize. "I'll deal with those cowards later." His tail flicked ominously behind him. "Kill the StarClan intruder."

CHAPTER 10

Rootspring looked out from the shadows of his prison. He could see, in the gloomy clearing outside, Mapleshade lounging on the dark earth. The tortoiseshell-and-white she-cat was stretched out, washing her foreleg with long, rhythmic laps, while Rushtooth stared idly out into the forest.

Houndleap had hurried after Ashfur, and Rootspring had wondered whether he could fight his way out with only Rushtooth and Mapleshade left to guard him. But just a few moments after Ashfur had left, Darkstripe had padded from the trees with Silverhawk at his tail. There was no way Rootspring could take on four warriors alone, so now he watched them, hoping for a distraction that might give him chance to escape. But with every moment that passed, his fear for Bristlefrost grew. Had Ashfur reached the StarClan barrier yet? Had he found her waiting there? His belly tightened at the thought.

"Move." Darkstripe nosed Silverhawk away from a patch of smooth earth and settled down, half closing his eyes as though he were lazing in a pool of sunshine. Silverhawk eyed him resentfully.

Rootspring padded back into the shadow of his prison. The

voice in his head had been silent since it had sent Ashfur racing for the barrier.

Frowning, Rootspring reached into his thoughts. *You're trapped in here with me,* he told the voice. *Any ideas?* He flexed his claws, frustrated by the silence. *Why start something you can't finish?* The voice still said nothing. *As far as I can tell, all you've done is put Bristlefrost in more danger. And I can't even help—*

At last, the voice interrupted. *I'm working on it.*

Working on it! Rootspring paced irritably. Did the voice know what it was doing? Was it even on his side? *Why did I trust you?*

The voice answered. *Because I'm trying to help you.*

Rootspring swallowed back anger. *I'd rather you were helping Bristlefrost. She's in danger.*

Get Darkstripe's attention.

Rootspring felt a twinge of alarm. *Why?*

Just trust me! the voice snapped. *This is your best chance.*

Doubtfully, Rootspring padded to the opening between the boulders. "Darkstripe." He forced back a shiver as the tabby warrior turned his head and looked at him. "I . . . I need to speak to you."

Slowly, Darkstripe got to his paws. Mapleshade didn't move, but she watched as Darkstripe padded to the cave entrance. Rushtooth pricked his ears. Silverhawk narrowed his eyes with interest.

"What do you want?" Darkstripe peered into the shadow of the prison, his eyes glittering.

Repeat what I tell you.

Rootspring forced his fur not to ruffle as the voice sounded again in his head. His heart pounded as he began to speak the words ringing in his thoughts. "Are you happy being Ashfur's lackey?" He met Darkstripe's gaze, hoping the fear that he felt surging beneath his pelt didn't show in his eyes as the tabby warrior scowled back at him.

"I'm no cat's lackey," Darkstripe snapped.

"Really?" Rootspring pressed on, repeating the words as he heard them. "First Tigerstar, now Ashfur." Suspicion sharpened Darkstripe's gaze, but he didn't reply. "Following orders is what got you killed. Aren't you ever going to stand up for yourself?"

Finally, the fur along Darkstripe's spine lifted. "What do *you* know about it?"

"Enough," Rootspring mewed. The truth was he knew nothing about it. He barely understood what he was saying.

"How can a kit like you know about Tigerstar?" Darkstripe demanded.

Rootspring repeated the voice's words. "Ashfur is just as evil as Tigerstar was. And he cares even less about what happens to the cats who fight for him."

"You know nothing!" Darkstripe growled, his expression hardening.

"You once said," Rootspring went on, "that every cat in the forest could turn to crow-food for all you cared."

The words seemed to hit Darkstripe like claws. He looked stunned. "I—I never said that to *you*!"

Rootspring ignored him. "But you're following *Ashfur*," he went on. "Why do you care so much what that fox-heart wants? Why would you help him, of all cats? Don't you realize he's leading you to your own destruction?"

Anger returned to Darkstripe's gaze. He thrust his muzzle closer. "Ashfur is a means to an end," he hissed. "I'll be able to live again once he leads us to the living Clans. After that, I don't care what happens to him. I don't care what happens to any cat. I'll be alive again. That's all I care about."

As Rootspring stared back at him, trying not to tremble, Darkstripe's face froze. "Your eyes!" The tabby warrior was staring at Rootspring in horror. "What's happened to your eyes? Is this a trick?"

He lashed out with a paw, and Rootspring ducked just in time to avoid its thorn-sharp claws.

Panic sparked in his pelt. *Are you sure you know what you're doing?* Rootspring demanded, but the voice didn't answer.

Mapleshade had gotten to her paws and was padding closer. Rushtooth and Silverhawk watched Darkstripe, their eyes sharp with interest.

"Look at his eyes!" Darkstripe hissed at them, backing away.

Rootspring's chest tightened. What did he mean? He blinked. What had happened to his eyes? He could see okay. They felt the same. *What's happening?* he asked the voice.

Keep going, the voice ordered.

"If you follow Ashfur, you'll never have a chance to live." As Rootspring repeated the words, fear spiraled in his belly. *Please let this work!*

Darkstripe curled his lip, the fear in his eyes turning to fury.

Mapleshade padded closer.

The voice answered. *There's going to be a fight!*

I can't fight them! Rootspring stared at the four warriors. *I'm outnumbered.*

It's okay. The voice sounded calm even as Rootspring's thoughts whirled. *I'll fight them.*

Why did this voice think he could fight these warriors?

I've been a warrior for far longer than you, the voice went on. *I can win this.*

Rootspring hesitated. Darkstripe was watching him like a hunter watching prey.

The voice spoke again. *Let me take over your body and I'll get us out of here.*

The voice wanted to take over his body? The words sent panic pulsing through Rootspring's paws. Was this just a trick to let Ashfur seize control of him?

Trust me, the voice mewed, *I'm not Ashfur. I want to get you to safety so you can save Bristlefrost.*

Rootspring hesitated. *How do I know you're not lying?*

Why would I lie to the cat who saved my daughter and her mate?

A chill ran down Rootspring's spine. Was this voice . . . ? Rootspring swallowed, hardly daring to finish the thought. *Are you . . . Firestar?*

Yes. The voice spoke with a clarity that rang in Rootspring's mind like the call of a blackbird. *Have you heard of me?*

Of course he had. Firestar was the cat who had restored contact between SkyClan and the other four Clans, back when SkyClan still lived in the gorge. There was no cat beside the lake who hadn't heard tales about the legendary leader of ThunderClan.

I won't let any harm come to you, the voice promised. *But you have to trust me. I want to save you, and Bristlefrost, and all the other cats threatened by Ashfur.*

Rootspring felt the fur lift along his spine. *Firestar* was here to help him. He didn't know whether to feel relieved or terrified. But he knew that this was his best chance to escape and get to Bristlefrost before Ashfur found her.

Pressing back fear, he closed his eyes. *You can take over my body . . . just for a little while.* He forced himself to relax, and in the dim shadows behind his eyes, he thought he saw a flame-colored pelt moving toward him. Then darkness swamped him.

Firestar breathed in the musty stench of the Dark Forest. After so long in the sweet-scented meadows of StarClan's hunting grounds, he found the pungent odor of rotting leaves sickening. He stretched his claws, getting a feel for Rootspring's body, then scrambled up and faced Darkstripe.

The tabby warrior was staring at him, confusion clouding his eyes. Mapleshade hung back, ears twitching with interest, while Rushtooth and Silverhawk peered around the edge of the boulders.

The sensation of real fur ruffling along his flanks and real paws at his command set Firestar's heart racing. This body was smaller and fluffier than his own, and pain throbbed in Rootspring's wounds. Firestar would have to make the most of the young warrior's strengths to compensate for his injuries, but as he shifted his weight, he sensed power in the muscles beneath Rootspring's pelt, and lightness of movement in his limbs.

"Hi, Darkstripe." Firestar looked past the tabby warrior. "Hi, Mapleshade." He glanced at the other warriors. "Rushtooth." He'd met this tom in the Dark Forest before. "How are you?"

Rushtooth bared his teeth but didn't reply, and Firestar flicked his gaze toward Silverhawk.

"It's good to see you."

Silverhawk snarled nervously.

"Why are you following Ashfur?" Firestar asked them. "You must know enough about him to realize he doesn't care about you. His plan to cut off StarClan from the living Clans will destroy the Dark Forest."

Darkstripe answered for the Dark Forest cats. "Who cares?" he growled. "We'll be safe in the bodies of living cats. What happens to the Dark Forest after that won't matter."

Firestar blinked at Darkstripe. He'd known the tabby warrior since he'd joined ThunderClan as an apprentice, and he knew Darkstripe wasn't a fool. "Is that what Ashfur told you?"

"He's proved it," Darkstripe hissed. "He took over Bramblestar's body."

Firestar snorted. "He slipped into a leader's body between lives," he mewed. "That doesn't mean every cat in the Dark Forest can steal any body they like."

Rushtooth shifted uneasily. "Why not?"

Firestar shrugged. "If it were true, why aren't you already

beside the lake? Why is Ashfur making you wait?"

Mapleshade whisked her tail. "He needs us to punish the Clans first." Her whiskers quivered excitedly. "And I'm happy to help him with that. Ashfur's vengeance will be my vengeance. I want to see them cut off from their precious StarClan. I want to see them destroyed."

Firestar pressed back rage, surprised at its power. It had been a long time since he'd felt like this. He struggled to control the surging anger and forced himself to return Mapleshade's gaze calmly. "If you hate the Clans so much, why do you want to live among them again?"

"Shut up!" Darkstripe thrust his muzzle closer.

Behind him, Rushtooth and Silverhawk were looking uneasy.

Firestar didn't flinch. "Let this young warrior go," he mewed.

Darkstripe frowned. "Which young warrior?"

"Rootspring."

"But *you're* Rootspring!"

Mapleshade pushed in front of Darkstripe. "Stop trying to trick us."

"I don't need to trick you," Firestar told her. "I'm warning you. If you don't let Rootspring go, you'll have to face the living Clans *and* StarClan."

A low growl rumbled in Mapleshade's throat. "StarClan?" she sneered. "Ashfur's going to destroy them, and we're going to help him."

"The only thing you're going to destroy is yourselves,"

Firestar told him. "Ashfur is a liar. Rootspring is trying to save you. Let him go."

"What do you mean, let *him* go?" Darkstripe nosed Mapleshade out of the way. "If you're not Rootspring, who *are* you?"

Firestar squared his shoulders and felt the muscles ripple along his flanks. "Haven't you guessed?"

Rushtooth backed away. Silverhawk edged behind Mapleshade.

Darkstripe stared at him. He lifted his head, peering down into Firestar's eyes. *That's right,* Firestar thought with satisfaction. *You've seen these eyes before, haven't you?*

Darkstripe's eyes slitted with disgust as he seemed, at last, to understand who he was talking to. "Firestar." His teeth glistened as he bared them. "What are *you* doing here? This is no place for a kittypet."

"This is no place for *any* decent cat," Firestar growled back.

Darkstripe snorted. "Even dead, you can't stop yourself from meddling in other cats' affairs?"

"Because I protect the Clans, and I always will." Firestar took a step closer. He'd been tripping over Darkstripe for too many moons. It was time he showed him that the Dark Forest could never win against the Clans.

Darkstripe flattened his ears. "You took Tigerstar from us twice! Now I'm going to destroy you once and for all." Satisfaction gleamed in his eyes. "I'm going to turn you and that little pest Rootspring into crow-food."

Firestar unsheathed his claws. He'd thought he'd never

have to fight again. But if these cats wouldn't listen to reason, he had no choice. With a yowl, he leaped through the prison opening and flung himself at Darkstripe.

The tabby warrior had lost none of the strength he'd had in life. As Firestar hooked his claws into Darkstripe's pelt, he felt muscle harden beneath the fur. But Rootspring's body was powerful, and he was able to thrust Darkstripe backward and aim a hefty blow at his muzzle. As his claws raked Darkstripe's jaw, he saw Silverhawk back away.

Firestar smelled blood, and the scent made his borrowed pelt bristle with energy. He eyed the others, ready for their attack, but Rushtooth seemed to be rooted to the ground, and Mapleshade simply watched, unmoving, curiosity in her gaze.

Darkstripe shook the blood from his chin and swung around, his eyes black with fury. Firestar had first seen that fury when he'd been an apprentice in ThunderClan. But he wasn't an apprentice anymore. He had battle skills now, which he'd learned and practiced over countless moons. Even in this unfamiliar body, he knew he was ready for this fight. Rootspring's paws obeyed him with a speed and strength that made his heart quicken with pleasure.

As Darkstripe attacked, Firestar lunged low and fast. He sank his teeth into the tabby warrior's foreleg and tugged it from beneath him. Darkstripe thumped onto his side, and Firestar grabbed him by the shoulders and churned his hind paws against his belly. Satisfaction welled in his chest as Darkstripe yowled with rage. He'd forgotten the thrill of battle.

Blood pulsed in his ears and excitement set his pelt bristling. This was too easy. He loosened his grip and let Darkstripe wriggle free.

Darkstripe scrambled to his paws and circled him like a fox. Firestar invited him to attack with a flick of his tail. "Come on, then."

Relish gleamed in Darkstripe's eyes. He leaped at Firestar with a snarl. Firestar ducked, but Darkstripe anticipated him, lashing out low with a forepaw that caught Firestar beneath his eye. The shock of it made Firestar gasp. He felt claws sink into his shoulders as Darkstripe hauled him backward and knocked his hind paws out from under him with a skillful kick.

Panic flared for a moment in Firestar's chest. He fell, and pain seared his leg as rough earth grazed Rootspring's wounds. Firestar fought back nausea. He couldn't lose—but Darkstripe was on him. The tabby's paw slammed into Firestar's muzzle, jerking it sideways. Blood welled in Firestar's eyes and dripped from his nose.

Young Rootspring's nose, he remembered. *I must protect Rootspring.* Summoning every bit of strength, Firestar heaved Darkstripe away, scrambling from beneath him and finding his paws. He turned on the tabby and began slashing at him, hitting out with blow after blow, so fast that Darkstripe couldn't find his balance. Backing away, the tabby dropped into a defensive crouch and flung out a desperate paw.

Firestar knocked it away and leaped on top of Darkstripe. Digging his claws into the tabby's shoulders, he pinned him to the earth. "Give up!" he snarled. "Ashfur will destroy you and the Dark Forest."

"I'd rather be destroyed than surrender to you." Darkstripe's hiss was sharp with pain. But no fear showed in it.

Firestar felt Darkstripe pushing beneath him, strength wound into every muscle. *This warrior won't stop until he's killed me.* A sickening sense of foreboding flooded his belly. *And if I go, so does Rootspring.* There was only one way to end this fight. The thought of it made him shudder.

But he would do what he had to do. A true warrior always did—and he had never stopped being a warrior.

He thrust his jaws close to Darkstripe's ear. "You've chosen this," he hissed. "You're going to suffer the same fate as Tigerstar." This time he wouldn't give the tabby warrior a chance. He sank his teeth deep into Darkstripe's neck and pressed down until he felt bone snap between them.

Darkstripe's body fell limp beneath him. Firestar closed his eyes. This warrior would never harm any cat again. He let his jaws loosen, regret tugging in his belly as his battle rage faded. Had he hoped, all these moons, that Darkstripe would eventually learn the error of his ways? He straightened and stepped back from the warrior's body. It was already fading into the gloom.

Firestar looked around. Mapleshade was gone.

Rushtooth was staring at him with wide, frightened eyes. He backed away. "I don't want anything to do with this." The light brown tom turned and hared into the forest, his tail dipping behind him as he disappeared among the brambles.

Silverhawk's ears twitched nervously. "Is it true?"

Firestar looked at him, the taste of blood still in his mouth. "Is what true?"

"Has Ashfur been lying to us?" Silverhawk's eyes narrowed. "Is it really impossible for us to live beside the lake again?"

Firestar held his gaze. "The only thing that's true right now is that if Ashfur has his way, the Dark Forest will disappear along with StarClan, and you will disappear with it."

Silverhawk glanced at Darkstripe's body. It was only a faint outline now—almost gone.

"You can help me stop Ashfur's plan," Firestar told him. "Join me and help me make sure the Dark Forest survives."

"Why would you do that?"

"To save StarClan and the living Clans."

Silverhawk hesitated. Then he dipped his head. "Okay," he mewed.

Firestar watched the Dark Forest warrior. Could he really trust him? "You must promise not to harm Rootspring when I let him return to his body."

"I promise."

"*Swear* it," Firestar ordered.

"I swear on Emberdawn's spirit," Silverhawk mewed.

"Emberdawn?" Firestar had never heard of her.

"She was my mate," Silverhawk explained. "She died."

Firestar hadn't seen Emberdawn in StarClan, and by the sound of it she wasn't here in the Dark Forest with Silverhawk either. He wondered if the mysterious she-cat had had anything to do with Silverhawk being here now, but there wasn't time to ask questions. He'd promised Rootspring that he'd protect Bristlefrost. It was time to give the young warrior his body back.

Firestar closed his eyes, his paws pricking with apprehension. He was entrusting his future, and the future of every StarClan warrior, to an inexperienced young tom. But Rootspring had come this far. He had courage and strength. Firestar was going to have to believe that Rootspring could finish what he started. He had to believe that StarClan would be safe. Focusing on the warmth of the pelt enfolding him, he let his thoughts slide into darkness

Rootspring felt pain in his leg. His muzzle stung and his muscles ached afresh. Had Firestar managed to fight his way free of the boulder prison? He opened his eyes, fearful of what he would see. He was standing in the clearing. Mapleshade and Rushtooth were nowhere to be seen. Darkstripe was nowhere to be found. Had Firestar killed them, or driven them away? Rootspring shivered, suddenly aware of the taste of blood in his mouth.

Silverhawk was staring at him, his pelt smooth. Rootspring began to back away before realizing there was no threat in the gray tabby's eyes.

"Where is Darkstripe?" Rootspring asked.

"Firestar killed him," Silverhawk told him.

Rootspring's pelt ruffled uneasily. His claws had killed a

warrior. Could they do it again, without Firestar?

Silverhawk went on. "He asked me to help him fight Ashfur."

"Did you agree?"

"Yes." Silverhawk glanced into the forest. "What do we do now?"

Rootspring drew in a long, slow breath. He knew exactly what he needed to do. "We find Bristlefrost," he mewed, heading for the trees.

CHAPTER 11

❧

Bristlefrost curled her claws into the earth as the spirit cats and the Dark Forest tom fanned out around Ashfur. The satisfaction gleaming in the dark warrior's eyes sent rage pulsing through her. His order rang in her ears. *Kill the StarClan intruder.*

Stemleaf dropped into an attack crouch. Willowshine flattened her ears. Their eyes were clouded like ice-covered water. As Berrynose and Softpelt edged forward, Bristlefrost moved in front of Needletail. There was no way she was going to let any cat harm the StarClan warrior.

"Wait." Ashfur flicked his tail.

Berrynose and Softpelt halted. Stemleaf and Willowshine froze as the other spirit cats watched in silence. Bristlefrost searched Stemleaf's gaze, hoping to see some sign of recognition, but he just stared back at her blankly, his ears swiveled toward Ashfur as he waited for the next order.

Ashfur's gaze fixed on Needletail. "You don't have to die here," he mewed smoothly. "You can join me."

Needletail stepped from behind Bristlefrost, her hackles lifting. She glared at the dark warrior. "Never."

"Really?" He widened his eyes innocently. "But we're so much alike, you and I."

"I'm nothing like you," Needletail snarled.

Ashfur didn't seem to hear. "You never truly belonged in StarClan," he mewed. "You were out of your depth there, just like I was. You never really believed in the Clans. You saw how weak their rules made them. You're a rebel like me. This is where you belong. I can give you life again."

Needletail showed her teeth. "I've heard empty words like yours before," she hissed. "I won't be taken in by them again."

"Okay." Ashfur shrugged. "Then you'll die here and never return to StarClan." He tipped his head. "Are the Clans worth it?"

"Always," Needletail spat.

Bristlefrost's heart sank as she noticed Maggottail, Redwillow, and Sparrowfeather edging away from her. Were they going to desert her to save themselves?

Then she would have to face this alone. "Why kill her?" she asked Ashfur as she padded forward. "There's no need. StarClan's crumbling. Why not let Needletail go back and be with her Clanmates to end her time?"

Ashfur's lip curled. "She's never going back."

Bristlefrost saw anxiety flit across the dark warrior's gaze. *Why?* She narrowed her eyes. *He's scared.* She glanced at Maggottail, Sparrowfeather, and Redwillow. These Dark Forest warriors had helped her get Needletail through the barrier. And Stemleaf and Willowshine had escaped his control for a while. Bristlefrost lifted her chin. *His plan is falling apart and he doesn't want StarClan to know.* If Needletail made it back and told StarClan that Ashfur's control over the Dark Forest wasn't as strong as he pretended, they'd send more warriors. *He knows he's not strong enough to fight the whole of StarClan.*

She leaned closer to Needletail. "You have to make it back," she breathed in the StarClan warrior's ear. "You have to tell them that Ashfur is weak."

"They already know he's weak." Needletail's eyes glittered with menace as she stared at the dark warrior. "I'm not running away." She padded toward Ashfur. "I've got this."

Ashfur blinked at her calmly, but his pelt pricked uneasily along his spine. "Kill her."

On his order, Stemleaf leaped forward. Berrynose lunged. Bristlefrost reared to defend Needletail. But the StarClan warrior turned and leaped for a tree. She landed on the trunk, dangled by her claws for a heartbeat, and then shot up it, faster than a squirrel.

Stemleaf stared up at her blankly. Berrynose looked puzzled, as though wondering who had stolen his prey.

Pelt spiking with rage, Ashfur watched as Needletail scurried from branch to branch and then leaped into the next tree. "Go after her, you mouse-brains!"

Like sleepers waking, Berrynose gave chase; Stemleaf scrambled after him. As Ashfur's forehead furrowed in concentration, the other spirit cats began to climb too, leaping into the branches around them as though weightless. In a moment, the trees were alive with cats. Conefoot pushed past Rosepetal. Softpelt leaped over Strikestone and flung herself into the next tree. Berrynose raced along a branch that reached deep into the withered oak beside it. All around Bristlefrost, branches shivered and dying leaves rustled as the spirit cats chased after Needletail.

Ashfur focused on them, his tail stiff, his body motionless as he willed them onward. Clearly, he was making his rage theirs. They raced recklessly through the trees, not seeming to care that a misstep could send them falling to their deaths.

Bristlefrost could see Needletail's lithe frame streaking along a branch in the distance. The stars in her pelt glimmered between the leaves. Berrynose was catching up. Stemleaf had taken a route that shadowed hers, and now he pulled ahead and turned, ready to cut across her path.

Alarm shrilled in Bristlefrost's pelt as the toms closed in on the StarClan warrior. There was only one way she could stop them from here. *I must break Ashfur's control.*

She leaped at Ashfur, hooking her claws into his shoulders. He felt as stiff as dead prey and fell as she hurtled into him. She clung on, glancing up at the trees, panic clutching at her heart as she saw Stemleaf stumble. *Don't fall!* High above, Berrynose faltered, as though suddenly aware of the drop beneath him. But Needletail didn't hesitate. Running faster, the StarClan warrior leaped into another tree and raced along a branch to the next.

Stemleaf! Holding fast to Ashfur, Bristlefrost's breath caught as Stemleaf's paw slipped and he slithered from his branch. She didn't want the spirit cats to get hurt! She tensed, relief swamping her as Stemleaf grabbed the branch below and dangled by his forepaws.

She felt the stiffness leave Ashfur as she clung to him. He twitched, and suddenly he was like a fish writhing beneath her. He flung her off with a growl, his gaze raking her like fire before he focused once again on the spirit cats, staring up into the branches.

But he was too late. Bristlefrost's heart soared as she saw Needletail vanish among the leaves.

Ashfur growled and glared at her. "You'll pay for that." His gaze flitted to Maggottail, Sparrowfeather, and Redwillow. The three Dark Forest warriors drew closer together, their tails low. Bristlefrost's mouth grew dry. They'd never defend her against Ashfur. She was on her own.

She backed away, glancing around frantically for an escape, when her gaze caught on Maggottail. The Dark Forest cat was looking straight at her. Surprise sparked beneath her pelt. Eagerness glowed in his eyes.

He darted to her side and faced Ashfur. "We can do this," he snarled as Sparrowfeather and Redwillow joined them.

Bristlefrost felt gratitude surge in her chest. "Thank you!"

Redwillow unsheathed his claws. "He's outnumbered."

Sparrowfeather growled softly. "Let's kill him."

Ashfur glanced toward his spirit cats. They had already stopped their pursuit. Now they turned and began to head back toward Ashfur, swarming through the branches as he flicked his gaze back to Bristlefrost and stared at her coldly.

Willowshine dropped lightly beside the dark warrior. Sandynose and Softpelt slithered like snakes down the trunks. Berrynose and Rosepetal leaped from the branches, their paws thudding softly on the forest floor. Closing in like wolves, the spirit cats lined up behind Ashfur.

Bristlefrost pressed back a shudder. "He's not outnumbered now," she breathed to Redwillow.

"Focus on Ashfur," Maggottail growled. "If we kill him, the spirit cats will stop fighting."

But as Bristlefrost nodded, Stemleaf dropped into an attack crouch. Berrynose drew back his lips. They glared at the Dark Forest warriors as though staring across a scent line at an enemy patrol.

Bristlefrost tried not to look at the spirit cats. She aimed her gaze at Ashfur. If she could reach him, she could stop him.

Ashfur blinked back at her, triumph in his eyes. He gave a tiny nod and his command sent the spirit cats surging forward. Conefoot slammed into Sparrowfeather so hard that he sent her sprawling into a pile of leaves. Stemleaf leaped at Maggottail. Sandynose dived at Redwillow. Bristlefrost saw cream fur flash at the edge of her vision as Berrynose grabbed her with outstretched claws and dragged her to the ground. She hit it with a thump that shocked her. With a yowl, she kicked out with her hind paws and caught him in the belly, knocking him away. Scrabbling back up, she glared at Ashfur.

The dark warrior stood at the center of a tight ring of spirit cats, directing them with his thoughts. Bristlefrost raced toward him, keeping low as she ducked a swipe from Berrynose. Strikestone broke from the ring and lunged at her, but she swerved to avoid him and, pushing hard against the earth, flung herself through the gap he'd left. She bared her teeth, ready to sink them into Ashfur's leg, but claws hooked her shoulder, and pain scorched through her as they lifted her off her paws. She gasped in surprise as Willowshine flung her backward. How could a medicine cat have such strength? Bristlefrost landed on her paws but skidded, unbalanced, and Willowshine leaped onto her, shoving her muzzle into the earth. Screeches and yowls exploded around her as the Dark Forest warriors tried to fight off the spirit cats. Bristlefrost pushed up with all four paws, thrusting the medicine cat backward. She felt her pelt rip as Willowshine's claws tore her fur, but this time she hardly noticed the pain as she spun and faced the medicine cat.

Willowshine glowered at her, her green eyes lit with hate. *Ashfur's hate.* There was no way Willowshine would ever be so malicious. "Look!" Bristlefrost nodded toward the StarClan barrier.

Willowshine dropped into an attack crouch.

"It's loosening!" Bristlefrost yowled. Surely the real Willowshine was still inside this cat? "We managed to make a gap!"

She saw Willowshine's tail quiver as the medicine cat prepared to leap.

"Needletail made it through!" Bristlefrost willed Willowshine to understand. "StarClan can help us. You have to fight Ashfur's control!"

Willowshine paused. Hope surged in Bristlefrost's chest as the medicine cat seemed to stiffen. Her eyes cleared, the brightness that had lit them in life glimmering there for a moment as she glanced at the barrier.

Bristlefrost hardly dared breathe. "Look." As she watched, a vine loosened and unwound just enough for a narrow branch to spring free. "We can save StarClan if we hope!"

But Willowshine blinked and dragged her gaze back from the barrier. *No!* Bristlefrost's heart plummeted as the spirit cat's eyes clouded once more. With a snarl, the medicine cat threw herself at Bristlefrost, raking her ear with a vicious blow.

Bristlefrost reared and thumped her paws down on Willowshine's spine. The gray she-cat rolled onto her side and wrapped her paws around Bristlefrost's legs. Tugging them from beneath her, she dragged Bristlefrost to the earth. Bristlefrost kicked out, catching Willowshine beneath the chin. As Willowshine yelped in pain, Maggottail tumbled past, clinging onto Stemleaf, his eyes slitted with determination. Sparrowfeather was beating Rosepetal back toward a tree, and Bristlefrost felt a jolt of panic as she suddenly realized what would happen if the Dark Forest cat killed her former mentor, or any spirit cat. Any cat who died in the Dark Forest died in real life—but they didn't go to StarClan's hunting grounds *or* the Dark Forest.

They simply ceased to exist.

Bristlefrost trembled and opened her mouth to call to Sparrowfeather just as Strikestone leaped for the spirit cat and pulled her away.

Bristlefrost's thoughts whirled. That had been a close call—Rosepetal easily might have been killed—but the Dark

Forest cats had to defend themselves. They were too heavily outnumbered, and no cat had managed to get near Ashfur. She couldn't risk any cat being killed—neither the spirit cats nor the Dark Forest warriors. If any of them died here, they would be lost forever.

"Retreat!" Yowling, she leaped to her paws. Willowshine regained her footing and lunged at her once more. Bristlefrost darted clear and, beckoning the Dark Forest warriors with a flick of her tail, pelted for the trees. "We have to get out of here."

A rivulet of dark water bounded the edge of the barrier clearing. She leaped it, glancing over her shoulder to make sure the others were following. Sparrowfeather batted Stem-leaf away and gave chase. Maggottail sprinted after them. Redwillow was already haring between the trees.

Bristlefrost took a path that dipped and rose through the forest. Every hollow ran with dark water, and Bristlefrost found herself leaping from rise to rise, terrified of getting her paws wet. Maggottail was at her heels, Redwillow and Sparrowfeather trailing, as they fled the spirit cats.

Bristlefrost's heart seemed to press up into her throat. *At least we survived,* she told herself. And Needletail had escaped. She leaped another rivulet, the path beginning to even out. It ran straight between the trees, and she pressed hard against the earth, making the most of the smooth terrain to out-distance the spirit cats. She looked back and saw movement between the trees. A yowl rang through the cold, dank air.

"I see them!"

Growls echoed after them. Paw steps pounded the earth. Bristlefrost ran harder. But the paw steps were closing in. She focused on the forest ahead, her muscles burning with the effort, her breath coming fast. *Keep going!* She lengthened her stride, half blind with fear, and glanced back again. Strikestone and Dappletuft were almost at Redwillow's tail.

As she turned to scan the path, her heart nearly burst with panic. A few strides ahead, a wide ditch cut across the earth. She was moving too fast to crouch and leap over it, but her momentum was too strong for her to make a sudden stop. Black water flowed along it, and she only pulled up just in time. As she scrambled to a halt, her pelt spiked in terror. "Watch out!" she shrieked, hooking Maggottail's shoulder with her claws and jerking him backward before he could hurtle blindly into the stream.

Sparrowfeather slewed to a stop beside them, her eyes wide with fear.

"Redwillow!" Bristlefrost screeched in horror as the tabby tom raced past. He was too fast to stop and she was too slow to grab him; he plunged into the water. Maggottail shrank away, and Bristlefrost ducked as black droplets showered around them.

"Redwillow!" Sparrowfeather teetered at the edge of the ditch. She stared in horror as Redwillow's shoulders disappeared beneath the water. The tabby tom flung his paws toward the bank, but it was too far away. His eyes rounding in terror, he opened his mouth to shriek. Water flooded in, and, silenced, he slid beneath the crow-black surface.

Bristlefrost stared, barely able to believe her eyes as he disappeared, and the water closed over the Dark Forest warrior as though nothing had ever disturbed it.

"He's gone," Sparrowfeather croaked.

A snarl sounded behind them. Bristlefrost turned in time to see Strikestone rearing over her, his face twisted with hate. His paw swung toward her, claws outstretched.

Bristlefrost froze, bracing herself for the blow. But Maggottail leaped from her side and flung himself at the spirit cat. He knocked Strikestone away with a hefty swipe that sent the brown tabby tom reeling.

"Quick!" Maggottail got a running start, crouched, and carefully leaped the ditch, and he beckoned Sparrowfeather and Bristlefrost over as Dappletuft and Softpelt thundered toward them.

Sparrowfeather got low and then jumped. Forcing herself not to think too hard, Bristlefrost crouched down and followed. Landing on the other side, she hit the ground running and pelted along the path. She tried not to think of Redwillow. He'd been alive a moment ago and now he was gone. But there was no time to mourn him. They had to escape.

"Get them!" Ashfur's order sliced between the trees. Yowls echoed from different points behind them as the spirit cats fanned out.

"Up here!" A mew from overhead made Bristlefrost snap her muzzle upward. The trees were denser here, and the leaves clustered thickly on the branches. She could just make out movement. Needletail! The StarClan warrior was running through the branches above them.

"Quick!" Needletail's hiss made her stop. "They won't be able see you from the ground."

Bristlefrost swapped glances with Maggottail as he slithered to a halt beside her. Sparrowfeather pulled up and glanced over her shoulder. They were in luck. The path had dipped, and a rise hid them for a few moments from their pursuers.

"Climb!" Bristlefrost hooked her claws into the nearest trunk and pulled herself onto the first branch. Maggottail followed. Sparrowfeather climbed the tree next to them. They leaped up from the branch, swishing through the leaves until the forest floor was barely visible beneath them. Bristlefrost stopped and froze, hardly breathing as paw steps pounded beneath her.

Sparrowfeather sat motionless above her. Maggottail crouched in the tree beside hers, his eyes round with panic. Needletail landed softly beside Bristlefrost and blinked reassuringly at her.

Ashfur's yowl sounded below. "Find them!" Rage hardened his mew. Bristlefrost glimpsed Softpelt and Dappletuft climbing trees nearby. She shrank against the bark, praying they wouldn't spot her between the leaves.

Needletail nodded sharply toward the trunk. Bristlefrost's heart sank as she saw Berrynose heave himself into the crook. The cream tom's eyes widened with triumph as he met Bristlefrost's gaze. He began to pick his way along the branch toward her.

Bristlefrost pricked her ears. Berrynose was the one

outnumbered up here. She only had to get him far enough from Ashfur and he'd be free of the dark warrior's control. Swallowing back fear, she straightened and darted toward him. His eyes widened in surprise and he gave a yelp as she grabbed him and pressed his chin against the branch. He tried to kick out with his hind legs, but Needletail leaped on top of him and pinned him down.

Helpless, Berrynose could only grip onto the bark as Bristlefrost pressed his head against the branch so hard that he couldn't open his jaw to wail.

After a few heartbeats, Bristlefrost felt the fight go out of him. He lay still, his eyes dark with rage, but she ignored him and glanced at Needletail. "Grab as many spirit cats as you can," she ordered.

Needletail nodded and eased herself off Berrynose. Bristlefrost took her place, squashing Berrynose down hard as the StarClan warrior hopped noiselessly into the next tree.

There, she signaled to Maggottail with a flick of her tail. The Dark Forest warrior glanced at Bristlefrost and seemed to understand. His eyes lit up as Stemleaf climbed onto the branch beneath him.

The white-and-orange warrior hadn't seen them. He tasted the air as he scanned the trees. Maggottail crept along the branch above him, then dropped on the unsuspecting tom. Stemleaf didn't have time to yowl before Maggottail pressed his muzzle against the branch. Holding him there, he blinked jubilantly at Bristlefrost.

Sparrowfeather must have seen what they were doing.

Bristlefrost's heart quickened with elation as the Dark Forest she-cat ambushed Willowshine. The medicine cat had been tiptoeing along a branch, but Sparrowfeather had followed her and overpowered her so nimbly that Willowshine had no chance to put up a fight. Now she could only squirm silently as Sparrowfeather held her down.

Don't let them make a sound. Bristlefrost's heart pounded in her ears.

Below, Ashfur's yowl hardened with rage. "Why haven't you found them?"

Bristlefrost looked down and glimpsed him between the leaves. The dark warrior was pacing, his pelt spiked along his spine as he scanned the forest. Conefoot and Rosepetal stood nearby, staring into the trees.

"They must have escaped over the rise." Ashfur padded away, his tail flicking ominously as Conefoot and Rosepetal headed after him.

Berrynose wriggled in Bristlefrost's grip, but she held him firm as the paw steps of their pursuers faded. Finally he gave a muffled mew, and Bristlefrost glanced at him.

The ThunderClan warrior was staring at her, his eyes pleading. Hesitantly, she loosened her grip enough for him to speak.

"Ow!" Berrynose mewed reproachfully. He twisted his head, trying to get free.

Bristlefrost held on, but not as tightly. "Is Ashfur still controlling you?"

"Nah," Berrynose managed to mew.

Sparrowfeather looked down from the branch where she was holding Willowshine. The medicine cat's green eyes were sparkling with indignation, but the blank hatred had gone. Stemleaf slapped his tail desperately against the branch where Maggottail had pinned him.

"I think they're back to normal," Bristlefrost called in a hushed whisper.

"Leh me go!" Berrynose strained against Bristlefrost's grip. She let go but backed away warily as he pushed himself to his paws and shook out his pelt, opening his jaws as though he was testing to see if they still worked. "I don't think my muzzle will ever be the same."

"Sorry." Bristlefrost dipped her head. "But it was the only way to free you."

Willowshine and Stemleaf were getting to their paws. Stemleaf looked stunned; Willowshine, relieved. They found a route along the branches and, with Needletail, Maggottail, and Sparrowfeather, joined Bristlefrost and Berrynose.

Stemleaf dipped his head to Bristlefrost. "Thanks."

Bristlefrost purred, delighted that her former Clanmate was free of Ashfur's control once more.

Willowshine looked at the forest floor. "Is it safe to climb down?"

"Ashfur must be out of range if he lost control of us," Berrynose mewed.

Needletail leaned over the side of the branch. "I'll go down first," she mewed.

Bristlefrost shook her head. "You can't. It's too dangerous."

Before the StarClan warrior could argue, she hurried to the trunk, lowered herself tail-first, and dropped onto the ground. She scanned the forest. There was no sign of movement. But streams of dark water crisscrossed the earth. What wasn't being engulfed by water was being swallowed by fog. She could see it, pale among the dark trees in the distance. She edged away from a stream that oozed between the roots of a nearby tree. "It's safe," she called up. "But watch out for the dark water."

The others climbed down to join her.

Sparrowfeather's pelt was bushed when she reached the ground. She glanced back the way they'd run, her eyes sharp with grief. "Redwillow," she whispered.

Bristlefrost met her gaze, pity welling in her chest. "He deserved better," she told Sparrowfeather.

Stemleaf looked at her in surprise. "But he was a Dark Forest warrior."

Needletail caught the tom's eye. "He had the courage to stand up to Ashfur," she mewed. "Not every cat is that brave."

Stemleaf frowned. "I guess," he muttered.

"Thanks for saving us." Berrynose rubbed his chin with his paw. "Though you could have been gentler."

Bristlefrost looked at him. "You tried to *kill* me a few moments ago."

"*Ashfur* tried to kill you," he told her. "Besides, I'm not sure I would have. It feels like Ashfur's mind control is getting easier to fight."

"Perhaps we're just getting better at it," Stemleaf mewed.

"Whatever," Willowshine mewed. "Let's not hang around to find out." She padded between the trees.

Bristlefrost followed her. "Where should we go?"

"Back to the barrier, of course," Willowshine told her. "If Needletail made it through, other StarClan warriors might follow."

Maggottail caught up to them. "Won't Ashfur be heading there too?"

Bristlefrost paused. There could be an ambush waiting for them already. She looked at Needletail. "Should we risk facing him again?"

A voice echoed from between the trees. "We'll need more cats."

Bristlefrost's tail bushed. She jerked around, looking to see who had spoken. Relief surged like cool wind through her pelt as she recognized the tom heading toward her through the trees.

"Rootspring." She raced to meet him, happiness fizzing in her paws. As she reached him, she thrust her muzzle into the soft fur around his neck and purred before pulling back and rubbing her jaw along his. "You're safe."

He purred loudly, pressing back. "So are you!"

They broke apart and gazed at each other, and Bristlefrost could see her joy reflected in his blue eyes.

Needletail padded toward them, her gaze curious. "Who's this?" She was staring at the ragged, pale gray tabby tom who was standing behind Rootspring. Bristlefrost blinked at him. She hadn't noticed him until now.

"Silverhawk." Maggottail stalked around him. "Have you joined us too?"

The gray tom dipped his head. "I didn't have much choice." He eyed Rootspring warily. "This warrior is a good fighter. He killed Darkstripe."

Bristlefrost's eyes widened. "Darkstripe?"

Rootspring looked sheepish. "It wasn't exactly me who killed him."

"What do you mean?" Did Rootspring have more allies?

"Do you remember the voice I heard beside the StarClan barrier?" he asked Bristlefrost.

"It was Leafpool, wasn't it?" Bristlefrost was confused.

"*Before* that," Rootspring mewed. "I heard a voice when we first got there."

Bristlefrost remembered now. He'd been the only one to hear it. "Who was it?"

"Firestar."

Bristlefrost's fur prickled. She'd heard so many stories about the great ThunderClan leader.

Rootspring went on. "He stayed with me, and when Darkstripe and Mapleshade held me prisoner, he took over my body and fought for me."

Bristlefrost stretched her muzzle forward and sniffed Rootspring curiously. He didn't smell any different. "Is he still with you now?"

"I guess so," Rootspring told her. "But he hasn't spoken to me since he gave me my body back."

"Firestar's with us?" Needletail was pawing the ground.

"I think so," Rootspring told her.

Needletail whisked her tail happily. "Then we've got nothing to worry about."

"I wouldn't say *nothing*," Rootspring cautioned.

But Needletail was already heading between the trees. "Let's get back to the barrier."

Bristlefrost hurried after her. "What if Ashfur's there?"

"Look!" Needletail glanced back at Maggottail, Sparrowfeather, and Silverhawk as they hesitantly followed. "We've got three Dark Forest warriors on our side, and three spirit cats, *and* a Clan cat who's carrying Firestar's spirit with him."

Bristlefrost blinked. Needletail was right. They were far better prepared to face Ashfur now than they had been before. She knew they might lose the spirit cats' support if they got close to Ashfur, but perhaps not right away; perhaps there would be time to get more help. All they had to do was reach the barrier. There might already be more StarClan warriors trying to break through. And the living Clans could be on their way right now, if Shadowsight had made it back to the Moonpool and persuaded them to send a patrol. They might be able to win this battle after all.

CHAPTER 12

Shadowsight paused for breath. The climb had been steep and his wounds ached, but he was almost there. He glanced up at the lip of the Moonpool hollow. Beyond it, the milky blue sky promised dawn. The sun would be rising soon.

Lightleap called down to him. "Hurry." Her mew was half whispered. She was supposed to come alone. The Sisters had ordered it. But Shadowsight had promised Dovewing he'd escort his sister safely to the hollow, hoping that by hanging back from the Moonpool itself, he would be doing enough to respect the Sisters' wishes. Though he and Dovewing knew that there was far more danger waiting for Lightleap once she reached the Moonpool than there would be on the journey through the Clans' territory, he could not let her leave on such a dangerous mission without saying good-bye.

Shadowsight scrambled up the last few boulders as his sister disappeared over the top. He followed her onto the smooth stone sloping down to the Moonpool, his heart aching. In the dawn light, the hollow looked as though it were underwater, swathed in blue shadow, waiting for the sun to lift over the enclosing cliffs and flood it with light He was surprised to see Graystripe and Squirrelflight waiting at the top beside Lightleap. Apparently they, too, had decided to bend the Sisters' rule. Mistystar and Reedwhisker were there too, shifting nervously in the half-light, and Shadowsight wondered which of them would be going into the Dark Forest. He assumed it must be Reedwhisker; Mistystar had seemed so conflicted about the plan earlier. Breezepelt was with Crowfeather, and Violetshine, Tree, and Needleclaw had come together. Which of them would be accompanying Lightleap on this mission?

As Tree dipped his head in greeting, Mistystar glanced in surprise at Lightleap, and then at Shadowsight's injured leg. "Which one of you is going?"

"I am." Lightleap lifted her chin.

Mistystar's ears twitched uneasily. Had she expected Tigerstar to send a more experienced cat? Or a warrior that wasn't his kin? Perhaps she thought *Shadowsight* should go, return to the Dark Forest despite his injuries.

Shadowsight glanced down the slope. The Sisters were huddled beside the Moonpool, their heads bowed together as they prepared for the ritual. There was still time for him to warn the volunteers what they would face. The Dark Forest had changed so much under Ashfur's rule that even the cats who'd traveled there during the Great Battle, like Breezepelt, could tell the volunteers little that would help them now. Shadowsight's knowledge was valuable, even if his injuries kept him from being a strong fighter. He wondered perhaps if that was also why he'd decided to come.

"Which of you is going?" He glanced around at the Clan cats.

"I am." Mistystar was the first to answer. Shadowsight nodded, trying to hide his surprise. *I suppose even leaders can have a change of heart.*

"And me." Violetshine dipped her head.

Crowfeather gave a curt nod, his eyes narrow, and Shadowsight guessed that this was the WindClan deputy's way of announcing his part in the mission. Breezepelt glanced anxiously at his father.

Shadowsight watched his sister, wishing ShadowClan's volunteer were any other warrior but her. She seemed so young and inexperienced beside the others. Was she really strong enough for the ordeal that awaited her? Her eyes were shining with excitement, though Shadowsight knew her well enough to see she was nervous from the twitching of her tail-tip. He was relieved. She would be safer in the Dark Forest if she was scared.

He leaned forward, looking gravely around at the volunteers. "When you get there, be careful of the dark water," he warned. "If you fall in, there's no escape. It will swallow you." These cats were senior warriors, except for Lightleap, and it felt strange telling them what to expect. But he knew what he was saying could help them. "The Dark Forest is shrinking. Fog and water are smothering it, so finding your way around will be hard. The old path between the Dark Forest and StarClan's hunting grounds is gone. Ashfur dug a new tunnel between them, then built a barrier across it. There's no sun or stars to guide you, and the barrier is deep in the center of the Dark Forest. You'll know when you're close because there are dark tree stumps dotted among the other trees."

Crowfeather frowned. "How will we find it?"

"Keep heading toward darkness, and away from fog," Shadowsight told him. "Watch out for the spirit cats. They're only in the Dark Forest because they can't reach StarClan, but you can't trust them. They might be controlled by Ashfur. If they try to harm you, it means Ashfur is nearby. A lot of the Dark Forest warriors are fighting for him too, but he can't control them directly." A shiver lifted the fur on his neck, as though claws were tugging at the edge of his thoughts *Can Ashfur sense I'm talking about him?* He shuddered, feeling queasy as he remembered his connection with the dark warrior and pushed the thought away.

Mistystar was frowning. "How does Ashfur control the spirit cats?"

"With his mind," Shadowsight told her. "He has to focus on them to make them do what he wants. If you break his concentration, it will break the connection, but he's strong and stubborn and you won't be able to break it for more than a few moments."

Reedwhisker looked nervously at the RiverClan leader. "Remember what we talked about," he mewed.

Mistystar met his gaze steadily. "I'm not going to change my mind."

"You're our leader." He glanced around at the other cats uneasily, as though wary of questioning his leader in front of them. But something compelled him. "If anything happens to you—"

She cut him off. "You've been a strong deputy, and you'll be a strong leader if I die," she mewed. "I have every faith you are ready to take my place."

Reedwhisker's eyes glittered with dread, and Shadow-sight remembered that he was not only Mistystar's deputy, but her kit.

Mistystar touched her muzzle to Reedwhisker's cheek. "You'll make me proud," she mewed softly. "I know it."

He closed his eyes for a moment, then pulled away, straightening. "I will try," he told her. "But I hope I don't have to."

Mistystar's gaze flitted around at the other volunteers. "Every one of us is risking our lives," she told them. "And our future in StarClan. But if we fail, our Clans will lose more. That's why they are sending us on this mission. Why else would ThunderClan even think of risking an elder as loved and valued as Graystripe?" She dipped her head respectfully to the gray tom, and he dipped his in return. Then she turned her gaze to Crowfeather. "As deputy of WindClan, you've proved your worth over and over again." She nodded to Violetshine. "And you're an honored warrior. You fought valiantly against Darktail, and no one will ever forget your courage and strength."

Shadowsight's throat tightened as the RiverClan leader turned to Lightleap.

"You're the youngest volunteer," she mewed. Lightleap glanced at her paws self-consciously. "Which means you're risking more than any of us. You have many moons as a warrior ahead of you. You may yet decide to take a mate and have kits. It isn't just your future in StarClan that you are risking, but your future beside the lake."

Heart pricking with grief, Shadowsight stiffened and looked away. The Sisters, he saw, had broken their huddle, and Flurry was padding up the slope. Would she scold them for accompanying their volunteers to the hollow?

Mistystar didn't seem to notice the she-cat's approach. "We are taking this risk because it is unthinkable not to do so. We must stop Ashfur and save StarClan. Squirrelflight was right when she spoke yesterday." She blinked gratefully at the ThunderClan deputy. "Our connection to our ancestors is what makes us warriors, and we must preserve it. I was wrong to question the idea of sending help, and I am glad that by joining this mission, I can prove my loyalty to StarClan."

As Violetshine's tail quivered, Crowfeather shifted his paws.

Graystripe turned his head toward Flurry, who had almost reached them. "We're ready," he told her as she stopped in front of the Clan cats.

Sunlight was glimmering at the top of the enclosing cliff. "We have no time to waste." She looked around the cats solemnly. "If you're not going into the Dark Forest, you should leave now."

Squirrelflight dipped her head to the Sister, then touched her muzzle to Graystripe's before the old tom padded away. Mistystar blinked fondly at Reedwhisker, then followed

Graystripe down the slope, pausing for a moment as though fixing her kit's face in her memory.

Tree leaned closer to Violetshine, pressing his muzzle into her neck. "Come back safely," he whispered.

Needleclaw brushed around her mother. "Take care," she mewed.

Breezepelt glanced at his father. "See you soon," he mumbled.

Crowfeather nodded, tapped Breezepelt's head with his muzzle, and headed after the others.

Breezepelt watched him go, his eyes glistening suddenly. He looked away self-consciously but made no move to leave.

"Good-bye." Lightleap blinked affectionately at Shadowsight. She was trying to look determined, but he sensed she was searching for encouragement as she gazed into his eyes.

"Be brave," he mewed, touching his nose to her cheek. "You're as strong as any warrior here. Trust your instincts and remember that we'll be thinking about you."

She purred, though her voice faltered, then she turned away before he could say anything more. His heart twisted in his chest. "Be careful," he called after her as she followed Flurry down the spiral path.

"We should go," Squirrelflight mewed, but she hesitated at the lip of the hollow.

Shadowsight's heart was pounding. "What if the ritual doesn't work this time?" he murmured. "What if they can't find Rootspring?" His mind began to spin as he imagined all the dangers waiting in the Dark Forest.

He felt warm breath on his ear. Needleclaw had padded to his side. She leaned close. "It'll be okay," she whispered. "Rootspring and Bristlefrost will get out of this, and Lightleap and Violetshine will too."

Shadowsight blinked at her, hoping it was true.

Breezepelt was watching his father as the patrol neared the Moonpool. He looked like a kit left alone in the nursery for the first time. Tree wove around him, trailing his tail comfortingly over the tom's shoulders. Shadowsight heard the yellow tom murmur something to Breezepelt but couldn't make out the words. Breezepelt dipped his head gratefully to the Sky-Clan tom, his eyes glistening anew.

The patrol lay down beside the water as the Sisters closed around them. Shadowsight pricked his ears, listening for the singing, but silence gripped the hollow. The tip of the sun was lifting over the cliffs. Surely they must start their song soon? "Perhaps we should go." He turned toward the edge, glancing one last time at the patrol. His heart was heavier than stone. *Take care, Lightleap.*

"Wait." Squirrelflight's mew made him turn back.

Flurry was hurrying up the spiral path toward them.

"We're leaving," he called to her, feeling guilty. They must be in the way. He searched her gaze, expecting irritation, but instead anxiety sparkled there. Then he realized that Lightleap was padding after the yellow she-cat, her brown striped tail drooping behind her.

Flurry stopped in front of Squirrelflight. "There's a problem."

Alarm pricked in Shadowsight's paws. Couldn't the patrol make it through? Lightleap seemed to shrink inside her pelt and Shadowsight tensed. What had happened? Had his sister done something wrong?

Flurry's gaze was clear and calm. She didn't look at Lightleap but addressed the group. "Not every cat has the quietness of mind to allow the singing into their thoughts," she mewed gently.

She means Lightleap! Shadowsight's heart ached for his sister. He hurried to her side.

Flurry went on. "Lightleap will not be able to make it through the Moonpool."

"It doesn't matter," he whispered into Lightleap's ear. "All that matters is that you were brave enough to try."

Lightleap pulled away. "I wanted to help. I just . . . can't push away the fear." Her mew cracked.

Flurry looked around the others. "If you want five cats to go, one of you must take Lightleap's place."

Squirrelflight lifted her muzzle. "I'll go."

"No." Tree lifted his muzzle. "Bramblestar will never forgive us if we let you go."

"I'll go," Breezepelt mewed.

Squirrelflight shook her head. "It would be too hard on your kin to risk you both," she told the WindClan warrior. She eyed Reedwhisker, as though warning him too.

Shadowsight padded forward. "I'll go," he mewed. He could still feel the ache of his wounds, but Puddleshine's ointment had eased them, and the medicine cat had wrapped enough cobweb over them to stop them opening again. He caught Lightleap's eye, willing her to understand that doing this was right, and that she shouldn't feel ashamed he was taking her place. "ShadowClan should be part of this," he told Squirrelflight.

Lightleap looked back at him, hurt flashing in her eyes, and guilt pressed so hard in his chest that he hardly heard Squirrelflight's anxious mew.

"Are you strong enough?"

He dragged his gaze away from Lightleap and looked at the ThunderClan deputy. "I'll have to be." And Lightleap would have to understand.

The decision made, his heart felt suddenly at ease, beating slower than it had when he'd thought Lightleap would go. This felt better, as though it was meant to be. He blinked at his sister, wishing Dovewing or Tigerstar were here to comfort her. But if they were, they might try to persuade him to stay, and he couldn't. He had to do this.

Lightleap blinked back at him. The hurt had gone from her eyes. There was only fear there now. He hesitated. What if he never saw her again? What if he never saw *any* of his kin again? He pushed the thought away before his heart could split in two.

Flurry whisked her tail. "We should start. The sun will be rising soon."

She headed back down the spiral path and Shadowsight hurried after her, squinting against the sunshine beginning to spill into the hollow. As he passed Lightleap, he ran his tail along her flank. "You were brave to volunteer," he whispered.

She touched her nose to his ear. "Come home safely."

She sounded so anxious that he wanted to stay and comfort her, but already a rosy glow lit the horizon. The sun was rising. He glanced hopefully back at Tree. Would the SkyClan tom offer Lightleap the same kindness he'd shown to Breezepelt?

Mistystar was pacing beside the Moonpool as Shadowsight reached it. Violetshine glanced at him and blinked reassuringly. Crowfeather's tail was twitching impatiently. Graystripe was sitting back on his haunches, giving his belly a quick wash as though this were just another day in camp, but as Flurry took her place among the Sisters, he got to his paws.

The Sisters closed around the patrol in a tight circle. Shadowsight's heart quickened as they blocked out the wash of color creeping across the sky. Mistystar and Violetshine lay down, Crowfeather dropped to his belly, and Graystripe gently lowered himself onto his side. Shadowsight lay beside him, comforted by the warmth seeping from the elder's thick gray pelt. He closed his eyes and, heart pounding, listened to the Sisters' voices rising in song around him as he prepared to return to the Dark Forest once more.

CHAPTER 13

✤

Rootspring followed Bristlefrost as she ducked under a low branch that twisted away into shadow. His shoulders ached. *Firestar must have fought hard.* It felt strange to have lent his body to another warrior. At least the taste of blood was gone now. He couldn't feel any new injuries, but his muscles still twitched with the memory of battle even though he couldn't remember the fight. *My paws defeated one of the strongest warriors in the Dark Forest.* He was eager to test them himself now that he knew what they were capable of. And yet the thought made him nervous. If there was a battle ahead, it would be a hard one.

He glanced anxiously at Bristlefrost as she led their patrol between two pools of dark water. He would protect her above all, even if it meant risking his own life.

The Dark Forest seemed to grow darker as they neared the StarClan barrier, and water brimmed in every ditch and hollow in the forest floor. As the path opened into a clear stretch of woods, Bristlefrost slowed to let him catch up. Needletail fell in beside them, the stars in her pelt lighting the shadows. Maggottail and Sparrowfeather were trailing with Silverhawk.

Berrynose and Stemleaf shadowed them, their ears pricked warily.

Willowshine halted, tasting the air.

Rootspring looked at her. What had caught her attention? "Is Ashfur near?"

Bristlefrost's tail twitched. "Is he trying to control you?"

"I don't think so." The RiverClan medicine cat peered into the shadows. "This place just gives me the creeps." She glanced at Stemleaf. "Can you sense him?"

"No." Stemleaf glanced over his shoulder. "But we should hurry if we want to get to the barrier before he does."

Rootspring hesitated. He hadn't been as eager as the others to return to a place Ashfur knew they would have to go. "We need more allies."

"We have them." Bristlefrost nodded toward the patrol.

Rootspring glanced doubtfully at the spirit cats, not wanting to point out that they couldn't be trusted.

Willowshine wasn't so hesitant. "Don't rely on us," she warned.

"Why not?" Needletail blinked at her.

"Have you forgotten Ashfur can control us?" Willowshine mewed.

Berrynose's pelt ruffled self-consciously. "We'll try to fight it, but Ashfur's power is strong here."

"But you're true warriors," Needletail insisted.

"That's not enough." Berrynose told her darkly. "Do you think we haven't tried to resist? If Ashfur is near and decides to control us, it's impossible to throw him off."

Stemleaf shifted his paws. "If we betray you, it won't be our fault."

Rootspring felt a jab of pity for the ThunderClan tom. It must be hard for a loyal warrior to admit. "I'm going to get you to StarClan," he promised. "If Needletail can make it through the barrier, so can you. You'll be safe there."

Stemleaf looked away, as though embarrassed that he needed protection.

Bristlefrost swished her tail. "If we work fast and stick together, Ashfur might not get a chance to use his power over you. He'll have to face us like a real warrior, and he'll be no match for us. And even if you can't resist him, we have Maggottail, Sparrowfeather, and Silverhawk fighting with us as well."

Rootspring eyed the Dark Forest warriors, wishing his safety didn't depend on such treacherous cats.

Bristlefrost must have noticed his doubt. "Maggottail saved my life," she mewed. "And, from what you say, Silverhawk didn't help Darkstripe when Firestar fought him."

"He didn't help Firestar either," Rootspring pointed out.

"We want Ashfur gone as much as you do," Sparrowfeather insisted.

Rootspring frowned. Was it true? "Let's say we *can* trust these warriors. It still isn't enough. You've seen how many Ashfur has on his side."

"We could recruit more Dark Forest cats." Needletail looked at Maggottail. "Do you know any others who might be willing to stand up to Ashfur?"

Maggottail shrugged. "Don't ask me."

Sparrowfeather's ears twitched. "It's difficult to know who to trust in the Dark Forest," she mewed. "It's not like a Clan. We don't hang out together. It's every cat for themselves here."

"I hardly know who's left in the Dark Forest," Silverhawk mewed. "Those I do know, like Thistleclaw and Rushtooth, keep to themselves. I don't know what they think or whether they'd be prepared to betray Ashfur."

"Thistleclaw would betray anyone," Sparrowfeather muttered.

Rootspring's heart sank. These cats didn't seem to have any sense of loyalty. Was it wise to rely on them at all?

"Come on, then." Bristlefrost started walking again. "Let's get to the barrier. It looks like StarClan is our best hope right now."

Needletail hurried after her. "What about your friend's mission to bring a patrol from the lake?"

Rootspring's pelt prickled anxiously. Had Shadowsight managed to escape the Dark Forest? "We can't be sure he made it."

Bristlefrost looked at him. "We'd know by now if he hadn't."

"How?" Rootspring was puzzled by her certainty.

"Ashfur would have been sure to tell us if he'd caught him," she mewed.

Rootspring narrowed his eyes. She was right—the dark warrior wouldn't have been able to resist the chance to boast.

Needletail looked hopeful. "So a patrol might already be on its way?"

Rootspring was still worried. He knew from experience how reluctant some of the Clan leaders could be to help each other. How quickly they'd turned on one another when Ashfur had been posing as Bramblestar. "*If* he can persuade the living Clans to send one."

"And *if* they can all make it here," Bristlefrost added.

Needletail's eyes darkened. "So you're right: StarClan *is* our best hope right now." She quickened her step as twisted stumps began to show between the trees "We're almost there."

"Be careful!" Rootspring called to Bristlefrost as she hurried after Needletail. They broke into a run. "Watch where you put your paws!"

Rivulets of dark water cut across the forest floor. His heart pounded as Bristlefrost leaped over them, and raced to keep up, terrified to take his eyes off her. Relief swamped him as they reached the barrier. Ashfur wasn't here, and there was no dark water in the clearing. He pulled up beside Bristlefrost, catching his breath as Stemleaf, Berrynose, and the Dark Forest warriors reached them.

Bristlefrost was padding eagerly around the barrier. "More of the vines have loosened."

Willowshine crossed the clearing and tugged one with her paw. It gave, unwinding just a little. "I think you're right!"

Rootspring sniffed the vines hopefully. The gap Needletail had squeezed through seemed a little wider, and the brambles around it had slackened.

Needletail nudged him aside and poked her nose through. "Is any cat there?"

"Needletail!"

The reply made Rootspring jump. A deep mew rang out behind the tangle of branches. Who was it? He pressed closer with Bristlefrost and Willowshine as they crowded around Needletail and tried to peek around her. Behind them, Berrynose and Stemleaf fidgeted in excitement while the Dark Forest warriors hung back, their eyes glittering warily.

"The Clans need help!" Needletail called back. "I can't do it alone."

The barrier shivered, as though some cat was trying to squeeze through. Bristlefrost hopped backward in surprise. Willowshine's eyes widened, but Needletail seemed to hesitate.

"It's dangerous here," she warned through the branches. "If you die in the Dark Forest, you'll be gone forever."

"We'll die if we stay *here*," the voice called back. "We must restore the link between StarClan and the living Clans and save our territory. Our forests have nearly disappeared."

A small brown paw, dotted with stars, reached through the brambles.

Rootspring's heart quickened. Was StarClan really coming to help? As hope surged in his chest, he heard Firestar's mew ring in his mind.

It's time for me to leave you.

No! Rootspring stiffened. *Stay and fight with us!*

Don't worry. Firestar's mew was calm. *Put your faith in StarClan.*

Would faith be enough? Rootspring closed his eyes. *But we need you!* he told Firestar.

You are strong enough without me, Firestar answered.

Am I? Rootspring wasn't sure. Could his paws defeat Ashfur without Firestar controlling them?

It's okay, Firestar soothed. *You can do this.*

Rootspring's chest seemed to grow hollow, as though his heart had suddenly emptied out. Firestar was leaving him. *No!* He dug his claws into the earth. *I need you!*

Beside him, the barrier rustled. Rootspring opened his eyes as a lithe brown tom, muscles rippling beneath his starry pelt, pushed his way into the clearing.

"Onestar!" Needletail whisked her tail happily. "You made it." She looked eagerly behind him. The barrier was trembling. A silver-and-black she-cat with piercing blue eyes slid through, shimmering with starlight.

"Hi, Silverstream." Needletail sounded delighted to see her, her eyes brightening even more as a second silver tabby followed, her fur as soft as cloud and her tail like a plume of smoke. "Feathertail."

Silverstream blinked at her, then glanced toward Bristlefrost. "You're ThunderClan, aren't you?" She didn't wait for an answer, her ears twitching eagerly. "How's Graystripe?"

"He's well," Bristlefrost told her.

Feathertail purred, her fluffy tail quivering. "Will you tell him we asked after him?"

"Sure." Bristlefrost wondered why these two cats were so interested in Graystripe.

Silverstream seemed to read her thoughts and brushed Feathertail's ear with her muzzle. "This is his kit," she explained. "And mine."

A tortoiseshell warrior pushed after her, followed by a black tom. "Redtail." Needletail greeted them in turn, her tail twitching with delight. "Larksong."

Redtail glanced darkly around the clearing. "I can't believe Ashfur has managed to cause even more trouble than Tigerstar," he growled.

Larksong looked at Bristlefrost, his eyes round with worry. "How are Sparkpelt and our kits?"

Bristlefrost blinked at him reassuringly. "They're safe," she told him.

His ruffled pelt smoothed. "I've been worried about them," he mewed. "It's been hard not seeing them since the impostor blocked our connection to the living Clans. I've been taking care of Flickerkit, but it's hard not being able to watch over the others. I'm sure they've grown by leaps and bounds."

"They have, and they're doing just fine," she promised. "Sparkpelt is a great mother."

Rootspring narrowed his eyes against the StarClan cats' sparkling fur. They lit the clearing, and he wondered if the Dark Forest had ever seen such brightness.

The barrier shivered again. Another StarClan warrior? Surely they shouldn't risk so many. "You know how dangerous this fight will be—" Rootspring began, but his words trailed away as he saw orange fur appear in the gap. Green eyes glistened among the brambles, and a large, flame-colored tom pushed through. Could it be? He held his breath as Needletail dipped her head low.

"Firestar," she mewed eagerly. "You've come!"

Firestar dipped his head. "I guess you could say I've been here a while." He padded toward Rootspring. "Thank you." He blinked warmly. "You were brave to trust me, but I'm glad you did."

Rootspring could hardly speak. He'd heard so much about this legendary warrior that even though he'd already carried his spirit, he felt self-conscious meeting him muzzle to muzzle. He glanced at the ground. "That's okay," he mumbled.

Firestar purred. "Don't be so shy," he mewed. "We're practically old friends. I've lived inside your thoughts." He glanced at Bristlefrost, his eyes sparkling. "A lot of them were about you." As she looked away self-consciously, he went on. "It's good to meet you at last."

Bristlefrost's pelt prickled. "It's—it's amazing to meet you," she stammered. "I've heard so much about you."

Stemleaf and Berrynose were staring at the StarClan warriors. Willowshine looked through the gap they'd made. "Does this mean we can go to StarClan once Ashfur's been defeated?"

Firestar looked at her. "You can go now if you like."

Willowshine shook her head. "I may be a medicine cat," she mewed, "but I'm not running away from *this* battle."

"Me neither," Stemleaf chimed.

"Nor I." Berrynose puffed out his chest.

Maggottail narrowed his eyes. "Why risk your place in StarClan?" he mewed sourly.

"I'd risk anything to save my Clan," Stemleaf retorted.

As Berrynose whisked his tail in agreement, Firestar

looked at Maggottail. "For true warriors, the Clans' future is more important than our own," he mewed.

Maggottail sniffed while Silverhawk eyed the spirit cats suspiciously, but Sparrowfeather was gazing at the StarClan warriors as though she was imagining what it would have been like to have a star-specked pelt.

Rootspring looked around the clearing, which was filling up rapidly. They had plenty of allies now . . . but would they be enough to defeat Ashfur?

Needletail's hackles lifted. Her gaze flashed toward the trees. What had she seen? Heart pounding, Rootspring jerked his muzzle around. Was it the dark warrior?

A shape was moving in the shadows. Needletail flattened her ears. Rootspring unsheathed his claws. Was it time to fight already?

But instead of the gray impostor, it was a skinny black tom who slunk into the clearing. Rootspring had never seen this cat before.

Needletail curled her lip. "Juniperclaw."

The tom looked around nervously. "Hello."

Firestar didn't move. Curiosity glittered in his wide, green gaze. "Saving Shadowsight's life wasn't enough to save you from the Dark Forest after you poisoned SkyClan's fresh-kill pile," he observed.

Juniperclaw ducked his head meekly.

"Why have you come?" Firestar demanded.

"There were rumors that strangers had come to the Dark Forest." The black tom avoided the gazes of the StarClan warriors. "I heard they planned to fight Ashfur."

Onestar glared at him, not disguising his disgust. "Why do you care?"

Juniperclaw flinched. "I want to help."

"Why should we trust you?"

Juniperclaw glanced at Maggottail and Silverhawk. "You trust them, don't you? They've done worse things than I have."

Maggottail's pelt lifted along his spine. "*You* poisoned a Clan's fresh-kill pile," he snapped. "What could be worse than that?"

"I thought I was doing it for the right reasons. But I know now that I was wrong." Juniperclaw shifted uncomfortably. "I want a chance to redeem myself."

"If you're looking for a way out of the Dark Forest, forget it," Needletail snapped. "You won't be forgiven for what you did."

"I'm not!" Juniperclaw mewed quickly. "And I know. I just want to prove that I'm a true warrior despite everything. To myself and to my Clan."

"It's a bit late for that." Larksong padded forward. "You put kits and elders at risk."

"You acted like a rogue, not a warrior," Redtail added.

"And that's why I want to help," Juniperclaw pressed. "I want to make up for what I did."

"Even if it could mean dying forever?" Redtail pressed.

"I don't mind dying for the Clans," Juniperclaw glanced at his paws. "It wouldn't be the first time I died to save someone else. My littermate Strikestone is a good cat, and he's trapped in the Dark Forest just as I am. If I help you, perhaps he, at least, will be free to enter StarClan's hunting grounds."

Rootspring felt a prick of sympathy for the black tom. Even though he didn't know the whole story, it sounded like Juniperclaw really wanted to make amends. But Maggottail was watching the black tom through narrowed eyes.

"Have some pride," the Dark Forest warrior growled.

Juniperclaw ignored him. His gaze was on Firestar. "Please. Let me help."

"It's fine with me." Firestar glanced around. "But I'm not the only cat who has a say here."

Needletail frowned.

"He did save Shadowsight," Rootspring cut in. They might not have made it this far without Shadowsight's help. And he was a friend Rootspring and Bristlefrost valued.

"I suppose we need all the help we can get." Onestar scowled at the other Dark Forest warriors. "No matter who's offering."

Bristlefrost stepped in front of them, chin high, like a parent defending their kits. "These cats are fighting to protect their home, and we should respect that," she mewed.

Onestar looked unconvinced. The other StarClan cats exchanged glances.

Rootspring padded to Bristlefrost's side. "I know you never expected to fight beside Dark Forest warriors," he told Onestar. "I'm not comfortable with it either, but we can't be picky right now. These cats want to stop Ashfur from destroying the Dark Forest." He nodded toward Silverhawk and Sparrowfeather. "It's their home, so there's a good chance they'll fight as fiercely as any StarClan warrior to protect it."

"I hope you're right," Onestar mewed darkly.

"Have faith in them," Firestar told the WindClan leader.

Onestar grunted. "I'm a StarClan warrior," he muttered. "They're supposed to have faith in *me*."

Rootspring stiffened. Unease was suddenly worming beneath his fur. Something was pulling at the edge of his thoughts. He swallowed as he heard a strange wail, like a cat yowling far away among the trees. His fur began to spike. Was it Ashfur calling to his followers? He looked into the shadowy woods, straining to hear more, but the sound died away, and silence hung once more between the trees.

He turned toward the others. "Did you hear that?"

Their pelts were bristling.

"Yes." Firestar scanned the forest.

Willowshine backed away. "If it's Ashfur, perhaps we should get going." She looked at Stemleaf and Berrynose. "I want to learn to fight his control, but I'm not confident yet. And if he gets close enough to control us, we might put the others in danger."

Berrynose fluffed out his fur. "I'm not running," he growled. "I told you, I want to fight this battle. If it means dying, I don't care."

Willowshine's eyes widened. "But if you're not ready—"

"That's a risk we're going to have to take." Berrynose cut her off. "How will we know when we're ready? All I know is that I let Ashfur control me when I was alive," he growled. "I had a choice then. Even though he was doing things Bramblestar would never do, and giving orders no warrior would ever give, I obeyed. It got me killed and I wish I'd resisted him. I'm going to try it now. I'm going to fight his control. I'm going to fight for the Clans and die again, forever this time, if I have to."

Bristlefrost blinked at the cream tom. "It might not work, but I'm glad you want to try." There was relief in her mew, and Rootspring guessed that Berrynose's betrayal of Thunder-Clan when he was alive must have hurt her. He felt suddenly even more protective of her. She'd been through so much, and she was still ready to support her Clanmates, even when they'd made mistakes.

But something needed to be said that he knew Bristlefrost wouldn't want to say. He looked at Berrynose. "You realize that if resisting Ashfur doesn't work, we'll have to fight you," he mewed. "We might even have to kill you."

"That's okay," Berrynose answered evenly. "If it comes to that, don't hesitate. You have to save the Clans."

"I have a confession too." Silverhawk's mew took Root-spring by surprise. "I've been here a long time," he mewed. "When I was alive, I tried to kill my leader so that my kit could take his place. I thought he'd been a deputy for long enough. All I succeeded in doing was getting us both killed. My time here has been darker than I could even imagine. But that's my fault. I chose to help Mapleshade and then Ashfur. I've made nothing but bad decisions. But now"—he glanced at Rootspring and then Bristlefrost—"I've seen what it is to be a true warrior and risk everything for others." He looked at

Firestar. "If I can make up for what I've done by helping you defeat Ashfur, then I will."

Maggottail's ears twitched disapprovingly. "You'll be begging them for a place in StarClan next," he muttered.

Silverhawk glared at him. "I don't deserve a place in StarClan. I never will. But I owe them, and the living Clans, something."

Redtail swished his tail impatiently. "Are we supposed to be impressed by these confessions?" he growled. "What's the point in being sorry? You shouldn't have done it in the first place."

"We'll see if you mean it when it comes to fighting," Silverstream agreed sharply.

"Talking like a warrior is easy," Feathertail chimed in. "It's acting like one that's hard."

Rootspring shifted his paws. Did the StarClan warriors have to be so harsh? Silverhawk was being earnest. His eyes shimmered with regret. Why confess if he didn't mean it? If he wanted to make up for what he'd done, StarClan should be pleased, surely. Rootspring remembered Snowtuft. The Dark Forest warrior had given up any future he could have in order to save living cats. Didn't any cat who finally became a true warrior, no matter how long it took, deserve to be accepted? Especially cats who'd been here longer than they'd been alive? If it were Rootspring's decision to make, Snowtuft would have a place in StarClan, and these cats would at least be given a chance to earn some sort of redemption. Some cat surely had to stand up for them. "Isn't it only fair to—"

A rustling sound between the trees cut him off. *Ashfur?* Firestar's hackles lifted. Onestar dropped into a defensive crouch. Bristlefrost glanced in alarm at the spirit cats.

Rootspring swung his gaze toward the trees. *Is he here?*

Cats were moving stealthily through the shadows. Rootspring could see their eyes gleaming in the darkness. His belly tightened. This time, Firestar wouldn't be fighting for him. He'd have to guide his own claws. Unsheathing them, he prepared to fight.

Firestar let out a warning growl. His muscles twitched as though they could barely contain the anticipation charging through his body. As Rootspring watched, the ThunderClan leader charged between the trees and leaped for the closest attacker.

CHAPTER 14

❧

Ashfur? Shadowsight froze as a large tom rushed from the clearing and charged at Graystripe. Had the dark warrior been waiting for them? *I can't fight.* Fear had pricked at the edge of his thoughts as the patrol had picked its way through the Dark Forest. It surged now into a flood of panic as the tom crashed into Graystripe, knocking the elder off his paws. *I shouldn't have come.*

Beside him, Mistystar's pelt bushed and Crowfeather's eyes widened. But they were hesitating. *Why?* Had the ferociousness of Ashfur's attack frozen them too? *Help him!* His thoughts whirled as Graystripe tumbled into a tree root. With a snarl, the tom lunged after Graystripe, ears flat, teeth glinting in the darkness. Time seemed to stop.

Shadowsight suddenly realized that the trees were shimmering as though starlight had broken into the Dark Forest. Then he saw more cats rushing toward the patrol. *Who are they?* Dark Forest warriors? Spirit cats? Shadowsight could barely think for the blood roaring in his ears. Why weren't Mistystar and Crowfeather attacking them? Why was Violetshine rooted to the spot? As their attackers charged, their fur seemed to light up the forest, and, in the glow, Shadowsight saw that the tom wrestling with Graystripe had orange fur. *That's not Ashfur!*

"Graystripe!" The flame-colored tom released him.

Shadowsight caught his breath as Graystripe yowled with joy.

"Firestar!" Purring so loudly that the dark trees seemed to hum with the sound, Graystripe rolled the orange tom over and over, licking his neck and his face as though he'd discovered a lost kit. "Is it really you?"

Shadowsight blinked. *Firestar?* Was this the legendary leader of ThunderClan? The cat who'd died moons ago, saving the Clans during a great battle with the Dark Forest?

"Firestar." Mistystar's pelt fluffed with delight. Crowfeather whisked his tail.

Firestar was purring too, pressing his muzzle into Graystripe's thick mane as he let the elder squash him against the ground. "You've put on weight," he grunted.

"I can't help it." Graystripe scrambled to his paws, his eyes nearly as bright as the star-specked fur of the cats who'd stopped a few tail-lengths away. "I'm getting old." His gaze flitted over Firestar's pelt. "But you look younger and stronger than ever."

"I'm not the only one who does." Firestar glanced toward the cats heading toward him between the trees.

Shadowsight's heart soared as he recognized the glimmering pelts. *StarClan* had come! They were here in the Dark Forest. Was the barrier untangled? He scanned the trees. Had Bristlefrost and Rootspring fixed it? Where were they?

He scanned the clearing and spotted Rootspring's bright yellow pelt. *There he is—and Bristlefrost right beside him, of course!* Shadowsight raced toward them, scrambling to a halt next to Bristlefrost. He was relieved to see that Stemleaf and Willowshine were still with them. And Berrynose! They'd rescued another spirit cat from Ashfur's control.

Purring, he blinked at Rootspring. The yellow tom seemed to have even more scratches than before and his fur was sticking out in clumps along his flanks. "Are you okay?"

"I'm fine." Rootspring fluffed out his pelt. "Things have been . . ." He paused for a moment. "*Interesting* since you left. But it looks like you made it to the Moonpool. Did you run into any trouble?"

Shadowsight shook his head. "Only once I'd reached the Clans. I didn't realize they'd be so hard to persuade."

Bristlefrost's eyes were shining. "You did it, though." She looked past him to where Firestar and Mistystar were escorting the Clan patrol toward the clearing. Delight dawned on her face when she spotted Crowfeather, Graystripe, and Violetshine. "You brought help!"

As she spoke, Violetshine broke into a run and raced for Rootspring. She pressed her nose to his head as she reached him, breathing in his scent, her tail shivering with happiness. "You're safe." She closed her eyes, as though her relief was too intense to bear.

A silver she-cat had followed the SkyClan warrior from the trees, her pelt ruffled excitedly. Shadowsight didn't recognize her. "Who's that?" he asked Bristlefrost.

"Needletail," Bristlefrost told him. "She was the first StarClan warrior to make it through the barrier."

Needletail was staring at Violetshine, her eyes glistening. She purred. "It's good to see you."

Violetshine turned to look at the StarClan warrior, her eyes shining in return. She touched her muzzle to Needletail's cheek. "I can never repay you for what you did for me. You let Darktail kill you so that I could escape. And because of that, I have a family now." She glanced at Rootspring. "This is my kit."

Rootspring nodded politely. "Hi."

"I'm so pleased to meet Violetshine's kit." Needletail ducked her head at him.

Violetshine nodded. "He has a sister," she mewed softly, leaning over to catch Needletail's eye. "Actually . . . I named her Needlekit."

Needletail's eyes widened. "Did you name her after me?"

"Of *course* after you." Violetshine nudged her old friend with her nose. "My kit deserves a true warrior's name."

Two StarClan she-cats were almost tripping over Graystripe's tail as Firestar guided him between the trees. Their silver pelts were so glossy that the starlight sparkling in their fur made them seem more like fish than cats. As they reached the clearing, they pushed past the ThunderClan leader and wound around Graystripe, tails high.

Shadowsight didn't recognize them. He nudged Bristlefrost. So much seemed to have happened since he'd left in the Dark Forest. "Who are they?" he whispered.

"Feathertail and Silverstream," she told him. "They're RiverClan warriors. Feathertail is Graystripe and Silverstream's kit."

Feathertail was purring. "Are you well?" she asked Graystripe.

"Of course," he mewed. "Better now than I've been in a long time."

Silverstream glanced along his flanks. "You've put on weight."

Graystripe puffed out his chest. "Why does everyone keep saying that?"

Firestar purred fondly. "I guess you still hate to see anything left on the fresh kill pile."

Onestar was padding eagerly around Crowfeather. "How is WindClan?" he asked.

"Prey's been running well, despite everything." Crowfeather dipped his head to the former WindClan leader. But his gaze was on Feathertail. Shadowsight saw wistfulness there and wondered why. They were from different Clans. Why did they seem to know each other so well?

Mistystar hurried to greet Willowshine. "I'm so sorry I let you take such a risk."

Willowshine dipped her head. "You couldn't have stopped me," she mewed. "I had to try."

Mistystar touched her nose to her medicine cat's head. "You are as brave as any warrior," she murmured.

As the StarClan cats greeted their old friends, Shadowsight noticed that there were other cats here he didn't recognize.

And they were clearly not StarClan warriors. They looked more like cats from the Dark Forest.

Rootspring seemed to notice him staring at them. "Bristle-frost recruited them," he mewed under his breath. "They used to fight for Ashfur. That's Maggottail," he added, nodding toward the largest tom. "The she-cat is Sparrowfeather, and that's Silverhawk."

Shadowsight narrowed his eyes as the Dark Forest warriors bunched closer together, staring uneasily at the Clan patrol. They looked strong, at least. But would they be loyal?

And was that Juniperclaw beside them? Shadowsight vaguely remembered the ShadowClan deputy who'd saved him from drowning as a kit. He must be planning to help too. Shadowsight's heart quickened. He looked around the clearing. StarClan was here, *and* the living Clans, along with fierce-looking Dark Forest warriors and other spirit cats. For the first time, he felt that they might really beat Ashfur. His paws tingled with excitement.

"Who's that?" He nodded toward a tortoiseshell StarClan warrior with a dark ginger tail. He was hanging back as though he didn't know any of the Clan cats.

Firestar answered, padding to join them. "That's Red-tail. He's even older than me. He died just before I joined ThunderClan."

Shadowsight blinked at the ThunderClan cat. "You were still a kittypet then, right?"

Firestar's whiskers quivered with amusement. "Yes," he

mewed. "I was still a kittypet. It's good of you to remind me."

Shadowsight felt suddenly hot. *Why did I say that?* As he shrank beneath his pelt, Firestar padded to the center of the clearing and called to the others. "We need to make a plan. Even with the barrier broken, the Dark Forest is still shrinking. Ashfur's thrown everything out of balance."

Crowfeather and Violetshine's gazes sharpened. Graystripe lifted his muzzle. Feathertail, Silverstream, and Needletail turned to face the ThunderClan leader as Onestar and Mistystar padded to join him.

"Ashfur came to hide in the Dark Forest," Onestar mewed. "But he won't be able to hide for long."

Mistystar flexed her claws. "This time, we're going to take the fight to *him*."

Bristlefrost spoke up. "How will we find him?"

"Surely, if we wait, he'll come to us," Willowshine mewed.

Mistystar glanced around uneasily. "I don't think we have *time* to wait," she mewed. "This place is shrinking fast." Channels of dark water gleamed between the trees, and the stream that edged the clearing was lapping closer to the barrier. Before long, this stretch of forest wouldn't be wide enough for the patrol of living and dead cats to stand in.

"There can't be many more places left to hide," Rootspring mewed. "And there'll be fewer before long."

Maggottail's pelt ruffled along his spine. "If it's shrinking for Ashfur, it's shrinking for us too. We need to find him fast."

A shudder rippled through Shadowsight's fur. Could he

use his connection to the dark warrior to locate him?

He leaned closer to Rootspring. "I'm going to look for Ashfur," he murmured.

Rootspring jerked his muzzle around, his eyes widening. "What do you mean?"

"I'm going to see if I can use my connection to him to sense where he's hiding," Shadowsight explained. "Keep an eye on me. Wake me up if I start to twitch or move." He met Rootspring's gaze solemnly. "If the connection grows too strong, I might try to hurt some cat."

Rootspring shifted his paws. "Are you sure you'll be okay?"

"It's the only way we can find him quickly," Shadowsight told him. Before Rootspring could argue, he tucked his paws beneath him and settled onto his belly. He focused his mind until he could sense Ashfur's presence, like the memory of a nightmare, tugging in his gut. Letting his thoughts drift from the clearing, he followed the feeling and let it expand until he could sense the dark warrior's anger like the heaviness before a storm, and feel frustration pressing inside his chest.

His ears pricked as he recognized a voice, deep inside his mind, and he fixed on it and let it swell until every thought rang with it. *StarClan must be destroyed.* It was the same voice that had told him the codebreakers needed to be punished, the voice that had persuaded him to kill Bramblestar. *I will get my revenge.*

He swallowed back dread and invited the voice in. *Ashfur.* He let his thoughts call out to the dark warrior.

He felt the air around him grow cold, as though leaf-bare

had rushed in without warning, and snapped open his eyes. He looked around. He was standing at the bottom of a steep hill, the forest behind him. The grass was muddy and tram-pled, the black sky starless. Dark water lapped at his tail as he looked up the slope. At the top, the silhouette of a warrior cut a shadow against the sky. The tom's back was turned, and Shadowsight called out.

"Ashfur?" Fear tightened his throat as the tom turned around slowly, his face lit with an eerie light that seemed to shine from within. As his gaze reached Shadowsight, his heart seemed to burst, and dread engulfed him.

It was his own face staring down at him.

Every hair on his pelt seemed to shrill with horror, and as he flinched, something hit him, slamming into him hard—a huge, invisible paw that threw him backward so sharply his breath caught and darkness closed around him.

CHAPTER 15

❦

"Shadowsight!" Bristlefrost stared at the unconscious medicine cat. What had happened to him? He'd yowled and twitched as he lay in the clearing, but his eyes had remained closed, and now a gash had appeared on his side and was beginning to bleed.

"Wake up!" Rootspring grabbed him by the scruff and shook him. Shadowsight grunted but didn't wake.

"What's wrong with him?" Firestar crossed the clearing. Bristlefrost could still hardly believe that the Thunder-Clan leader had come. It felt unreal that the cat she'd heard so many stories about was here and ready to fight alongside them. He thrust his muzzle close to Shadowsight. "Why won't he wake up?"

Mistystar pressed in next to him. "Is he having a vision?"

Rootspring let go of his scruff. "He was looking for Ash-fur," he explained as the others crowded around him, their pelts bristling with alarm. "They've got some kind of connection, and Shadowsight thought he might be able to track him down in a dream."

"Wake up, Shadowsight." Willowshine crouched close to the

medicine cat and licked his cheek fiercely. "Come back to us."

With a groan, Shadowsight blinked open his eyes.

Relief swept through Bristlefrost. "Are you okay?" She searched his gaze. It was cloudy for a moment, then cleared.

"Yes," he mewed weakly.

Willowshine sniffed the gash along his flank. "Did Ashfur do this to you?"

"I don't know." Shadowsight pushed himself to his paws, flinching as he did so. He looked at the wound and sniffed it gingerly before shaking out his pelt. "But I'm okay."

"It must hurt." Willowshine glanced around the clearing as though looking for something she could use to treat the wound.

"It's all right," Shadowsight told her, but Bristlefrost could see pain flashing across his face.

Firestar was watching the ShadowClan medicine cat, his ears twitching. "Did you see where Ashfur was?"

"I couldn't tell," Shadowsight mewed. "I thought I saw him, but then he looked like . . . me." He sounded confused. "I don't know where I was. It looked like the Dark Forest, but it felt like somewhere else, somewhere I've never been before." His eyes darkened. "We might not be able to reach him."

Bristlefrost felt suddenly lost. This was hopeless. What were they doing here? How could they ever defeat Ashfur in this shifting Dark Forest, where the darkness he fed off only poisoned them and sucked away their courage? *We're going to die, and StarClan will disappear forever.*

Rootspring padded to her side. "It's going to be okay," he whispered.

She blinked at him. Could he tell how she felt? She saw affection in his gaze, and her heart ached in reply. She touched her muzzle to his ear. "I hope so," she mewed softly. She ignored the tug at her belly to be home again, where it was safe and familiar and she was surrounded by her Clanmates. At least while she was here in the Dark Forest, she could be with Rootspring.

Firestar straightened, his green gaze suddenly dazzling. "Don't worry," he told Shadowsight. "You were brave to try to find Ashfur, but we don't need visions. We're warriors and we're trained to hunt. We'll find him like we find any prey— with skill and experience."

He seemed so certain and unafraid. How could she give up hope when Firestar was with them? And look how many allies they had now. Her gaze flitted around the patrol. If everyone stayed strong and focused, perhaps they could do this. Perhaps they *could* defeat Ashfur and get out of here and back to the living world.

Firestar spoke again. "If the water's rising, Ashfur will make for higher ground. Let's look for him there." He headed into the forest where it sloped upward into shadow and began to climb. Graystripe followed, Onestar and Mistystar at his heels. The spirit cats hurried behind them while the Dark Forest warriors fell in with the rest of the patrol and began to make their way between the trees.

Bristlefrost hesitated as Rootspring padded after

Violetshine. Should she join him? Perhaps she should catch up to Stemleaf and Berrynose instead. She was worried Violetshine would see how close she and Rootspring had become. Surely she'd disapprove. Bristlefrost was from another Clan.

Rootspring glanced back at her, beckoning her with a flick of his muzzle. "Hurry up."

She nodded warily toward Violetshine, who was hopping over a tree root. *Will she mind?*

Rootspring seemed to read her thoughts. He shrugged. "The patrol needs to stick together," he mewed.

Violetshine turned. "Come on, Bristlefrost. Don't get left behind."

Bristlefrost felt a flicker of surprise. Violetshine had spoken to her like a Clanmate. She hurried to catch up, swapping looks with Rootspring as she fell in beside him. His eyes sparkled. Was he swallowing back a purr?

The Clan cats picked their way stealthily between the trees, avoiding the pools of dark water, their ears pricked as though patrolling, but the StarClan warriors were less careful. Silverstream and Redtail let their paws swish through fallen leaves, and it was clear that it had been a long time since they'd had to cross enemy territory. Didn't they realize Ashfur or his spies could be listening? Silverhawk and Juniperclaw seemed more cautious, treading lightly, but Bristlefrost still feared they weren't trying hard enough to stay hidden. It was as if they had forgotten that this forest was no longer theirs but belonged to a far more dangerous spirit.

Bristlefrost's paws pricked with anxiety. Could Ashfur hear

them? Worse, could he sense them? She remembered how the dark warrior had said he knew everything that happened in the forest. Perhaps it made no difference how quiet the patrol was. Perhaps Ashfur already knew they were there and was biding his time before he ambushed them.

No. She pressed back a shiver. She mustn't believe that. She must hold on to hope. Ashfur was a liar. He'd proved again and again that nothing he said could be trusted. And yet unease still wormed beneath her pelt.

She realized that, ahead, the patrol had stopped. Firestar was standing beneath a silver birch. Its bark was white, like stripped bone, and stood out starkly among the blackened trees. He looked around the patrol, his green eyes oddly bright in the darkness of the forest.

Bristlefrost noticed that ahead of him the trees opened onto a stretch of dark water. She glanced one way, then the other, and saw that it stretched as far as she could see in both directions, a river cutting off their way forward. How far to the other side? She strained to view the path through the darkness but could only make out shadow where she hoped to see the far shore. Had they traveled as far as they could in this direction?

"Stay clear of the water," Rootspring warned. "I fell in once and nearly died. It's not like real water. It will try to crush the spirit out of you."

Mistystar gazed at it in consternation. "If we can't swim in it, how do we cross?"

Onestar picked his way along the shore, as though hoping to find another route.

Sparrowfeather headed in the other direction and returned a few moments later. "It's spreading around us." Fear edged her voice. "It'll cut off our retreat soon."

"No cat's going to retreat," Graystripe growled.

Bristlefrost pressed her paws into the earth, fighting fear. "We need to get to higher ground."

"How?" Silverstream stared at the dark river lapping at the shore.

Graystripe glanced around. "We could make a crossing." He hurried to a boulder sticking up from the ground. "With stones."

Shadowsight looked doubtful. "How could we move stones big enough to keep our paws dry?"

"The water might be shallow," Graystripe mewed hopefully. A smaller stone was wedged in beside the boulder. He clawed away the earth holding it and tugged it out with his forepaws, then rolled it toward the water. He pushed it in, but his tail drooped as it disappeared, the surface closing over it as silently as black fog.

"Let's head back before we're completely cut off," Crowfeather mewed.

"No." Firestar gazed across the water. "If higher ground is over there, that's where we'll find Ashfur."

Bristlefrost blinked at him. He sounded so certain. But how would they reach it?

Crowfeather grunted. "If we can't *get* to him, it makes no difference where he is."

Firestar's gaze didn't waver. "We'll find a way." He looked at Crowfeather, his wide green eyes showing no glimmer of doubt. Bristlefrost's pelt suddenly felt lighter. She could feel her heart beating strongly in her chest, and imagined for a moment that it was beating in time with Firestar's. They'd *have* to find a way. The future of the Clans was at stake. And they'd made it this far, hadn't they?

Firestar leaned toward Graystripe and began murmuring quietly to his friend. Mistystar and Onestar joined them, and as the senior warriors conferred, Bristlefrost looked around. The trees farther downstream were overhanging the water. She headed for them and padded around their trunks, examining their branches.

Rootspring stopped beside her. He followed her gaze along an oak branch that stretched into the darkness. "Are you wondering if it reaches the other side?"

She shook her head. The branch looked thin. "I don't think it's long enough."

Her heart quickened as she spotted a tree farther down the shore that was leaning out over the water. She hurried to examine it. The land here had contracted, pushing two trees together. An elm had slammed into the roots of a beech, forcing them up and out of the ground so that the trunk tilted across the water, the roots clutching the muddy bank like an animal clinging to safety. "We could climb that," Bristlefrost suggested.

Rootspring narrowed his eyes. Bristlefrost saw doubt there. The tree wasn't leaning over far enough, and even if it did, would it reach the far shore?

"If we could push it over more," she mewed hesitantly, "the highest branches *might* make it to the other side."

Rootspring sniffed at the roots, which snaked in and out of the ground like a half-woven den.

Bristlefrost jumped down among them and scraped out a pawful of earth. "If we work together, we could dig out enough to loosen its grip." She didn't wait for Rootspring to comment. This was the best chance they had. She hurried back to the group. "I've got an idea."

Firestar looked at her. "What is it?"

She felt suddenly self-conscious. "I don't know if it will work."

Rootspring caught up to her. "I think it's worth a try," he told Firestar.

Firestar blinked at her. "Tell us."

Bristlefrost jerked her muzzle toward the leaning beech. "I thought we might be able to push that tree over and use it to cross the water."

"Push a *tree* over?" Crowfeather's ears twitched.

"It's already half out of the ground," Rootspring told him. "We can dig out more of the earth around the roots."

Bristlefrost nodded. "It's barely clinging to the bank," she mewed. "If we work together, we can loosen it."

Firestar whisked his tail. "Show us."

Bristlefrost headed toward the beech, hardly daring to

breathe. Firestar might take one look at the tree and decide it was impossible. She hung back, letting the older cats inspect the roots.

Graystripe nosed his way between them and began to dig. "The earth's crumbly enough," he mewed.

Crowfeather and Mistystar hopped in beside him and began to claw at the soil.

Firestar looked along the slanting trunk. "We need cats to push on the trunk as we dig out the roots," he mewed.

Berrynose and Stemleaf reached up with their forepaws and began to push. Willowshine and Sparrowfeather crowded in beside them with Violetshine and Silverstream. Firestar began to dig with Graystripe.

Bristlefrost glanced up. The branches at the top of the tree began to tremble as the patrol worked around its roots. Would they be strong enough to tip it over? She pressed in beside Violetshine, pushing at the trunk.

The tree creaked. More roots were pushed from the earth as the cats dug among them. With a groan, the trunk leaned a whisker closer to the water, but it held fast to the bank.

Bristlefrost looked along the trunk to where the branches trembled but stayed stubbornly above the water. Her paws itched with frustration.

Graystripe looked up from his digging. "If only it were heavier at the top."

Bristlefrost's heart pounded. She had to make this work. "I'll make it heavier." She scrambled up the tree, past Sparrowfeather and Silverstream and, standing on the trunk, looked back. "I'll climb to the top."

Rootspring's eyes widened in alarm. "It's too dangerous!"

Violetshine's fur bushed. "What if it doesn't reach the other side?"

"What if you fall?" Needletail gasped.

Bristlefrost blinked back at them, aware of Firestar's steady green gaze. She'd come this far. She couldn't give up now. "I can do this," she insisted. "I won't fall in. And if it's not long enough, I'll just run back." Even as she spoke, she knew she was only hoping for the best. There might not be a chance to run back if the tree collapsed into the water and sank beneath the surface. *It can't.* She curled her claws into the bark. *It won't.* This was the patrol's best chance to cross the water and find Ashfur. She had to take the risk.

She avoided Rootspring's gaze. The fear sparkling in his blue eyes scared her. Instead, she turned and began to pick her way along the trunk. "Keep digging!" she called back. "And push harder!"

Bark crumbled beneath her paws as she crept onward. Splinters fluttered down and disappeared into the matte-black water. She slowed as the trunk divided and split into thinner and thinner branches, putting one paw carefully in front of the other as though picking her way through a thistle patch. Her breath grew shallow until she realized she was hardly breathing at all. Pausing, she steadied her thoughts and deepened her breath. She could do this. She had to.

The tree was shivering beneath her now, and she looked back to see Maggottail and Juniperclaw hop out from around the roots and join the cats straining against the trunk. The branches were so thin now, she didn't dare go farther. Instead she stopped and sank her weight into the bark, rocking the tree deeper toward the water. Digging her claws in, she hung on, trying not to look down.

The tree grew still beneath her, as though taking a breath. Then, slowly, it began to dip. A groan sounded from the roots, then a whine that grew to a screech as wood twisted and split and the trunk suddenly dropped beneath her. With a jerk it plummeted, falling so fast that Bristlefrost felt wind streaming through her fur. Her heart exploded with panic as she clung on and closed her eyes. *If this is the end for me, please let the others make it.*

But the tree crashed to a halt, juddering between her paws, branches quivering around her as it hit solid ground. It must have reached the other side! Behind her, branches splashed into the water and Bristlefrost flinched as droplets sprayed around her. Alarm shrilled through her fur. *I can't let them touch me!* They pattered down without splashing her and, relieved, she pushed herself to her paws and picked her way to the end of the branch. With a surge of triumph, she leaped onto the far shore and gazed back into the shadows. She couldn't see the patrol. "It's safe!" she called into the darkness. "You can cross."

A moment later, Rootspring appeared from the gloom, his pale fur moving like mist among the branches as he hurried along the trunk.

"Be careful!" Bristlefrost stared at him as he scampered along the branches like a squirrel. "There's no hurry!"

He reached her and pressed his muzzle to her cheek. "You scared me," he mewed.

"But it worked." Bristlefrost purred and pulled away. The others were following.

Needletail hopped down beside them. "You were so brave," she told Bristlefrost, her eyes shining.

Graystripe and Willowshine reached them, then Stemleaf, who wound around her, purring.

"That was amazing," he mewed happily.

One by one, the patrol filed across and jumped onto the far bank, each cat blinking at her admiringly as they landed. While they murmured to each other, clearly pleased and relieved to have made it across the dark water, Shadowsight alone stared nervously up the slope.

Firestar crossed last, his paws thumping lightly onto the ground as he landed beside Bristlefrost. "That was a great idea," he told her. His eyes lit up the gloom. "You were brave to risk the climb."

Bristlefrost nervously met the ThunderClan leader's gaze. "I had to do it," she murmured. "After we tried so hard to bring you here, I had to find a way across."

He dipped his head and turned to the rest of the patrol. Shadowsight was staring up the slope, his eyes wide with fear. Beyond the river, the forest thinned and the land stretched up toward a field of long, swaying grass where gnarled trees poked up here and there, and the black, starless sky pressed down upon it like a gathering storm. "We should be quiet," Shadowsight murmured. "Ashfur's close by." Bristlefrost's paw pricked nervously as he went on. "I can feel him."

Was he still connected to the dark warrior from his vision? She pressed back a shiver. There was no time to be afraid. They'd come here to face Ashfur. This was their chance.

"Okay." Firestar nodded. He glanced at Stemleaf, Berrynose, and Willowshine. "You should hang back," he told them. "If you see Ashfur, or feel him start to take control of you, run away."

Berrynose bristled indignantly.

"No cat here will think any less of you if you leave," Firestar told him. "We have plenty of warriors, and we're strong fighters. We'll be okay without you. The most important thing is to stop Ashfur getting more powerful. The fewer cats he controls, the weaker he will be."

Berrynose sniffed. "Fine," he mewed stiffly, and hung back as the rest of the patrol began to follow Firestar up the slope.

Bristlefrost fell in beside Rootspring and Violetshine as they swished through the long grass. She felt Rootspring's pelt brush hers as they walked. He didn't look at her, but the warmth from his fur was comforting.

"That was the bravest thing I've ever seen." Violetshine glanced at her. "You frightened us half to death when you climbed up the trunk, but I don't see how else we could have moved it."

Bristlefrost felt a rush of pride. Now that she was on firm ground once more, she could hardly believe she'd done something so daring. Just knowing that she could be so brave filled her with hope. And she was sure she wasn't the bravest cat here. Suddenly she could imagine winning this battle and going home. Her heart ached with a longing to be back in the ThunderClan camp. She could almost smell the musty scents of the forest and see the lake glittering between the trees. Ahead of her, the patrol slowed. She tensed. Had they seen something?

She glanced over her shoulder. Stemleaf, Berrynose, and Willowshine had frozen behind her, their ears pricked with alarm.

She called in a hushed mew to Stemleaf. "What's wrong?"

"Ashfur." Stemleaf's pelt bristled along his spine.

"Is he trying to control you?" she asked.

"Not yet." Stemleaf's mew was barely more than a whisper. "He hasn't realized we're here."

She hurried on, slipping softly through the grass. She felt Rootspring's breath at her tail, and as she nosed her way past Maggottail and Silverhawk, she saw Firestar and Graystripe. They were crouching against the earth. Needletail, Redtail, and the others had fanned out and waited in the long grass, motionless as stones.

Bristlefrost hurried to Firestar's side. The ThunderClan leader was peering from the grass. A clearing opened ahead. On the far side, a dense thicket of trees, crushed together and tangled by the contracting earth, formed a wall as impenetrable as stone. In front of it, Ashfur was prowling, pacing one way and then the other.

He was alone and seemed unaware he was being watched. "I'll make them pay."

Who was he talking to? Bristlefrost scanned the clearing.
She couldn't see anyone else. *Is he talking to himself?* She tasted
the air and smelled the rotten stench of carrion.

"I'm make them all pay," Ashfur growled. "They thought
they could humiliate me, but I'll make them grovel before
they die."

"What's he doing?" she whispered to Firestar.

"I don't know." The ThunderClan leader's eyes were narrowed. "But it's weird that he's alone. Surely he must know it's
dangerous to make himself so vulnerable."

"Maybe he doesn't realize we have help now," Bristlefrost
whispered.

Graystripe sniffed. "More like he's lost touch with reality,"
he growled. "Ashfur always had bees in his brain."

"It could be a trap." Firestar flicked his tail and the rest of
the patrol spread out farther, creeping noiselessly around the
edge of the clearing.

Bristlefrost glanced at Rootspring. He'd stopped a tail-
length away and was staring between the stems of the grass,
his hackles high.

"When do we attack?" he whispered.

"Wait." Firestar blinked at Graystripe. "Can you smell any
other cat-scents?"

"Only our patrol," Graystripe told him. "I think he's really
alone here."

Bristlefrost's pelt fizzed with hope. This was a perfect
opportunity. If they could kill Ashfur, it would break his hold
on the spirit cats, and the Dark Forest warriors would have

no one to follow. They could untangle the StarClan barrier and everything could return to normal. She leaned forward eagerly, tensing, ready for Firestar's command.

"Follow me." The ThunderClan leader crept slowly from the grass and beckoned the patrol into the open. "Hold your line."

Ashfur jerked around. His eyes widened as he saw the StarClan cats and Dark Forest warriors emerge from the grass. As they slowly advanced, he held his ground, his tail to the tangled thicket.

Bristlefrost's heart quickened. *He's trapped!*

She searched Ashfur's gaze, wanting to see fear in his eyes. He'd caused so much suffering, she wanted him to be afraid. He had to understand what he'd done. He should suffer in return.

But there was no sign of fear. He blinked eagerly at Firestar. "You're here! Good!" Was that a purr in his throat? It should have been a growl. *What's wrong with him?* "I'm pleased to see you."

Bristlefrost stared at him. Why wasn't he scared?

Ashfur lifted his tail. "This is perfect. Better than I'd ever imagined." Bristlefrost exchanged a puzzled glance with Firestar. She could tell he was as confused as she was by Ashfur's eagerness. Did he think he could win this battle? "We can finish this once and for all."

Firestar stared at him. "Don't you feel any remorse for what you've put the Clans through?"

"Remorse?" Ashfur looked puzzled. "What for?"

"We've forgiven you so many times," Firestar mewed. "StarClan gave you a place among us. A chance to change. And you've repaid our kindness by trying to destroy us. By trying to destroy *everything*."

Ashfur sniffed. "It's not my fault if StarClan is full of fools. Why should I feel bad because you forgave me? I never forgave *you*."

Bristlefrost could hardly believe her ears. Didn't this cat know when he was beaten?

Ashfur went on, his eyes shining. "I've never forgiven anyone. I'm not weak. I never forgave Bramblestar for taking what was mine. And I'll never forgive Squirrelflight for rejecting me over and over again. I gave her love and she betrayed me. As though my love was worthless." He scowled. "I'm going to make her suffer more than any other cat. And I'm going to enjoy it."

Firestar let out a long, low hiss. The stars in his pelt quivered as though fury possessed every muscle in his body. He looked as powerful as a badger, and Bristlefrost wondered why Ashfur thought he could defeat this cat by himself.

Ashfur stared at him scornfully. "I see that your time in StarClan has not dented your confidence. You and Bramblestar are so alike. You both think you're the greatest warriors who ever walked the forest. Your arrogance makes my pelt crawl. It's about time the Clans saw how weak you really are. And when I'm done with you, I'm going to find Squirrelflight and I'm going to—"

Graystripe cut him off. "Stop babbling," he growled. He

padded closer. "You've lost, can't you see that?"

"Have I?" Ashfur stared at the ThunderClan elder. "Don't you realize that StarClan isn't special?" He looked at Crowfeather. "The only difference between you and them is that you're alive and they're dead." His gaze flicked to Violetshine. "They're just a bunch of corpses who can't bear to give up control. They don't care what happens to you. They just like telling you what to do so you serve them instead of yourselves."

Mistystar seemed to freeze as the dark warrior glowered at her.

"What did following your dead ancestors ever bring you except trouble?" he snarled. "They invent problems and then ask you to risk your lives solving them. If you ignored them, you'd be living happily in peace now instead of fighting."

Crowfeather's ears twitched uneasily. Was the WindClan deputy actually listening to this nonsense?

"You could all live in peace if you ignored StarClan," Ashfur pressed. "They're just keeping you busy so you don't realize what's good for you. You'd be better off without them."

Violetshine's pelt ruffled. "It's hard to believe we ever thought you cared about the warrior code," she hissed.

Ashfur gave her a withering look. "The trouble is that you'll believe anything." He lashed his tail. "That's why you're here now, fighting another cat's battle." He looked around at the other living cats. "Help me destroy StarClan. You can free yourself from their dumb schemes and live as you want to. You can rule the forests without owing anything to any cat."

Mistystar was staring at him without speaking. Bristlefrost

stiffened. Had he convinced her? Nervously, she glanced at Crowfeather and Graystripe. Were they going to agree with this outrageous cat?

Relief washed her pelt as Mistystar snorted.

"You don't even deserve a warrior name," she growled.

Crowfeather glared at Ashfur through slitted eyes. "You're a fool," he growled.

Violetshine flicked her tail. "What are we waiting for?" she asked Firestar. "Let's kill him."

Bristlefrost flexed her claws. She was ready for battle. She looked at Firestar. *Give the order.* The sooner they put an end to this fox-heart, the better.

Ashfur's eyes sparkled with amusement. He looked pleased with himself. Didn't he realize this was the end for him?

The grass behind them swished. Bristlefrost snapped her gaze around. Her eyes widened as a muscular white tom slid from the bushes.

"Darktail!"

Mistystar's hiss set fear sparking in Bristlefrost's belly. *Darktail?* Wasn't he the rogue who had nearly destroyed the Clans before she'd been born?

Needletail's fur was on end. Onestar's eyes widened. Around the clearing, the patrol bristled with alarm as Darktail padded into the clearing. More cats slunk from the grass, one after another until Bristlefrost's throat tightened with fear. The patrol was surrounded by cats she didn't recognize. Their pelts were matted and mangy. Scars crisscrossed their muzzles. Hardly one had an ear that wasn't torn or a tail that didn't look half shredded. Who were these cats?

Darktail stopped and met Ashfur's gaze. "They came right to us, just like you said they would," he mewed smugly.

Onestar's tail twitched. He snarled at the white tom. "What are you doing in the Dark Forest? You're not a warrior. You don't belong here."

Darktail's eyes glittered. "Oh, my father. I lived long enough among warriors to earn my place here." He tipped his head to one side, his eyes rounding. "Don't you think?"

More cats padded from the grass, and Bristlefrost's heart sank as she saw Sandynose, Dappletuft, and Softpelt with the other spirit cats, staring blindly ahead like sleepwalkers.

Ashfur had planned this all along.

Darktail went on. "I was surprised as any cat to find myself here, but it's all worked out. Ashfur has given me a chance for revenge. I failed in life, but in death I can finally destroy the Clans."

Firestar curled his lip. "You should never be allowed to walk among warriors, not in life or death. Not even among warriors who harmed their own Clans."

Graystripe's ears flattened. "How did you bring *rogues* here?" He looked around Darktail's patrol in disgust.

"They died recently, like your Clanmates," Ashfur told him. "Their spirits were fresh. It was easy enough to bring them here while StarClan was . . ." He hesitated, as though looking for the right word. *"Busy."*

Darktail's whiskers twitched with amusement. "Aren't you glad they managed to find somewhere to rest after such difficult lives?" he asked.

Firestar hissed. "You're just using them!"

Ashfur lifted his tail. "Really, Firestar," he scolded. "You're so naive. Why *wouldn't* I use anything I could to destroy the Clans?"

Darktail blinked expectantly at Ashfur. "Shall we begin?"

Bristlefrost felt a chill enfold her as though the air itself had turned to ice.

"Yes." Ashfur nodded. "Let's do this."

As he flicked his tail, Darktail reared, and the patrol of rogues and spirit cats surged forward, yowling like a pack of hungry dogs.

CHAPTER 16

❧

Rootspring froze. Time seemed to slow as he watched Darktail streak across the clearing. Ragged, snarling rogues poured after him from the long grass, like a wave of dark water sweeping across the battlefield. Mistystar and Crowfeather disappeared under the flood, and panic shrilled through Rootspring's pelt as he saw Softpelt and Dappletuft burst from cover to join the attack. Had Berrynose, Willowshine, and Stemleaf succeeded in resisting the dark warrior's control? He tried to glimpse them among the mass of pelts. Perhaps they'd managed to get away before Ashfur could take control of them.

He saw Houndleap, Rushtooth, and Thistleclaw shoulder to shoulder with the rogue spirits. Ashfur clearly still had the loyalty of plenty of Dark Forest warriors. Sandynose lunged at Violetshine. Strikestone raked claws across Silverstream's muzzle as Clawface and Mapleshade sprinted toward Ashfur and fell in beside him, their teeth bared.

The Clan patrol was outnumbered. Rootspring lashed out at Rushtooth as the Dark Forest warrior sped past him, but the brown tom hardly seemed to notice. His slitted gaze was fixed on Redtail. Rootspring's mind whirled as terror threatened to overwhelm him but, as Bristlefrost reared up beside him and slammed her paws into a mottled gray rogue's flank, his thoughts sharpened likes claws unsheathing. He would not let any of their patrol die here.

He flung out a paw and hooked the mottled rogue's leg as she turned on Bristlefrost. Unbalanced, she stumbled, and Bristlefrost leaped onto her back. As yowls exploded into the icy air, he spotted Shadowsight.

The medicine cat turned, eyes wild, and lashed out clumsily at the rogues as they streamed around him. *He can't fight. He's a medicine cat.* The fresh wound inflicted in his vision gleamed wetly, and the cobwebs around his hind leg fluttered as they fell away. *He won't survive a battle.* Rootspring glanced at Bristlefrost. She'd pinned the rogue to the ground and was tearing at her pelt with her hind claws. She could manage for now. He darted across the clearing, dodging around Needletail and ducking Houndleap. "Shadowsight!"

The medicine cat jerked his muzzle around as Rootspring called his name.

"Run!" Rootspring crashed into a ginger she-cat as she reared over Shadowsight, sending her staggering backward. He nodded toward the tangled wall of trees behind Ashfur. It was the only place to hide.

Shadowsight met Rootspring's gaze, then looked past him. His eyes flashed with horror. Rootspring turned. Houndleap was rushing at him. The Dark Forest warrior leaped, snarling, and sank his claws into Rootspring's shoulder. Rootspring fell, thumping to the ground, pain searing his pelt. He saw

Shadowsight start toward him. "No!" Thrashing beneath Houndleap, he stared desperately at his friend. "You're not trained to fight!" he yowled. Shadowsight paused, confusion in his eyes. "Just hide!" Rootspring yelped. "We can't fight them *and* protect you!" Shadowsight seemed to understand. Relief swamped Rootspring as he watched the medicine cat turn and race for the trees, scramble up the closest trunk, and haul himself into the branches.

Rootspring turned his attention back to Houndleap, who was pressing him into the earth. Rootspring curled his hind legs beneath the Dark Forest warrior's belly and thrust him away with a vicious kick. He felt the tom's claws rip free and scrambled to his paws. The ginger rogue glared at him as she recovered her footing. Hissing, she leaped to join Houndleap as he rushed Rootspring for a second attack.

Rootspring ducked, sliding beneath Houndleap's outstretched paws. The Dark Forest warrior stumbled over him and crashed into the ginger she-cat. They spat angrily at each other. Rootspring felt a flash of hope. These cats were vicious, but they clearly weren't used to fighting together. As the rogue turned on him once more, he lashed out and raked her face with his claws. Houndleap grabbed his hind leg, but Rootspring shook him free, jerking around to give the Dark Forest warrior's forepaw a powerful bite. Houndleap recoiled, pain glittering in his amber eyes as the rogue she-cat lunged for Rootspring again. This time she hit him with such force that he staggered. His paw skidded on the slippery earth and he fell. Thinking quickly, he rolled out of reach, finding space to escape as Maggottail crashed past him, batting back a rogue.

As Rootspring tumbled clear of the ginger rogue, he heard water softly lapping the earth. He froze, mid-roll, then slowly turned his head, his heart pounding as he saw, a whisker away from his muzzle, a dark pool opening like a wound across the ground. It was spreading from the long grass, eating away at the edge of the clearing. The battlefield was *shrinking*!

He scrambled to his paws, his pelt bristling with alarm. As he backed away, another cat smashed into his hindquarters. The force sent him sprawling forward. Terror ripped through his chest as he stumbled toward the edge of the water. He dug his claws in, gripping as though at the edge of a cliff as he felt the other cat's paws pushing him harder from behind. He glanced over his shoulder. The ginger rogue had come after him. Her eyes were shining hungrily as she tried to push him into the water. He dropped, thumping onto his belly, and let his body go limp. The rogue's eyes widened with surprise. Her forepaws buckled and she lurched forward. Rootspring twisted onto his spine, hooked his hind paws beneath her, and thrust her up and over his head. With a grunt, he flung her into the water. She hit it with a wail of horror. Her expression twisted into shock for a moment, and then she disappeared, the puddle of dark water swallowing her as though it were a lake.

Icy fear crept through Rootspring's fur as the water grew smooth. Not even a ripple showed that a cat had fallen there. He remembered, with a jolt of horror, falling into the water beside the island, and felt the dark water closing over his head all over again. He felt sick, but pushed the thought away. Behind him, screeches of pain and rage split the air apart. He leaped to his paws and turned, ready to rejoin the fight.

A mottled rogue barged past him and leaped at a ginger-and-white tom. Rootspring stiffened. *Stemleaf?* He hadn't managed to get away. He scanned the clearing and saw Berrynose near the center. *Both* warriors were here! Rootspring hesitated. Had they seen the size of the enemy patrol and come to help? His belly tightened. Was Ashfur controlling them? Then he realized that Berrynose was fighting Strikestone with a flurry of well-aimed blows. He blinked as Stemleaf leaped at the mottled rogue and knocked him backward. They were fighting *against* Ashfur's cats. Rootspring felt a rush of excitement. *They're on our side!*

Rootspring darted over to Stemleaf, rearing up beside him as the tom lashed out at Rushtooth. "Don't get too close to Ashfur," Rootspring said, nodding toward the dark warrior, who was crouching in front of the tangled wall of trees while Mapleshade and Thistleclaw blocked him from the battle. "He might take control of you again."

"Do you think I don't know that?" Stemleaf grunted. "It's not like I have much choice." He glanced toward an ominous shadow seeping across the earth. It was dark water, oozing from the other side of the clearing, pushing them back toward the trees. Rootspring pressed away panic. They needed to finish this battle quickly, while there was still enough space to fight.

"Stay strong," he told Stemleaf.

Stemleaf nodded. "I've been thinking of Spotfur." His eyes burned with determination. "I hope that if I can just focus on her and our kits, I'll be able to resist Ashfur's will."

As Rushtooth dropped into an attack crouch in front of them, Stemleaf nudged Rootspring away. "I've got this," he growled.

Rootspring nodded. He wasn't going to muscle in on Stemleaf's fight. Another warrior might need his help. He just hoped that Ashfur was too busy trying to manage the other spirit cats. If he did manage to take control of Berrynose and Stemleaf too, they'd be even more outnumbered.

Scanning the clearing again, Rootspring spotted Firestar fighting shoulder to shoulder with Graystripe as the two old friends faced a ring of rogues. A tabby darted forward, excitement gleaming in his eyes. With a swift jab, Firestar raked his claws across his muzzle. Another took his place, but Graystripe batted her back with a swinging blow while Firestar kicked out with his hind paws, thrusting away a ginger tom who lunged at them from the rear. As though sharing the same thoughts, the two old friends kicked and swiped at their attackers, turning in a rapid circle, their paws working together to meet every muzzle and claw with such perfect timing that it seemed as though they'd trained for exactly this moment. Between swipes, Firestar's gaze flitted toward Ashfur. The Thunder-Clan leader was clearly trying to edge the fight toward the dark warrior, but the ring of rogues kept them at bay. Meanwhile, Mapleshade and Thistleclaw guarded Ashfur with slitted eyes and flattened ears, as though he were their kit.

Perhaps, Rootspring thought, if he joined Firestar and Graystripe, they might gain the advantage and push their way through to Ashfur. He headed toward them, dodging Feathertail as she rolled past, a snarling tom held in her fierce grip. He leaped past Crowfeather as the WindClan warrior dragged Houndleap to the ground and held him there. Rogues snapped and hissed like a swarm of rats as Rootspring wove between them. There were too many to fight, but if they could get to Ashfur, the dark warrior's patrol might abandon the battle.

As he neared the ring of rogues, an anguished yowl rang over the clearing. Rootspring froze. It was his mother's cry. It pierced his heart like a thorn and he swung his gaze around. At the edge of the clearing, hemmed in by dark water, Violetshine faced two rogues. A tabby tom battered her with outstretched claws. A black she-cat tore at her tail. But Violetshine was fast. She swung her foreleg at the tabby, knocking his paws away, and thrust him backward with her head. Then she spun and slashed the she-cat's ears.

As blood sprayed the earth, Violetshine's desperate gaze flitted across the stretch of dark water. She yowled again. "Needletail!" Panic edged her mew and Rootspring followed her gaze. Her cry hadn't been for herself but for her friend. Needletail was on her belly, crouched defensively beside the water, her eyes round with fear as Darktail loomed above her.

Rootspring hared toward Needletail. Claws raked his flank, but he ripped free and dragged his paws clear of snapping jaws as he ran. Darktail lifted his forepaws and began to swing them down, his face twisted with malice. Rootspring pushed harder against the earth and leaped, skimming the surface of the dark water like a hawk, and slammed into Darktail before the rogue's paws could reach Needletail. He shoved Darktail backward as hard as he could.

The white rogue met Rootspring's gaze as he staggered away. Rootspring followed, flinging his paws around him to wrestle him to the ground. Darktail's eyes lit with shock for a moment, and then he collapsed like a rotten corpse beneath Rootspring's paws. Surprise sparked through Rootspring. Unbalanced, he staggered. Then Darktail reared. Rootspring froze as the powerful tom rose like a crow against the starless sky and swung a forepaw down toward him, spiked with claws as long as blackthorns.

Rootspring dodged them as they flashed toward his cheek, then ducked, cutting one way, then another, to avoid the flurry. He heard claws slice the air beside his ear, and twisted just in time to escape the blow, half blind with panic. Dread hollowed his belly. Where was the water?

Dizzy, he glanced down. He saw a dark puddle beside his paws and, heart lurching, sidestepped right into a vicious swipe. Pain burned his ear as he felt it tear and saw his own blood spatter the earth. He felt Darktail's claws hook the fur on his shoulders. With a yowl of triumph, the rogue hauled him off his paws and flung him to the ground. Rootspring kicked out with his hind paws but felt only air as Darktail pinned him. He struggled against the rogue's powerful paws, agony screaming through his pelt. He was beaten, unable to escape, the dark water merely a whisker from his cheek.

Darktail's eyes shone excitedly. "Good-bye," he snarled.

Rootspring gave a last desperate push as Darktail's teeth flashed toward his throat. Then he glimpsed silver fur. Needletail had grabbed Darktail's scruff. She yanked him backward. But Darktail was as strong as a fox. He held fast to Rootspring with his claws, choking him.

Rootspring thrashed desperately but couldn't escape. His courage vanished as though dark water had swallowed it. How had he thought they could ever win this battle? This was the Dark Forest. Cats like Darktail and Ashfur thrived here, growing ever stronger on the misery and hopelessness that tainted every breath of fetid air and every blackened branch. Rootspring felt hope fade like the dying light of the evening sun as Darktail's eyes glittered with a wild viciousness Rootspring had only ever seen in Ashfur's gaze.

We're going to die. We're all going to die. He glanced across the clearing. *Bristlefrost!* His heart seemed to crack in two. He'd let her down.

Suddenly, black-and-white fur flashed at the edge of his vision. Violetshine was leaping over the dark water. She landed beside Needletail, her pelt bristling with rage. With a yowl, she sank her teeth into Darktail's neck and hauled him backward.

The ragged white tom's eyes widened in surprise as he let go of Rootspring. Needletail had his hind leg between her jaws and was dragging him down onto his belly as Violetshine swung a hefty blow at his ear. It sent Darktail rolling across the ground.

Needletail leaped after him. "You're going to pay for making me suffer." She struck him across the muzzle with outstretched claws.

Darktail grunted and scrambled up.

Needletail hit him again. "And for the pain you caused Violetshine!"

Violetshine darted past her, grabbing Darktail's throat with her forepaws and thrusting him back to the ground. She held him there, churning his belly with her hind paws. "Haven't you brought enough misery to the Clans?" Her eyes burned with rage. "I'll never forgive you for what you did to me and Needletail."

She rolled off him and landed beside Needletail. Both she-cats watched with cold hatred as Darktail hauled himself up and swayed on his paws. Then Needletail lashed out, her claws raking his eye. Darktail gave an agonized yowl, reeling away, too stunned now to defend himself. Violetshine slashed his cheek, then Needletail, as they drove him back toward the long grass.

Rootspring dragged himself to his paws, shaking out his bloody pelt. He watched, hardly breathing as his mother and Needletail swung blow after blow at the evil rogue until his paws buckled and he collapsed.

"Is he dead?" Violetshine stared at him, her teeth bared.

Needletail leaned down and sniffed his muzzle. Then, as

fast as a snake, she clamped her jaws around his neck. Dark-tail twitched once more, then fell still. Drawing back, her jaws bloody, Needletail looked at Violetshine. "He is now."

Rootspring could suddenly feel the icy air reach through his fur. He pressed back a shiver. Behind him, the patrol was still fighting. Their screeches echoed over the clearing. He turned. Was that a rogue disappearing into the long grass? Darktail had seemed to command the spirit rogues. Would his followers flee, now that he was dead?

As hope flickered in his chest, he spotted Bristlefrost. She was wrestling a tabby, her eyes flashing with fury as a gray tom sank his teeth into her tail. Houndleap was heading toward her, his eyes slitted. The battle wasn't over yet.

Rootspring charged across the clearing. This time he didn't swerve or dodge. He barged his way through the fighting cats, ignoring the jaws snapping at his tail, shaking off any claw that hooked his pelt. As he raced past Juniperclaw, a rogue she-cat tried to reach for him, but the former ShadowClan deputy seized her and dragged her away. Rootspring blinked at Juniperclaw, grateful the Dark Forest warrior was on their side. Then he charged after Houndleap. He grabbed the scrawny black tom with his claws and flung him away. Then he pulled the tabby off Bristlefrost.

"Thanks." Bristlefrost blinked at him, exhilaration in her eyes, and scrambled quickly to her paws. Pressing in beside him, she kicked out at the rogue tearing at her tail and knocked him away. As the tabby reared for another attack, Root-spring darted forward and nipped his hind leg. He staggered backward. As Rootspring straightened, he felt Bristlefrost's flank against his. She caught his eye and gave a nod.

Together they lashed out at the rogues, driving them back with well-aimed blows. Was this how it felt for Firestar and Graystripe? Rootspring felt he could anticipate her every move and weave his own among them. They knocked a gray tom out of the way and sent a tortoiseshell running for cover with a barrage of blows. As they beat a path through the battle, cats began to back away.

Rootspring's heart soared. The pain of his wounds seemed to fade. They were going to win. He was fighting beside Bristlefrost and they were working together as though they'd shared a mentor. Suddenly he knew that she was more important to him than anything. Why had he ever hesitated? If there was any cat he'd give up his Clan for, it was her.

And if they escaped the Dark Forest, that was exactly what he would do.

CHAPTER 17

❧

Shadowsight gripped the slippery bark of the branch he'd scrambled onto, digging his claws in as the tangled thicket of trees shuddered around him. The earth beneath was buckling under their roots. Was the Dark Forest shrinking even more? Dark water was oozing faster from the edges of the clearing, cutting swaths across it. Around the clearing, the wide stretch of shadowy grassland seemed to rise and fall, heaving like an ocean.

He hardly breathed as he watched the battle below, shoving down every urge to scramble down to defend his friends. *I'll only get in the way.* The thought made him cringe with shame. But it was true. He had no battle skills, and the fresh wound in his flank stung even more than the gash on his hind leg. It had been hard enough climbing into the trees. The thought of jumping down made him flinch. And, though it was humiliating to hide up here, he knew that he would only distract his friends if he put himself in danger.

But hope was starting to flicker in his chest. He'd seen Violetshine and Needletail kill Darktail. Since then, rogues had started to slip away into the long grass. A few of the spirit cats seemed to have lost heart as well, as if Ashfur's control of them was slipping, and he had apparently not even tried to retake control of Stemleaf and Berrynose. Dappletuft had slunk quietly away, and Sandynose had been chased from the clearing by Stemleaf while Berrynose drove Conefoot, snarling, for cover. The StarClan warriors had managed to strip Ashfur of his guard. Even now, Feathertail and Onestar were pushing Mapleshade back, and Redtail and Needletail had sent Thistleclaw racing for the shelter of the grass. Shadowsight could see it rippling around the clearing as the beaten cats fled.

As Bristlefrost and Rootspring fought back a group of rogues, Firestar, Graystripe, and Mistystar were slowly advancing on Ashfur. The dark warrior seemed unaware of the danger. He was pacing beneath the tangled thicket, his pelt ruffling along his spine as he snarled to himself.

"You'll suffer for what you've done to me," he growled. He seemed to have lost focus on the battle. No wonder the spirit cats were taking their chance to flee.

Shadowsight shifted on his branch, watching Ashfur as Firestar, Graystripe, and Mistystar closed in, their eyes narrow as they blocked any chance of escape. But Ashfur didn't seem interested in escaping. He barely even seemed to notice as Firestar and Mistystar hung back while Graystripe padded closer.

"You're scared of StarClan's anger," Ashfur muttered to himself. "But you think you can do what you like to me without ever having to pay. I'll show you how wrong you are." Did he even realize he was losing?

As Graystripe reached him, Ashfur paused and blinked as though he didn't understand where the ThunderClan elder had come from. Perhaps now he'd see that his allies were deserting him. Shadowsight leaned forward, straining to hear as Graystripe stopped in front of the dark warrior.

"I've got a message from Squirrelflight," Graystripe growled.

Ashfur pricked his ears. "What is it?" Was that *hope* in his eyes? Did he still believe Squirrelflight had anything *good* to say to him?

Shadowsight held his breath as Graystripe went on.

"She wants you to know that she cared about you once." Graystripe stared unwaveringly at the dark warrior as he passed on Squirrelflight's message. "She considered you more than a Clanmate. . . . She kept on caring about you—even *loved* you—as a friend until she discovered you were willing to kill the cats you believed to be her kits."

Ashfur's eyes rounded, as though he was struggling to understand.

Graystripe went on. "That was when she realized she could never, ever have loved you. And that your love was rotten. It wasn't even love. You just wanted to possess her. She wants you to know that, whatever way the battle went today, it would always have been Bramblestar she chose. She wants you to think about why she'd always choose him. She wants you to finally understand why Bramblestar is and always will be the cat she truly loves."

Disbelief began to cloud Ashfur's gaze. "But I came back from the dead for her."

Graystripe snorted. "You should have stayed dead, because Squirrelflight will never love you. She loves Bramblestar, and ThunderClan, and nothing you can do will—"

Ashfur's hackles rose as though, at last, he understood. Ears flattening, he let out a sharp screech and lunged at Graystripe. Shadowsight's heart lurched as the ThunderClan elder was flung backward. Firestar darted forward, but the dark warrior had hauled Graystripe to the ground before he could reach him and was tearing at his pelt like a vicious hawk, opening deep gashes in the elder's belly. Firestar tried to drag Ashfur off, but Ashfur knocked him away, fury fueling his frenzied attack.

Shadowsight pressed back nausea as the smell of Graystripe's blood rose above every other scent of battle. Then his pelt spiked. The long grass was rustling. A moment later, rogues began streaming back into the clearing. Mapleshade and Thistleclaw followed, driving the ragged cats into battle once more.

Violetshine and Silverstream jerked their muzzles toward the attacking mob. Bristlefrost turned, shock clear on her face. Rootspring backed away, his bloody pelt rippling in surprise. They exchanged glances, then charged forward, meeting the fresh wave with angry yowls.

Panic jabbed Shadowsight's heart. Could the Clan cats fight off the dark warrior's horde a second time? Berrynose and Stemleaf were still farther off, chasing rogues through the long grass. Needletail and Onestar were gone too. Had the rogues' retreat been a plot to draw the StarClan warriors away?

"Help!" Shadowsight yowled into the icy air. "They've come back!" As his screech rang out over the shadowy meadow, he felt the branch tremble beneath him. He froze, gripping harder to the bark. The branch was moving. He heard it creak. The tangle of trees clattered around him. The earth around their roots buckled tighter, and, as it did, Shadowsight's tree began to lean. The branch he clung to ripped away from the trunk, enough to tip Shadowsight off balance. His hind claws lost their grip. His legs slipped over the edge, and, heart pounding, he dangled, his paws waving helplessly over the clearing as rogues swarmed beneath him. Any cat could reach up and drag him down. He scrabbled, trying desperately to clamber back onto the branch, the pain in his wound like fire. But the branch was tearing farther away from the trunk, the wood splintering, until, with a crack, it broke off and Shadowsight felt himself falling.

Terror burst across his mind. Flailing, he dropped and hit the sharp spine of a rogue. He felt its pelt beneath him for a moment, then slithered onto the ground. Agony blinded him as he collapsed onto his injured leg. Bodies thrashed around him. Pushing himself to his paws, he struggled to see through his pain as the fresh wound in his flank stretched and opened. A shoulder thumped into his cheek, sending him reeling. A hip crashed against his as he tried to recover his balance. He could not tell friend from enemy in the chaotic whirl of pelts.

Teeth snapped beside his cheek. He recoiled. Claws sliced the air behind his head. Snarls and shrieks filled his ears.

As he crouched, frozen with fear, he felt the ground roll beneath him. It seemed to rise, and he wondered if he was imagining that it lifted him above the other cats and carried him back like a wave. He closed his eyes. Perhaps the rest of StarClan was watching over him even here. Perhaps they'd rescued him. But, as he opened his eyes once more, he could see that he wasn't safe. The earth had lifted and pulled him clear of the fighting cats, but dark water encircled him.

He stared at it, dread hardening in his belly as the stream widened. His tail bushed as the ground began to drop. It sank lower, the water closing in as it quickly swallowed the earth around him. He had to escape before it reached him. He stared across the stream, his flank throbbing, his leg stiff. Could he jump that far? He had no choice. Drawing up every whisker of energy, he gritted his teeth and leaped. As he flung himself over the dark water, pain stabbed deep, like vicious thorns in his leg. He landed clumsily on the dry ground and staggered to find his balance. *StarClan, help me!* His strength seemed to drain away, and he swayed backward.

As he tried not to fall, a tabby rogue caught his eye. The rogue's whiskers twitched with pleasure as he fixed his gaze on Shadowsight, like a hunter glimpsing prey. Turning toward him, he began to charge, and he knew at once what the rogue intended. He glanced back at the dark water. *He's going to push me in!* Terror gripped his heart like eagle claws. He tried to run, but his hind leg buckled. Fighting to find his balance, he felt the water yawning greedily, reaching toward him, ready to suck him down as the rogue pounded nearer. Unable to flee, Shadowsight closed his eyes. *I'm going to die.* He was abandoning his friends in this place. He had been little help to them, but now he was leaving them forever. *I'm sorry.*

Pale gray fur flashed in front of his eyes. It brushed his muzzle, a scent sweeping over him like a warm breeze. *Bristlefrost!* She blocked the rogue's attack, hissing out of the corner of her mouth. "Run!"

Shadowsight found his paws and fled, pain flaring in his wounds. He scrambled, half running, half limping past the dark water, running for safety at the edge of the clearing, away from the fight. Shame tugged in his belly. He hated how scared he was. He hated running away.

Frustration boiled beneath his pelt, but as he neared the long grass, he faltered. Every thought seemed to drain from his mind, every feeling seemed to die as energy flooded out of him like blood gushing from a wound. He slumped to the ground, the battle growing hazy around him. Only gratitude remained. Bristlefrost had saved him.

He felt his head loll and darkness press at the edge of his vision. Was he dying? As consciousness ebbed away, he saw Ashfur. The dark warrior was running toward him, his gaze fixed with purpose. He shouldered his way through the fighting cats, and yet it seemed that no one else saw him. Shadowsight felt horror flood his body as Ashfur pounded nearer. Gasping with shock, he felt the dark warrior crash into him, before he was swept away by unconsciousness.

He opened his eyes into what felt like a dream. Silence surrounded him, the air thick, as though a storm hovered close. He was standing on four steady legs. Looking around, he saw that the gloomy meadow had disappeared. There was no battle here, no tangled thicket of trees, only gray cloud above, around, and below. It enveloped his paws and swirled around him. *Am I dead?*

Not yet. Ashfur's voice answered him, filling his thoughts like an owl crying in the night.

Shadowsight jerked around, scanning the grayness. Ashfur's eyes flashed in the murk, and the dark warrior padded forward, gleeful spite in his gaze. He stopped in front of Shadowsight.

"Where are we?" Shadowsight fought back rising panic.

"In your mind," Ashfur mewed. "We're connected, don't forget. This place is as much mine now as it is yours."

Shadowsight shook his head. "Get out!"

Ashfur purred. "You're dying," he mewed. "If I leave you here, there will be nothing left to tie you to life."

Shadowsight stiffened with anger. "If I'm dying, let me die."

"You don't have to die." Ashfur padded around him, trailing his tail along Shadowsight's spine.

Shadowsight shuddered and shook it off. He eyed the dark warrior. He could sense Ashfur scheming. "Leave me alone."

Ashfur wasn't listening. "You can join me," he mewed smoothly, still pacing around Shadowsight.

"Why would I join you?" Shadowsight glared at him.

"I can get you out of here. You can live." Ashfur's ears twitched excitedly. "All you have to do is kill Bristlefrost."

"You're bee-brained!" Shadowsight stared at him. "Why would I do that?"

"It would end the battle," Ashfur mewed. "You'd sacrifice one life to save many." He stopped in front of Shadowsight. "She'd never see it coming. Her guard would be down. It would be so easy, even *you* could do it."

"I would never—"

Ashfur ignored him. "Once Bristlefrost is dead, Root-spring will be too heartbroken to fight. Finishing him off would be like plucking a baby mouse from its nest. He'll be gone, and so will Bristlefrost, and *you'll* be on my side." Ashfur purred. "With you three out of the way, even Firestar will lose heart. The battle will end. There will be peace." He thrust his muzzle close to Shadowsight's. "Don't you want that?"

Shadowsight met his gaze. Peace. Of course he wanted peace. Every cat in the forest wanted peace after the chaos of the past moons. But not like this. "I want the battle to end," he mewed slowly. "But only because you've been defeated."

Ashfur's eyes widened and glittered with rage. He drew away sharply, his lip curling. "You really think you're one of them, don't you? You think you belong in the Clans."

"Of course I belong in the Clans!" Shadowsight snapped back. "My father is Tigerstar. I'm a ShadowClan cat to my bones. I've risked my life to help them."

"ShadowClan?" Ashfur's whiskers twitched. "Your mother is from ThunderClan. You're a half-Clan cat. And you've been weird since you were a kit. If your father wasn't their leader, do you think your Clan would accept you?" His tail flicked ominously. "You have visions but you don't even know who sends them. You can't fight. You helped me escape. You *killed* the leader of ThunderClan." His gaze flicked over Shadowsight, who shifted his paws self-consciously.

Everything he said was true, but that didn't mean Shadowsight didn't belong.

Ashfur went on. "Do you think your precious patrol didn't see you back there in the battle? Do you think they didn't notice you hiding in a tree while they were risking their lives? Do you think they don't mind having to rescue you over and over again?" He snorted with scorn. "You're no help to them. You're a liability."

Shadowsight forced himself not to back away. He wanted the grayness to enfold him and muffle this warrior's words. There was too much truth in them. And yet he knew his friends valued him. Bristlefrost had just saved his life, hadn't she? He trusted her. He trusted Rootspring. But this cat? Shadowsight met Ashfur's gaze and held it, staring deep into its corrupt depths. This cat was a liar. No cat could trust him. And his taunting was not going to work. Shadowsight narrowed his eyes. "You won't ever convince me again that I don't belong in the Clans," he mewed slowly. "Or that no cat cares about me. They do. I have kin. I have Clanmates. I have friends. I know where I belong."

Ashfur's gaze seemed to falter. The dark warrior backed away. Then he began to fade, dissolving into the gray cloud until he was barely visible. Suddenly his eyes flashed one last look of hate. "We'll see about that," he snarled and disappeared.

Shadowsight blinked, relieved that the dark warrior was gone. But the clouds still swirled, and the air grew thicker until it seemed to smother him. He shook himself. He couldn't stay here. If he did, he would die. But how could he escape? Had he gone too far? Was there any way to make it back to life?

CHAPTER 18

Bristlefrost ducked. The rogue's claws nicked her ear. Ignoring the sting, she darted forward and slid between the tabby's legs. As she thrust her head up hard into his belly, the rogue grunted and flicked his hind legs into the air. Twisting on his forepaws, he faced Bristlefrost once more.

Bristlefrost wanted to look over her shoulder. Had she given Shadowsight enough time to run clear? This rogue had been about to push him into the dark water.

The rogue lashed out with outstretched claws. Bristlefrost batted him away before he could reach her muzzle. Pushing hard with her hind paws, she flung herself at the tabby, hooked her claws into his pelt, and hauled him, wriggling, to the ground. She held tight, rolling the rogue onto his spine and holding him so close that he couldn't fold his hind legs into his belly.

Every wound stung; every muscle ached. She'd thought this battle was over when Firestar and Graystripe had surrounded Ashfur. But the fleeing rogues had returned, and the clearing was filled once more with the smells and sounds of battle.

The rogue pushed himself free of her grip. Bristlefrost

scrambled to her paws. She walked backward, luring the rogue away from the dark water that was seeping ever farther across the clearing. The rogue stalked after her, narrowing his eyes, ready for a fresh attack. Bristlefrost glanced past him. Shadowsight was near the long grass, safe from the water. But he was stumbling. As she watched, he collapsed. Her heart seemed to stop. Shadowsight was injured!

The rogue leaped toward her. She reared to defend herself, but the rogue lunged for her hind paw and sank his teeth in, hard. Bristlefrost yowled as pain arced up her leg. She swung her paws down onto the rogue's shoulders and grabbed his pelt. Digging in her claws and tossing him to the side, she forced him to release her paw, then pressed him to the earth and leaped onto his back. Churning her hind paws against the rogue's spine, she glanced again at Shadowsight.

Her pelt spiked in panic. Ashfur was beside him. The dark warrior had grabbed Shadowsight's scruff between his teeth and was hauling him toward the dark water.

No! She had to save Shadowsight before Ashfur threw him in.

The rogue thrashed beneath her. She felt power in his muscles. As he pushed against the earth, she slid from his back. There wasn't time for this. She had to finish this fight now. She thrust her muzzle toward his neck and bit down. The rogue jerked beneath her, then fell limp.

Spitting fur from her mouth, Bristlefrost leaped up and hared toward Shadowsight. Ashfur was dragging the medicine cat's unconscious body closer to the dark water. A small black-and-brown splotched tom loomed in front of her, hissing with his teeth bared. There was something familiar about him . . . *Antfur!* He was a ShadowClan warrior who had died in newleaf, but now he was under Ashfur's control. She hooked his forepaws from beneath him and, as he fell, shoved him away and kept running. Another tom crashed into her flank, unbalancing her, but she let herself fall, rolled, and, as the rogue leaped on top of her, gripped him and raked his belly with her hind claws. He yowled with pain and she threw him off, jumping up and pelting once more for Shadowsight.

The medicine cat was only a tail-length from the water. Ashfur's ears were flat, his eyes slitted as he dragged the helpless tom closer.

"Leave him alone!" Bristlefrost batted another rogue out of the way as he lunged at her, her focus never leaving Shadowsight. She had to get to him. Her muscles burned with the effort. She barged past Houndleap as he wrestled with Silverhawk, then pushed her way between Rushtooth and Silverstream. "I'm coming!"

Claws hooked her hind leg and she fell sprawling onto the ground. She twisted her head and saw Thistleclaw. The Dark Forest warrior's teeth glistened as he drew back his lips. He leaped at her, the force of his attack so fierce it knocked the wind from her lungs. She struggled to get free, but he pinned her shoulders to the earth. Kicking out with her hind legs, she tried to push him away, but he held her firm, snarling in her ear.

"Are you ready to die?"

Panic pulsed in her blood. She reached up and sank her teeth into his foreleg. His grip loosened and she writhed, feeling her pelt tearing free of his claws. As she fought to find her paws, something heavy thudded against her cheek. She felt more claws slash through her fur and turned to see Mapleshade glaring at her. The Dark Forest she-cat grabbed her scruff, lifted her up, and raked her claws along her neck. Bristlefrost's head swam, and her vision blurred as she felt blood spurt from the fresh wound. She staggered and dropped to her belly, frustration clawing at her chest as the weight of Mapleshade thumped onto her back. Paws were all around her now, swiping and clawing. She felt Thistleclaw's teeth in her tail as Mapleshade pressed her muzzle into the earth. She was helpless, gagging as blood filled her mouth.

"Shadowsight!" She strained to see past the blur of pelts, but they blocked her view. How could she free herself from so many cats? As despair dropped like a stone in her chest, she heard a yelp of surprise. The weight was lifted from her back.

She pushed herself up, her flanks heaving. Turning heavily, she saw Violetshine and Rootspring. Gratitude flooded her. She shook the blood from her mouth, and as Thistleclaw dived at her again, she knocked his paws from beneath him. Violetshine was forcing Mapleshade back toward the middle of the clearing, jabbing at her with quick, vicious swipes. Rootspring leaped at Thistleclaw, shoving him down and raking his muzzle.

Bristlefrost wanted to thank them, but Shadowsight was in trouble. There was only enough time to catch Rootspring's eye as he pushed Thistleclaw's muzzle into the dirt. She had so much to say to him, so much that she should have said before the battle. Her heart ached as he returned her gaze, his eyes widening when he saw the wound in her neck. Then he glanced past her to the dark water.

Shadowsight was at the edge, Ashfur standing over him. Beyond them, the pool was widening, spreading across the clearing. Bristlefrost flattened her ears. She had to stop Ashfur. He had hurt so many cats already—she couldn't let him kill Shadowsight. Her nostrils flared as she remembered all the time she'd spent wanting to please the impostor, even as his demands became stranger and stranger. She knew him better than any Clan cat, except, perhaps, Shadowsight. She knew how truly dangerous he was.

As Ashfur shifted his weight, she saw her opportunity. *But I have to move now.* There was no time to second-guess herself. She knew, deep in her bones, that this was right.

Without thinking, she glanced at Rootspring. *I'm sorry!* Rootspring's eyes flashed with alarm, as though he guessed what she meant to do. She blinked at him. There was no way to tell him everything she wished she could. *I have no choice.* Without wasting another second, she spun and raced for Shadowsight.

Rootspring's yowl echoed behind her. "Wait!" His cry was desperate, but she couldn't stop. Ashfur had his paws against Shadowsight's flank. One shove and the medicine cat would be gone forever.

StarClan help me! The thought seemed ridiculous. StarClan was *here*, fighting beside her.

When she reached Shadowsight, she pushed her hind paws harder against the earth than she'd ever done before and launched herself at Ashfur. The dark warrior was silhouetted against the reflectionless surface of the widening pool. Ducking her head low, she crashed into him, and as he collapsed, she tumbled over him, and over Shadowsight. Her heart seemed to slow along with time, and she looked down and saw the dark water yawn below her. There was no way to avoid it.

She hit it like breaking through ice. Cold wrapped itself around her, gripping so hard that it thrust the breath from her body. She sank, darkness closing around her. *Fight!* She knew she should kick. She should thrash against the freezing blackness. She reached for thoughts of Rootspring. She tried to see his sky-blue eyes. She tried to hear his gentle mew. If only she could hold on to him . . .

She felt movement beside her and twisted, her fur billowing around her. Something was flailing a tail-length away. *Shadowsight?* Had she sacrificed herself for nothing? Panic flared in every hair. She struck out, ready to fight. She would save him. She had to.

But when she saw the face of the cat beside her, she froze. It wasn't Shadowsight who'd fallen in. Ashfur was thrashing his paws as he fought to reach the surface.

No! I can't let him escape the water. . . .

Bristlefrost lunged, taking two clawfuls of the dark

warrior's fur and letting her weight sink into her hindquarters, turning her body to the side and pushing him away with all her strength. She watched him sink toward the darkness below. His face was distorted by the water, and yet the terror in it was clear. Bristlefrost felt a surge of triumph. They'd done it! Ashfur was scared at last. He saw her, his eyes rounding with disbelief for a moment before he slipped from sight and vanished into shadow. All that remained was his last breath as it bubbled past her to the surface and disappeared.

He was gone. It was over. She had done what she had always wanted to do, from the time she was a tiny kit: She had saved her Clan.

She had saved *all* the Clans.

Bristlefrost turned and glanced back toward the surface. It looked very far away now. Her struggle with Ashfur had dragged her body down into the very depths of the dark water, and she felt the last of her strength ebbing out of her from the gash in her neck. The surface, the living world, the Clans—they were out of her reach.

Her body relaxed, and the pain of her wounds eased. The dark water no longer horrified her; it felt warm and soothing, engulfing her like an embrace.

It's time to rest.

But she looked up once more at the vanishing surface. Were those faces, peering in? She couldn't be sure. *Violetshine?* She thought she saw black-and-white fur moving beyond the water, and a yellow pelt beside it. *Rootspring?* Her heart ached with love, and she felt a stirring inside her. How could she leave him? She tried to reach out a paw and pull herself up, but there was nothing to grip but water, and the water would never let her go. Grief pierced her heart, not for herself, but for Rootspring. Her work was finished, but he had loved her, and now he would have to live without her. *I'm sorry.* Her mind grew hazy. *But we beat him. We destroyed Ashfur. We saved the Clans.*

Thoughts of Rootspring filled her mind. He was pressing beside her beneath a spreading willow, the warmth of him seeping into her fur. Was it a dream or a memory? She couldn't tell. Now they were hunting, running through the forest, side by side, so close their pelts touched. And then she saw herself cocooned with him in a nest. Had they shared one after all? Surely they had, she thought, with a rush of love. Tails entwined, they were gazing proudly at three tiny kits. Of course it was real. Of course these were memories of the life they must have shared.

The cold that gripped her seemed at last to let her go. She closed her eyes and in her last moment felt only warmth. Only love.

CHAPTER 19

❧

"No!" A wail tore from Rootspring's throat. He spun, paws slithering, rage pulsing through him as he tore free from his mother's grasp at the edge of the dark water.

Violetshine was staring at him. "You can't save her. You'll only put yourself in danger, too."

"I have to!" Panic pulsed beneath his pelt. As he turned back to the water, Violetshine grabbed his scruff between her teeth as though he were a kit and hauled him away.

She flung him backward. "She's already gone!"

He stared at her, his thoughts frozen. She couldn't be. Bristlefrost couldn't be dead. It was impossible. He darted back to the water and stared into the reflectionless pool. Violetshine pressed close, her body stiff as though ready to grab him again if she had to.

The water was still. The splash had left no ripples, but as he watched, a bubble opened the surface for a moment.

Then it was gone.

Violetshine was right. Bristlefrost, too, was gone. He couldn't save her. His heart seemed to open, spilling out pain so unbearable that he could hardly breathe. He could feel Violetshine pressing her muzzle into his neck and feel her breath, warm in his fur, but it meant nothing. It changed nothing. Bristlefrost was dead.

He was vaguely aware of the battle slowing around him. Dappletuft pulled away from Needletail. The RiverClan tom glanced around the clearing, alarmed, as though mystified at why he was here.

"He's gone!" Stemleaf lifted his tail jubilantly. "Ashfur is dead!"

Violetshine rounded on him, her mew sharp with pain. "So is Bristlefrost!" she wailed. "She pushed him into the dark water to stop him killing Shadowsight, and it swallowed her too."

Shock showed in Stemleaf's eyes. It seemed to leap like fire, setting light to the gazes of warrior after warrior as they faltered and stopped fighting and turned their faces toward the dark water where Bristlefrost had disappeared.

A gray she-cat struggled free from Firestar's grip and stared at him, confused. *Smokehaze,* Rootspring realized sadly. He hadn't recognized her during the battle. The WindClan warrior had died fighting the false Bramblestar. Now her gaze switched to Houndleap and darkened with fury as if she had just realized who her true enemy was.

Rootspring could hardly breathe.

As Crowfeather dragged his gaze from the water and faced his attacker once more, Thistleclaw shrank into a defensive crouch and began to back away. Mapleshade's eyes glittered with alarm. She edged toward the long grass, her pelt rippling uneasily. Maggottail and Berrynose padded slowly toward her, their ears flattened menacingly, and she turned and, with a final hiss, fled. Thistleclaw pelted after her.

Around the clearing, the rogue spirits exchanged glances and moved closer together, eyeing the StarClan warriors warily. Redtail's ears twitched ominously, Feathertail shook out her fur, and as Onestar's cold gaze swept over them, one by one, the rogues turned and slunk away, the grass closing behind them like water.

The great oozing pools of dark water began to soak away, disappearing into the earth as the tangle of trees at the back of the clearing creaked and groaned. The ground beneath them unbuckled and the trees slid back into place, their branches unknotting as they settled into old, familiar soil.

Rootspring stared blankly around the clearing. His mind seemed frozen, as though his thoughts were encased in ice.

Violetshine shifted beside him. "It's over," she whispered.

As she spoke, a star-pelted warrior pushed her way from the long grass, panting as though she'd been running.

"Leafpool!" Firestar hurried to greet her. "Do you have news?"

"The barrier that separated StarClan's hunting grounds from the Dark Forest is gone." Leafpool looked around at the StarClan warriors, her eyes sparkling. "StarClan is returning to normal." She blinked at the spirit cats as they clustered together. "Our connection to the living world is restored."

Stemleaf whisked his tail as Conefoot and Dappletuft exchanged glances and Softpelt wove around them.

Heavily, Rootspring turned back to the dark pool. There was little left of it now, just a puddle that was soaking quickly into the soil. Hope clawed in his belly. Would it leave Bristlefrost behind? He stared desperately at the dwindling water, willing it to reveal the gray pelt he'd loved so much. But it left no trace, only darkened earth where it had been.

Please. Rootspring dropped onto his belly and pressed his muzzle to the ground. He would listen to the earth. It would tell him where she was. If he reached deep enough, he could find her. He'd done it before beside the lake. The Sisters had taught him to sense, through the deepest energy of the earth, any cat connected to him. Closing his eyes, he felt for her. The warmth of her spirit must be somewhere, and he'd find it. He had to.

But the ground betrayed nothing except the coldness of the Dark Forest. Rootspring felt the emptiness like unendurable pain. Bristlefrost hadn't only lost her life; she'd lost her chance to live on in StarClan. He would never see her again.

She was gone from his life, and his only wish now was that his own spirit would seep into the earth and join her.

CHAPTER 20

"Our connection to the living world is restored."

As Leafpool lifted her tail in triumph, Shadowsight gazed around the clearing. He'd struggled out of the dark dream Ashfur had drawn him into, pushing his way through the grayness that had engulfed his thoughts, and opened his eyes to see . . . that the battle was over?

He sat up straight, fighting disbelief. But it was true. The rogues were gone, the Dark Forest warriors with them. He should be happy, but something was wrong. He felt an emptiness in his chest, as though his heart had been hollowed out. Firestar's green eyes were shining. Onestar's pelt prickled excitedly. Graystripe was pushing himself heavily to his paws.

Shadowsight tensed. *Where's Bristlefrost?*

Softpelt was weaving around Dappletuft.

Conefoot was looking eagerly at Leafpool. "Does this mean we can go to StarClan now?"

Leafpool blinked at him. "Yes."

Murmurs of relief rippled around the spirit cats, but Rootspring was crouched beside a damp stain on the earth where the dark water had been. Violetshine and Stemleaf were watching him, their faces horror-stricken. Shadowsight felt dread creep beneath his pelt. He tried to catch Rootspring's eye, but Rootspring's muzzle was pressed against the ground.

Shadowsight's mouth grew dry. He no longer had to ask where Bristlefrost was. He knew by the grief glittering in Violetshine's eyes, and from the expression on Stemleaf's face as he stared at the damp earth. There was only one reason they would both look so shattered. The dark water had claimed her.

Thorns seemed to pierce his heart. Had Ashfur pushed her in? Had he killed her after Shadowsight had refused to? He padded softly to Stemleaf's side. "What happened?" he whispered.

"Bristlefrost pushed Ashfur into the water." Stemleaf looked at him, pity in his eyes. "He was trying to kill you. She saved you, but she fell in too."

Shadowsight felt dizzy. The ground seemed to shift beneath his paws. *I killed her after all.* Ashfur's words rang suddenly in his mind. *You're no help to them. You're a liability.* The dark warrior was right. He shouldn't be here. He didn't belong. He turned to look at Rootspring, wishing he could change what had happened—wishing Bristlefrost had let him die instead.

"Shadowsight."

Shadowsight looked up into a pair of familiar eyes. *Spiresight.*

"You saved me," the small black guardian cat mused. "Without you, my spirit would have been trapped in this terrible place."

Shadowsight winced. *I saved you, but I killed Bristlefrost.* "I'm glad for you, Spiresight," he said, "and I'm grateful for everything you've done for my family. But I don't feel like a hero right now."

Spiresight tilted his head as he stared at the young medicine cat, his gaze suddenly intensifying. "You mustn't let them claim you," he growled.

Shadowsight backed away. He loved Spiresight, but he didn't feel up to a confrontation with the strange cat. "I hope you're happy in StarClan," he blurted out, then ducked away.

Further down the hill, he spotted Leafpool heading back into the long grass. "Let's go," she mewed. "We're done here. You've all stayed in this terrible place too long."

Shadowsight's gut twisted. How could she leave without Bristlefrost? How could any cat leave? But, one by one, the spirit cats followed, with the rest of the patrol trailing behind them. Graystripe seemed to have some trouble getting up, but Firestar helped him, supporting his old friend with his shoulder. Though he left the grass darkened with blood, Graystripe was soon limping across the clearing.

Numbly, Shadowsight watched Violetshine nudge Rootspring to his paws, murmuring softly to him. Rootspring seemed to have no will of his own as she steered him after the others.

Shadowsight wanted to run after him and apologize. *She died saving me.* The thought brought a fresh wave of grief so sharp that it lifted him for a moment from his daze. But it was too soon to talk to Rootspring. He couldn't push his own pain onto his friend—the young SkyClan warrior clearly had enough to carry on his own.

Maggottail was watching the other cats disappear after Leafpool. "Does she want us to follow?" he asked Sparrow-feather.

The mottled she-cat shrugged.

Silverhawk narrowed his eyes. "Probably not. They don't need us anymore."

"We should at least say good-bye to them," Juniperclaw mewed. "And thank them."

Maggottail eyed him. "Shouldn't they be thanking *us*?"

"They saved the Dark Forest," Juniperclaw reminded him.

Maggottail sniffed. "They couldn't have done it without our help."

Juniperclaw flicked his tail. "And without *their* help, the Dark Forest would have disappeared and taken you with it." He turned to Shadowsight. "Are you coming?"

Shadowsight stared back at him blankly for a moment, then shook out his fur, trying to rid himself of the sorrow that seemed to weigh him down like water.

Juniperclaw's gaze flitted over him. "You should get Willowshine to look at your wounds."

Shadowsight was faintly aware of the sting from the gash along his flank, and the wound in his leg ached; but the pain in his heart was worse. "Puddleshine will treat them when I get home." *Home.* The ShadowClan camp suddenly seemed far away and strange, as though it were a dream he'd once had.

Juniperclaw let the Dark Forest warriors go first into the long grass before guiding Shadowsight after them with his tail.

Shadowsight wondered why the black tom was being so kind. *He saved my life once. Perhaps he still feels responsible for me.* A darker thought struck him. *He died saving me, just like Bristlefrost.* He blinked at Juniperclaw. "I never had the chance to thank you." *If only I could have the chance to thank Bristlefrost too.*

Juniperclaw looked at him. "What for?"

"For saving me when I was a kit." He didn't remember clearly what happened, only that a black tom had appeared beside him in the swirling flood and pushed him up, out of the water.

"It was the least I could do to try to make up for what I did to SkyClan," Juniperclaw mewed.

Shadowsight glanced at him. "You mean, poisoning their fresh-kill pile?"

Juniperclaw looked ashamed. "Yes."

"Why did you do it?"

"I thought it would end an argument between the Clans." His pelt, black as the starless sky, twitched. "But it was a cowardly thing to do. Not worthy of a warrior, or of ShadowClan. I brought shame on my Clanmates."

Shadowsight pressed back a shiver. He knew how Juniperclaw felt. He'd been the one to allow Ashfur to take over Bramblestar's body. He'd insisted he was right, even when the other Clans had objected, but he was just being used by Ashfur and had been too proud and foolish to realize. Because of him, ShadowClan would be remembered forever as the Clan that helped Ashfur return to the living forest. And now he'd caused the death of Bristlefrost, his friend and one of ThunderClan's bravest warriors. She'd risked everything for the Clans, and now she was gone. He hung his head, hardly seeing where he put his paws, letting Juniperclaw lead the way through the grass.

As they emerged on the other side, he saw the patrol had reached the bottom of the slope, where dark water had blocked the way. The tree they'd pushed down still bridged the bottom of the valley, but there was no water now, only an empty ditch.

Leafpool hopped across it easily, and the others followed as she led them into the forest.

"Let's hurry." Juniperclaw quickened his step, but Shadowsight trailed behind.

Do I belong with these cats? The hollowness he'd felt when Leafpool had announced that the connection with StarClan had been restored grew sharper. The landscape seemed suddenly empty, like a sky leached of color, or prey drained of life. The great swath of grass seemed gray, the ground beneath his paws cold. The trees at the bottom of the slope were as pale as ghosts. Shadowsight watched as the patrol disappeared among them. The cats he'd grown so close to seemed like strangers, and he realized with a sickening sadness that it was not the Dark Forest that had changed, but himself.

He was no longer the same cat who had entered the Dark Forest. What had happened?

Juniperclaw looked back at him. "Are you coming?"

"I don't belong with them." Shadowsight blinked back at him, his heart empty of everything but grief.

"Don't be mouse-brained." Juniperclaw beckoned him with a flick of his tail.

Shadowsight swallowed against the tightness in his throat. "I killed Bristlefrost."

Juniperclaw padded toward him. "You can't blame yourself," he mewed. "It was a battle. Sometimes warriors die."

"They shouldn't die because of me." Anger surged in Shadowsight's chest. "I shouldn't have been there. I shouldn't have been any part of this. Bristlefrost would be alive if she hadn't had to save me. Ashfur would never have found a way to the living forest. I've done nothing but cause the Clans pain. And it got my friend killed."

"You risked your life to protect the cats you love," Juniperclaw mewed sharply. "It was the same decision Bristlefrost made."

Shadowsight was barely listening. "I'm an outsider," he growled, anger at himself swelling. "I always will be. I was supposed to be a great medicine cat, but I turned out to be a curse on the Clans."

Juniperclaw's eyes darkened. "I saved you from the flood because I knew you'd do great things. What was it that Spiresight said about you? That you'd see into the shadows? You've done that, haven't you?"

"But seeing into the shadows only brought trouble!" Shadowsight swallowed back a wail of despair.

"Trouble would have come no matter what," Juniperclaw told him. "Ashfur would have found another way to harm the Clans. But because you saw into the shadows, they *defeated* him."

Shadowsight's thoughts tumbled over each other so fast they barely made sense. All he was sure of was that he had brought darkness to the Clans and that he wasn't like his Clanmates. "What if I can see into the shadows because I belong in them?"

Juniperclaw stiffened. "What are you talking about?"

"I can't go back to the lake," Shadowsight's mew cracked. "Ashfur did something to me. He changed me."

Juniperclaw frowned. "*Changed* you?"

"He found a way to connect with me," Shadowsight murmured. "A way he couldn't connect with any other cat. He became . . ." His mew trailed away as he looked for words Juniperclaw could understand. "He became part of me. Or I became part of him. I still am. I must be. I feel like he's emptied me out. I don't belong beside the lake anymore. I belong here now, in the darkness he created."

Juniperclaw stared at him. Below them, the last of the patrol disappeared into the trees.

Shadowsight shifted his paws miserably. "I can't go home."

Juniperclaw growled. Shock sparked along Shadowsight's spine as the black tom's eyes slitted with anger.

"You fool!" Juniperclaw leaped at him. Bundled backward, Shadowsight hit the ground with a thump, breathless with surprise as the ShadowClan tom pinned his shoulders to the earth. His muzzle was a whisker away, his eyes burning furiously as he glared down at Shadowsight.

"What are you doing?" Shadowsight gasped.

"You must *never* think that way," Juniperclaw growled. "You have to snap out of it. The Dark Forest is getting inside your head. This place can turn a good cat bad. Don't let it. You risked your life to save the Clans. You don't deserve to stay here. You deserve to be beside the lake with your Clanmates." He loosened his grip. "You were injured, and you have no battle skills, but you still came. They couldn't have defeated Ashfur without you."

"All I did was get in the way."

"You reached into the shadows for them," Juniperclaw snapped. "You dared to go places they couldn't follow. And even if you *have* harmed them in some way, you should make up for it. You can't disappear. You have to go back to the lake and spend every day trying to make up for what you've done. You must give them your best." He gave Shadowsight a small shake, then released him and sat back on his haunches. "I'd give anything to have another chance," he muttered. "To prove myself worthy of being part of ShadowClan. But I can never go home again." He blinked at Shadowsight. "*You* can. You have Tigerstar and Dovewing there, and Lightleap and Pouncestep. They're all waiting for you. Your whole Clan is waiting for you."

Shadowsight didn't move. "Do you think so?"

"Yes!" Juniperclaw snapped. "How do you think Dovewing or Tigerstar would feel if you never returned?"

Shadowsight slowly got to his paws. Juniperclaw was right; they'd be devastated. "But I feel so strange. I thought Ashfur's death would be a relief. But there's only emptiness. It's like . . . a shadow under my heart."

"The Dark Forest does the same to every cat." Juniperclaw growled. "I struggle against that feeling every day. But once you've left, it will fade. And if any trace remains, use it as a warning—a constant reminder that you never want to end up here."

Shadowsight blinked at him. Guilt tightened his belly. This warrior had suffered despite having saved Shadowsight as a kit, and he was still trying to help him even though he'd never be free of the Dark Forest. He felt a wave of gratitude. "Thank you," he whispered.

Juniperclaw nudged him after the patrol. "Just keep up with the others. They'll be waiting for you."

Shadowsight followed him into the valley and the woods beyond. The trees had spread out again, and even though the woods were gloomy and filled with the dank scents of decay, the mist had vanished. The Dark Forest seemed to have returned to its own kind of peace.

After a while, he spotted Spiresight lingering beside a rotting tree stump. The guardian cat was clearly waiting for Shadowsight. He felt a pang of guilt for how he'd treated his old friend earlier. "Spiresight, I—"

But the dark tom simply nodded at him. "The shadows are dispersing."

Shadowsight narrowed his eyes. Spiresight would make an

excellent StarClan cat: He was already terribly hard to understand. Yet he had an idea what the tom meant. "I hope so," he breathed. But still, as they fell into step together, his heart ached with grief.

They trailed behind the others, walking deeper and deeper into the woods until, at last, Shadowsight saw the blackened stumps that marked the way to the StarClan barrier.

He followed Juniperclaw into the clearing, his eyes widening as he saw that the tangled knot of vines and brambles had fallen away completely. Branches littered the ground, and the opening they'd hidden was so bright that Shadowsight had to screw up his eyes. He padded closer and, as his eyes adjusted, stared inside. Ahead, a long tunnel stretched away into shimmering light.

Maggottail pushed past Sparrowfeather and looked in, his tail flicking uneasily. "Is that StarClan?"

"Yes." Silverstream purred as she gazed toward the light.

Willowshine sniffed at the edge of the tunnel. "If StarClan and the Dark Forest have always been connected like this," she wondered, "what stops Dark Forest warriors from traveling to StarClan whenever they like?"

"Until Ashfur blocked it, there was a difficult and dangerous path between StarClan and the Dark Forest that only StarClan cats could travel, but this is a new connection." Leafpool's tail was twitching nervously. "Ashfur dug this tunnel so he could travel directly from StarClan to the Dark Forest. He was the only cat who knew about it, and by the time we discovered it, he'd blocked it and there was no way to follow him through."

Willowshine frowned. "Should we block it up again?"

Leafpool shook her head. "What's done can't be undone," she mewed. "If we block it, we risk unbalancing the Dark Forest and StarClan again."

Firestar narrowed his eyes. "We can't leave a direct pathway open between the Dark Forest and StarClan," he mewed. "What if another cat tries to take advantage of it like Ashfur did? We never should have left the other pathway unguarded."

Onestar padded to his side. "We need to find a way to manage it." His mew echoed along the smooth, bright walls of the tunnel. "To stop cats from getting through."

Maggottail sniffed. "Who says we want to get through?" The Dark Forest warriors were lingering at the edge of the clearing, keeping their paws in the shadow where the light of the tunnel hadn't reached. He exchanged glances with Silverhawk, who dipped his head in agreement.

"We've been here so long, we're not interested in going to StarClan," the ragged gray tabby mewed.

Juniperclaw's ears twitched. "Unless, of course, we're *invited* to go."

Shadowsight looked at the ShadowClan tom. Was he hoping he'd earned a place in StarClan?

Firestar and Onestar exchanged glances.

Leafpool didn't seem to have heard. She was looking at Shadowsight. He straightened self-consciously and glanced at

Spiresight, wondering what she was thinking.

"How do you feel?" she asked him.

Shadowsight's heart seemed to skip a beat. Did she know about the hollowness Ashfur had left in his chest? He'd thought Spiresight could sense it because they'd always been connected. But what if it was visible for every cat to see? "What do you mean?"

"Ashfur made a connection with you, didn't he?" she mewed. "Like this tunnel reaching from darkness into light. You must feel strange now that he's gone."

He swallowed. "I didn't *want* to be connected to him," he mewed quickly. "It just happened."

"I know," Leafpool replied. "Ashfur used you. He reached into your thoughts and exploited your goodness for his own ends."

Shadowsight blinked at her. Shame washed his pelt. "Now that he's gone, it's almost like I miss him," he confessed.

"You don't *miss* him," she told him. "What you're feeling isn't loss, only absence. The emptiness will heal, like a wound." She padded toward him and touched her muzzle to his head. "You've been very brave and suffered a lot," she mewed gently. "But you can rest now. You've fulfilled your destiny. It's over."

Shadowsight pulled away and searched her gaze. "Does that mean I'm of no use anymore?"

She blinked kindly. "Of course not," she mewed. "Your Clan will always need you. But only as a healer. You will never have a connection with StarClan. You never really did. Your connection was with shadow, not light. And when Ashfur disappeared, he took that connection with him."

Shadowsight felt a pelt brush his own and turned to see Spiresight, wordlessly offering his support. He turned back to stare at Leafpool. Was he supposed to feel relieved? "But how can I be a medicine cat without StarClan?"

"You can still mix herbs and care for your Clanmates," she told him. "You're a good medicine cat, and you'll become a better one."

He stared at her, his eyes pricking. Had he never been a real medicine cat?

She rested her tail on his spine. "Shadowsight." Her mew was as gentle as breeze. "Never lose your courage. StarClan will always be with you. Keep us in your heart even though you can't share it with us. You have always been different. You've known it since you were a kit. It's your challenge, but it's also your strength." He felt the earth beneath his paws, and the cold air of the Dark Forest flowing around his pelt, as she went on. "You've seen into the shadows, just as you were meant to. But that part of your life is over now. You can begin anew."

To his surprise, as she lifted her tail from his spine, he felt as though she lifted with it the whole weight of the forest. It was over. He had fulfilled his destiny. Now he might not have a connection with StarClan, but he was free to make his own path and decide where his paws would lead him. Closing his eyes, he felt the darkness that had clung to his heart for so long dissolve into nothing. *I'm free.*

"The shadows," Spiresight said again, laying his tail across

Shadowsight's back. "They're gone."

Shadowsight turned, pressing his head to the black tom's chest. "Thank you, Spiresight."

The guardian cat had always belonged in StarClan. Shadowsight hoped both of them would walk in the light now. He, at least, had spent far too long in the shadows.

CHAPTER 21

❧

Rootspring gazed blankly into the bright light flooding from the tunnel to StarClan. The vines and branches that had blocked it lay in a heap on the ground, but he felt no joy. This was what he had fought for. It was what Bristlefrost had died for. But she would never see it. She was gone. The victory seemed so hollow, he wanted only to yowl his grief into the shimmering hole.

Graystripe limped toward it and slitted his eyes against the brightness as he peered inside. "Am I allowed through?" He looked at Firestar. "I know I don't belong there yet, but there are so many cats I want to see."

Firestar padded to his side. "Normally, living cats aren't allowed in, but . . ." He glanced at Leafpool, then looked around at the Clan patrol. "I think you have all earned a chance to see StarClan once."

Leafpool dipped her head in agreement and Crowfeather pricked his ears. Mistystar's tail twitched.

Rootspring felt Violetshine shift beside him. She hadn't left his side since the battle had ended. She looked at him now, her gaze glistening, and he guessed there were StarClan cats she'd like to see too. Hope fluttered in his heart like a creature stirring from sleep. Was there a chance that Bristlefrost would be there? Perhaps she'd been spared from the fate he'd feared. Perhaps the Dark Forest hadn't claimed her entirely.

Juniperclaw padded forward. His green eyes were round with hope.

Firestar seemed to guess what the ShadowClan warrior was thinking. "Dark Forest cats are forbidden from setting paw in StarClan's hunting grounds."

Juniperclaw wilted. "But I was a noble warrior for many moons," he pressed. "And I honored StarClan as much as any cat."

Firestar glanced at Leafpool again. With a nod, they apparently came to a silent agreement. "Very well," he mewed. "You fought bravely today, so we will make an exception. But you can't stay there. You will have to return." The ThunderClan leader's mew contained a warning. "The Dark Forest might be harder to bear once you've seen StarClan. You'll see what you can never have."

But Juniperclaw was staring eagerly into the tunnel. "I want to see it." His tail quivered. "I know that I must stay in the Dark Forest. I have only myself to blame for that. I just want to see StarClan once, so that I can carry the memory of it with me. It would make staying here *easier* to bear, not harder."

Rootspring glanced at the other Dark Forest warriors. Did they want to visit StarClan too?

Firestar must have been wondering the same thing. He turned to face them. "You fought bravely for us," he mewed. "All three of you. Do you wish to see StarClan once before we leave?"

Maggottail had been watching Juniperclaw through narrowed eyes. "Why get a taste for something you're not allowed to eat?" he grunted.

Sparrowfeather's eyes clouded wistfully. "It would be worse to see what I'm missing."

Silverhawk nodded. "I just want to go back to my life here," he growled. "I've been here so long, it feels like home."

Firestar dipped his head. "Thank you for your help," he mewed.

Maggottail grunted. "We didn't have much choice." He headed toward the trees.

Sparrowfeather hurried after him. "Can't you be civil for once?" she mewed.

Silverhawk nodded to Firestar. "Thanks for helping us save our home. I'm sorry you lost Bristlefrost. She was brave." He headed toward the trees, glancing over his shoulder. "I just hope that tunnel doesn't mean StarClan cats are going to start sticking their noses into our business whenever they like." With a flick of his tail, he disappeared into the forest after Maggottail and Sparrowfeather.

Rootspring watched them go. It was Bristlefrost who had recruited them. She'd inspired loyalty from cats condemned for their treachery.

Graystripe stretched his muzzle into the tunnel, the light illuminating his bloody mane. His eyes were bright. "Can we go now?"

Leafpool padded past him. "Follow me." With a flick of her tail, she beckoned the patrol after her and headed into the light.

Crowfeather slid quickly past Graystripe and fell in beside Leafpool, pressing so close against her that that starlight in her fur seemed to spark into his.

Rootspring hesitated as the patrol headed into the tunnel after them.

"Are you coming?" Violetshine looked back at him.

"What if she's not there?" His throat tightened.

Violetshine blinked at him sympathetically. "You know she can't—"

"Hurry!" Juniperclaw called to them over his shoulder, and Violetshine turned away without finishing her sentence. Rootspring was glad she didn't. He still wanted to hope for a little longer, no matter how vain his hope was. Forcing his paws to move, he followed Violetshine.

The smooth sides of the tunnel felt like the soft inner casing of bark beneath his paws. The scent of fresh grass funneled from the far end and washed his pelt. He could smell the musky aroma of prey too, and the air grew warmer with every step. Ahead he saw the patrol disappear into a wall of light, and he slitted his eyes against the glare as he reached it. Hardly seeing, he stepped through the shimmering haze and emerged into a wide, sunny meadow. Pine forest bounded one side of the grassland and oak forest another. Blue sky stretched overhead, and in the distant fields he could see the star-specked pelts of StarClan warriors.

Stemleaf and Willowshine were already heading down a grassy slope toward a wide clear pool with the other spirit cats. Their pelts twitched with excitement, and Rootspring thought he saw starlight begin to glitter in their fur.

Firestar purred as Graystripe looked around, his eyes wide with wonder. Silverstream wove around them, as though eager to show Graystripe her territory. Beside them, Juniperclaw stood stiffly, his nose twitching. Onestar and Redtail sat down and gazed across the meadow, clearly relieved to be home.

Mistystar followed the spirit cats downslope, and Needletail followed, beckoning Shadowsight after her.

"Come and taste the water," she called. "It's sweeter than any water you'll taste beside the lake."

As Shadowsight padded after them, Rootspring noticed a gray tabby she-cat bounding up the slope, a sleek brown she-cat beside her.

"Graystripe!" The gray tabby lifted her tail. "What are you doing here?"

Rootspring noticed Silverstream stiffen as Graystripe broke into a purr.

"Briarlight is Millie and Graystripe's daughter," Needletail whispered to Rootspring. "She couldn't walk after her back was hurt by a falling tree, but in StarClan she can run again."

"Millie! Briarlight!" Graystripe started toward the she-cats but faltered, swaying a little on his paws.

Millie darted toward him. "Are you hurt?"

Graystripe blinked at her. "A little," he mewed. "But I'll be okay. I'm just visiting before I return to the lake."

"It's good to see you." Millie pressed her muzzle deep into his mane. Briarlight purred.

Silverstream glared at them for a moment, then looked away. She beckoned Feathertail with a jerk of her muzzle. "We should leave them in peace."

She sounds hurt. Rootspring narrowed his eyes.

Feathertail didn't seem to have heard her mother's mew. She was watching Crowfeather, her pelt ruffled as though she was annoyed that he was standing so close to Leafpool.

Was she jealous, too? Rootspring sensed tension crackling in the air. There was clearly more to the relationships between these cats than he knew; he was relieved when Silverstream nudged Feathertail away. "Come on," she sniffed. "They'll join us soon enough."

As the two silver she-cats padded away, Graystripe nuzzled Millie. "Your scent hasn't changed a bit." A deep purr rumbled in his throat.

Millie returned it. "Nor has yours." Her gaze flitted over him. "Has your pelt grown thicker?"

Graystripe purred louder. "Aren't you going to tell me I've gained weight? Every other cat has." He looked at Briarlight. "I've missed you both so much."

As Millie nuzzled him again, a speckled white she-cat came springing over the grass toward the group.

"Violetshine!" she called out as she neared.

Violetshine lifted her tail. "Pebbleshine!" She ran to meet the white warrior, then turned to blink excitedly at Rootspring. "This is my mother!"

The StarClan warrior's green eyes reminded him of Twigbranch, but the soft line of her shoulders and her long, thick tail looked like Violetshine. He dipped his head. He should be happy to meet her, but his heart was still heavy with grief. Where was Bristlefrost?

Beside him, Leafpool and Crowfeather were talking softly together. He could barely make out the words, but Leafpool's mew was warmer now than it had been in the Dark Forest, and she was leaning affectionately against the WindClan tom. Had she been waiting for Feathertail to leave? Her mew thickened as she touched her nose to Crowfeather's ear. "Despite everything, I never stopped missing you."

As Crowfeather touched his nose to Leafpool's muzzle, Rootspring felt a fresh pang of loss. He'd touched Bristlefrost's muzzle like that once.

Was she here? He scanned the distant meadows, straining to make out her familiar pelt. Was that pale gray pelt hers? Or that one? With each flash of hope and jab of disappointment, panic started to spiral in his chest. There was no sign of her. Perhaps she was in one of the forests, or so far away he couldn't make her out. He opened his mouth, letting the air touch his tongue, tasting for her scent. But he smelled only the unfamiliar scents of cats he'd never known. He felt suddenly sick with loss.

A pelt brushed his and he jerked his muzzle around,

disappointment sweeping him as he saw Firestar gazing at him, his bright green eyes round with sympathy.

"She's not here." The ThunderClan leader's mew was gentle. "She won't be. Any cat who dies in the Dark Forest is . . ." He paused, as though wishing for a better word. "Gone," he mewed finally.

Rootspring felt himself sway. Hope drained from him as though he'd fallen into the dark water. He closed his eyes, frozen. He never wanted to move from this spot. He never wanted to think or eat or breathe again. The emptiness breaking open his heart felt so vast that he wanted only to fall into it and lose himself in its darkness.

"I'm sorry." Firestar ran his tail along Rootspring's spine. "You and Bristlefrost were so brave throughout this ordeal, braver than many cats ever could be."

Rootspring stared at him blankly, thinking the words should comfort him, but they didn't. Firestar dipped his head and padded toward the others beside the pool. Graystripe and Crowfeather followed with Leafpool and Millie, leaving Rootspring alone on the hilltop.

Blind to the rolling meadows and the wide blue sky, Rootspring stood like a rock, his thoughts only on Bristlefrost and the future he'd imagined with her. Since he'd decided to give up his Clan, he'd imagined himself in ThunderClan, patrolling with her, sharing her nest, and perhaps one day visiting her in the nursery and watching their kits be given their apprentice names. How had he dared to dream so much? The warm breezes of StarClan rippled through his fur, but he barely noticed as he let himself sink into his loss. Only when he felt that his grief had entered every hair on his pelt, and every drop of blood sang with it, did he pull himself back. He couldn't give up. Bristlefrost would have wanted him to go on—to be the best warrior he could be, to take care of his Clan and one day learn to be happy again. He had to say goodbye to those dreams. Lifting his gaze to the distant forest, he pushed his grief aside.

Grief could wait.

He looked down the slope to where the others were gathered beside the wide blue pool. Blinking away the tears that had welled in his eyes without his realizing, he padded toward them.

"This is where we go to see our loved ones in the living world, and to communicate with the medicine cats at the Moonpool," Leafpool explained.

"That's fascinating," Violetshine mewed, leaning close to take a look. "Does that mean it leads directly to the Moonpool?"

"Not exactly," Leafpool replied. "Squirrelflight once used it to travel between worlds, but it doesn't work quite that way. We think it draws on our connection to our loved ones, and the connection of the three worlds, to show us what we wish to see. *Usually*. As you know, sometimes the connection between our worlds is . . . not as clear as it could be."

Crowfeather's whiskers twitched in amusement. "You mean when we need a clearer sign from you than a foggy day or a red sunset?" he asked.

Leafpool shook her head as if she were dismissing his words, but her eyes shone with affection. "Anyway," she went on, "when Ashfur built his barrier between our hunting grounds and the Dark Forest, our pond became so clogged with branches and vines that we couldn't see anything. But look now." She gestured to the water with a sparkling paw.

Rootspring couldn't help peering curiously into the water.

"It's perfectly clear," Graystripe noted, just as Rootspring realized the same. He didn't see any cat from the living world, but the clear blue water seemed to go down forever.

But when Rootspring looked up at the other cats, he saw that Mistystar didn't look terribly pleased. She was looking accusingly at a sleek gray StarClan tom who had joined them. "Why did you let Ashfur join StarClan in the first place?"

"It wasn't Gray Wing's fault." Another tom defended him. This cat's pelt was lighter, and the starlight sparkling in his fur made him shine like silver beside the water. "We were all to blame."

Gray Wing dipped his head. "Skystar's right," he mewed. "We decided together to give Ashfur a chance."

Crowfeather scowled angrily. "Why? He wanted to kill his Clanmates!"

"We thought he'd atoned for it," Skystar mewed.

"'Atoned,'" Juniperclaw growled. "If that was all a warrior needed to do to join StarClan, the Dark Forest would be empty."

Rootspring reached the group but hung back, feeling unsure next to these important cats. *Do I have anything to say that's worthy of the founder of SkyClan?*

Onestar lifted his chin. "Deciding who can join StarClan and who should be in the Dark Forest is a hard decision, and we don't take it lightly. A gathering of StarClan warriors discusses every cat to try to understand what is in their hearts, and to judge whether they should be allowed to join us."

"Sometimes we are wrong," Firestar mewed with a sigh.

Rootspring nodded thoughtfully, remembering Snowtuft. Despite feeling intimidated, he had to speak up for his Dark Forest ally. No other cat would. "Is it possible to change your decision once it's been made?"

Skystar looked puzzled. "Why would we?"

"A Dark Forest warrior saved my life," Rootspring told him. "He saved it twice and sacrificed his whole existence to let me and Bristlefrost escape from Ashfur. Surely a cat like him deserves a place in StarClan?"

Onestar sniffed. "If he's gone, it's irrelevant."

Juniperclaw narrowed his eyes. "But what if other Dark Forest cats change like Snowtuft did? Is there really no way to earn a place in StarClan even after death?"

Gray Wing looked thoughtful. "We are all judged on what we did in our lifetime. It's no use being sorry afterward. It's more important not to break the warrior code in the first place."

Rootspring thought this was too harsh. "Surely every warrior has done *something* wrong." He looked around the others. "Is there any cat here who can say for sure they've never broken the warrior code?"

The cats exchanged glances.

"Ashfur definitely broke it," Graystripe growled.

Firestar shifted his paws. "No system is perfect," he mewed. "We just try to be as fair as we can be."

Onestar nodded. "We try to consider not so much *whether* they broke the warrior code," he mewed, "but why. And we try to decide if, despite everything, their hearts are still true."

"I had to *persuade* StarClan to accept me," Leafpool mewed. "I stood in front of some of the greatest warriors the Clans have ever known and convinced them that, despite my code-breaking, I was worthy of being a StarClan warrior." Her pelt prickled along her spine as though the memory of her trial still made her uneasy. "They accepted me." She looked at Mistystar, whose eyes were narrowed doubtfully. "If breaking the warrior code stopped every cat from joining StarClan, the Dark Forest would be overflowing, and these meadows"—she paused to sweep her gaze over the rolling landscape—"would be empty."

Crowfeather nodded. "There's more to all of us than the rules we've obeyed and the rules we've broken," he mewed. "And we change as we grow older. Rules we broke as apprentices seem more important when we become warriors, and rules we'd never dare break as apprentices come to seem more flexible."

Firestar winked teasingly at Crowfeather. "Like crossing borders, for example."

As Crowfeather fluffed out his fur, Violetshine spoke, her mew soft as though she was shy in front of so many StarClan warriors. "Perhaps some of StarClan's rules aren't as important as they used to be." She looked at her paws as their gazes swung toward her. "I just mean that, after the trouble with Ashfur, perhaps it would a good idea to think about which parts of the warrior code are most important. So that we don't make the same mistakes again."

Skystar and Gray Wing exchanged glances.

"We can't just pick and choose which bits of the code we like." Gray Wing spoke sharply. "What kind of warriors would we be?"

Skystar nodded. "The Clans would start to question *every* rule if we changed one."

"I just thought . . ." Violetshine's mew trailed away and she seemed to shrink beneath her pelt.

Rootspring moved closer to her. "The warrior code didn't protect the Clans from Ashfur," he reminded them. His paws pricked uncomfortably. He was arguing with StarClan cats. But he had to defend his mother. "He used it to harm us."

Leafpool tipped her head to one side. "That's true." She turned her gaze toward Gray Wing and Skystar. "Of course *all* the rules are important, but aren't some of them more gestures of respect, like thanking StarClan for prey? Others— like being loyal and defending kits and elders—are vital for the safety and well-being of the Clan."

The well-being of the Clan, Rootspring mused. Hadn't Bristlefrost died for that? She hadn't risked her life because she wanted to follow the warrior code. She'd risked it because she had valued the safety of the cats she loved above her own.

"The warrior code isn't about rules." He found himself speaking again. "It's about not being selfish. Bristlefrost sacrificed her life—and her place in StarClan—to save the Clans." His heart was pounding. The StarClan warriors were staring at him. "Some cats get lost in meaningless battles for power, and some are willing to hurt other cats just to get something for themselves. Bristlefrost was never like that. A *lot* of warriors are never like that. They believe they should defend their Clan, even with their lives. But Bristlefrost didn't just give her life for ThunderClan; she gave it for SkyClan, ShadowClan, WindClan, and RiverClan too. She understood that following the warrior code meant taking care of every cat, not just her own Clanmates."

Graystripe nodded. "If there's one thing we ought to learn from Ashfur, it's that if . . ." He seemed to need to catch his breath before he went on. "If we want to survive, we must protect not just our own Clans, but *every* Clan. And the warrior code should reflect that."

Firestar moved closer to his friend. "I agree," he mewed. "I've seen how, over the moons, the Clans have learned to support each other, so that it's unthinkable now for a warrior to attack another Clan's fresh-kill pile." He glanced at Juniperclaw. The black tom's fur prickled uncomfortably along his spine as Firestar went on. "And it's become clear that a Clan strengthened by deceit or dishonesty, or one that takes unfair advantage of a weaker Clan, isn't truly strong. The strong fight fairly. Only the weak cheat."

Crowfeather was frowning. "That all sounds very

impressive, but does it mean we should think about changing some of our rules or not?"

"Of course." Graystripe lifted his muzzle stiffly. "Things have changed since the times we fought petty battles over borders and prey. We should decide what it means to be a warrior *now*, not what it meant countless moons ago."

"The code is like a living thing," Leafpool chimed. "It changes and grows as it needs to." She looked thoughtful. "But perhaps we don't need to *change* it." She glanced at Skystar. "Perhaps we could just reorder the rules so that the most important ones come first."

"Defending all the Clans should be first," Graystripe mewed.

Firestar nodded. "But each Clan still has the right to be proud and independent. . . ."

Needletail cut in, quoting another rule. "And an honorable warrior does not need to kill other cats to win their battles, unless they are outside the warrior code or it is necessary for self-defense."

Eager murmurs rippled around the gathered cats.

"Elders, queens, and kits must be fed first," Silverstream offered.

Onestar whisked his tail. "A Gathering of all five Clans is held at the full moon under a truce that lasts for the night."

"No warrior can neglect a kit in pain or danger, even if the kit is from a different Clan," Redtail mewed.

One by one, the cats listed the rules of the warrior code, ordering them and reordering them until every cat seemed satisfied.

Only Skystar looked unconvinced. "So the rule on boundaries comes last now?"

Gray Wing looked at the SkyClan leader. "Perhaps it should have come last all along."

Skystar stiffened, as though ready to argue, then looked away. "Perhaps you're right," he mumbled.

Shadowsight lifted his muzzle tentatively. "No cat has mentioned whether the rules our leaders make have the same power as the warrior code."

"Surely they must," Mistystar mewed. "How can they lead if their Clan doesn't take their rules seriously?"

"Following our leaders' rules hasn't worked these past moons," Stemleaf reminded her. "Look how Ashfur used rules to turn us against each other."

Shadowsight nodded. "The rules a leader makes are only as good as the leader who makes them."

"A bad leader makes bad rules," Leafpool agreed.

"Perhaps there should be a way to challenge a leader," Firestar mewed. "If they lose the trust of their Clan." His gaze flicked around the living cats, settling finally on Mistystar. "Perhaps the Clans should think about it. Would three moons be enough time to come up with a plan for getting rid of a leader who isn't serving the best interests of their Clan?"

Mistystar nodded. "Okay," she mewed. "We'll start discussing it at the next Gathering."

"Surely that should be something for StarClan to decide," Skystar muttered under his breath. But no cat responded. Instead, Crowfeather cleared his throat.

"There's still no clear rule about relationships between cats from different Clans," he mewed.

Rootspring pricked his ears. That was something he'd thought a lot about over the past few moons.

"We don't need a rule," Mistystar mewed. "A warrior who has a relationship with a cat from another Clan is disloyal. It's as simple as that."

Rootspring looked at her. *Simple?* Didn't she realize how complex a cat's heart could be? "Do you think I'm disloyal after I've fought so hard to save the Clans?" he asked.

Violetshine bristled. "Of course not! No one does!"

Murmurs of agreement spread among the others.

"And yet I loved Bristlefrost." Rootspring's throat tightened, his voice growing husky as he went on. "I tried not to love her. I knew I'd be betraying my Clan. I tried reasoning with myself, but it was impossible. When we got home, I was going to join ThunderClan to be with her." Violetshine jerked her muzzle toward him, her eyes rounding, but he went on. "No warrior, no matter how brave and loyal they are, is strong enough to fight love."

"What cat can control his own heart?" Graystripe agreed.

Mistystar looked at Rootspring, her eyes glistening. "I know how much it hurts to lose a cat you love," she mewed softly. "And I would never accuse you of disloyalty. But if we allow cats from different Clans to become mates and have kits, it'll undermine every Clan."

"Not if they make a choice and stick to it," Rootspring mewed.

Stemleaf fluffed out his fur. "I think a warrior who chooses love over his Clan is braver than most cats."

Leafpool dipped her head. "Perhaps this is something else the Clans should think about over the coming moons." She looked at Mistystar. "Do you think, between you, the Clan leaders can come up with a way to allow cats to switch Clans?"

Mistystar's gaze narrowed. "We can try," she mewed doubtfully.

"In three moons," Firestar mewed, "tell us your decision." He looked up the slope toward the tunnel entrance. "For now, it's time you went home."

Rootspring shivered at the thought of returning to the Dark Forest. But it was the only way back to the lake. He dipped his head to Willowshine. "Thanks for your help." He looked at Stemleaf and Berrynose gratefully. They might not have won the battle without their help.

Stemleaf blinked back at him. "I wish Bristlefrost had made it." He held Rootspring's gaze, and Rootspring felt strangely comforted. Bristlefrost would be remembered, at least.

He noticed Shadowsight glancing at him but couldn't bring himself to return his gaze. If only Bristlefrost hadn't seen that the medicine cat was in trouble. He pushed the thought away. He was being selfish. Pressing back grief, he followed the others up the slope, keeping close to Graystripe, who was still limping.

At the top, Skystar nosed his way through the group and stared into the tunnel, wrinkling his nose. "I can smell evil," he growled.

Gray Wing slid in beside him. "How will we stop Dark Forest warriors from using this?"

"Some cat should guard it," Skystar mewed. "A cat both sides can trust. Guarding it would become their entire life."

Juniperclaw's ears pricked. "I can do it."

"Really?" Firestar eyed him thoughtfully. "It'll be lonely work. You won't belong either in StarClan or the Dark Forest."

"I'd be honored," Juniperclaw mewed. "At least I'll have some connection with StarClan. And I want to keep you safe."

Mistystar stared solemnly at him. "You can't let any cat pass from one world to the other."

Juniperclaw dipped his head low. "I promise." As he looked up, his eyes shone happily. "I will do my best. I want to show StarClan that I truly am sorry for what I did."

As he spoke, Graystripe lurched suddenly. Firestar's gaze flashed toward the ground beneath the old tom's paws. Rootspring followed it. The grass was glistening with blood.

"Shadowsight!" Firestar mewed in alarm. "Graystripe needs help!"

Graystripe sat down heavily, and Shadowsight darted to his side, sniffing first at his flank, where a gash showed, and then at his belly. He drew back sharply. "Are there any cobwebs here?" he asked Firestar.

"No cobwebs," Firestar told him. "But there's moss."

Silverstream was already racing to the pool, where she began tugging great clumps from the edge.

Firestar stared in dismay at the long open wound gaping

on Graystripe's belly. "I didn't realize you were so badly hurt."

"I didn't want to worry you." Graystripe was breathing heavily.

Silverstream was already racing back up the hill. She scrambled to a halt and dropped the moss she was holding between her jaws.

Shadowsight scooped it up and began to pack Graystripe's wound. The old tom's eyes glittered with pain. "It should hold until he gets home," he mewed, leaning back to look at his work.

"Jayfeather will have enough herbs to heal him, won't he?" Mistystar mewed hopefully.

Shadowsight met her gaze but didn't answer.

Millie hurried to his side. "Oh, Graystripe." Her eyes darkened with pity.

"It's okay," Graystripe soothed. "I've lived a long life."

She blinked at him. "Will you stay here with us?"

"I need to go home first," Graystripe murmured. "My body is there, like many of these brave cats'. I'm sure my friends are wondering about my injuries. I need to reassure them that I'll be all right . . . and say good-bye."

Mistystar's eyes clouded. She stared at Graystripe. "We can't lose you. The Clans won't be the same."

"I'm sure they'll manage." Graystripe forced a purr, wincing as he spoke.

Firestar touched his nose to Graystripe's ear. "You're welcome in StarClan," he murmured. "Whenever you arrive."

"No!" Rootspring pressed back a shiver. The ThunderClan

tom couldn't die. They'd lost so much already. "After everything he's done, he doesn't deserve to die."

"I've had a good life," Graystripe told him. "I've had great friends and loyal Clanmates. I've loved and been loved." He glanced affectionately at Millie and Silverstream. "And I've had kits that I'm proud of." He looked at Feathertail and Briarlight. "A warrior can't ask for more than that. I'm just grateful I had one last chance to protect the Clans."

Firestar's green eyes glistened with emotion. "You were the first warrior I ever saw," he mewed. "I hope you will be the last. You'll be remembered by the Clans for moons to come. And though they'll be losing you, I won't be sorry to hunt beside you again. You were, and always will be, my best friend."

Graystripe's whiskers twitched. With a husky purr, he nudged Firestar's muzzle away. "You always did talk like a soppy old kittypet."

CHAPTER 22

♣

Shadowsight pushed hard, shoving Graystripe through the starlit water of the Moonpool while, above him, Rootspring and Mistystar dragged the ThunderClan elder up to the surface. Shadowsight broke through a moment after them. There was a moment of confusion as every cat besides Rootspring located their sleeping form on the edge of the Moonpool and prepared to reunite with it. Shadowsight thought he noticed Graystripe hesitating—no doubt alarmed by the reality of his injuries. Shadowsight moved toward his own body. He closed his eyes and felt a warmth coursing through him, followed by a jaw-clenching pain. He opened his eyes to find himself looking out from his body once more. His injuries ached far more here than they had in the spirit world, but Shadowsight stifled a moan, knowing that Graystripe must have it so much worse. When his vision focused, he saw that Rootspring looked stricken and followed his gaze to where Bristlefrost had lain.

She was gone.

Not dead. Not injured. Just . . . *gone.*

Their kin had come to meet them, looking eager and confused. Tree and Needleclaw were there, and Breezepelt, pacing nervously beside Mothwing. They probably hadn't gone far from the Moonpool hollow since the patrol left for the Dark Forest. Lightleap was there too, and Tigerstar and Dovewing had joined her. Shadowsight felt a surge of happiness as he saw them. It seemed a lifetime since he'd been home. But his happiness fizzled away as he noticed Ivypool staring at him, eyes narrowed. "Where is she? Where has she gone?"

Shadowsight moved his mouth to answer, but he had no idea how to begin. His vision bleary from the swim, he watched Bramblestar and Squirrelflight rush from the back of the crowd over to Graystripe.

"Is he dead?" Bramblestar glanced quickly at Mistystar before grabbing Graystripe's scruff between his teeth. Shadowsight knew that he was asking not about Graystripe, who groaned weakly as Bramblestar pulled him onto the stone, but about Ashfur.

"Yes." Mistystar fell back, exhausted after the long climb out of the Dark Forest. "We won the battle."

Bramblestar laid the elder gently on the stone and looked at Rootspring. "Did we lose any cat?"

"Did we lose Bristlefrost?" Ivypool was staring at Rootspring now, her gaze intense, but her jaw trembled. "She was sleeping there, and I took my eyes away for a moment. When I looked back, she had just . . . *disappeared.*"

"I've never seen anything like it," Mothwing added.

Rootspring stared at Bristlefrost's mother, shock and pain in his eyes, as though the ThunderClan warrior had turned on him and raked claws across his muzzle.

"Yes." Mistystar answered for him, lowering her mew to a whisper that Shadowsight could hardly hear. But he knew what she would say next. "Bristlefrost died a hero." The River-Clan leader's gaze flitted toward Ivypool, whose face seemed to crumple. "She pushed Ashfur into the dark water and fell in with him."

As Bramblestar froze, his eyes darkening with anguish, Squirrelflight touched Graystripe's bloody, wet pelt with her nose. "And what of Graystripe? Who did this to him?" she asked.

"Ashfur." Mistystar was still watching Ivypool.

Mothwing darted forward and began to examine the wound on Graystripe's belly. Some cat had packed it with moss, probably when it had first appeared, but that had come loose when Graystripe's spirit had reunited with his body and he'd stirred. The wound was pouring blood, just as it had in the Dark Forest.

"Look for cobwebs!" Mothwing called to the Sisters, who were hanging back on the rock.

Flurry nodded and quickly led Snow, Furze, and Tempest toward the shadowy cliffs. Shadowsight watched them go, his heart pounding. Would cobwebs be enough to save the ThunderClan elder?

"Shadowsight!" Dovewing called from the edge of the Moonpool. "You're safe!"

At his mother's mew, he walked away from the other cats who'd battled in the Dark Forest with him and shook out his fur. For a moment, among all this loss, it was a relief to be fussed over by his mother.

Dovewing nosed around him, undaunted by the spray, and sniffed him like a newborn kit. "Is this a new injury?" She blinked at the gash on his flank.

"Yeah, but it's fine," he reassured her, trying to pretend it didn't hurt.

Tigerstar nosed past Dovewing and pressed his muzzle to Shadowsight's head. "It's good to have you back."

Lightleap blinked at him. "Thank StarClan you made it." She sounded relieved, but there was a quietness in her mew that made him wonder if she would ever feel entirely easy about him taking her place in the patrol. "Are you hurt?"

"Of course he's hurt," Dovewing fretted. "Look at him." The water pooling darkly at his paws smelled of blood.

"I'll recover," Shadowsight promised. He glanced toward Graystripe, fearing the same would not be true of the ThunderClan tom.

Breezepelt hurried to his father as he rose and got to his paws. "Are *you* hurt?"

Crowfeather nudged him away and shook out his pelt. "Just a few scratches," he mewed.

After some time, Ivypool broke her silence. "We don't even have her body to bury," she mewed softly, staring into the Moonpool.

Tree and Needleclaw were winding happily around Violetshine, but Rootspring drew away, his gaze fixing on Ivypool.

Shadowsight saw grief glisten in his blue eyes and watched, barely aware of Tigerstar and Dovewing, as the SkyClan tom padded toward Ivypool.

"I'm so sorry," he told her softly from the edge of the pool. "She gave her own life to kill Ashfur."

Ivypool stood like a stone by the water, her gaze fixed on Rootspring, though Shadowsight guessed she wasn't focusing on anything but the pain slicing through her heart.

Rootspring padded slowly into the pool and nudged her toward the shore. "If I could have taken her place, I would have. But she died as she lived: bravely, willing to give it all for her Clan," he told her, his own eyes shimmering with grief.

Ivypool blinked at him, then looked back at the Moonpool as though Rootspring might be wrong and Bristlefrost would appear spluttering above the surface at any moment. "It can't be true."

"If there were any chance she was still alive, I wouldn't have come back." Rootspring's mew was hollow with grief. "I would never have left without her."

Shadowsight's throat tightened. He knew that, eventually, he'd have to go to Ivypool and explain that Bristlefrost had given up her life for his. If there was any way he could honor her sacrifice, he would. But not now. He pulled away from Tigerstar and Dovewing. There wasn't time for grief. "I have to help Mothwing."

Graystripe was lying on his side, his eyes closed, his flanks barely moving. Shadowsight could see that he was in pain. The Sisters were hurrying from the shadows, cobwebs in their jaws and wrapped around their forepaws.

As Flurry reached Mothwing and peeled off a clump for her to use, Shadowsight joined them. "Can you stop the bleeding?" he asked.

"I don't know." Mothwing was already wadding cobweb into the wound that sliced Graystripe's belly open. Her eyes were dark and her paws drenched in the tom's blood.

Shadowsight scooped up another clump and trailed it over the gash, but it was like trying to block a river with leaves. He grabbed another pawful and pressed it into the gap.

Graystripe grunted, his eyes flickering open.

Squirrelflight crouched beside him. "We'll get you through this," she promised.

Graystripe blinked slowly. "I don't think so." There was no fear in his mew, or regret. "I'm going to StarClan." His eyes were clouded. "It isn't sad. I've lost so many cats I loved, and now I can be with them again."

Squirrelflight's whiskers quivered as she fought back grief.

Bramblestar leaned down and touched his nose to Graystripe's ear. "ThunderClan has been lucky to have you for so long," he murmured.

Graystripe gave a soft grunt as though trying to purr. "I've been lucky to have them. Tell them that I wouldn't want to have belonged to any other Clan and that I'll miss them. Say goodbye to my kits for me, and tell them I'll be waiting for them in StarClan after they have long, happy lives." He turned his head stiffly and looked at Squirrelflight. "I gave Ashfur your message," he rasped. "He carried it to his death."

"Ashfur's gone forever," Shadowsight added. He wanted to make sure Squirrelflight knew that she'd never have to deal with the dark warrior again. "Bristlefrost made sure of that. And we broke down the barrier to StarClan. We can contact them again." A twinge of regret jabbed his heart. *We.* The word sounded hollow. He'd never contact StarClan now. He'd lost any connection he'd had with them. Ashfur had destroyed it. He glanced at Mothwing. "The medicine cats should meet here tomorrow and share with them."

"Okay." She nodded but didn't take her eyes off her work.

Graystripe pawed at her weakly, pushing her away. "It's no good," he murmured. "Let me go."

Mothwing didn't fight him. She leaned back as he laid his head down and closed his eyes.

Shadowsight's heart seemed to drop like a stone in his chest. His paws were still on Graystripe's belly when he felt a sudden stillness he'd only ever felt in prey.

Mothwing sat back on her haunches, then put a paw to Graystripe's chest. A moment later, she nodded gently. "He's gone."

Silently, slowly, Bramblestar crouched beside Graystripe's body, then let out a long, low yowl. As it echoed around the hollow, Squirrelflight joined him until every stone rang with their grief.

CHAPTER 23

❧

The next night, as he crouched beside the Moonpool, Shadowsight felt a hollowness inside him like hunger. The wound Ashfur had opened had not healed as Leafpool had promised. But perhaps he just needed to wait a little longer.

The other medicine cats were here—all of them beneath the bright white moon—but, after Graystripe's death, there seemed to be a chill in the Moonpool hollow that neither warm pelts nor clouding breath could chase away.

The Clan cats had carried the message home to their Clans that Ashfur had been defeated and the connection to StarClan restored. They had arranged for the medicine cats to meet here. They'd told them that they'd be able to share with StarClan again. Shadowsight knew that they'd been longing for this moment for moons, and that they'd be delighted and relieved to be here. They would be comforted tonight, but Shadowsight wondered whether his own emptiness could ever be healed if he would never be able to share with his ancestors.

He crouched guiltily at the water's edge. Should he tell the other medicine cats what Leafpool had told him? That he'd never have the same connection with StarClan that they had? Would they stop him from coming here? He fluffed out his fur against the night's chill. *Mothwing* came to the Moonpool meetings even though she didn't share with StarClan. Why couldn't *he*?

Shadowsight glanced at Mothwing as Puddleshine chatted eagerly with the other medicine cats.

"Tigerstar has ordered extra hunting patrols so that we can celebrate with a feast," he mewed.

"Harestar too," Kestrelflight told him. "If StarClan approves, we'll celebrate Whistlepaw becoming my medicine-cat apprentice—but there are already so many reasons to celebrate."

Shadowsight's former mentor had patched up his wounds, treating them with so many herbs they felt numb now. The absence of pain was one relief, at least. If only Puddleshine had some cure for the loss of Bristlefrost and Graystripe, and of StarClan.

Puddleshine blinked at Mothwing. "You'll be traveling back to the RiverClan camp after the ceremony, then?"

She nodded. "It's time I went back. RiverClan needs a medicine cat, and Mistystar has finally apologized for banishing Icewing and Harelight for so long."

Kestrelflight rubbed a paw over his muzzle. "Are they going back with you?"

"They're already there," Mothwing told him.

"The ShadowClan camp seems empty without them,"

Puddleshine mewed. "Although Yarrowleaf's complaining that we'll never get the smell of fish out of the warriors' den."

Jayfeather sniffed. "If Yarrowleaf's complaining, it sounds like life is getting back to normal."

Puddleshine purred. "About time too."

Alderheart's eyes shimmered anxiously. "Do you really think we'll be able to share with StarClan tonight?"

"There's only one way to find out." Jayfeather padded to the edge of the water and crouched beside it.

Alderheart settled next to him and Puddleshine lay down beside Shadowsight as the other cats took their places around the Moonpool. Only Mothwing hung back, her gaze flitting distractedly around the moon-shadowed cliffs.

Should I be sitting beside her rather than here? Shadowsight glanced at Puddleshine, feeling shame wash his pelt. He should have told his former mentor, at least, what Leafpool had told him. That he would never be able to share with StarClan. But the words had stuck in his throat. ShadowClan had been so pleased that he was back and that Ashfur had been defeated, he hadn't wanted to spoil their happiness with bad news.

Jayfeather closed his blind blue eyes and touched his nose to the water. As Puddleshine joined him, Shadowsight quickly dipped his muzzle to the chilly surface of the pool. Perhaps StarClan would share with him after all. It wasn't fair that he'd never get to speak to them. Even if he'd fulfilled his destiny and seen into the shadows, couldn't he have the chance to say good-bye?

Behind his closed eyes, he saw nothing but darkness and heard nothing but his own thoughts. He tried harder, reaching as far as he could, as though he was trying to remember where he'd seen a fresh clump of chervil growing in the woods. But nothing came. His thoughts remained empty.

He sat up, his heart aching. Mothwing looked at him, puzzled, but said nothing and began to wash her belly. *She* seemed content without sharing with StarClan. Perhaps he was asking too much.. He'd actually walked in StarClan territory and seen the forests and meadows and StarClan warriors. He'd spoken with *Firestar.* Could any medicine cat want more than that?

As the cold air began to reach through his pelt, the other medicine cats began to move. Alderheart's tail quivered as he blinked open his eyes. Jayfeather sat up, his pelt rippling, and Kestrelflight stretched.

Puddleshine got to his paws and looked at Shadowsight. "What did you see?"

Shadowsight froze. What should he say?

Relief flooded him as Alderheart answered first.

"I saw Graystripe." The ThunderClan medicine cat looked at Jayfeather. "He's glad to be with his old Clanmates. And he says he's enjoying catching up with Briarlight and Millie."

"Good." Jayfeather purred. "He's earned his rest."

Kestrelflight's eyes were shining. "StarClan told me that Whistlepaw will be a fine medicine cat. And that we must learn from what happened with Ashfur."

"Me too." Puddleshine whiskers twitched. "They said we should think about the changes to the warrior code, and take it seriously. They hope everything that's happened will bring the Clans closer together and help us rebuild and become stronger." He looked eagerly at Shadowsight. "Did they tell you that too?"

Shadowsight's pelt seemed to burn as the medicine cats looked at him expectantly. He dropped his gaze, wishing he could disappear.

Mothwing padded closer. "Shadowsight's been through a lot," she mewed. "Perhaps he's too tired for visions."

"Really?" Puddleshine sounded surprised.

Shadowsight's heart was beating so loudly he could hear nothing else. He forced himself to meet Puddleshine's gaze. "I saw only blackness," he confessed.

Puddleshine frowned. "I guess Mothwing's right," he mewed. "You must be tired."

"No." Shadowsight shook his head. "It's not that." He curled his claws against the stone. "It's because I don't have a connection with StarClan."

Jayfeather pricked his ears. Kestrelflight frowned.

"What do you mean?" Puddleshine sounded confused. "You helped destroy the barrier. Of course you have a connection with them."

Shadowsight swallowed as he remembered Leafpool's words. *Your connection was with shadow, not light.* "Leafpool told me that I've never really shared with StarClan at all," he admitted. "I just *thought* I could share with them. My destiny was to see only into the shadows. My visions all belonged to Ashfur, and when he disappeared, my visions went too." He shrank beneath his pelt. "I'm sorry," he mewed, too ashamed to look at the other medicine cats. "I'm not a real medicine cat at all. Ashfur just used me to get back to the Clans. It's my fault he caused so much trouble. It was me who let him in. I'm so sorry."

Puddleshine hesitated, his eyes darkening for a moment before he fluffed out his fur and mewed brightly, "What do you mean you're not a real medicine cat? You're a perfectly fine medicine cat. In a few moons you'll almost be as good as me."

Shadowsight looked up. Surprise flashed through his fur. Puddleshine was purring.

Mothwing swished her tail. "There's more to being a medicine cat than sharing with a bunch of dead warriors," she mewed.

He blinked at her. "But you were so angry with me for bringing Ashfur back."

Mothwing sniffed. "I had to be angry with some cat," she mewed. "I'm sorry I was so hard on you. I was grieving for my place in RiverClan and needed some cat to blame. And I suppose, in some way, you represented my worst fear—that living cats would go against their own instincts to follow the dangerous instructions of some long-dead cat. But Ashfur could have used any cat. It wasn't your fault he chose you, and I shouldn't have acted like it was. If he'd chosen me, I might have been fooled too. But I don't think I would have been brave enough to follow him into the Dark Forest." She glanced at the wounds in Shadowsight's pelt, where his fur was still matted with dried blood. "Even when you were injured, you went back there to help defeat him once and for all. How could any cat be angry with you?"

Shadowsight's heart lifted, and he glanced hopefully at the other medicine cats. Did they feel the same way?

Jayfeather tutted. "I don't know why you're making such a fuss," he told Shadowsight. "Mothwing gets along fine without sharing with StarClan." He turned his blind gaze on Mothwing, with just a touch of apology in his expression. *I suppose he's sorry for revealing her secret to a whole Gathering,* Shadowsight mused as the ThunderClan cat went on. "As for Ashfur, what's done is done. Perhaps you *were* a mouse-brain, but you were young. You still are! I'm sure you'll make plenty more mistakes. But your heart's in the right place, and you've more than made up for whatever harm you did."

Kestrelflight nodded. "If we've ever made you feel like you didn't deserve to be a medicine cat, we're sorry. Thanks to you, StarClan has returned and the Clans are safe. If that doesn't make you a medicine cat, nothing will."

Alderheart flicked his tail. "You're one of us and nothing will change that."

Shadowsight looked around at his fellow medicine cats. They were gazing at him with a respect he'd never seen in their eyes before. The emptiness in his heart seemed to fill as joy flooded it. He felt suddenly sure that the darkness Ashfur had pulled him into had dispersed forever.

For the first time, he didn't feel like an outsider. He was accepted at last.

Chapter 24
❧

"Bramblestar! Bramblestar!"

Rootspring gazed up at the Great Oak while the Clans lifted their voices together to chant the name of the returned leader. On the long, low branch, Bramblestar shifted his paws self-consciously, but his eyes were shining. He was clearly pleased to be back. The island clearing, warm under the biggest full moon of greenleaf, seemed to fizz with happiness. Despite their losses, the Clans were relieved that order had been restored, along with their connection to their ancestors. But Rootspring couldn't share their joy. In the half-moon since he'd returned from the Dark Forest, grief had weighted every paw step and dragged at every breath. It had soured the flavor of prey and muffled the companionship of his Clanmates so that he felt like no more than a spirit cat haunting the camp.

He joined in the chant, but the ache in his heart hardened until his mew trailed into silence.

Needleclaw nudged him. "Are you okay?"

"Yeah." He met her anxious gaze, widening his own to reassure her. She blinked at him sympathetically. Over the past half-moon, she'd stayed close to him in camp, brought him prey from the fresh-kill pile, and asked to join his patrols. He was grateful for his sister's care. But some days it seemed too hard to pretend to be fine, and he wished he could leave his Clan for a while and mourn alone in the forest.

His Clanmates had been through enough, though, and he wasn't going to worry them by disappearing. So he'd joined every patrol, though he'd wanted to stay in his nest; he'd hunted with his denmates whenever they'd asked. And when Beekit and Beetlekit had begun to follow him around camp with wide, admiring eyes, asking him questions about his time in the Dark Forest, he'd done his best to hide his sadness as he'd told them how bravely Bristlefrost and the other warriors had fought.

"Thank you!" Bramblestar's mew cut through the chanting and the voices ebbed into silence.

In front of Rootspring, Kitescratch and Turtlecrawl pricked their ears. Beside him, Violetshine and Tree leaned forward. On the far side of the clearing, the ThunderClan cats shifted eagerly while ShadowClan and WindClan whispered to each other, their expectant gazes never leaving Bramblestar.

"The Clans have passed through some of their darkest moons," Bramblestar mewed.

"I thought it was the end," Tawnypelt called.

"It nearly was!" chimed Shimmerpelt.

Bramblestar went on as the Clans murmured in agreement. "But we survived. We drove out the impostor and reconnected with StarClan." Gratitude glistened in his gaze.

"Thank you for bringing me back, for seeing what needed to be put right and being prepared to do whatever was necessary to make it happen." He looked at Squirrelflight. "Thank you," he mewed. "No warrior has ever had such a loyal deputy or mate. Without you, I would have been lost. You never gave up on me, and you put yourself in harm's way over and over again to save me and protect your Clan. You led them when they needed leadership most. I will always be grateful to you."

A fresh wave of approving murmurs rippled through the Clans. Rootspring's ears twitched uncomfortably. He looked around and saw pride shimmering in the eyes of the warriors around him. Had they forgotten how easily they'd turned on each other and how far they'd gone in driving out codebreakers under Ashfur's command? Not to mention the warriors who'd insisted that the real Bramblestar was gone and that they should kill Ashfur even though it risked leaving Bramblestar's spirit with no body to return to. *Bramblestar must know this.* He'd watched the Clans as a ghost. Rootspring felt a new rush of respect for the ThunderClan leader. He was being generous with his speech.

"But we must remember . . ." Bramblestar's gaze hardened. "Ashfur nearly destroyed the Clans by using our code against us. We must remember how close we came to putting those rules above what it truly means to be a warrior." He looked at Tigerstar. "You understood from the start that using rules to exile and condemn loyal warriors was wrong. You refused to follow Ashfur, even before you knew who he was, and gave a home to exiled warriors when no other Clan would." He dipped his head to the ShadowClan leader. "I never thought I'd say this, but you showed courage and wisdom above all the Clans."

"Tigerstar!" Blazefire called out his leader's name.

Tawnypelt called it too, along with Scorchfur and Whorlpelt, until a chant rose from the ShadowClan cats that spread across the gathering as the other Clans joined in.

Tigerstar glanced at Dovewing, and Rootspring's heart ached as he saw the pride in the ShadowClan leader's eyes reflected by his mate's. He pressed back the resentment that jabbed his belly. Why had their love worked out when his hadn't? He was ashamed that he could begrudge any cat happiness. He didn't want to be bitter, but anger sometimes threatened to overwhelm him. How could life be so unfair? Why had Bristlefrost's bravery been rewarded with death?

Tree moved closer as though sensing his pain. "Let them celebrate," he whispered gently. "They've suffered too."

Rootspring glanced at his father. He knew Tree was right and leaned against him, grateful for his warmth.

Bramblestar raised his voice once more. "We must thank the brave warriors who risked their lives to defeat Ashfur. Let's remember the early rebels who gave their lives to oppose the dark warrior: Conefoot, Stemleaf, Dappletuft, Sandynose, Frondwhisker, and Strikestone. And the unfortunate warriors who met their deaths because they'd been fooled by the impostor: Rosepetal, Berrynose, Smokehaze, and Softpelt. They deserve our sympathy as well. All are with StarClan now, thanks to the courage of Mistystar, Crowfeather, and

Violetshine, who joined a patrol to enter the Dark Forest to fight Ashfur and free StarClan. And I am grateful to Shadowsight and Rootspring, who not only rescued me from the Dark Forest, but returned there to defeat Ashfur once and for all." A cheer rose from the crowd, filling the night air with yowls.

"Rootspring!"

"Shadowsight!"

Rootspring caught Shadowsight's eye across the lifted muzzles and saw there a glimmer of anguish. He guessed that Shadowsight was remembering Bristlefrost, too. She should be with them, hearing this.

Bramblestar waited for the cheering to end, then went on. "We've lost many good cats—Willowshine, whose courage we will never forget, and Graystripe, who was one of the bravest cats the Clans have ever known."

Rootspring's heart pounded. He knew the moment was coming when the ThunderClan leader would acknowledge Bristlefrost. Would he have the strength to swallow back his grief?

"Graystripe and Willowshine are in StarClan now," Bramblestar went on. "But there is one cat who gave up everything, including her place in StarClan, to fight for the Clans." Rootspring's breath caught as the ThunderClan leader's gaze sought his. "Bristlefrost was a young warrior, but she had the courage and wisdom of a cat many moons older. Her sacrifice will always be remembered, and I give my sympathy and thanks to those cats who will miss her most."

Rootspring glanced toward the ThunderClan cats. Ivypool

was watching Bramblestar, hollow-eyed, while Fernsong pressed against her, his eyes glistening. Beside them, Bristlefrost's littermates, Thriftear and Flipclaw, huddled together.

Bramblestar hadn't finished. "I want to honor the cats who entered the Dark Forest to save the Clans with a special title. From now on they will be known as the Lights in the Mist."

"Lights in the Mist!" Kitescratch called out the words, and this time the Clans seemed to join him as one, chanting the new title so loudly that the trees seemed to shiver.

Turtlecrawl glanced over her shoulder, her eyes round with admiration as she looked at Rootspring. His pelt prickled self-consciously as Kitescratch glanced at him, and then Harrybrook did as well. His Clanmates were clearly proud of him, and he wished he could enjoy their gratitude. But his heart could only ache at the memory of Bristlefrost. What did a title mean when he had lost her?

Bramblestar moved back, and Mistystar edged forward on the branch. As the RiverClan leader's gaze swept over the Clans, they grew quiet once more.

"When I visited StarClan . . ." She ignored the murmurs of amazement bubbling through the crowd. Surely by now every cat had heard about the Dark Forest patrol's journey to StarClan's hunting grounds? "We discussed with Firestar and Leafpool how to make the warrior code more relevant to our lives beside the lake. You will know now that StarClan agreed to reorder the rules so that we know which parts of the code they value most. Loyalty is at the heart of every true warrior, and a willingness to protect those weaker than themselves.

But there are issues the code still does not cover, and which StarClan has asked us to consider."

"We know." Breezepelt's yowl was indignant. "You want us to allow cats from different Clans to become mates!" He looked around the gathered cats. "I can't believe StarClan would ever approve of a plan that would undermine every Clan!"

"StarClan doesn't see the divisions between us quite as clearly as we do," Mistystar told him. "Don't forget, there are no borders in StarClan."

Kitescratch narrowed his eyes. "Encouraging cats from different Clans to become mates will send a message that betrayal can be forgiven!" he called out.

Among the RiverClan cats, Shimmerpelt raised her muzzle. "I thought StarClan believed loyalty is at the heart of a true warrior," she grunted. "What's loyal about choosing a mate from another Clan?"

Tigerstar bristled. "Loyalty is not that simple!" he called from beside Mistystar.

"Perhaps it should be!" Lionblaze yowled back.

Rootspring saw pelts ruffling around the clearing. Cats were beginning to flatten their ears. Tails were flicking angrily. He lifted his chin. "Nothing about being a warrior is simple." He'd spoken loudly, and his paws pricked self-consciously as muzzles jerked in his direction. Eyes widened as warriors of all Clans turned to look at him. He forced himself to go on. "Would any of you question my loyalty?"

Kitescratch blinked at him. "Of course not."

"You're one of the Lights in the Mist," Shimmerpelt called.

"And yet I was willing to leave my Clan for a cat I'd fallen deeply in love with," he mewed.

Kitescratch stiffened, surprise rippling through his fur. Around the clearing, Rootspring heard gasps.

"Leave his Clan?"

"Who was he in love with?"

Rootspring steadied his breath. He would share what he'd been through. It might help others. "I loved Bristlefrost. I was going to join ThunderClan to be with her." He pressed on before anyone could speak. "But I never got a chance to tell her that. She died believing that I'd chosen my Clan over her, and I will never see her again or have a chance to let her know she was more important to me than even my own Clanmates."

Rootspring saw eyes rounding with sympathy. "I don't need your pity," he mewed quickly. "I just want things to change. If I hadn't spent so long trying to choose between my Clan and Bristlefrost, we could have spent what little time we had left together. Instead we spent it torturing ourselves over where our true loyalty lay." He looked up at Mistystar. "My loyalty would always have been with her, and if it meant moving to her Clan, then my loyalty would have been with her Clan, because what was important to her was important to me."

Harestar was frowning. "And what about the Clan that raised you? What about your loyalty to it?"

Rootspring had no answer. What would he have done if ThunderClan had faced SkyClan in battle? Could he have fought his old Clanmates? Or his own kin?

As Rootspring hesitated, Crowfeather spoke. "The truth is, cats have had feelings for warriors from other Clans since the Clans began," he mewed. "But if they'd switched Clans every time they developed a crush, there would be no Clans left."

Dovewing's tail quivered angrily. "No true warrior would even think about switching Clans for a *crush!*"

Rootspring bristled. "My feelings for Bristlefrost weren't a crush!"

"I know." Crowfeather returned his gaze solemnly. "You are loyal and brave, and you've proved that you are willing risk your life for the good of the Clans. I know you must have thought long and hard about leaving SkyClan." He turned back to the leaders. "Choosing to leave your Clan for love should never be taken lightly. It must never be done on a whim. But some loves are worth switching Clans for. Leaving your Clan for love should no longer be forbidden, but neither should it be easy. The Clans have dealt with cats who wished to switch Clans in different ways, but perhaps we need a formal solution that all the Clans agree on. It is something we need to think about seriously before we come to a decision."

The ruffled pelts around the clearing began to smooth. Eyes narrowed, not with indignation now, but thoughtfully. Rootspring saw Kitescratch gazing at him.

"I didn't realize your feelings for Bristlefrost were so strong," the reddish-brown tom mewed.

Rootspring stared back at him. "I loved her," he breathed. "I loved her so much."

Mistystar was talking again, but he barely heard the words.

She was saying something about finding a way to remove a leader who had lost the trust of their Clanmates so that a cat like Ashfur could never abuse his power again. But Rootspring didn't care. It had felt a relief to declare his love for Bristlefrost out loud, in front of all the Clans, but grief had tightened its grip on him once more, and he stared blindly ahead as the Clans talked and talked.

At last, Tree nudged him.

Rootspring looked at him blankly.

"Are you staying for the vigil?" Tree asked him.

"The vigil?"

"The Clans are sitting vigil in honor of those who died." Tree nodded toward the Great Oak, where the leaders were climbing down. Around the clearing, the Clans were pulling back to the edges, leaving a space in the middle.

Needleclaw shifted beside him. "We can sit over there." She nodded toward a space at the edge of the clearing where a tree overhung a patch of grass.

Violetshine was already heading toward it. As Needleclaw followed, Tree nosed Rootspring to his paws.

"Come on." Nudging him gently between the other warriors, he guided Rootspring toward the grass patch. Violetshine and Needleclaw made room for him, then huddled close on either side as he pressed his belly against the earth. He felt that he'd been sitting vigil for Bristlefrost every day since she'd died.

Nestled among his kin, Rootspring let sadness overwhelm him. Not fighting it, he gazed at the empty space in the clearing where moonlight washed the bare earth with silver light.

His heart seemed to break as he pictured Bristlefrost there, a ghost among the living warriors. Her spirit should be with him at least, but it never could be. She was gone.

Gradually the Clans settled in a wide circle, and silence fell as they paid their quiet respects to their fallen Clanmates. The stars turned slowly above them as the night passed. Rootspring felt Needleclaw's breathing soften beside him. She was sleeping and he let her. She must be tired after watching over him for so many days and nights.

A figure moved in the darkness a few tail-lengths away. Rootspring watched a she-cat pad heavily toward him. As she slid from the shadows, he realized it was Spotfur. She was heavy with kits, her flanks bulging.

He blinked in surprise as she stopped in front of him. "Can you make Stemleaf appear?" she whispered. Her eyes were round with hope. "I just want to talk to him one last time."

She was asking because of his power to bring dead cats into the living realm for a few moments. But it wouldn't work now.

"He's in StarClan," he told her. "I can only make stranded spirits appear."

"Won't you try?" Spotfur stared at him hopefully.

"Will you try for us too?" Ivypool's mew took Rootspring by surprise. She'd crossed the clearing with Fernsong and was staring at him. "Can you make Bristlefrost appear?" She must have guessed what Spotfur wanted.

Rootspring blinked at the ThunderClan she-cat. "I can't reach her," he mewed. "I wish I could, but she . . ." He couldn't finish the sentence. It seemed too cruel to tell Bristlefrost's kin that she couldn't be reached now, that they'd never see her again.

"Please try," Fernsong mewed softly.

Spotfur was gazing at him. "Please try."

Rootspring understood their pain. They wanted one last chance to see their loved one. He knew what that felt like. But he knew too that both Stemleaf and Bristlefrost were beyond his reach. He couldn't make them appear, no matter how hard he tried. He met Spotfur's gaze. "You meant so much to Stemleaf," he told her. "He knows about your kits and he's watching over you from StarClan." As her eyes glistened, he went on. "You'll see him again, but I can't make him appear. You must wait until you join him." *At least you'll have that chance.* Yet he knew it must be little comfort. For now, she would have to live every day in ThunderClan without Stemleaf and raise their kits alone. But she seemed to accept Rootspring's words.

She dipped her head. "We have both lost so much." Sadness welling in her eyes, she turned and padded away.

Ivypool and Fernsong were still watching him hopefully.

"Bristlefrost's not in StarClan, is she?" Fernsong mewed.

Rootspring shook his head.

"She must be somewhere." Ivypool's mew was edged with fear. "Mustn't she? I know what happens if you die in the Dark Forest, but . . ." She ducked her head as her voice gave out.

Fernsong nuzzled her gently, his eyes on Rootspring. "Perhaps you could try," he suggested. "It would bring us such comfort."

Rootspring couldn't bring himself to refuse, even though

he knew that reaching Bristlefrost was impossible. The sun was beginning to lift behind the moors, bathing the island in pink light. Around him, the Clans were beginning to move. Warriors got to their paws. Elders stretched stiffly. Apprentices began to pace, impatient to return home after their long night.

He met Ivypool's gaze. "I'll try," he murmured.

He closed his eyes and touched his muzzle to the grass. Pressing his paws against the ground, he let his thoughts reach deep into the earth. She wouldn't be there, but he searched for her anyway. His heart trembled in his chest as though it still believed she must be there somewhere, listening for his call. Suddenly, images streamed through his mind—of Bristlefrost leaning against him beneath a willow tree, running beside him through the forest, curled with him in a nest with three tiny kits, two pale gray like her, one yellow and white. It was as though the earth held memories of what should have been as well as what was. Or perhaps it was simply showing him what he'd hoped for with all his heart. Lifting his muzzle, he opened his eyes, sadness engulfing him anew.

Ivypool and Fernsong were staring at him. Every hair on their pelts seemed to quiver with hope.

He shook his head. "She's not there," he whispered hoarsely.

Fernsong dipped his head. "Thank you for trying." There was calm acceptance in his mew. He touched his nose to Ivypool's cheek. "She's gone," he mewed quietly.

Ivypool blinked at him. "She'll always be in our hearts, though?" She spoke as though it was a question.

"Of course she will," Fernsong reassured her. "Beside the lake and in StarClan. Her spirit will live on as long as ours do, because she will live inside us."

Ivypool's pelt smoothed. Relief showed in her tired face. "Thank you," she mewed to Rootspring, and, turning, let Fernsong guide her away.

Needleclaw stretched beside Rootspring, the warmth of her pelt seeping into his as she leaned against him. He wondered how long she'd been awake. Tree had already gotten to his paws, and Violetshine was giving her face a quick wash before she got ready to head back to camp.

"Come on." Needleclaw nosed Rootspring up. "Our Clanmates are leaving."

She nodded to where Leafstar was leading Harrybrook, Kitescratch, and Turtlecrawl into the long grass that led to the tree-bridge.

Rootspring cast one last look over the clearing, his eye falling on the spot where Shadowsight sat beside Pouncestep and Lightleap. The young medicine cat stared back, his amber eyes seeming to shimmer with both grief and exhaustion. Then he nodded.

Rootspring nodded back. Then he turned and followed Needleclaw as she padded after Violetshine and Tree.

Her spirit will live on as long as ours do, because she will live inside us. Fernsong's words rang in his mind. His heart still ached at the thought that he'd failed to save the life of the cat he'd loved most. She was gone, and not even her spirit remained. No warrior would see her in StarClan. No warrior would feel her love again. Or hear her gentle mew. Or feel their paws guided by hers. But as long as cats remembered her, Bristle-frost would live on. Not just in her parents' hearts but in his heart too. She could never truly be gone. She would always be with him.

As he nosed his way into the soft grass, and the sun began to spill light across the lake, he felt grief at last begin to loosen its grip on his heart.

WARRIORS

HARPER
An Imprint of HarperCollinsPublishers

warriorcats.com